The Darkness Cycle

Legend of Darkness

Sam Verney

Teen Author
Boston

Published by Teen Author
www.teen-author.com

Library of Congress Control Number: 2009938515
ISBN: 978-1-936184-15-6

First edition, October 2009

Printed in USA

To my parents, whose whole-hearted support made this possible,
and to Mr. C for lighting the fire.

Contents

Maltesque

Rocky Outcrop

Barren

Great Sage

Poisonsap Forest

N

Cavernous Cliffs

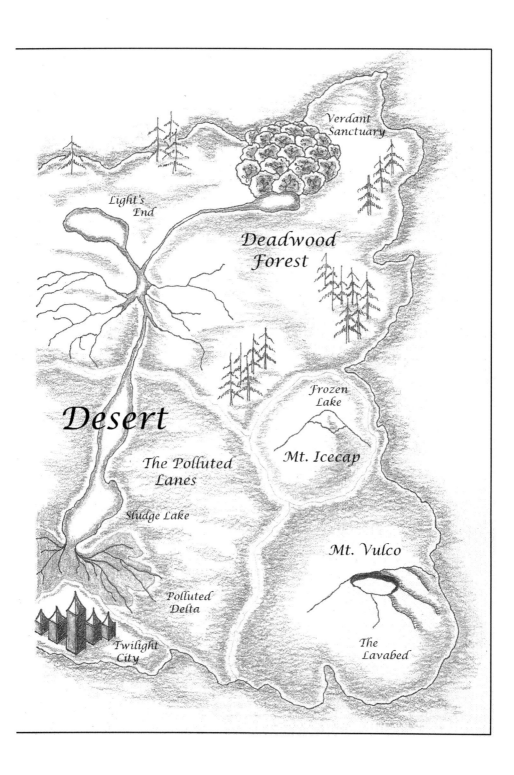

Verdant
Sanctuary

Light's
End

Deadwood
Forest

Desert

Frozen
Lake

The Polluted
Lanes

Mt. Icecap

Sludge Lake

Mt. Vulco

Polluted
Delta

Twilight
City

The
Lavabed

Prologue

It was a night of darkness, a night that would change a world forever. A harsh wind blew across a barren desert landscape. Storm clouds gathered overhead. Suddenly, a bolt of black lightning struck the ground with tremendous force. The sand where the bolt had struck had crystallized into an ebon glass. The winds picked up once more, disintegrating the crystal into black sand, which then mixed with the other sands of the desert. The storm clouds dissipated, and the cycle began again. Such was tonight on the planet of Genesis, which, despite its title, was entirely barren of life. *Almost* entirely.

The storm cycle ended abruptly, and all was silent. An eerie voice cut through the still night. It was a voice that would drive any mortal man mad it so reeked of evil. "Kronos," it whispered, "you have proven a valuable servant on your recent assignment, therefore I feel it is only right to entrust you with a very... special... mission."

The voice paused for effect. "The mission is simple but important, incredibly important. All you need do is take a little... *trip*... for me."

Again the voice paused. "You see, the universe that we reside in may seem large to a mortal such as yourself, but when you see as I do, when you fully grasp the concept of infinity, you see that our universe is a very small infinity indeed. Genesis resides in-between two much larger infinities. Our universe is one of infinite darkness, as is the one to our right, but to the left lies a universe of infinite light. I have been gaining power as of these recent years, and I believe that I have almost enough energy to be reborn. As you know, my last escapade did not go as planned. I am giving you the assignment of bringing me light energy, which I require for my reincarnation. And while we're at it, why don't we destroy the universe of light?"

As the voice paused in its monologue, the man it was speaking to, Kronos, spoke with a low, yet scratchy, voice.

"My lord, your word is my law, as always, but can it be done?"

"You dare doubt me, Kronos?" the voice roared. " I see that I was wrong to trust you, *Ulysses*!"

Kronos cringed at the sound of his name from days gone by. "My lord, I won't fail you, I merely wanted to know the plan!" he cried. "I swore my loyalty to you, and my word is my bond!"

"I see that your old name still holds power, as all names do," laughed the voice. "Nevertheless, Kronos, I think, that we would be better off if I were to give you incentive. I shall transplant some of my dark energy to you, to see that you don't stray from my gentile guidance. For if you do, I shall crush your mind like an eggshell! This universe was once composed of chaos, both dark and light, and when you arrived, plucked from your old world, you fought on the side of light, and against me. I am worried that you might opt to side with your old friends, who will be destroyed along with the light universe."

At this, Ulysses went to carry out his master's bidding.

A short cackle cut through the night, and the storm cycle began again.

***

Years later, Ulysses returned to Genesis. Though nearly a decade had passed, Ulysses looked no worse for the wear, due to the power of his master. "My liege," he began, "I have done your will. The trap is set. The die is cast. If fate smiles upon our endeavor, the one we seek will come to us."

"Well, if nothing else, this mission has taught you to speak in a dramatic fashion," jeered the voice. "Unfortunately for you, I have yet another task set for you, Kronos. You have once again earned that title..." The voice paused. "I wish for you to oversee the collision. Fate usually leans on the side of light, and something will undoubtedly go wrong. But this time, I can't afford a mistake. After all, if things go as I have planned, this will be far more than just a trap. You see we, well, more like I, have planned a collision between the dark miniverse, the incredibly small universe of darkness that you created, and the universe of light. One could conceivably call that an infection. This is far more than a trap," the voice sneered, "this is a virus."

***

The dark miniverse was moving through the fifth dimension, the space between universes, at a frightening rate. It is impossible to describe how it was moving, or the direction that it was moving in, for we, unlike the dark voice, do not grasp the concept of infinity, or the existence of higher planes. One can only say that it was moving towards the universe of light at a speed that cannot be described. Kronos was flying toward the miniverse at a greater speed than the miniverse itself was traveling at. When Kronos caught up to it, he plunged into the dark void. There was nothing but pure darkness, and if a mortal were to venture there, it would drive him mad as surely as the dark voice would.

Once inside, Kronos sent a mental call to his master, through their dark energy link. As the infinite void began to give Kronos a headache, he pleaded his master to grant him some sort of human dwelling.

Upon hearing Kronos' request, the dark voice snickered, "But of course, dear Kronos! Your feeble, semi-mortal mind cannot stand up to infinite darkness, so you request a building? Naturally, naturally. I should have thought of that myself."

At that moment, a steel tower appeared. "I hope you are satisfied," said the dark voice through his mental link with Kronos. "I have even created thirteen people for you to chat with. I think you will find them most... *entertaining*. You should be crashing into the universe of light very soon."

Kronos braced for the impact. He never felt a thing. If Kronos could have been outside the miniverse, in the fifth dimension, he would have observed the miniverse suddenly grind to a halt, but some invisible force absorbed the impact, so the miniverse was spared.

The miniverse gently bumped into the much larger universe, sending a small (to the eyes of Kronos) shudder through both. Then, very slowly, the miniverse began to merge itself into the universe of light.

"Kronos, you actually expected me to let you get hurt, didn't you!" exclaimed the voice. "You have so little faith in me that it's insulting! Not that I blame you. I usually let people down..." The dark voice punctuated the last remark with a cackle. "I am currently merging you with the outer edge of the universe of light. From there, the dark energy in this miniverse will spread like a virus. The countdown to checkmate has begun..."

1

A Cosmic Quake

It was the first day of freedom, the first day of winter vacation, for Adrian Cantor, and he was already up to his neck in trouble. It had begun at breakfast, when he got pulled into an argument with his older sister, Serena. She was being very obnoxious, as was often the case, and Adrian finally got fed up with it, as he usually did.

"And you, my disgusting little brother, will stay in your room all during the party. Unless further instructed, you will do nothing that might frighten the guests, like walking out of your room. I do hope you don't mind."

As Serena said this, she flashed her ravishing smile at her parents, who would never dare disagree with her. It had been this way since Adrian could remember, but he was not sure why.

"Can it, Serena," snarled Adrian, knowing full well that he would be in trouble with his parents if he dared disagree with his *darling* sister. "I have every right to come to our neighborhood party! Heck, the party was my idea in the first place!"

"Yes, but you'll make me look bad in front of our guests. After all, you're no more than a baby," pouted Serena.

"Yes, Adrian, your sister is right. You tend to make a mess of these things, and I have to do all of the cleaning," Mrs. Cantor hastily agreed with her daughter. "Besides, your sister knows more about what's best for her popularity. We would never want your dear sister to feel unpopular, *would we,* Adrian*?!*"

Adrian chose to take his chances and ignore his mother. "For heaven's sake, Serena, you're two lousy years older than me! You can't call me a baby without calling yourself a toddler. None of you seem to appreciate me, so maybe I should just leave!"

"Adrian, *how dare you argue with your sister?*" thundered Mr. Cantor.

"No, father," Serena smiled at her dad. "Let me handle this. So Adrian, you think you know better than I?" Serena's questioning gaze held more than just a hint of malice in it as she turned towards Adrian. "You claim you are no longer a baby? Then how about you prove it," she suggested, her voice softening to a mere whisper.

"All right, I will!" shouted Adrian. "What is it that you want me to do?"

"Something that a baby couldn't," mused Serena. "Oh, I know! Why don't you take an hour-long visit to the Southwest corner of town? I hear the folks there are very entertaining..."

Even Adrian had to shudder at the thought of visiting the darkest corner of town. Years ago, on Halloween night, a small girl had ventured there, and never was seen again. Not long after that, the girl's brother went to look for her. The father then went after the brother. The boy returned home, but the father remained missing. The remaining family members moved away. Every citizen of Adrian's town knew of this, and all but those who could afford to live nowhere else avoided the Dark District (as it was now called) at all costs. Adrian was especially frightened by this tale, for he had known the family before they had moved. Not well, of course, but well enough.

"You can't be serious, Serena," stammered Adrian. "That place is dangerous! How would you feel if I disappeared? What if I never came back?"

"Sounds like excuses to me," smiled Serena.

Serena had dared Adrian to do just that sort of thing before, and Adrian always lost his nerve at the last minute. His mind was suddenly flooded with memories of Serena mocking him when he failed to carry out his dare. It was this torrent of visions that hardened his resolve.

"If that's the way you feel about it, I'll go! And maybe I won't come back!" stormed Adrian, as twelve years of annoyance at his sister came pouring out, steeling his determination.

Now, any self-respecting parent would have stepped in at this point, but Adrian's parents did nothing to stop it. Secretly, Adrian was hoping that one of his parents would put their foot down. Serena was hoping for no interference whatsoever. Their parents knew both of them well enough to know what they both wanted, and they sided with Serena.

"Well? Don't either of you have anything to say about this?" Adrian directed this question at his parents. Neither of them had anything to say. "Fine!" snapped Adrian. "Serena, time me. I'll be back in an hour or more!" With this, Adrian left for the Dark District of his town, Pilfershire.

***

As Adrian took his first couple of steps into the Dark District, he began to feel as if he had made a huge mistake. Most of the buildings were small shacks, barely more than huts. The larger buildings were abandoned, and, well, dying. Ever since the girl and her father disappeared, everyone that could afford to had moved out of the district. Adrian had heard that there was still an orphanage in the area, but he didn't believe the rumor.

"Well, the very thought of an orphanage here is ridiculous, but I may as well see if there's any truth to that rumor," thought Adrian as he strolled down the street.

As a well-dressed young boy, Adrian was beginning to attract some attention. Old widows and ancient men alike began to crawl out of their huts to see who this bold adventurer was, and what brought such a well-dressed man to the poorest part of town.

"Them's a mighty fine pair o' trousers yeh got there, sonny!" nodded an old lady. "I don't suppose yeh'd care to donate 'em to me?"

"By the look of you, I'd venture you've got some spare cash, m'boy. Care to give some to this old geezer?" inquired a man who probably should be in a museum.

"Sorry, sir, but I don't have any right now," mumbled Adrian, trying to keep his cool.

"Whaddaya mean yeh don't got no trousers, sonny? They're on your legs right now! And what do you mean by callin' me 'sir', anyways?" asked the old woman, who clearly thought that Adrian was still talking to her.

"I'll betcha ya do got some cash, and ya jus' don' wanna give it up!" snarled a middle aged man, who began to roll up his sleeves. Adrian could sense that they were going to get what they wanted, no questions asked. Now, Adrian was no coward, but he turned and ran.

Adrian ducked into an alleyway to avoid the crowd, but his trick only worked for a few seconds. The mob came pouring into the narrow street, but the lack of space slowed them down enough for Adrian to escape. He ran out into the main street again, and gave his antique pursuers a little bit of time to get out of the alley, a plan forming in his mind. As the throng charged out of the narrow street, Adrian led them up Main Street a ways, and then ducked into another alley, larger this time, and led his pursuers back in to the street where they had started. He then led them back through the first alley, leading them in a circle, but always staying just out of their sight. He did this three or four times, and finally, he ran off in a different direction. The crowd did not notice, and kept running in a circle. Adrian then checked his watch, and, much to his dismay, discovered that he still had a half hour to go.

***

As he rounded a corner, Adrian was struck by a fantastic sight. All of the other buildings were old and decrepit, but this one's appearance made it look as if it was almost as old as time itself. If the other buildings were dying, then this one was already dead. There was a thin black line around the building, which Adrian supposed meant, "DO NOT ENTER". Worst of all, this building still had people living in it. Some, nay, most, of the people were children.

"This must be the orphanage!" gasped Adrian, horrified.

"Lookin' fer somthin', honey?" wheezed the old crone from before, stepping out from behind a building.

"Yeah, watcha doin' here, punk?" inquired a tough-looking man. Worse yet, he was carrying a gun. "An' I ain't afraid to use it, ya freak!" growled the gunman, seeing Adrian looking him over. Adrian then noticed that some of the people from the crowd were coming to watch this spectacle. Suddenly, the orphanage didn't seem so bad to him.

"Get inside, kid!" shouted a boy from inside the orphanage. The boy was about Adrian's height, but scrawny. He was wearing glasses, and had a mop of blond hair that looked too long for him. He had a slight air of geekiness about him, but he seemed better than a gun-toting mobster and a mad old lady to Adrian.

"Kid, you ain't goin' nowhere!" roared the gunman. As he went to draw his gun, the most violent earthquake ever felt in Pilfershire struck the city. And Pilfershire is right on a fault line.

The gunman was knocked off his feet. The old crone fell to the ground with her hands clasped in what seemed like prayer. Even Adrian fell flat on his back. Some of the buildings began to collapse. A very deep crack etched itself down the street. Oddly, the orphanage, despite being the oldest building in town, was barely even trembling.

"Get in here!" the scrawny kid shouted. "This building is built to withstand earthquakes. Quickly, before the gunman gets up!" Adrian needed no further encouragement. Leaping to his feet, he attempted to dash into the building, only to be foiled by the lurching ground. Slowly this time, Adrian crawled into the building. As he entered, the old crone burst out, "This is a sign from above! The boy with light blue eyes will ruin us all!"

"What's your problem with blue eyed people?" shouted Adrian as he ducked through the orphanage door.

"You okay?" asked the scrawny kid. "I was trying to get you to come into the building before the earthquake hit. My name's James, by the way. At least, that's what people call me."

"Wait. You knew the earthquake was going to hit?" inquired Adrian fuzzily.

James' face paled. "Perhaps I've said too much. You can stay here until the earthquake passes, then you must go."

At that moment, a piece of debris fell from the ceiling. Adrian lunged at James and pushed him out of the way. Unfortunately, this meant that the debris fell on him instead. As Adrian fell unconscious, he began to wonder why he had saved James.

**

In unconsciousness, Adrian's mind began to dream. Fleeting images flashed through his head, as if his mind was trying to find something to focus upon. Then, it found a focus point: Yesterday morning.

**

A harsh wind whipped sand into Adrian's face as he stood upon what appeared to be a large dune. He was painfully aware that someone was watching him, but there was nobody anywhere near him. Storm clouds gathered overhead, and a black bolt of lightning struck the ground mere feet away from him. Suddenly, a black voice shouted, "Bring me the Lightseeker!" Adrian awoke from his dream within a dream with a start, and rolled out of bed with a crash loud enough to be heard in Alaska.

Adrian's door burst open, and his mother stalked into the room, scowling heavily at the reason she was awake.

"Adrian, would you be quiet?" she hissed, glaring at her son. "Serena is trying to sleep, and you might wake her up! She needs to say goodbye to her friends, especially Eric, and she won't be able to do it properly with only nine hours of sleep."

"Nine ho- I was up until midnight doing her homework, then I had to do mine! And now I fall out of bed at three in the morning, and you yell at me that Serena needs her beauty sleep? What do you have against me? I'm your lousy son, for crying out loud! I'm sick of you and Dad constantly siding with Serena! Whatever happened to equal treatment? I demand the respect that I deserve!" shouted Adrian.

"Do not take that tone with me, young man! We will discuss this later, but right now, we both need our sleep," hissed Mrs. Cantor.

**

As Adrian sat down at the breakfast table, he could see that the events of the early morning were still fresh in his mother's eyes, for a gorgon could not deliver a more piercing glare. Though Adrian longed to lash out at his family with all of the scathing words he could muster, he decided that his best option was to play it safe.

"So, er, Serena, how did you sleep last night?" inquired Adrian in a desperate attempt to be friendly.

"Though it is none of your business, disgusting maggot, I slept very well. I ascended into my comfortable bed at 5:50, and promptly fell asleep at 6:00 sharp. Life is so much easier when you have no homework to do," responded Serena. Adrian knew that she was baiting him, for he had gone to sleep at about 1:00 on a lumpy mattress after slaving away until midnight at Serena's homework. "I had no interruptions while sleeping," continued Serena, and Adrian breathed a sigh of relief. "Except for when a certain someone fell out of bed at three A.M. I could not fall back asleep for a half hour!" exclaimed Serena, and Adrian knew that he was in deep trouble.

"Adrian, we need to discuss this matter elsewhere, where we shall not disturb the rest of the family," growled Mrs. Cantor. She grabbed Adrian's wrist and dragged him out of the kitchen and into the living room. "I told you that you were going to disturb your sister! Now, thanks to you she only got eleven and a half hours of sleep!"

"I got *five* and a half hours of sleep!" exclaimed Adrian, his constantly thin temper wearing down. "You expect me to go over and apologize to that monster, when she's the reason I don't get any sleep at night! And you, you call yourself a mother when you let your daughter boss me around like a servant?"

"Adrian, don't tell me how to raise my child, er, children!" stumbled Mrs. Cantor.

"See!" cried Adrian. "You don't even treat me like your child!"

"That's because —" started Mrs. Cantor, who was cut off by her husband.

"Keep it down in there!" bellowed Mr. Cantor. "Some of us are trying to eat a peaceful breakfast in here! Adrian, just get ready for school."

***

After his father brought a rushed end to the discussion, Adrian found himself waiting at the bus stop several minutes before the bus would be considered reasonably early. Serena, of course, would be driven to school by her doting parents just a few minutes before school began, as they only lived about a minute away. Adrian, however, was forced to take the bus, as Serena could not bear being seen by her monster of a brother, as she put it. Today, however, Adrian was a little bit early in being out of the house, so he decided to walk.

Adrian lived in the only luxurious house in the neighborhood, since his father was the CEO of some large insurance company, but had a taste for a more scenic house. Because of this, they moved into the more undeveloped part of town, so most of the buildings were still works in progress. However, Adrian did have a next-door neighbor, named Mr. L., with steel-gray hair, and eyes the hue of the sky. Adrian did not know his full last name. He was presently moseying down his driveway to fetch the paper.

"Mornin' there, Adrian!" he called, waving at Adrian. "I'm a-gonna weed m'garden t'day, 'n case you was wonderin' Ah see thet yus is gonna walk to school t'day. Did'ja get inta a fight with your older sister?" For a man of seventy-three, thought Adrian, he's remarkably perceptive.

"Yep," answered Adrian. "She lost a half hour of sleep because I rolled out of my bed around three this morning. My parents are royally ticked at me, so they made me get out of the house early."

"Well, ain't they the dotin' parents, hmm?" inquired Mr. L. "Always braggin' 'bout their perfect daughter, and how good they parented her. I ain't never seen them talk 'bout you."

"Thanks," scowled Adrian, taking the comment to heart as he stalked off to school.

"Adrian, don't worry about the small things. They'll work out. If you only knew what was coming..," Mr. L's voice faded into a mere whisper as he retreated into his house.

***

While Adrian was walking towards his school, he noticed that even fewer people than usual were walking outside today. He assumed that it had something to do with the "severe earthquake warnings", as Mrs. Cantor had put it while explaining to Serena why she couldn't go on the late-night canoe trip with her boyfriend Eric. Adrian didn't know if she was telling the truth about the warnings, as he was not allowed to watch television, but people did seem a bit more tense these days. He resolved to ask one of his friends at school about it, and then, with a groan, he recalled that although he once had a large group of friends surrounding him, Serena had pulled them into her army of admirers, one by one. He decided that he would ask a teacher about it, and then he remembered that, because Serena did very poorly in school, and was constantly disrespectful to her teachers, Adrian had been labeled as a troublemaker from day one, and his teachers actively looked for ways to punish him. As Adrian had no means to resolve the issue, he decided to let it rest for now.

Suddenly, a car careened past, skimming the sidewalk and narrowly missing Adrian. The driver stuck his head out the window as he drove away, shouting some choice words at Adrian. Adrian thought about shouting back, but he saw one of his classmates that was notorious for tattling on others, so he decided against it. He waited until a red light to cross, and made it to school without further incident.

***

As Adrian stepped into his school, he saw Serena gliding down the hallway, flocked by her admirers, with a smug look on her face. Adrian spotted a few of his past friends in her pack, all seeming to have forgotten the second Cantor at the school.

"Hey loser!" shouted Serena as she swept past. "I don't see any adoring friends surrounding you!"

"Serena, you may be the most popular person in the school, and I may be the least popular, but at least I have the brains to support myself, and I can see a much better future for me than I do for you. How will being popular help you when you're living alone in some old apartment, unable to pay the rent because you don't have the skills to hold a job! Just because-"

"That will be quite enough, Mr. Cantor," said a voice from behind Adrian. Adrian spun around, and had to wonder who in heaven was out to get him. Any other teacher in the school despised Serena much more than Adrian, and would have sided with Adrian, but no, the teacher that was standing in front of Adrian had to be Mr. Luigi, the only teacher in the school to positively adore Serena. "See me in my office after your class. I do believe that some extra homework during your winter break is in order. I shall discuss that with your advisor." And with that, Mr. Luigi stalked off.

***

"Mr. Cantor, you are late for class," sniffed Adrian's teacher as he walked into the room.

"But I'm the first one here!" exclaimed Adrian, still fuming after his encounter with Mr. Luigi. Adrian's teacher, Mr. White, glanced around the classroom, and saw that Adrian was indeed the first person to arrive.

"Well, perhaps you are too *early*, then. And I'm sure that you're plotting something to disrupt the class, and I won't have it. When you return to school, you will have a detention."

"What for?!" exclaimed Adrian.

"Well, now you have two, and one is for arguing with your teacher. The other one is for possible disruptions that may occur during class. Now please take your seat."

***

The rest of Adrian's classes went somewhat like the first one, with the teachers giving punishments for every little thing, and Adrian felt a wave of relief when the bell rang for lunch. At Adrian's school, you could either buy a lunch, which Adrian couldn't do, as his parents kept all of his money, or bring a lunch, which Serena always did, but Mrs. Cantor only made one home-cooked lunch a day. Initially Serena and Adrian had alternated, but, one way or another, Serena got the home-cooked meal every day. What this meant was that Adrian often went without a lunch. However, today Adrian had found a five-dollar bill on the ground, so he could have lunch.

As he sat down and was about to begin to eat, Serena walked over to him and said, "So, where did you steal the money from?"

"The ground," huffily replied Adrian. "Even though you try to starve me by depriving me of lunch, I can still find a way to eat. If you were in my position, would you, being the royal brat that you are?"

"Is that all you think of me as?" asked Serena, appearing to be hurt by the comment. "Sure, I may have done some mean things to you, like making all of your teachers and your parents hate you, stealing your lunches and your friends..." Serena's voice trailed off and a look of dawning comprehension spread across her face as she realized what a mess her brother's life had become.

"Hey, Serena! Aren't you going to eat lunch with me?" called a boy from the other side of the cafeteria.

"But I don't care, as long as I have a boyfriend like Eric!" said Serena, more to herself than to Adrian, as she stalked away.

***

When Adrian awoke, he could not recall who, where, or why he was. Then it all came back to him: The bet with Serena, the gunman, the earthquake; all of this returned in an instant. He slowly opened his eyes, and was met by the sight of James staring worriedly down at him.

"Are you alright?" James' voice was laden with concern. "A piece of iron hit you on the back. Any higher and it could have killed you..." His voice trailed away into nothingness.

"Why?" managed Adrian fuzzily.

"Why what?" asked James, surprised that Adrian could already talk.

"Why won't you tell me how you knew that the earthquake was going to hit?" replied Adrian, his brain clearing.

"I didn't think I could trust you," answered James shamefully. "I can see that I was wrong. You saved my life. Thank you."

"Well, can you tell me now?" asked Adrian. A small smile slid across James' face.

"Not quite yet. I'd like for you, or rather your family, to do one more thing for me."

"What's that?" curiously asked Adrian.

"Adopt me."

"Nope. First you tell me then I'll see if I can talk my parents into it. I don't really have a lot of power in my family," explained Adrian "James, look. I saved your life. The least you could do would be to give me your crackpot theory."

All right, fine. I'll tell you," scowled James. "That, whatever you believe, was no earthquake. It was something far worse. I would call it a cosmic quake. Ours was not the only planet to be affected by it. Billions of other solar systems felt that tremor. We got off lucky. Some planets were probably torn apart by it. Some stars probably supernova'd. Unfortunately, I can't prove any of that. We won't see the effects of that cosmic quake for centuries."

"Then why bother telling me?" asked Adrian, caught off-guard. He had sort of expected James to have proof for everything.

"I wasn't finished!" exclaimed James, irritated. "As I was saying, though we won't see that evidence in our lifetime, I have other proof. I would have to, otherwise, how would I have known that all of this was going on? Do you know what a seismograph is?"

"No."

"Well," said James, "It's an instrument that records seismic waves, or disturbances in the earth's interior. There has been one consistent wave going on ever since, or maybe even before, I set a few up."

"Wait," said Adrian, confused. "You set some up? Aren't they expensive?"

"They're makeshift ones," replied James sheepishly. "Anyways, there have been small crescendos in the energy level of the wave. However, each crescendo is followed by a decrescendo, but a smaller decrescendo than crescendo. Also, the crescendos have been getting bigger consistently. We will have more cosmic quakes, and each will be bigger than the last."

Adrian remained skeptical. "How do I know that your data is real? You could easily have faked it. Besides that, you have yet to tell me the cause of the earthquakes. Where's the epicenter?"

"I'm not sure," said James, stroking his non-existent beard. "I would need to check my seismographs. If you could give me a few more minutes..."

"All right, but hurry," scowled Adrian. "If you could take me to the epicenter you might convince me."

"I can do that," grinned James.

***

In James' room was one of the most interesting contraptions that Adrian had ever seen. James seemed to have built his seismograph using the water current from the pipe to turn the paper. Adrian could see that James was right; there was one constant wave going on.

James took out a map of the town. Using the data from the seismograph and a chart he had with him, he drew a circle on the map. It was surprisingly small. He also took the piece of paper off of the seismograph.

"Odd. It looks like the epicenter is somewhere near the building," James muttered. "Gotta check the other seismographs..."

James took Adrian to another room on the ground floor, and, using the data from that seismograph, drew another circle on the map. It intersected the first circle at two points, both of them inside the orphanage. "Now that is really odd," murmured James. He took Adrian to the last seismograph, and drew the last circle on the map. James then took out a second map, one of the orphanage.

"Adrian, that is really, really odd. The focus is right beneath our building, but our solar system is still here. It should have been destroyed!" exclaimed James.

"I think you just proved your theory wrong," stung Adrian.

"Not necessarily. Like I said, the building is built to withstand earthquakes. Still, there's something wrong with this picture. I'll try to show you the epicenter, if I can.

***

James showed Adrian to a room that looked perfectly ordinary. Adrian had thought that the room would look slightly different from the others.

"Hmm. That's not what I expected," mused James. "Well, this may be the epicenter, but what I really want to see is the focus. It's probably in the basement."

As James and Adrian descended the stairs to the basement, they both felt a chill in the air. Both of the boys shivered.

"I'm not sure about this," whispered Adrian to James.

"Don't be stupid!" snapped James, but he too felt a strange desire to flee.

When they reached the bottom of the stairs, a very strange sight met them. There was what looked like a small pool of shadow, and rising out of the pool was the spire of a skyscraper. Oddly, parts of the spire were missing. The spire seemed to be pulsating, moving out of the pool, and then, Adrian assumed, going back in. Both James and Adrian felt a slight gravitational pull towards the pool.

"I recognize that pattern!" gasped James, pointing at the spire. "That's the same pattern as the seismic wave! When it comes up, the wave crescendos, and when it goes back into the pool, the wave decrescendos!"

James turned on the light switch to get a better look at the spire. The moment the light turned on, a tendril of darkness reached out of the pool, no, James and Adrian could now see that the pool was more of a bubble, and grabbed the light bulb. A dark spark of electricity rapidly climbed the tendril, and, when it reached the light bulb, exploded into a million other sparks, all around the light bulb. There was suddenly a flash of black light, and the bulb exploded. In the few seconds that the light had been on, Adrian had seen that there were multiple tendrils holding up the building, and keeping it safe from the earthquake. The tendril crawled back into the pool, or bubble, but two more came out, and they both reached for the boys.

"Run!" shouted Adrian, but James needed no more incentive. As the tendrils approached, the boys slammed the door to the basement shut.

"What... the... heck... was... that?" panted Adrian.

"No... clue," answered James. "Whatever I expected, it wasn't that. Well, now we know the cause of the earth... no, cosmic, quake."

"Weird though that may be, you have yet to show me proof that it was a cosmic quake. It might have just been a strange earthquake."

"Dang!" cursed James. "I was hoping that you wouldn't spot that. I have more evidence."

"Really?" questioned Adrian, though he had sort of suspected that. "Why didn't you tell me earlier?"

"I didn't tell you because you could claim credit for the theory if I gave you too much information. But I can see that I was wrong. I can see now that I can trust you."

"Thanks," said Adrian, sarcastically pretending to be flattered.

"Anyways," continued James, "I built a three-dimensional seismograph. I can tell that this is a cosmic quake because the exact same signals are coming from outer space."

Adrian let these words sink in. If James was right, which he probably was, a cataclysm could be right around the corner. Armageddon could be approaching, and no one, save two boys with zero political influence, knew a thing about it. "I believe you James," he said at last.

"You didn't ask for proof!" exclaimed an intrigued James.

"I believe you," stated Adrian once more.

As James and Adrian were having this cozy little chat, time had been ticking away as normal, and it was now over 10 hours since Adrian had first ventured into the Dark District. Serena, whatever she may seem, was no monster, and she was beginning to worry about Adrian. Though her parents didn't really care about Adrian in the slightest, he was her brother, or so she thought, and she felt some obligation towards him. She, with her strange power over her parents, was now forcing them to call the police.

Back at the orphanage, both James and Adrian cried out as the door to the basement broke open, and two tendrils of darkness came out.

2

An Unexpected Guest

The two boys screamed in terror as the tendrils shot out towards them. They could see that there was only one escape route — through the window. James wrenched it open, and then he dove out, closely followed by Adrian. Adrian slammed the window shut on the tendrils. The severed ends of the tendrils glowed for a moment, and then they exploded in a flash of black light.

The boys could see that they had little time; a dark spark was traveling up both tendrils. Neither of them shouted the command, but both ran without a second thought. The window shattered in a brilliant black flash, but Adrian and James were both too far away to see it. However, night had fallen. The tendrils were in their element, and could have sensed the boys even if they were on the other side of the earth. So it should come as no surprise that the tendrils followed the boys even when they were out of sight. The tendrils made a point to stay far enough away that they could not be seen.

"I think we lost them," panted James. "Those things are made up of pure darkness. Technically, they shouldn't be able to move at all. Heck, they shouldn't even be able to retain a shape! They are being controlled by something else."

"Did you hear that?" gasped Adrian. "I thought that I heard a cackle! Someone's spying on us! Let's get back to my house, fast!"

"What? Oh, right. I'm used to returning to the orphanage after an adventure. Of course, none of them compare to this," said James hurriedly, catching Adrian's quizzical glance.

As the boys had been talking, the tendrils had been approaching them from behind. A deep-rooted instinct told Adrian that he was in danger. He quickly spun around, and then ran. James wasn't so lucky. As he saw the tendrils approaching, he let out a piercing scream. Adrian spun around, and accidentally knocked over some boxes abandoned at the side of the road. A high-wattage flashlight fell out and landed on its battery pack, short-circuiting. A blinding flash of light shot out of the flashlight, and collided with the tendrils! Tendrils of darkness have a weakness to high-powered light, and they exploded at the touch of it.

"Adrian, thank you! You saved my life again! Plus, you found the tendril's weakness. They hate light!" joyously exclaimed James.

"You think you've outwitted me?!" shouted a rough voice from the shadows. "My master is too smart for the likes of you to comprehend. Neither he, nor I, can be beaten so easily! Your torment has only just begun..."

"Who are you? Show yourself!" shouted Adrian. "Why are you coming after us?"

"Part of the answer is, you're too nosy for your own good. You have seen that which should have gone unseen." The voice faded away into nothingness.

"What the heck was that?" asked James.

"You're supposed to be the one with the answers!" shouted Adrian, clearly shaken. Something about the voice had rung a bell in his head, but he couldn't put his finger on it.

Right then, another cosmic quake struck. The boys had grown accustomed to the constant vibration, so they had little warning. Buildings toppled. The street fragmented. Suddenly, pieces of asphalt began to shoot into the air, proving that this was no ordinary earthquake. Debris from buildings was doing the same thing. Everything within district limits was being lifted into the air by some tremendous force. Even the orphanage, which James had credited as being nearly indestructible, was beginning to rise. And as for the two boys? They had managed to escape the district before it rose into the air.

***

As the boys ran like mad for home, James realized that the strange behavior of the district might help him find the truth about the cosmic quakes. He stopped Adrian and forced him to turn and look. The entire district had risen into the air. Then, with a crash, it plummeted down to earth. What had once been the most feared part of town was now just a pile of debris. James coul just barely see the spire at the farthest corner of the district.

Unfortunately, the spire was not harmed in the slightest. Worse, James could see that it had come farther out. He could also see that there were other fragments of the building floating around the spire. Then, one by one, they shot towards the spire, and vanished. James took out his prized invention, the portable seismograph, and set it on the ground. He then took out the data from the other seismographs, and compared them.

"There's been a change in the rhythm of the wave," shuddered James. "The crescendos and decrescendos are moving at the same rate in proportion to each other, but at a faster pace!"

"What?" asked a blank-faced Adrian. "I don't speak geek."

"Hmph. Wise guy," muttered James. "What I said was, *the spire is rising faster.* And a faster spire means more earthquakes, if that's simple enough for you"

"Well then, that's a problem!" cried Adrian. "What can we do?"

"Well, the only thing that I can think of would be to go back to the tower," mused James. "No, no, not now, tomorrow. The darkness gives the tendrils an edge," hurriedly explained James, catching Adrian's worried look.

At that moment, a shrill scream pierced the night. "Run!' shouted Adrian. Normally, he would have helped the endangered person, but he was more concerned for his own safety right then.

After a few minutes, the boys got back to Adrian's house. They were quite the sight; two bedraggled youths walking into a fancy party.

"Adrian!' gasped Serena, running over to him.

"Adrian, who in the world do you have with you?" stiffly asked Mr. Cantor. "And why are you so messy? Go change!"

"Dad!" exclaimed Serena, shocked. She knew her parents always leaned towards her side in an argument, but she had never really thought of them as being outright mean. "By the way, Adrian, I changed my mind. You can party all you like."

"Thanks Serena!" said Adrian, taken aback. "Oh, dad, meet James. He comes from the orphanage in the southwest corner of town. I was wondering if we could adopt him..."

"Adrian, adoption requires a lot of paperwork, and I don't think..."

"Nonsense, Mr.— Adrian, I don't know your last name," whispered James.

"Cantor," whispered Adrian back.

"Hm. Funny last name. As I was saying, Mr. Cantor, there's no need for paperwork, because I technically don't exist. I have no birth certificate, so I don't think that anybody particularly cares about me. There are no adults at the orphanage, for some reason, and nobody there officially exists."

"I don't know," muttered Mr. Cantor.

Serena, on the other hand, had her mind made up. She had always taken Adrian for granted, and had never realized that he had any worth at all. But now that she had almost lost him, she finally realized that he was family too. "Welcome to the family, James!"

Adrian, for the first time in his life, gave his big sister a hug.

Suddenly, the door slammed open. In the doorway stood a person in a brown raincoat that covered her entire body. She had her head turned down, so it was impossible to see her face. Then, the person turned her face up, and

Adrian could see that it was a girl. She had dark hair, and a fair complexion. However, Adrian could see that something was wrong. Her brown eyes were wide in terror, and she suddenly gave a piercing scream. The same piercing scream, Adrian realized, that he had heard on his way home. Then, she fell on her knees.

At that moment, Adrian's father turned the porch light on, and Adrian could see that right behind her, there were three tendrils, all poised to strike. James caught sight of them too.

"H-help me!" stuttered the girl. She had a pretty voice; very delicate, like the soft peal of church bells on Christmas Eve. Suddenly, the tendrils shot out at her, and they vanished into her body! Her eyes opened even wider (if that's possible), and she gagged.

Unexpectedly, a new voice came from her mouth. "Adrian, do you now see that I will stop at nothing to find you? You have seen what you should have not. I *will* find you. And though your house is too bright for me to properly function in, I can lure you away!"

With this, a dark tendril shot out of the possessed girl's hand, and wrapped itself around Serena! "If you wish to see your sister again, come to the spire by noon tomorrow!"

Adrian could only stare in horror as he watched his sister carried away by the darkness. His eyes followed the possessed girl down the street, and out of sight. A single tear rolled down his cheek as he thought about Serena. He hoped that she would be safe. A day ago he would not have cared, but things had changed in the past few hours.

"Did... wha... Adrian, what just happened?" asked Adrian's dazed mother. Adrian's father could only stare blankly out of the door.

James put his hand on Adrian's shoulder. "Adrian—" he began.

"James, how do we stop this thing? It has no concept of mercy. It has no weakness," Adrian cut James off.

"Adrian, don't worry. I have a plan. Interested?" asked James.

"Fire away," answered Adrian, trying to act brave.

"Alright. This dark force isn't from our universe. That pool of darkness we saw is a different universe merging with ours. The dark force will corrupt more people, this much is clear. But darkness has one fundamental weakness: light," explained James.

"But how does this help us? We don't have any light strong enough to pierce *solid* darkness!" lamented Adrian, as another tear ran down his face. "That flashlight in the alley used up all of its energy in seconds, and it was above full power!"

"Adrian, you need to have more faith in your brother! If I can build a seismograph, then I can build a powerful flashlight! If I start working tonight, I might finish it in time," explained James.

***

As Adrian lay in his bed, he pondered the events of the past day. He was at last glad that he had a sister, and wanted her back very badly. He had actually made a friend, who was now his adopted brother.

His mind suddenly shifted gears. He wondered who the voice controlling the shadows was, and who his master was. He pondered the purpose of the steel spire, and of the dark universe that it resided in. And, above all, he wondered why the master of the shadows needed him. Him, out of all people. Him, regular old Adrian Cantor!

***

Kronos knelt in a pool of darkness, his eyes closed.

"My master, there has been a slight, ah, *complication*. Please do not be too angry with me!"

"Kronos, you fool!" bellowed the voice. "Your so-called 'complication' was actually in the plan! Or did you forget?"

"My lord, you never told me the plan! I just did what you told me to!"

"Ah. Well then, Kronos, I apologize, although that is not in my nature. Perhaps I could fill you in on the details..."

***

Dawn broke over a blonde boy, asleep at his workbench. James had been constructing the flashlight all night, and was taking a short nap before embarking upon his perilous journey into the unknown. Adrian was also asleep, for he had stayed up until midnight worrying about tomorrow, which was now today. His parents had barely managed to cry themselves to sleep; they were so worried about Serena. Thus, when James awoke, it was 11:30, which is a bit of a problem if your deadline is 12:00. This led to a frantic scramble, in which Adrian's parents were completely forgotten. After throwing the flashlight, some bottled water, a bit of dried fruit, and some other assorted items into James' backpack, it was 11:42, leaving them with eighteen minutes to get to the spire. As they left the house, no one even thought to leave a note telling Adrian's parents where to go.

Adrian and James dashed down Main Street until it took them to the Dark District (or what was left of it), and then made their way through the rubble.

Just like last time, the boy with good clothes and blue eyes began to attract attention, but this time, the attention he received was immediately hostile. The antique lady from before was the first to reach James and Adrian.

"Stay away!" she screeched. "Beat it! Scram! You've ruined us all, with your cursed light-blue eyes! You'll bring nothing but more disaster to us all!"

"What's your problem with light blue eyes?" asked Adrian, feeling annoyed.

"My boy, I have only seen one other man with eyes like yours, and —" the old crone was cut off by a boy, no younger than eight, who shoved her aside, trying to get to Adrian, presumably to pickpocket him.

"Adrian, hurry up!" whispered James. "We've got, like, thirteen minutes 'til twelve!"

"Coming," said Adrian, as he raced away from the crowd.

***

It took James and Adrian about twelve more minutes to get to the spire, but they made it in time.

"So, you've returned..." mocked the harsh voice from the shadows. "I have your sister right here. All you need to do to get her is step inside the bubble."

Without a second thought, Adrian clenched his eyes shut and charged in. If he had not closed his eyes, he would have been driven mad, for, as I said before, infinite darkness would drive a mortal man mad. Nevertheless, Adrian had a nauseous feeling as he plunged into the darkness. He groped for the spire, and, as luck would have it, found it. Suddenly, he felt his feet alight upon solid ground once more, and the feeling of nausea vanished. He looked up.

"Welcome to my humble domain," laughed the harsh voice. Adrian found himself looking at a man with long black hair that was pulled back. Part of his hair was pulled into two spikes that leaned backwards, making look like a dog with its ears pulled back. He was wearing a gray T-shirt with an unzipped black leather jacket, and two black leather gloves. His face was covered by a mask, but his eyes still showed, one green as a forest, the other black as night. He wore black pants and black boots, giving him a gothic sort of look. "My name is Kronos," he said.

"Where's Serena?" shouted Adrian.

"Oh, you mean your sister? Why, she's right here," smiled Kronos. Serena was held against the spire by two darkness tendrils.

"Adrian, help me!' she cried.

"Now that you are here, Adrian, I have no use for that particular distraction." Kronos snapped his fingers and Serena was swallowed up by the darkness.

"Serena!" cried Adrian, who swung around to look at Kronos. "What did you do to her, you monster?"

"As we speak, sweet Serena is feeding the darkness. Her life force is being absorbed by the... ah... tendrils of darkness, as I believe you call them. The energy provided by her life should be enough to posses thousands of people, as I did to that girl last night," calmly explained Kronos, as if he was teaching a two year old the alphabet.

Adrian, shocked and terrified, ran for it. Only then did the possessed girl step out from behind Kronos. She tackled him from behind, and Adrian shouted, "James!"

James had been standing outside the bubble, and though he could not hear everything that was being said, he heard Adrian shout his name, and James tossed the backpack into the bubble. Adrian quickly took the flashlight out, aimed it at the girl, and turned it on. The result was a brilliant flash of light, unlike anything he had ever seen before. It purged all remnants of darkness from the girl, freeing her. Her eyes widened, and she then collapsed. Adrian felt her forehead; it was feverish.

While Adrian's hand was still on her forehead, his other hand resting upon the backpack, a tendril of darkness shot out at him from Kronos' hand, and the three of them disappeared.

***

James had no notion that anything had changed, or that Adrian had vanished from inside the bubble, but he did notice that the spire vanished. "Where the heck did that thing go?" James asked himself.

"Am I too late?" gasped a voice from around the corner. "Is Adrian alright? I just heard-"

"OK, I don't have a clue who you are, so you're going to have to tell me your name before I tell you anything," said James. "For all I know, you could be the voice that we heard in the alley last night."

"Very well," sighed the voice, and as he stepped out from behind the ruin of a building, James could see that he was an old man, maybe in his early nineties. The man saw James staring at his shabby appearance and said, "This isn't what I really look like. I've been wearing a mask to hide from the very man you mistakenly took me to be. His name is Kronos, but he works for a much more dangerous entity. As for me, Adrian has thought of me as his kindly old neighbor, Mr. L, for years. But my true name," with this he pulled off his mask, revealing himself to be a man around age sixty, "Is Ajax Lightseeker. I am Adrian's grandfather. And speaking of Adrian, where is he? "

"He entered the bubble a few minutes ago to rescue his sister, and he called out to me, so I tossed a backpack filled with supplies to him. However, there was a spire-"

"Yes, yes, I know all about the spire," said Ajax impatiently. "But what happened to Adrian?"

"All I know is that the spire vanished. Do you know what that means, Mr. Lightseeker?" finished James.

"Damn! If the spire vanished, that means that Kronos escaped with Adrian! We'd best get out of here," sighed Ajax.

"Kronos kidnapped Adrian?!" gasped James. "Where did Kronos take him?" "Adrian has, probably, been taken to Kronos' hideout in the universe called Genesis. I have a certain connection with Adrian, though, and I should be able to use that to track-"

Ajax's comment was cut short by the sudden eruption of tendrils of darkness from the darkness bubble. They streamed out towards all of the citizens who had gathered around this new addition to town, the bubble, and possessed them. Then, the tendrils shot into the alley where James stood with Ajax, and into all of the surrounding alleys and streets.

"Run for it!"

***

James rushed after Ajax without the slightest notion as to where he was going, desperately hoping that Ajax knew the way. Worse, as James had tossed the backpack with the flashlights into the bubble for Adrian, he had no weapon against the darkness.

"Where are we going?" shouted James to Ajax as they passed the wreckage of what was once a general store.

"To somewhere where the darkness tendrils won't be able to find us," responded Ajax.

***

"This is it?" cried James. "This place looks like a disaster area! I thought you said you had somewhere *safe* that we could hide! This place could be blown over by a gust of wind!"

James' comment was perfectly justified. Ajax's hideout was a two story house that looked as if it had been knocked down, sloppily rebuilt, burnt down by a fire, and rebuilt again using the charred pieces of wood by someone who barely knew how to hold a hammer.

"James, mind your tongue, or I'll cut it out!" snarled Ajax angrily. "I would never even step inside a building like that! Inside the house... Actually, it'd be easier to show you."

Ajax stepped inside the house, and beckoned James to follow suit. Inside the house was a steel dome that seemed to be holding the house up. James could see the remnants of an old staircase climbing up the fractured wall of the old house. There were raised spots on the floor were some of the old walls had been. Bits of wood protruded from the wall once it reached a certain height. James assumed that it was the remnants of the second floor. "Are you quite finished sightseeing?" sneered Ajax. "Come on, inside the dome." And with that, he grabbed James and pulled him into the silver dome.

For a second, James was somewhat disoriented. He hadn't seen a door from the outside, so how had Ajax pulled him in? Then he saw that there was indeed a concealed door that must have blended in with the rest of the dome from the outside. The inside of the dome was rigged with some kind of security system, with wires and hidden cameras everywhere. There was also a computer to which all of the wires were connected. Attached to the computer were a microphone and an eye scanner.

"Name?" asked the computer.

"Ajax Lightseeker and company," responded Ajax.

"Name of guest(s)?"

"James," answered Ajax. Suddenly, a hidden paned slid open in the floor, and an elevator rose up from below. "Come," said Ajax, clearly happy to be home. They stepped into the elevator, which resembled a five-foot by five-foot square of steel with a metal railing attached.

"How does this thing work?" asked James, puzzled. The vast majority of elevators that he'd seen were closed boxes.

"Air pressure," said Ajax in his usual gruff manner. "A vacuum system either propels it up with a blast of pressurized air, or sucks the air back in."

"Then how come it doesn't fly out of the floor?"

"There's a magnet on the ceiling. The positively charged end is sticking out, and it repels the positively charged metal elevator," explained Ajax, obviously proud of himself. "Well, enough yapping, just get in the dang thing!" he ordered, returning to his usual unpleasant manner.

As the elevator descended, James suddenly began to feel somewhat claustrophobic. The elevator was in a glass box that perfectly fit the metal square. Above James, the hidden panel in the floor (ceiling?) closed with a snap. The elevator hit the floor, and Ajax pushed open a nearly invisible glass door. The two comrades, young and old, strode into Ajax's hidden abode.

"Good grief, what did you sell to build this place?" cried James. At first glance, he counted about twelve computers on one section of the many walls.

Each computer seemed to be controlling a different test, or doing various computations. "And what in the name of sanity are all of these computers working on? It looks like they're working on a thousand separate projects, but they all seem to be centered on some primary focus. I really, really..."

"Good god, James, do you want me to answer you questions or not?" snapped the ever irritable Ajax. "To answer your first question, I am the inventor of the laser and the particle accelerator. During my experiments, I found other uses for some of the things that I created, so I patented them, and made a fortune."

"And what exactly were you trying to build"

"That, my friend, I will explain to you right now!" said Ajax with the air of someone who has much to be proud of. "The only weakness that the darkness has is high intensity visible light. That in itself presents a problem, for high intensity light shifts into ultra-violet, x-rays and such. So the issue is how to pack energy into visible light without it shifting into U.V. Your solution, or so I surmise, was to get as close to U.V. as possible without actually causing the light to become U.V. That'll work in the short term, but, to defeat the heart of the darkness, we need to find a better energy source. Luckily, I have.

"The secret lies in a currently obscure, yet very promising, theory in physics. It's called string theory. Actually, I haven't been keeping up to date with science, so maybe it's more well known now... oh well. Anyhow, it doesn't matter. The idea is, there are eleven dimensions, but some of them are wrapped up so small that we can't see them. So, my idea is to pack energy into the smaller dimensions, and use them to power the light ray.

"Up until today, there was a serious problem with the light laser: The vast concentration of energy would actually rip a hole in the fabric of space-time. However, now that means that we could use it to rescue Adrian!"

"And, Ajax, how exactly do you plan to pack energy into the higher dimensions?" wondered James.

"Well, the technology hasn't been invented yet, but I believe that I know what purpose the people possessed by Kronos are meant to do," explained Ajax. "Kronos and his master will be looking for a way to spread the darkness virus throughout the rest of the universe, and I'm sure they'll have the possessed people take care of it for them. So they'll do our research for us, and in the meantime, we'll hide in here."

"Does Kronos know something you don't?" asked James thinking that if he didn't, then they could do all of their work in Ajax's lab.

"Of course he does, James! If he didn't, why would we need to steal info from them?" exclaimed an immediately exasperated Ajax. Suddenly, he gasped, and fell to his knees. "Stupid link takes more out of me than it used to," he muttered. "James, Adrian never lets me down. He caused something to go wrong, and they crash-landed on a remote plane, or universe, called Maltesque. He should be safe there. If you're wondering how I knew that, remember, I have a connection with Adrian." Ajax wheezed out the last words, and then fainted on the floor.

3

Maltesque

As Adrian hurtled through the fifth dimension, paralyzed by fear, he examined Kronos more closely, and began to get the feeling that he had seen him once, long ago. He was looking in the other direction, but Adrian couldn't suppress the feeling that his anime-like hairstyle was vaguely familiar. Something about a Halloween party...

Adrian shook the feeling from his head. He couldn't afford to sympathize with his captor. He glanced down to his right, and saw that the girl was still unconscious. He noticed that she would have looked unusually beautiful in normal circumstances, but after her ordeal, she was drenched in sweat, and covered in bruises. As he looked past her, he saw discombobulated images flash by. Adrian saw the ever-present clashes of life and death, fire and water, light and darkness. He saw past, present, and future separate and combined as one, and he saw death in his family. He tried to tear his gaze away, but the sight pulled him back again and again. Adrian was unwittingly looking into the fifth dimension, which no mortal should ever lay eyes upon. He began to feel his grip on reality, bolstered by his terror, slowly slip away. He lost his mind in the swirling void, and looked up with hatred into the face of Kronos. With a howling scream, he charged at the object of his anger.

As Adrian let loose his blood-curdling roar, Kronos swirled around, and he lost his intense focus upon maintaining the transportation bubble. Without the combined focus of him and his master, the bubble would destabilize. Fortunately for Kronos, he was extremely close to his destination, Genesis. But when Adrian barreled into him, Kronos, instead of landing on the plane of Genesis, lost control of the bubble and crash-landed on the obscure plane of Maltesque. In between the universe of light and the universe of Genesis, there were multiple isolated worlds remaining from the creation of the multiverse. The worlds had no knowledge of each other's existence, as there was no simple way to travel between them. Maltesque was one of these numerous worlds.

***

Adrian recovered from his temporary insanity in order to find himself in a dimly lit prison cell, chained to the wall. The walls were composed of steel, and the floor was built of expensive marble. The air seemed thin to Adrian, and he figured they were high up. In another cell down the hall, he could hear the desperate moans of the girl he had freed from the darkness. Adrian's stomach rumbled, and he desperately wished for food and drink. More than anything, he just wanted to fall back into unconsciousness. As he let his mind wander, he wondered idly if he was in the building underneath the spire. He had no idea why he wasn't still hurtling through that mesmerizing void. The last thing he remembered was staring past the rescued girl and then-

Howls of insanity joined moans of agony as Adrian slipped back into his former state.

***

Adrian awoke to find himself being force-fed stale bread and filthy water. However, he was so exhausted that he couldn't find the will to object to his rough treatment. He felt himself being unchained, and was then shoved by the guard down a silver hallway, which, though he was much too tired to pay attention, was very luxurious and oddly well-furnished for a prison. He felt a chill emanating from his guard. He was led into a room with a beautifully polished mahogany floor and a red carpet, with the girl unconscious upon it. The intense color was too much for him, and he passed out cold.

Once again, Adrian awoke. He felt oddly refreshed this time, and guessed that he had actually been asleep for longer than he wished he had been.

"Did you sleep well?" sneered a mocking voice. Adrian found himself looking into the eyes of Kronos, his kidnapper. "We wouldn't want you to be too tired before the home stretch, now would we? After all, your sacrifice will be the final step in my master's rebirth, and the start of his rule over all things."

"So that's what you want of me," whispered Adrian. "And do you think that I'm just gonna give up my life to suit the will of your insane master?" Adrian's voice crescendoed into a shout that banged against Kronos' eardrums. A strange rage seemed to overcome both of them.

"YOU HAVE NO SAY IN THE MATTER!" bellowed Kronos. "I have no desire to see your life go to waste either." Kronos doubled over, clutching his head. He straightened up, and said, "What I meant was, you and the girl are going to my master, whether you like it or not, and I don't give a d—"

"Why are you taking her? She never did anything against you, and she already served as your pawn." Adrian suddenly felt himself losing his grip on things. He struggled to keep his hold on things, and as he did, Kronos took the initiative in the debate.

"Yes," he mused to himself. "Why *does* she need to come..." Suddenly, his hand flew up to his head once again, and he went rigid. "Because my master commands it!" he shouted, answering himself and Adrian. "We will leave for Genesis immediately, and this time, I'll take a few shadow soldiers with m—"

He stopped himself mid-sentence, and whirled around. He could see something outside the window...

Suddenly, a blast of air shattered the wall, and Kronos managed to grab onto the arm of his chair, which was bolted to the floor, before being thrown out of the window along with everything else. Over the tempest, he heard someone shout, "For Benevolaria!" Adrian and the girl, however, were not so fortunate.

As they were flung out of the building, Adrian had time for one thought: "Why?"

***

Adrian awoke to find himself being checked for a fever by the girl he had rescued from the darkness. "I seem to be waking up a lot lately," he mused to himself with a chuckle. He seemed to be lying on a piece of the floor of the carpeted room which was floating on a dark river.

"Hey, you woke up!" exclaimed the girl, obviously relieved. "I thought that I'd lost you!"

"And why would that be of any consequence to you? You don't owe me anything."

"Are you kidding me?" she laughed. "You saved me from the darkness. It's had a hold on me for years. I owe you everything."

"Um, right. So, uh, what's your name?" asked Adrian, suddenly flustered.

"Rose Cores," she said. Adrian was suddenly besieged by a torrent of memories.

"You-you-y-you're that girl! The one that vanished in the dark district years ago! So all this time... You've been out there, but no one was looking for you!" Adrian felt an incredible wave of pity for Rose, and sat up and hugged her.

"That's not true," she said quietly, and Adrian wondered if she was denying reality. "My father looked for me, but the darkness that took me and used me as a spy whisked him away from me, and sent him to serve the lord of darkness as an enforcer of his evil verdicts. He fought, but the darkness overpowered him." Adrian could see different emotions battling for control of her, and held her closer. And so they drifted down the murky river, the two children whose lives had been stolen by the darkness.

***

After hours of sitting on the piece of driftwood, occasionally engaging in conversation, the scenery began to change. Instead of the barren wasteland that had accompanied them beforehand, they began to see dead trees and foliage litter the banks. They held each other even tighter than before, for they could see things moving in the trees, and Adrian guessed that anything on this god-forsaken world that kept to the shadows wouldn't be too friendly to two defenseless strangers. However, the water seemed to deter them, and the creatures turned the other way.

As they sailed into the heart of the forest of dead trees, Adrian saw the occasional living thing, and some how the feeling of danger eased. They came to a fork in the river, and for the first time in hours, Rose spoke.

"Adrian, I really think that we should take the right path. I think that I hear a waterfall the other way."

Adrian listened closely, and did indeed hear the sound of rushing water. He jumped into the river, and paddled their driftwood boat towards the right lane, though the current put up a good fight, Adrian, even in his weakened state, was able to fight harder.

The river carried them to a small pond, barely fifty feet across. The river was blocked from proceeding any further by a dam, and beyond the dam, Adrian and Rose saw... life. There seemed to be a very small forest of trees, which was a shock to see in this wasted world.

"Well, we escaped Kronos," sighed Adrian, leaning up against a tree. "After forcing myself to stay awake so as not to fall off the raft, I don't think I can make myself take another step, and I haven't taken all that many."

"Speak for yourself," muttered Rose. "I haven't had anything to drink in god knows how long." She bent down and drank from the pond. Suddenly, she twisted to the side and wretched.

"Water, water everywhere, but not a drop to drink," chuckled Adrian, quoting.

"Yeah, I guess you're right," said Rose. She sat down next to him, rested her head on his shoulder, and they both went to sleep.

***

Adrian opened his eyes to see a lavishly carved wooden ceiling, and to find himself lying in a bed with a feather mattress. He had been sleeping underneath several silk blankets. To his left, he saw that Rose had also been sleeping in a luxurious bed. If there was one thing he had specifically expected not to see, this was it. His mind wandered, and he wondered who had rescued them.

Adrian suddenly realized that he was famished and parched, and he rolled out of bed to try to find his host. As he wandered the halls, he saw multiple wooden sculptures, all with the theme of nature. He looked down and saw, to his surprise, that the floor was composed of dirt. *Must be some kind of naturalist*, he thought to himself. He came to a wooden door, the first one he had seen. He opened it, and stepped outside, into a clearing, seemingly in the middle of the woods. At the edge of the clearing, he saw a man, robed in green. As Adrian walked towards him, he slowly turned around.

"Good morning!" he exclaimed cheerfully. "I was beginning to think that you and your friend would never wake up!" Adrian wondered who the heck this odd person was. "I suppose I ought to introduce myself," he said, and Adrian wondered if he could read minds. "My name is Vitalius Viridia, last of the druids."

"Druids?" asked Adrian. "So you're, like, a plant guy?"

"I suppose 'plant guy' will suffice. However, please call me by name. I'm very proud of it; it means Keeper of Life. Since my wife died, I'm the last of my order, as neither of my children are interested in greenkeeping."

"Greenkeeping?" inquired Adrian, confused. "What exactly is greenkeeping?"

"You're not from around here, are you?" observed Vitalius.

"Well, truth be told, I don't have a clue where here is, other than not Genesis, wherever that is," admitted Adrian. "Can you tell me where I am?"

"You, my friend," began Vitalius, "are in the world of Maltesque." Adrian shuddered at the name. "Surely you've seen that ours is a dying world. It was once lush, and verdant, like this grove of trees. Sadly, our world has been torn apart by nature's worst enemy: man."

"There once an order of druids, charged with keeping nature safe from harm. This task was dubbed greenkeeping. However, the Order was also charged with keeping people safe from nature, as this world used to be somewhat barbaric. But, thousands of years ago, a man from another world came to Maltesque, then called Benevolaria. He introduced himself as Ulysses, and taught the people how to create electricity. Then, he mysteriously disappeared. But the damage was done. A few members of the order of druids decided that it would be easier to keep nature in check if we used the tools brought to us by Ulysses. So they began to re-route the magma flow of the world to power their new city. When this began to destroy plant life, a war of the druids began. It nearly wiped out the order, thus allowing the people to run amok. They polluted the river with waste from their city, and, over time, forced the river to run in the opposite direction, spreading pollution throughout the world. Thankfully, some of the last druids, myself included, heard of this, and dammed off the water, so it wouldn't reach this grove of trees, which we... I... call the verdant sanctuary. The trees get water from the ocean, which flows though an intricate machine that filters out the salt."

"Wow," was all that Adrian could manage. He resolved to be a lot less wasteful if he ever got back home. "So, um, how long can we stay here with you?"

"As long as you like!" smiled Vitalius. "However, I think you have something else that you need to do. I saw how you mustered up the effort to paddle the boat, if you can call it that, towards the sanctuary. One cannot muster such a feat of strength without something to work for. But there seems to be something holding you back, leeching your strength away."

"There is," said Adrian. "When I was kidnapped and brought to this world, I saw a chaotic, swirling realm. If I think about it, I go mad. But, even when don't think about it, I can still feel the memory ebbing away at my strength. Also, from time to time, I'm assaulted by headaches. I had one while floating down the river. I've never had one before, though. And as for what I should do with my life, I have no idea. How do you start life anew?"

"Once, after my wife died, I too didn't know where to go, or who to turn to," explained Vitalius. "But, there was one thing I did that helped me. I hiked out to the rocky outcrop, and there my path became clear to me. Legend has it that the outcrop is haunted by a spirit, who often shows people their path in life. Perhaps you should, too."

"I'm there," said Adrian, walking out of the clearing and into the wood.

"Perhaps you would like a map?" inquired Vitalius with a slight smile.

***

As Adrian consulted the map given to him by Vitalius, it struck him how small Maltesque really was. It was barely the size of Rhode Island, and yet it was an entire world all to itself. He could easily imagine one big city completely screwing the world up.

He was nearing the small pond where he and Rose had fallen asleep under the tree. He recalled fondly the warm feeling of her head resting upon his shoulder, and then shook the feeling from his head. He didn't know if his path was the same as hers, and he didn't want to hold her back from making a life for herself with Vitalius. Vitalius had recommended staying near to the beach, so as not to attract unwanted attention from the things that lived among the trees. Following his advice, Adrian turned north, and skirted the edge of the sanctuary.

When he reached the beach, the scar of his memory of the fifth dimension had taken a toll on his body. Though the walk was short, it caused him to fall down, and a massive headache assaulted him. He saw a dark figure emerging out of the forest of dead trees, or deadwood forest, as the map called it. He forced himself to crawl behind a sand dune, so as not to be seen by the shadowy figure. The figure looked around, and, apparently satisfied that no living thing was on the beach, turned around and left. When it had looked around, the sheer fear of an unknown menace sent shivers down Adrian's spine. Adrian felt his headache subside as it left. Nevertheless, he rested behind the dune for a number of minutes, to recover his strength.

After a number of hours, Adrian was faced with a natural wall of stone, the base of the outcrop. Adrian felt as if an unknown presence was watching him. He whirled around, but as he looked for the shadowy figure, he noticed that his memory wasn't acting up, so it had to be something else. Then he remembered Vitalius telling him that the outcrop was haunted, so Adrian figured it was the spirit. After all, a ghost wasn't any more unrealistic than any of the other things that Adrian had seen in the past few days. The sheer unbelievability of his plight made Adrian laugh. He wondered if he had really just gone insane, and was just imagining all of it. A quick scratch on the arm quickly dispelled that idea as he brushed up against a thorn bush.

Adrian turned left, and climbed up a somewhat flat hill as he re-entered deadwood. He was only in the forest for a few minutes, but in that time, he was cut by too many branches to count. He emerged to see a truly incredible sight. The rocky outcrop was a plateau of sheer granite, polished smooth by the elements. Along the edge were multiple jagged rocks, most about waist height. As he stepped onto the outcrop, light shone on the rock, revealing layers of mica inside the granite. A cloud passed over the sun, but the rock was still shining brightly.

Suddenly, a voice in Adrian's head whispered, *"Come, lost one. Step forward so I can get a better look at you. Though you cannot see me, I am in the middle of the outcrop, and my eyes are weak."* Adrian looked into the middle of the outcrop, and suddenly a massive headache overtook him, and he felt as if his head was about to explode. Then, strangely, his headache vanished, and he looked up to see that he could not, except for a ghostly woman standing at the center of the outcrop. He looked away, and his vision returned to normal. *"So, lost one, you have gazed into the fifth dimension. Though this is a weakness now, with practice, you could turn it into strength, and you would be very powerful if you did. I will lessen the pain so as not to hold you back too much. You will travel to the city, and then the Great Sage will aid you. Go now, I, Virda, first of the druids, have spoken."* Adrian felt a great light envelop him, and he heard a girl's voice call his name before he passed out.

***

Adrian had a strange feeling of déjà vu as he woke up to see the finely carved wooden ceiling. He glanced to his side to see Rose sitting in a chair next to him. She had her head in her hands, and seemed to be crying. Adrian sat up, and, to his relief, was not besieged by a massive headache. He tapped Rose on the shoulder, and she gasped as she looked up.

"Adrian! You're all right! Oh, thank god! When I found you passed out against the rocks, I assumed that..."

"Calm down, Rose! I'm okay, and in the company of one of my best friends," said Adrian, with a smile. Tears welled up in Rose's eyes, and she leaned over and embraced Adrian. Adrian hugged her back, and then Vitalius came into the room.

"Ah, young master Adrian, I'm glad to see that you're awake! Rose told me your entire story, and I realized how foolish it was to send you off alone, so I sent her after you. When she told me she found you on the ground, and dragged you back here, I immediately tended to you, and it appears that my remedies worked! Did you speak with Virda?"

"I did indeed!" laughed Adrian. "She set me on the right path, and I intend to head out for the city as soon as possible. She told me that I could turn my sight of the fifth dimension into a strength, instead of a weakness. Though I have no idea how that could be possible, she implied that I should head to the city to find the truth, and that I should speak to the Great Sage. Any thoughts?"

"While I have no idea who this Great Sage is, I think that traveling to the city sounds like a good idea," commented Vitalius. "After all, if you want to learn the truth about this Kronos character, I think that you would have the best chance if you confront him directly. If you travel to the city, my two boys, Arrow and Joshua, would be more than willing to help you. Perhaps they have heard of this Great Sage of yours. However, if you plan to leave, it would be better to leave sooner as opposed to later. Rose saw something that she might want to share with you."

"When I was walking out to find you, I thought I saw someone in the shadows. I don't know who he was, but at the time, I though it was you. I walked towards him, and he stepped back and hissed at me. Then he just, well, vanished," narrated Rose.

"I saw him too!" exclaimed Adrian. "He cornered me on the beach, and I hid behind a sand dune. And good thing too, as he didn't look like he had the best intentions for me."

"This evil of which you speak," began Vitalius, "has not been seen in Maltesque for years. They appeared a thousand years ago, days before Ulysses disappeared. They are known as necrossis in the ancient language of the druids, and their name means 'soldiers without life', although you could translate it more loosely as soldiers of shadow, or shadow soldiers. While we are not sure of their full power, we can accurately assume that they are very dangerous beings. While you are on your journey, be on the lookout for them. Whomever they serve probably has little mercy to spare for strangers to our world. But let us not worry overmuch about these demons, for you most likely won't run into them again. We should begin to prepare for your journey. Ideally, you should be able to set out tomorrow!"

Adrian regretfully turned to Rose. "Well, I guess that this is where we part."

"Adrian, what are you talking about?" laughed Rose. "I'm coming with you. I told you, I owe you my life!"

"Really?" sighed Adrian with relief. He had been dreading leaving her behind. "You'd be safe here, with Vitalius. Do you really want to put yourself in danger for me again?"

Rose rolled her eyes. "Adrian, please. Vitalius is a wonderful host and acquaintance, but not a best friend. You, however, are my best friend, and family in a way."

"Um, Rose, not that I don't appreciate all of this, but we've known each other for, like, two days. I don't think that..."

Adrian stopped himself as he saw a shameful look creep across Rose's face. "You may have only known me for two days," she said, "but I've been watching you for years. I told you that the darkness used me as a spy. What I didn't tell you is that they asked me to spy on you."

"Me? Why would the darkness show any interest in me?" exclaimed Adrian.

"I don't know!" exclaimed Rose, starting to cry. "They just used me as a tool, and didn't tell me anything. But all the while I admired you, admired how you put up with your sister and your parents, and that gave me strength to carry on. I..." Rose lost her composure, and burst into sobs.

"So it's settled then," said Adrian as he wrapped his arms around Rose. "She comes with me."

***

As Adrian double-checked his backpack, making sure that he had everything, Vitalius spotted the flashlights.

"You won't need those," he said. "The tendrils of darkness, as I believe you called them, won't be stopped by the flashlights." Adrian opened up his mouth to protest, Vitalius stopped him by holding up his hand. "Yes, they'll be able to hold them off for a while, but if the tendrils find you, I doubt that these flashlights will make much of a difference. I'm sure that Kronos has other dark things to do his bidding. Besides, you'll need room for food in your pack. Nothing grows further out, and you don't have the strength to hunt. You might be able to fish near the ocean, but you should probably avoid the sea. You might run into another necrossis, and that's a risk that we can't afford."

"Fine," scowled Adrian. "We leave the flashlights. Anything else?"

"Nope," confirmed Vitalius. "It looks like you'll be all set come morning."

"Adrian!" shouted Rose, bursting into the room. "I saw one! A necrossis! He was headed a little to the north, but I think that he saw me!"

"Adrian, you cannot wait until morning!" commanded Vitalius. "You must leave at once. How near is he?"

Rose glanced out the window. "He's entering the clearing! Do something!"

"Well, nobody's ever going to accuse Vitalius of deserting a guest!" he said with a chuckle. "I'll distract him, and you can slip out the back door." With a swish of his robe, he stepped out the front door.

"Rose, grab a flashlight!" commanded Adrian. Even if we shouldn't put it in our backpack, we should still bring one for protection."

Rose conceded, and they rushed out the back door. As they reached the edge of the clearing, Adrian spun around to see if the necrossis was following them, but what he saw instead would haunt him for months.

***

Vitalius' eyes were a deep shade of green, with no pupils or whites. A viridian glow surrounded him, and extended to the plants at the edge of the clearing. Thick vines twisted around the necrossis' limbs, pinning him in place. The viridian aura seemed to be fighting with a black aura cast by the soldier. As Vitalius' aura extended to the trees around the clearing, a few of them uprooted themselves, and crawled towards the fight. Suddenly, as soon as it began to look like the soldier might lose, it stopped struggling. The necrossis was immediately possessed by another force, and suddenly, tendrils of darkness exploded from it. The tendrils wrapped themselves around Vitalius, and squeezed. Vitalius loosed a harsh cry, and then slumped over. Green energy flowed from his corpse, and forced the tendrils back into the soldier's body.

"Vitalius!" screamed Adrian. Rose tried to hold back a torrent of tears. The necrossis looked in the direction of the scream, and, with a snarl, began to tear apart the vines holding him in place. Adrian and Rose turned and ran.

***

After running south for a while, Adrian and Rose stopped to catch their breath. "Do you think we lost him?" panted Adrian.

"Hope so. If they can do that to someone as powerful as Vitalius..." Rose stopped talking to choke back a sob. Adrian reached out his hand to comfort her, but she slapped it away. "It's all your fault!" she suddenly shouted, throwing a venomous look at Adrian. "I don't know what you did, but somehow you got the darkness' attention. If they hadn't needed me to spy on you, they might have let me go. Maybe this whole mess never would have happened! Maybe Vitalius would still be..."

"Rose, I never did..." started Adrian, but he was swiftly cut off by Rose.

"Just leave me alone!" she cried, and rushed away to the north, possibly heading back to the sanctuary.

"Rose!" cried Adrian, not wanting to lose yet another friend. He was about to run after her when he was struck by a massive headache. He turned around in time to see the beat-up necrossis stumbling towards him. Despite his headache, he ran away, following the sound of Rose's sobs.

4

At Light's End

Adrian ran away from the necrossis as fast as he could, and though the shadow soldier was still injured from the battle with Vitalius, he could still match Adrian's pace. He navigated between remnants of trees long dead, signaling that he had once again entered deadwood forest. Adrian's headache didn't help matters, and he began to feel Virda's protective spell being overrun by the shadow power of the soldier. Rose's sobs had died out a few minutes ago, or was it hours? Adrian had lost track of time. He headed to where he had guessed Rose's last sob was, which was near the waterfall, or light's end, as the map called it. The name sent shivers down Adrian's spine.

Adrian was running upon what he took to be a path through the dead trees, but he lost his footing, and tumbled into a ditch lined with thorns. A thorn bush scratched his face as he hit the ground, raking lines in Adrian's face. The necrossis must not have noticed, however, for Adrian's headache began to subside. He allowed himself a moment to recuperate, gasping for breath, but as he sat there, he heard a low growl to his left. He swung his head around, and saw what appeared to be an oversized cat staring him down. It was a pale orange, and multiple thorns were firmly lodged in the cat's fur, along with several twigs. Adrian slowly stood up, and the cat took a few steps towards him, growling.

Adrian's mind raced, trying to think of a way out of this perilous situation. If he ran, the cat would pounce. If he walked forwards, the cat would pounce. If he stayed where he was, the necrossis would surely return. He took a step towards the cat, and the cat tensed its back leg muscles, preparing to pounce. Adrian slowly reached into his backpack, drawing a snarl from the cat, and took out a piece of fruit, which the cat eyed hungrily. It slowly paced toward Adrian, and opened up its mouth to take the fruit. Suddenly, Adrian's headache returned with a vengeance, and his arm spasmed, ejecting the fruit from his hand onto the path. The cat dove after it, barreling headfirst into the necrossis, who had realized his folly, and returned. As the two of them fought with claw and shadow, Adrian sprinted toward Light's End.

***

As he sped away, Adrian heard an agonized yowl from behind him, and realized that the cat had lost the fight. He redoubled his pace in fear that the necrossis might catch him again. The dead vegetation began to thin out, giving way to various rock formations. He smelled a faint amount of water in the air, giving it a sweeter taste. Adrian tripped over a small hill of stone, falling flat on his face. He heard labored breathing behind him, and sprang to his feet. Small streams of water flowed between the rock formations, slowing him down as he strove to avoid them.

He suddenly came to rapidly moving stream, the same one that he and Rose would have gone down, had he not paddled the boat away. The thought of one of his best friends in danger gave Adrian the resolve to carry on. He trudged through the mud near the riverbed, trying not to trip over the numerous rocks that just seemed to be everywhere.

Adrian slipped on a patch of mud, and fell into the river with a splash that reverberated for miles. "Well, there goes any chance of inconspicuousness," thought Adrian. He could feel the current trying to drag him under the surface, but he fought with all his might to stay afloat. With an acute feeling of dread in the pit of his stomach, Adrian heard the crashing of the waterfall ahead. The dirty water started to seep into the scratches on his face, and stung like a horde of enraged wasps. He struggled to swim to the shore, but the current dragged him back to the center time and time again. Suddenly, his feet struck the bottom, and he fell further into the water, completely submerging himself. The river dragged him into ever-shallower water, and after a while, he stood up. After shaking the water out of his eyes, he saw that he was but a few feet from the drop. The water was so shallow, it barely passed the soles of his decrepit shoes. Rocks stuck up at weird angles, spraying water everywhere and blocking his passage to the hundred-odd foot plunge.

Adrian laughed to himself as he stumbled to the bank of the river, which was just as rocky as everything else. However, there was a certain amount of living vegetation in between the stones. Rose had been right about the waterfall, but Adrian doubted that their makeshift raft could have made it to the plunge. Adrian looked up and saw that Vitalius was correct; there was a constant cover of cloud.

***

"Why do they call it Light's End?" Adrian had asked, eyeing the map.

"Because it is the end of light," Vitalius said simply. "Due to the pollution, most of Maltesque is covered by a constant blanket of toxic cloud. But because of the sea breeze, which was much stronger in the days of old, the perimeter of the island is constantly besieged by sunlight. Light's end is where the cloud layer starts. Also, the lake to which the waterfall falls into is always shrouded in fog."

***

Tears flooded Adrian's eyes as he thought of Vitalius, who would never again see the sanctuary he loved so much. Rose's accusations poured back into his mind, and a small sob racked his body. Adrian wondered if Rose was right, and he had somehow made an enemy of the darkness by one of his actions. He pointed out to himself that he had never had the freedom to make an enemy of somebody, but a lingering doubt still remained.

His period of reflection was broken by the snap of a twig. Adrian swung his head around, and was accosted by a sudden headache. The necrossis stumbled toward Adrian, a hideous grin on its face, which seemed to have been the cat's main target. Adrian seemed to recall that Vitalius had mentioned a series of tunnels behind the waterfall, and he desperately looked for the entrance. Vitalius had said that the tunnels had been used for growing phosphorescent plants that thrived in the dark.

He found it hidden amongst a clump of rocks, blending in with the other formations of stone. It was a medium sized opening in a jagged wall of rock. The gateway was surrounded by jagged stones, creating the appearance of a huge mouth, just waiting to swallow an unsuspecting traveler.

Adrian made a break for it. The necrossis lurched towards him, but Adrian was too fast for it. He made it to the tunnel with the necrossis several yards behind him. Though the light was dim outside, the inside of the tunnel was comparable to the interior of a black hole, only darker. The floor was littered with jagged stones that pierced the bottoms of his shoes, and dug into his feet. The further Adrian proceeded into the tunnel, the harder it became to see, and he bumped into the rough tunnel wall a couple of times. The shadow soldier's demented laughter reverberated through the tunnel, making it hard for Adrian to tell how far behind it was. After he had run into a wall so hard that he knocked himself over, he lamented the loss of his flashlight, which Rose had been carrying. There were many different exits to the tunnel, but Adrian stuck with the main path, which was on a steadily downward slope.

Adrian found himself at a noticeable fork in the tunnel, one that split the tunnel right in half. He didn't know which way to choose, but he thought that he saw a faint light emanating from the one on the right. He took his chances, and headed toward the faint light. As he rounded a corner, he thought that he heard the sound of rushing water up ahead.

Adrian saw that he was right, there was stone above and below him, and on one side, but the other side of the tunnel was completely exposed. Clear water, the filth removed by the upward slope above, rushed over the gap, forming the fourth wall of the cave, and splashing water into the tunnel. Adrian stuck his hand into the waterfall, and discovered that the fast moving water stung his hand. He decided that it was best not to take any chances of the necrossis catching up, so he continued to walk forwards.

As he reached the end of that portion of the tunnel, the necrossis lurched around the corner behind him. Adrian felt his headache pick up again, and felt his strength begin to wane. As the soldier reached Adrian, he spun around and stuck his arm into the flowing water. The water ricocheted off his forearm, and into the necrossis' face. It seeped into his wounds from the fight with the cat, and stung his face. It also bounced into his eyes, temporarily blinding him. The soldier screamed in agony, and while it was distracted, Adrian made his escape.

***

Adrian did not see a sharp turn in the tunnel, and ran into the wall. He turned around, and failed to notice that he was walking in the wrong direction for a few seconds. He only noticed his mistake because the wrong tunnel began to lead him uphill again. After he corrected himself, he observed that it was difficult to keep his balance, as the floor was increasingly slippery. He figured that he must be near the bottom, since the moisture was presumably from the fog that shrouded the pond, or so Vitalius had claimed. As he was distracted by these thoughts, he slipped on a spot of mildew, and went careening down the tunnel on his back. He fell upon the floor with a thud, and thought he felt something break near his nose. Clutching his face, he stood up, and saw that he was out of the tunnel. Vitalius had not lied; the lake was indeed under a deep cover of fog.

"Rose?" shouted Adrian, and a spasm of pain wracked his face. Adrian thought he heard a faint response, but he couldn't be sure. His headache began to pick up again, and he thought that the necrossis had returned. Then he realized that it was just from exhaustion, and he sat down to catch his breath.

"Adri—" called a voice that gave out midway through the word. Adrian recognized it as Rose's voice, and forced himself to get up, and walk toward the sound. It was hard to see, but he could still make out the outline of the lake. Surrounding the lake were rocks jutting out at odd angles, just like at the top of the waterfall. Adrian stumbled over a tree root, which, he reckoned, shouldn't have been there, since there were no trees around. In between the rocks was the occasional sunken pit. It was in one of these pits that Adrian found Rose, bound and gagged.

"Rose!" he shouted, shocked to see her in such a state. Her body seemed to relax at the sight of Adrian, but her eyes suddenly widened in horror at something behind Adrian, and he was tackled from behind, knocking his backpack to the ground.

Adrian crashed to the ground, and wondered why his nose had to take such a beating. He rolled over, and gazed into the eyes of one who lost his sanity years ago, and no longer cares.

"Nasty, pesky, outsiders have come to bother me!" cackled his shriveled, old assailant with glee. "No one to hear their cries of pain, as I do things that others would never think of. I need some oil, yes much oil, and something dry to burn. I've had lots of time to think, oh yes, years and years of just thinking. I can only think, yes I can. I was shunned by every living thing, made into a stranger by family, my family! The trees had it coming! They did hold us back, yes they did! I, Democritus, created the second order of druids. I'm a hero, yes I am!" Suddenly, his eyes became less clouded, and he seemed to become sane. "What have I done? I created this world, this hellscape. I destroyed the order of druids, and condemned myself to this cursed fog. God, the fog! It presses in from all sides, and holds me here. My weak eyes can't take light anymore, no they CAN'T!" He regained the mad glint in his eye, and ran away cackling, to fetch something that would burn.

Adrian stood up and limped over to Rose. He untied the knots binding her, and the rope gagging her. She wrapped her arms around him, and held him tight. Tears of relief streamed down her face. "Adrian, thank god! Well, if there is one. With our luck, I'm just not sure. When that lunatic found me, I thought for sure that I was done for! I was terrified of never seeing you again. I thought I would die alone, like I've lived my whole life..." She stopped talking, and started to cry. "Adrian, I was scared! There was no telling what he would do..."

"Rose, um, the whole hugging thing, don't you think it's kind of, well, I don't know, babyish? No, that's not a good word," pondered Adrian.

"Sorry," frowned Rose. "If you want me to stop, I will."

"Oh, alright. Just this once," laughed Adrian, and hugged her back, happy to see her. "Um, by the way, do you have the flashlight?"

"Sorry," she said, with her eyes cast towards the ground. "The lunatic took it. He said something about clearing the fog, then he went into a quiet, brooding mood. Then, when I started to shout your name, he gagged me."

"Well, that's a pity. The necrossis followed me here, so the flashlight would have helped to protect usssauggghh!." Adrian's last word transformed into a groan of agony as his headache returned in spades. The necrossis lurched out from the moss-covered rock behind which it had been hiding, and Rose let out a scream.

"Adrian, run!" she cried, leaping to her feet. The necrossis stepped closer, and Adrian's headache intensified to the point where he lost the ability to move. Rose grabbed Adrian's shoulders, and started to drag him away. A tendril of darkness extended from the soldier's hand, wrapping itself around Rose. Rose struggled as hard as she could, not wanting to become a slave of the darkness once again. Kronos' voice came out of its mouth.

"Well done, Adrian, and whatever your name is. To elude me for this long is truly a feat worthy of congratulations. I possessed this necrossis, and I have twelve more at my command. This one shall return you to twilight city, and I shall personally oversee the transportation."

With this, the tendril reached out to Adrian, and wrapped itself around his arm. Adrian let out a shriek of pain, and suddenly, and unexpectedly, a white aura suffused his body. Lightning flowed down his arms, emptying into the tendril, and traveling up the tendril, into the necrossis. The soldier dissolved in a burst of white light, and three screams shattered the night, one from Adrian, one from Kronos, who was being attacked by white lightning, and one on Genesis, where Kronos' master's hold on him was nearly broken.

***

Rose crouched on the ground, panting. She had no idea how Adrian had conjured lightning to destroy the necrossis, but the incident had just increased her respect for him. Maybe it had something to do with his sight of the fifth dimension, but Rose really had no idea. She had dragged him to the tunnel from which they had both entered the lakeside area. She had to stop to rest occasionally, and she was doing so now. She mustered up the strength to carry Adrian a few more feet, but the last few days had taken a toll on her. The allure of sleep became too great, and she set Adrian down. She curled up into a ball next to him, and was thankful that they were both okay.

***

Adrian had been awake for a while, but he had no desire to open his eyes. He could hear the muttering of the old man from before, and could feel something sharp poking into his back. These two things suggested anything but pleasant surroundings.

"Pesky little things, yes they are," the old man sang to himself in an oddly high voice. "Burn in the big fire to keep away the fog, yes they will! Keep out the trees, burn the trees!"

Adrian forced his eyes open. He was lying on a stack of wood at least ten feet tall, and all he could see above him was black. He judged himself to be in a tunnel, and a dry one, at that. It was not one that he had been in before, for it was dimly lit by a torch of unknown whereabouts. The strange old man danced about in a white robe, not unlike Vitalius'. Adrian didn't see anything preventing him from getting down, so he descended the side of the pile. He reached his foot down to the floor, and realized, with a start, that the floor wasn't there! His foot flailed wildly, but to no avail. He climbed back up to the top, and realized that they were on a circle of stone, cut off from the rest of the cave floor by at least twenty yards. The old man had gone, probably to fetch something to worsen their situation.

Adrian shook Rose. "Wake up! Come on Rose, get up!" Adrian saw that it was futile, as she wasn't stirring. He could hear Democritus walking back, and he was out of ideas.

"Keep away the fog, keep away the fog!" sang Democritus happily. "Burn in the fire to keep away the fog, yes they will." He seemed to be carrying some sort of container, which he then emptied the contents of into the pit. "Now they can burn!" He picked up the torch, and tossed it onto the wood.

Adrian freaked out. Desperately, he tried to wake Rose up, but she refused to stir. With no other options, he was going to try to throw Rose to safety, but as he lifted her up, a voice shouted, "STOP!"

"Stay there! I'll see if I can get you across!" Adrian looked down in surprise to see that it was Democritus that was shouting up to him. "Here, I've got some rope, though I'm not quite sure why... I'll toss it up to you, and you can climb down!" Adrian followed his orders, tying his end of the rope to a firmly lodged piece of wood, and climbed down.

"What about Rose?" shouted Adrian over the crackling fire.

"I have some water by my, er, nest, if you will. The less sane side of me is not very organized. If you hurry, we may be able to wake her in time!"

Adrian ran as fast as his legs would carry him to Democritus' "nest", and saw that the description was fitting. It looked not unlike the room of a fifteen year old. There was a loosely stuffed mattress lying upon the floor, and a table, complete with a chair. On the table sat a jug of water, the very one that he sought, next to some paper and dried fruit. Surrounding the table were multiple cooked animals, and a couple off books. He saw his backpack on the floor, presumably taken by Democritus.

Adrian hastened back to the fire as fast as possible without dropping the jug. He arrived to see that the flames had climbed nearly halfway up the pyre, but, thankfully, no higher. Adrian guessed the flame's slow progress was due to the unusual amount of moisture in the air.

Adrian held the jug of water tight under his arm as he climbed up the rope. He reached the top and saw, to his dismay, that Rose had somehow managed to stay asleep. Though Adrian had spilled at least half of the water, there was still enough that when he poured it on Rose, she woke up.

"Adrian! What- Where- How- Adrian, what's going on?" she stuttered.

"Rose, just do as I say. Grab onto the rope, and climb down." Rose, not understanding, nodded frightfully. The flames had begun to lick at Adrian's shoes by the time Rose reached the floor. Adrian grabbed the rope, and climbed down. The flames began to assault the rope. When Adrian was but a few feet away from the edge of the chasm, the end of the rope that was tied to the wood was burn away. The rope severed, and Adrian was thrown into the wall of the chasm. He felt something break, and then he lost his grip. With a scream, he hurtled into the depths of the abyss.

***

Rose sat upon the bed, crying her heart out. Watching her best friend plummet to his death while not being able to aid him in any way was the most terrible thing she could imagine, and the fact that Adrian had saved her a few times did nothing to ease her pain.

"Why is it, Democritus," she mumbled in-between sobs, "that I have to endure so much? I never did anything to deserve this? Why-"

"There, there," said Democritus patting her on her back. "I told you, once you collect yourself, I have something to cheer you up."

"I really doubt," started Rose with a sob, "that anything could cheer me up right now. But tell me, why do you have the occasional lapses of sanity?"

"Well, if you, as you say, have met Vitalius," this brought another sob from Rose, "then he has no doubt told you about the coming of Ulysses, and the fall of the order of druids. Now, though he may not have called it by this name, he probably mentioned the second order of druids. These were the ones who were originally charged with keeping nature in check. Eventually, however, they rebelled, as they thought that the technology of Ulysses could ease both their jobs, and the rest of the order disagreed with that. Eventually a war of the druids began, and that wiped out both orders, and led to the downfall of Benevolaria, and the creation of Maltesque. I was the leader of the second order of druids."

***

"But we *need* to use the tools! Ulysses was sent here for a reason!" raged Democritus, furious with Vistus, leader of the druids. "Just hear me out. If we re-route the magma flow out from under the mountain, it will limit the amount of space that anything can inhabit, thereby easing our jobs! And if we keep the people horded up in the our new metropolis, Sunlight City, it will limit the contact between the two factions, further easing our work."

"We will not do anything to lessen our burden at the cost of others!" decreed Vistus. "We shall not use the alien technologies to shift the natural balance. That would go against our code! Or have you forgotten your days of learning as a youth?"

"I have not forgotten them," growled Democritus. "However, my opinions on the lessons taught have changed. But I can see that you will not be swayed on this matter, so I shall do what I see fit, with or without your permission!" And with that, he stalked away.

***

Rose looked at him with an astonished expression. "You led the second order? Then you're responsible for..."

"The re-routing of the magma, the end of nature, and many other things. However, I have seen the error of my ways since then. At the end of the war, the spirit of the first druid, Virda, appeared on the opposing side."

"I've heard of Virda!" exclaimed Rose. "Adrian spoke to her! She told him to..." her voice faltered, and Democritus stepped in.

***

"And you, Democritus! You led the rebellion, dooming the world! Were I a mortal arbiter, I would sentence you to death. However, since my powers far transcend those of a mortal, I shall instead sentence you to something far worse: eternal life!" screeched Virda.

A confused look came upon Democritus' face. "Eternal life is a blessing, not a curse. However, if that is your verdict, I shall respect your judgment."

"Ignorant fool!" yelled Virda, losing her patience. "I shall sentence you to eternal life in Fog Lake, and you shall not be able to leave, until you have seen the error of your ways! But I doubt you shall ever truly comprehend what you have done here today, so you shall rot in Light's End forever. For after years, that is indeed what the lake and currently nonexistent waterfall shall be called!" Democritus vanished in a flash of light, and was thrown violently into Fog Lake.

***

"Anyhow, Virda banished me here, and forbade me to leave. She cursed me with eternal life, and in the first hundred years or so, I went insane. I slowly watched the flow of water in the lake reverse itself, and saw the formation of Light's End. After a few more years, I came to my senses, and repented for my crime against the world. But my darker side still festers; still believes that nature should be suppressed."

Though Rose felt very sorry for Democritus, the thought that someone had endured worse than he strangely cheered her up. "Alright Democritus, I've stopped crying. Now what was it that you wanted to tell me?"

"I wanted to tell you," smiled Democritus, "That there's a chance that Adrian may still be alive."

5

Into the Abyss

Rose had no idea where Democritus got his rope from, but he seemed to have an excessive supply. He certainly hadn't gotten it from their backpack, which Rose now carried, but he said he needed it to rescue Adrian. "Explain to me again," she demanded, "how Adrian could have survived the fall?"

"Well," began Democritus, "When these tunnels were created by the first order of druids, though back then they were underneath a lake, they had a secret sublevel. The tunnel that we're in now was thought to be the lowest one, but they had a secret tunnel, codenamed The Abyss, beneath this one, unbeknownst to the rest of the world. It speaks of this in the atlas that I have back in my nest. During the floods, multiple books were swept into the lake, which is how I have acquired so many of them."

"What kind of books?" asked Rose. "I didn't know that you even had books here on Maltesque."

"Well, actually, Ulysses introduced them, and explained briefly how to make paper out of trees. Though he never really elaborated on the matter, paper became an extremely valuable and rare commodity here on Maltesque," explained Democritus. "Of course, books were handwritten at first, but in the past couple hundred years, a couple more books have been swept into the lake, and it appears that Maltesque has seen the invention of the printing press."

"So what kind of books?" reiterated Rose.

"Well, at first they were mostly confined to scientific topics, such as biology and cartography, but eventually they settled into the realistic fiction niche, and then they started to explore the realm of fantasy," explained Democritus. "Then, as the more recent additions to my collection lead me to believe, literature began to cover all of the aforementioned topics, leading to the widely varied range of subjects that I believe controls Maltesquian book lore today."

"Back to the topic of Adrian…" prompted Rose impatiently.

"Anyhow, the pillar that I built your fire on, commonly known as the sunken pillar, is a natural phenomenon. When it was discovered by the druids, they carved stairs out of the side of the outside crevice wall. The top of the stairs were destroyed by the second order when we organized a raid on these tunnels, but the stairs start about ten feet under where Adrian fell. I didn't think of it at the time, but it came to me after we returned to my nest," finished Democritus.

"Whatever. Now, what can we tie the rope to?" inquired Rose, getting straight to the point. Democritus pointed to a stalagmite growing out of the floor, and Rose promptly tied the rope around it. She tied the other end around her waist, and began to descend into The Abyss. After climbing down the rough wall for a few minutes, while trying very hard not to lose her grip, her foot touched the top stair. It felt rough to her feet, thereby proving Democritus' story of the raid on the tunnels was true.

"Democritus!" shouted Rose.

"Did you find the first stair yet?" he yelled back. "I'll toss the torch down, unless you're yelling up because you need help."

"No, Democritus," smiled Rose. "Toss the torch down." Democritus gave no response, save for the fluttering light of the torch as it fell to the ground. It landed but a few inches from Rose's feet. Rose picked up the torch and saw that Democritus was right; Adrian had landed on the top stair. There was a good deal of dried blood where Rose assumed Adrian had landed, and then a dim trail leading down the rest of the stairs. A faint thud told her that Democritus had climbed down the rope, and landed next to her.

Rose's eyes welled up with tears. "Thank you, thank you, thank you! Thank you, Democritus! I don't know what I'd do without you. I mean, I'd still think that Adrian is dead, and..." Rose stopped trying to express her gratitude with words, and flung herself onto Democritus in a passionate embrace.

After Rose had expressed her thanks, she began to descend the stairs. However, somehow Democritus had become entangled in the rope when she had hugged him. He fell over, and the sudden shock was enough to reduce him to his insane form. He writhed about upon the ground, and Rose spoke soothing words to him. He attempted to bite her, but she leapt back. Eventually, with much snarling, griping, and mad howling, Democritus returned to his sane state.

"Rose, perhaps it would be better if we left me tied up like this. On the off chance that I should happen to go insane again, it would be better if I were unable to do any harm. You can carry me, as I weigh very little. I haven't eaten in weeks, so I'm even lighter than usual," concluded Democritus, who Rose had now officially pegged as long-winded. However, she agreed, and carried Democritus down the stairs.

When they reached the bottom, Rose noticed that the trail of blood was beginning to die down. She also saw that Democritus had not called it The Abyss for nothing; even with the torch burning brightly, she could barely see three feet in front of her. Eventually, however, she began to see a strange glow emanating from the walls.

"Democritus," she began timidly, "what sort of plants did the druids grow down here?"

"Well," started Democritus, "I'm not entirely sure. Obviously they glow, but no one's been down here for millennia. I'm not positive what a millennium's worth of unsupervised plant growth will yield, and I'm not sure I want to find out."

Rose's question was answered in a far more satisfactory manner by the sight of the next room. Luminescent trees covered all four walls of the room, all of which were linked by vines, and in the middle of the room was what appeared to be a person, completely shrouded in vines. "I recognize him!" exclaimed Democritus, horrified. "If you look closely, you can kind of see his face. He was part of the second order, and I was banished here before Virda judged him. He must have been sent here too!"

Suddenly, the figure twitched. Slowly, the mouth opened, and a horribly aged voice groaned, "Democritus. My old friend. Leader of the second order. The reason I'm here." He lurched forward, and Rose saw that to her horror, one of his arms was completely replaced with vines. Whether or not the same applied to the rest of his body, she could not tell. A fiery look came into his eyes and he shouted, "We all have our demons, Democritus, and mine are these vines! Virda cursed me to remain here until I could better understand the needs of flora, at the cost of my own body. I've become one with the vines, and they've given me strength far beyond that of an old man such as yourself! I've seen what your actions did to this world, and you must pay." With that, he leapt at Rose.

She jumped back, and accidentally dropped Democritus as a result. He suddenly began to thrash about and shouted, "Burn the vines, yes I will! Kill the vine man, yes I will. Burn! Burn with fire, bright fire, yes they will! I almost made a good fire, yes I did, but — "

He was unable to finish his sentence, as the vine man leapt at him. Democritus tried to tear through his ropes, so as to fight his adversary, but to no avail. The vine warrior struck Democritus in the abdomen, sending him hurtling back. However, one of the thorns on the vine warrior's arms sliced through the ropes that bound Democritus, and he threw the rest off in an instant. He leapt to his feet with a snarl, and pointed himself at his enemy. He launched himself at his opponent, arms stretched out. He flailed wildly, tearing through some of his adversary's vines. Rose fled in terror as the two members of the second order fought to the death.

***

Democritus had been carrying his torch, as Rose's hands had been filled with, well, him. He had dropped it when Rose dropped him, and his old friend had failed to notice it. Democritus slashed at him, but even in his insane state, he could see that that was getting him nowhere. He saw the torch lying on the ground, and saw the connection between a tree and his assailant, and he knew that trees burned. With a vicious snarl, he kicked his old friend in the stomach, and, as his friend recoiled from the blow, Democritus pushed him into the flames. As the flames consumed him, he screamed, and shouted with his own voice, and the voices of the vines he wore, "Democritus! You've burnt me! My plant parts are dying, and it won't be long before I will tooooooaaaauggghhh!" In his dying moment, he reached out with his mind to the rest of the plants, and told them, in no uncertain terms, to avenge his death.

Democritus, of course, was entirely unaware of this as he danced around his fallen foe, arms waving madly in the air. "Kill the nasty man, yes I did, yes I did! Find something to burn! Yes... I will find something, and he will burn! Burnburnburn! He will burn, yes he will!" Suddenly, the ancient madman became aware of motion in the chamber around him. The vines that covered the walls seemed to come to life, and surged towards Democritus.

"Back! Back!" he shouted crazily, swatting at them with his torch as the vines converged on him. Though a few of them caught on fire, dozens more took their place. Democritus was soon surrounded, and he screamed as he was absorbed in a sea of green. A vine wrapped itself around his mouth, and though he struggled violently, he could not free himself. He felt himself slipping away, and his lungs began to burn from a lack of oxygen. He felt a slight pain around his legs, and then everything went black.

***

Democritus awoke to find himself dangling from a mass of vines. He screamed as his senses returned, and he felt thousands of thorns clawing away at the flesh on his legs. He looked down, and saw that glowing thorny vines were twisting around his legs, and were beginning to encase him in a coffin of thorns. A shriek of agony tore itself from his lips, and he lost his grip on sanity. His eyes suddenly widened, and he pushed as hard as he could on the thorns, tearing the skin on his hands. He ripped his legs out of their thorny vice, at the price of a thousand rips in his skin.

He fell to the ground, and crawled away from the vines. As he crawled, he looked at his legs, which were in a fairly bad condition. Most of the skin was ripped, and a couple of the deeper scratched penetrated down into the muscle, and one particularly deep scratch on his left leg went all the way to the bone. However, none of the muscles were completely useless, and he was just able to crawl, at great pain. Some of the nerves had been killed by the damage to his skin, though, and Democritus grabbed the torch, though it had long gone out, and waved it at the vines, envisioning them burning. As the plants in the room had not moved for millennia, their reflexes were somewhat sluggish, and that allowed Democritus sufficient time to escape.

He crawled into the next room to see the girl sleeping on the floor. "Nasty girl, she should burn in the fire, nice big fire, to keep away the trees and the fog, yes she will. She should have burnt before, yes she should have, yes," he muttered. He crouched on the floor, and found two pieces of rock, and struck them together, in a vain attempt to light the torch again. After he failed, he whispered to himself, "She'll burn just as well dead, won't she? Yes she will." He moved forwards to strangle her, but as he reached out his hands, he was tackled from behind.

***

Rose ran down the tunnel, shrouded in the pale glow of the luminescent plants, and followed by the sound of battle coming from behind her. She tripped over a rock, but regained her balance before she hit the ground. She straightened up, but as she did, she heard a sharp crack from behind her, and it sounded to her like one of them had come into contact with the floor in a very rude manner. She heard Democritus' adversary scream in pain, and heard the spread of flames. An orange glow crawled down the tunnel, telling her that she was right, there was fire burning in the other room. Suddenly, she felt the mood in the tunnel change. The plants began to sway, though there was no breeze, and the tunnel wall slowly began to collapse, spraying debris everywhere. Rose screamed as a piece of rock the size of Democritus came crashing to the floor, just barely missing her. However, she was less lucky with the other, smaller, pieces, which crashed into her head, rattling her vision. The plants about her seemed to surge towards the tunnel where Democritus lay, driven by some unknown force.

Rose ran out of the tunnel, and into a room untouched by plant life. However, there was a pool in the center of the cavern, and Rose could see dots of light decorating the bottom. She strode over, and peered into the pool. She could see fish swimming about, and she saw that they were the source of the light. They had odd tentacle-like appendages, each of which had a luminescent bulb at the end. However, there was not much else to notice about the room, and she searched for the exit. She found it hidden between two stalagmites, each fully embracing the ceiling. She turned around and looked about the room one last time, and saw something she had missed at first: the figure of a boy huddled up against one of the stalagmites.

***

Adrian did not know where he was, only that he did not want to be there. For a few seconds, he entertained the possibility that he was dead, for the last thing he remembered was falling down into a seemingly bottomless pit. A quick pinch to the arm quickly dispatched that notion, for he was fairly sure that dead people could not feel pain. He looked about him, and, in the dim light, saw that he was standing atop what appeared to be a large staircase. He decided that the best course of action would be to follow the stairs down, for they might lead to a way out. As he stood up, he was besieged by pain from both his arm, which felt broken, and his head, which was in shock from the fall. His memory of the fifth dimension began to leech away at his strength, and he felt slightly ill. Nevertheless, he proceeded down the steps.

When he reached the bottom, he felt just about ready to drop dead, but a strange force of will kept him going forwards. He proceeded down a tunnel, bracing himself against the wall with his hand, and eventually came to a cave filled with glowing trees. The soft light burnt his eyes, and his headache intensified a thousand-fold. He dashed through the chamber, ignoring both the pain in his arm and the man-like plant growth in the center of the room. He came out into a similarly glowing chamber, though the light was less intense. He raced through this one as well, disregarding the pain in his arm. He came out of that tunnel, and came into a chamber with a glowing pool. This time, the light soothed his aching eyes, and he decided to take a rest in this room. However, he saw the door, and whatever force was giving him the will to keep walking was also doing its best to keep him from stopping. He walked towards the door, but his legs gave out from under him. He crawled over to a stalagmite, and closed his eyes.

***

Rose force-fed Adrian a piece of dried fruit, after failing to wake him after many vigorous attempts. She was exhausted, as she always seemed to be these days, but she kept herself awake for Adrian's sake. In the few minutes in which she had believed Adrian to be dead, she had promised herself that if someone else were in trouble, she would do everything in her power to help that person. Now that she knew Adrian was alive, she resolved to do everything in her power to help him, as she had promised herself she would. After feeding him, she poured some water down his throat. She had made a sling for his arm after finding it to be broken, and after she had attempted to set the bones. She didn't think she did a terrible job, but she was sure any doctor could do a better one.

For no apparent reason, Adrian began to stir. He slowly opened his eyes, and murmured, "Rose?"

Rose, suddenly overcome with emotion, slapped him. "Adrian, don't ever scare anyone like that again! We thought you were dead! If Democritus hadn't-" she lost her composure, and hugged Adrian tightly, as if she would never let go. Adrian let her stay there for a few minutes, but the strange foreign will willed him on.

"Rose, we should really get going. I'm tired of tunnels, and being underground, and of breathing old air. Plus, I feel some sort of strange consciousness here, and it doesn't feel, well, human." he shuddered. Rose let go of him, then hugged him one more time, and let go again.

"Wait," she said suddenly, struck by a thought. "Adrian, we should get Democritus!"

"What, the old lunatic?" Adrian laughed weakly.

"He's not always like that!" protested Rose. "After all, he saved my life, and helped me to find you. But once in a while, he goes insane, but is that really so bad? Anyhow..." Rose was unable to finish her sentence, as she was attacked by a fit of yawns.

"Tell you what," smiled Adrian. "You rest up here, and I'll go look for, uh, Democritus, I believe you called him."

***

Adrian walked down the hallway, slowed down by his sling, and the rocks scattered about the floor. He had never actually broken a bone before, so the experience was new to him. The inability to move his arm irked him a good deal, and his less than pleasant thoughts distracted him from the task at hand. Suddenly, he heard labored breathing, and a voice muttered, "Burn the vines with the girl, yes I will." He recognized the strange use of 'yes I will' as something done by Democritus, so he flattened himself against the wall, so as not to be seen.

The strange old man passed him by, crawling, and Adrian held his breath, hoping that he had not been seen. However, Democritus proceeded unabated, and Adrian assumed he had not seen him. He followed Democritus down the tunnel, and into the room cavern. Once they reached the cavern, Democritus stood up. He seemed not to notice the pool, but made straight for Rose.

"Nasty girl, she should burn in the fire, nice big fire, to keep away the trees and the fog, yes she will. She should have burnt before, yes she should have, yes," he muttered. Adrian kept close behind him, preparing to strike. However, Democritus did something very strange: he picked up two pieces of rock, and began to bash them together, with his unlit torch underneath him. Adrian presumed that he was trying to start another fire, but he seemed to fail. "She'll burn just as well dead, won't she? Yes she will," whispered Democritus. These words sent shivers down Adrian's spine. Democritus bent down, presumably to attack Rose, and Adrian tackled him, with the positions of their original encounter reversed.

***

"Getoffgetoffgetoff!" shouted Democritus, flailing wildly. Adrian held on tight, trying to force him to the ground. The shouting woke Rose, and she sat up with a start. She blinked confusedly for a moment, and then she came to her senses.

"Adrian, what're you doing?" she cried preparing to break them up, as she seemed to need to.

Thankfully, Democritus shouted, "Burn you both, yes I will!" Rose could see that Democritus had lost his sanity, and she saw, to her horror, that his legs were horribly mangled, though apparently not bad enough to prevent him from fighting Adrian. A grim smile played its way across her face as she decided what to do, and she tackled Democritus by the legs. "Let gooooooo!!" screamed Democritus, flailing more wildly than before. However, his weak legs gave out from under him, and he fell to the floor.

"Rose, do you have any rope?" shouted Adrian, trying to hold down the flailing Democritus.

"I think he put some in my bag!" she said, and ran over to her bag and opened it. There was indeed a good deal of rope, and she tied Democritus up while Adrian held him down. He thrashed around and cursed for a few minutes, but eventually he settled down, and began to whimper.

"What do we do with him?" asked Adrian, bewildered.

"Well, we can't just leave him here," mused Rose, crossing her arms. "However, I don't think he'll return to sanity." Adrian shot her a quizzical look, and Rose pointed to his legs. The thorns had torn off virtually all of the skin, leaving a good deal of muscle showing. His legs were nothing but a bloody mess, and Adrian wondered how he had managed to stand at all. "Pain robs him of his sanity," explained Rose.

"Then I guess it stands to reason that he won't be coming to his senses anytime soon," mused Adrian. "I'll carry him out of the tunnel, and we'll decide what to do with him then." Adrian leaned down to pick up Democritus, and Democritus attempted to bite off part of his face.

"I guess that we should gag him?" suggested Rose. Adrian nodded, and Rose reached into her bag, and pulled out some more rope. Adrian tied it around their captive's mouth, resulting in much thrashing. However, Adrian was now able to pick up Democritus without having to fear for the well being of his face, though with only one arm fully usable, it was still a bit of a challenge. Adrian and Rose walked side by side into the last tunnel.

***

"Ungh, how long does this tunnel go on for?" groaned Rose. She figured they had been walking for at least a half hour.

"I don't know," began Adrian, "but I think that I can see light ahead!" He and Rose picked up their pace, quickening into what was almost a run. They burst out of the tunnel into a brightly lit cavern. The walls were smothered by luminous vegetation, but there was a clear path through it. In the center of the path was the last thing Adrian expected to see: a tree root, sticking out of the ground and reaching a few feet into the air. Then, the tree root did the last thing he expected it to do: it spoke.

"Greeting, Adrian Lightseeker, Rose Cores, and Democritus Deveridia. Welcome to my home, on behalf of the Great Sage," spoke the root in a low voice, projecting its words directly into their minds.

"First off, my last name isn't Lightseeker. Secondly, you're the Great Sage?" inquired Adrian, skeptical.

"No, not the Great Sage, merely his ambassador," explained the root. "He has ambassadors such as myself in all corners of the world."

"So he works with plants?" asked Rose, her curiosity aroused.

"He aided Virda with the founding of the order of druids," began the root, "and he is considerably more knowledgeable about plants than the greatest of the druids. So, to answer your question, yes, he works with plants. However, that is not my prime concern. I was assigned here by the Great Sage so I could keep an eye on Democritus, should he try to slip out before he learned his lesson."

"Burn the trees, yes I will!" shouted Democritus through the plant's mind link.

"From what I have seen, he has not!" judged the ambassador. "Therefore, he must remain here. At least, that's what I would have done, had he not slain another member of his second order. For now, the penalty must be death!" The root sent a mental call to the plants around the room, and thorn vines began to attack Democritus.

"STOP!" ordered Rose, and everything froze. "Democritus has learned his lesson. At least, the real Democritus has. This twisted thing here," Rose pointed to Democritus, "is not the real Democritus. This is the other side of him, the darker side, but he tries his hardest to repress it! Please, just listen to me!"

"Allow me to see if this is true," said the root. He reached out to Democritus with his mind, and seemed to draw the information he needed. "You are indeed correct, Rose Cores. However, were I to remove the darker side of Democritus, it would go directly against Virda's wishes, and it might cause him irrevocable harm. I must consult with the Great Sage about this." With that, the root became still, and seemed to retreat into its own mind.

"Adrian, what should we do?" asked Rose, as Democritus thrashed about on the floor.

"We'll see what the Great Sage's verdict is. Then we'll decide what to do," whispered Adrian, as the plant seemed to come back to life.

"The Great Sage," began the plant, "has decided to let Democritus live. However," said the root, catching Rose's jubilant expression, "there is a condition. Democritus' legs will be healed, and then he will be instructed to go to the City of Twilight, where you two seem to be going also. If he has rid himself of his dark side on the journey, he will be spared. However, if he has not, he will instead be slain. This is the will of the Great Sage."

Suddenly, vines shot out towards Democritus, and wrapped themselves around his legs, beginning to heal them. "The healing process may take longer than I thought," mused the ambassador. I believe that he will have to have those vines on his legs for a while longer, as they continue to heal him."

"Burn the vines. Getoffgetoff! Yes I will!" shouted Democritus, clawing at the vines wrapped around his legs. However, they seemed to be very firm, and they did not give.

"Perhaps you should leave him?" suggested the root. "He's quite capable of taking care of himself, and he'd just be a burden for you."

"Maybe he's right," whispered Rose, mostly to herself. "He'll just be a burden and he can survive on his own, especially with his legs healed."

"We should leave him," said Adrian, his mind made up. "The ambassador is right, he'll just slow us down." Rose nodded. "Ambassador," began Adrian, "Could you do me one more favor? I would really appreciate it if you could heal my arm. I broke it when I fell down here."

"Very well," sighed the ambassador.

Vines wrapped themselves around Adrian's arm, and in a few seconds, it was healed, though it still pained him. "It will most likely continue to hurt for about a week or so," explained the ambassador.

"Well, tell the Great Sage that we're coming to meet him," nodded Adrian, heading towards the exit from the cave. "I'm afraid that we have to be on our way. It was nice meeting you."

Adrian and Rose turned in unison and walked out of the cave, glancing over their shoulders at the Sage's ambassador. Promptly, however, their attention returned to getting out of the long and winding cave, and within minutes Adrian felt a cool breeze rustle through his clothes. He and Rose picked up their paces, and soon Adrian's vision was gifted with a burst of sunlight.

***

Adrian stumbled out of the cave, slowed down by his exhaustion. He felt the alien will lift from his mind, and gave into his own will, which was telling him to sit down and rest. He sat down underneath a tree, and looked up at the sky. There didn't seem to be a moon gracing the sky of this world, and he wasn't entirely sure how he had missed this intriguing fact before. He remembered the last time he had seen the sky of his own world: the night he had run home from the orphanage with James. Once again, he wondered who was controlling Kronos, and why he needed to sacrifice Adrian, as opposed to any other boy. After all, if he hadn't specifically needed Adrian, he could have just grabbed some other boy, and been off. However, he had sent the necrossis after him, and the words from Adrian's dream from days — or was it weeks? — ago: "Bring me the Lightseeker," still echoed in his mind, enhanced by the fact that the root had called him by that very name. This, coupled with the fact that Adrian had somehow summoned white lightning to ward off the necrossis, suggested to him that he was involved in something beyond his control.

"Adrian, do you know where we are?" inquired Rose, piercing his period of reflection.

Adrian consulted his map, and responded, "I'm not sure, exactly, but I have a general idea. If you look kinda closely you can see a cloud of fog in the distance, and I think that's Light's End. Do you have a compass?"

"Vitalius might have put one in the bag, I'm not sure," replied Rose. She too sat down, and rummaged through the backpack. Triumphantly, she pulled a compass out of the bag, and handed it to Adrian. He held it out flat, and rotated himself so that he was facing north. "We're at the outskirts of the Deadwood," he answered with conviction. "We're a little further east than when we were at the Verdant Sanctuary, but that's okay. But can't we rest for a bit before continuing our trek?" Rose nodded, and sat down next to Adrian. In a few seconds, they were both asleep.

***

"Just a few more minutes," mumbled Adrian, who was being prodded. In the fuzziness of being half-awake, he assumed that it was his mother prodding him, presumably followed by a lecture about why it was good to wake up before the sunrise. However, when he opened his eyes, he found himself staring down a- well, he wasn't quite sure what it was. It looked sort of like a person, but with longer limbs. Also, it was made entirely out of vines, which Adrian noticed with a start. It didn't have a face, *per se*, but Adrian was fairly sure that it could see him just fine. And though Adrian was pretty sure that he should feel scared, the vine thing just didn't feel dangerous. Adrian sat up slowly, and the creature jumped back a few feet. It took a timid step towards Adrian, and then reached out what seemed to be its arm in a gesture of friendship. Adrian took the thing's arm, and shook it. The thing seemed off-put for a second, but then it shook Adrian's hand in return. Adrian pulled himself up and saw that the vine thing was actually a good deal shorter than him. Then Adrian looked around and saw, to his dismay, that Rose was gone. However, the vine thing was pulling on Adrian's arm, apparently trying to lead him somewhere. Adrian looked up, and saw that he was right at the edge of the cloud layer. He picked up his backpack, and began to walk after the vine thing, which seemed to be leading him in a southwesterly direction. Sunlight poured down on his face as he followed the strange creature. He heard a branch crack to his left, and turned to look. To his surprise, he saw Rose walk out of the brambles.

"Adrian!" she shouted, and jumped back a few inches. "Wow, you took me by surprise! I was just taking a look around, since you seemed to be determined to sleep. I tried to wake you, but you resisted."

She looked down, and seemed to notice the vine-person for the first time.

"Adrian, who's your, um, friend?" inquired Rose, sizing up the vine thing. It pulled vigorously on Adrian's sleeve.

"I'm not entirely sure, but he seems friendly enough," responded Adrian. He gave into the tugging, and allowed the vine thing to lead him further into the forest. He realized that he had been led out from the sunshine, and was now under the constant shade of the cloud layer. A shiver involuntarily crept down his spine as the warmth of the sunlight vanished. Rose shivered harder, and hugged herself. The thing, however, seemed undeterred, and continued on at its previous pace. The trees became much more thickly bunched, and Adrian saw things dart from tree to tree.

Suddenly, a large cat erupted from the bushes, snarling fiercely. It was like the one that he had fought before, but bigger and meaner looking.

The cat took a step towards Adrian, and the vine thing stepped in front, presumably to protect him. The cat lunged, catching Vinetia, as Adrian had dubbed his new acquaintance, off-guard. A shriek sprung from its lips as it fell back, and Adrian took a step forwards. He tried to call up lightning, like before, but it appeared that he could only achieve that task under specific circumstances. Adrian guessed that this cat would not be placated by a piece of fruit. Out of ideas, Adrian wildly charged at the cat, desperately hoping something would happen. He was not disappointed.

Vinetia seemed to meditate, calling upon some hidden power. Vines erupted from the ground, twisting themselves around the cat. In the moment that the cat was immobilized, Adrian locked onto it with a stranglehold. The cat thrashed about at first, but then allowed itself to be subdued, whimpering. Adrian let go, seeing that the cat was no longer a threat.

"What else lives around here?!" exclaimed Rose as the cat walked away. Vinetia pulled at Adrian's arm again; he was clearly intent on getting Adrian wherever he was leading him as quickly as possible. Adrian was beginning to wonder exactly how long the walk was when Vinetia led him to a clearing. In the middle of the clearing was a hut, surrounded by at least twenty more vine people. They all seemed to be intent on repairing the hut, which seemed to have sustained a good deal of damage, somehow.

Adrian saw how the house had been damaged very quickly. A flock of birds had been circling the clearing, but Adrian had failed to notice them. Suddenly, they dive-bombed the hut, cawing ferociously as they tried to tear it to shreds. All the vine people, except for Vinetia, screeched and hid themselves. Adrian, however, charged at the flock.

"Shoo! Go away! Scram!" shouted Adrian as he beat at the birds with his good arm. One of the birds rammed him in the chest, and Adrian felt the skin give way as the beak entered his chest. He winced, and pulled himself away, and picked up a stick. He ran at the birds, swinging his branch about wildly. They scattered when he came near, and flew away.

"What were those?" panted Adrian, trying to stop the blood from leaking out of the puncture wound. As Rose had no answer, he walked back towards the hut. He suddenly heard a vicious caw from behind him, and turned around to see another, bigger bird flying straight at him. He held up his arm to protect himself, but Vinetia intercepted the bird in midair. The beak tore right through the vines that made up his body, but the bird suddenly fell down to the ground, weighed down by the vine man. The bird's spine seemed to shatter at the impact, and it became limp.

"Vinetia!" cried Adrian, rushing over to the fallen vine man.

"Welcome to my home, strangers of Maltesque," smirked a strange man in a somewhat high and whiny voice, stepping out from the hut. He was very tall and skinny, with greasy black hair. He was sneering, and was slightly stooped over. "Well, I bid you welcome, Adrian Cantor."

"Wait," said Adrian, confused. "How do you know my name?"

"I overheard you talking with the ambassador, silly," smirked the man. "I've been keeping tabs on our friend, the ambassador. I overheard his conversation with you."

"Who are you?" asked Rose, confused as to how that was possible.

"I serve Necropheus the Great, lord of all that lives in this barren world," began the man. "I'm his informant. As to how I keep tabs on the root, let me show you. Just step into my hut, and you'll see."

As the spy stepped into his hut, Rose asked, "Should we trust this guy?" to Adrian.

"I don't know," responded Adrian, "but I'm curious about his spying on the ambassador, and thus the Great Sage himself. If he's a potential threat, we should definitely warn the root."

Adrian stepped into his hut, and what he saw shocked him to his core. A root, just like the ambassador, was in the center of the hut. At least thirty ropes were pulling it in different directions, and multiple knives were driven into the root. Some sort of red sap was seeping out from several wounds, and two syringes were forcing what appeared to be poison into the root. Adrian could have sworn that he heard a faint voice shouting, "Help!"

"What- Why-" Adrian was at a loss for words. Rose seemed similarly shocked.

However, the spy seemed to take their reactions as awe, as opposed to horror. "I hope that you can see the brilliance of my work. With the will of this ambassador repressed, I can spy on all of the others. Yes, this poor, damaged root used to be an ambassador of the Great Sage. However, after years of work, I broke the spirit of this root, by inflicting enough pain upon it to drive it mad, but not so much as to kill it. Now, by using the powers granted to me by my master, I can force my way into the ambassador's mind, and use its connection to the other roots on Maltesque to observe the goings-on of the world. So, what do you think?"

Adrian could very clearly see that he was dealing with a very dangerous man, and acted accordingly. "I think," he began, "that this is a work of genius!"

Rose looked at him with a horrified expression, and was about to open her mouth to violently object to Adrian's comment, but she suddenly seemed to catch on. Shakily, she said, "Well, I agree." Lying wasn't her thing, however, and the spy gave her a quizzical look before Adrian redirected the man's attention to himself.

"Well, sir, I thank you for your hospitality, but my friend was injured in the battle with the birds that attacked your house. I would really appreciate it if you could heal him, or, her. I can't really tell."

"Your friend," inquired the spy, confused. "Oh, you mean the guide I sent to fetch you. She's expendable. You needn't worry about her."

"Please, sir, save her!" exclaimed Rose. "She was hurt protecting us, and I'd feel awful if she died."

"Very well," sighed the man, shrugging. "But please stop calling me sir. My name is Blaise, and I'd really like it if you called me that."

They stepped outside, and Blaise walked over to Vinetia. He knelt down before the vine-woman and seemed to meditate, like Vinetia had done while fighting the cat. He was surrounded by a pulsating green glow with splotches of gray and darker green mixed in, and extended it out to Vinetia. The wounds seemed to stitch themselves together, and Vinetia began to breathe normally again. Blaise began to pant, and he remained in his kneeling position for a few moments. "I never was very good at Greenkeeping," he muttered, forcing every word out. He staggered to his feet, and said, "There! Happy? I healed your friend. Now, what should I do with you two?"

"Well, we'd be happy to be on our way," suggested Adrian, eager to get away from this Blaise character.

"No, that won't do," mused Blaise, stroking his chin with his hand. "Perhaps I should take you to see Necropheus. I'm sure he'll be happy to meet you."

"Well, where does he live?' inquired Adrian, figuring that if he lived in the right direction it wouldn't hurt to have a guide on their journey.

"His house is to the south," wheezed Blaise, suddenly exhausted. "He lives in the center of the Deadwood, by the river. Will you come?"

"Yes, we will," answered Rose, with the same intentions as Adrian. However, she was also fueled by curiosity as to the identity of this Necropheus character, and was wondering why Blaise described him as the 'lord of all'.

"Well, do you agree?" asked Blaise to Adrian in the manner of a moderator of a presidential debate.

"I do," firmly stated Adrian.

"Then it's settled," murmured Blaise. "We'll set out tomorrow, as soon as I get some rest. Do you two mind sleeping out here? I hope not, as there's only enough room for me in my hut." With that, he walked back into his house.

"Adrian, what are we going to do about him?" asked Rose, once she was sure that Blaise couldn't hear them.

"I don't know for sure," murmured Adrian. "I do have an idea, however. We let him take us to the house of this Necropheus guy, and then we'll ditch him. He doesn't look like a fast runner, so we should be able to outrun him."

"Well, that sounds like a good plan to me," concurred Rose. "I am vaguely curious about this Necropheus character, but Blaise scares me. How could he do that to a peaceful ambassador?"

"We'll need to warn the Great Sage if we get the chance. Anyways, we'd have to be nuts to trust Blaise. Be on your guard. If he finds out that we-"

Adrian jumped as the door to the hut slammed open, and Blaise came out. "I thought that you might appreciate having a blanket to sleep under." He tossed them the blanket, and he went back inside.

"How much do you think he heard?" asked Rose, shaking.

"Not much, I hope," responded Adrian, frightened by the encounter. He and Rose lay down, and put the blanket over themselves.

6

Under Ajax

J ames was furious. He had spent an entire week under the command of Ajax, and what had they accomplished? Nothing! The thought of Adrian in peril, and Ajax just sitting around, doing nothing, was enough to make James want to smash all of the intricate devices in Ajax's hideout, or, as James had begun to call it, the lab.

"Ajax, I still don't see what all of this sitting around is doing. Adrian is in danger! Kronos is probably setting all of his efforts on finding him, and I don't think it's going to end well if he does," stormed James, venting his frustration.

"I told you, James, Adrian is perfectly safe," began Ajax. "You are, however, right about Kronos attempting to find him. Don't let that go to your head, though. I felt a surge of light energy emanating from Adrian a few days ago, a reaction which could only have resulted from contact with darkness. My guess is that Adrian managed to escape from Kronos somehow, and Kronos' master gave Kronos one of his most feared creations: a necrossis, with which he was to track down Adrian."

"How do you know so much about Kronos?" asked James, finally summoning up the courage to ask the question that had been bothering him from the start.

"You are very bold to ask me that; a bit too bold, perhaps. I will not answer that, however. Maybe, if you prove yourself, I can tell you. But you're not quite there yet," answered Ajax, in his typical grouchy manner.

"Also, what does all of this waiting around accomplish? If we're trying to build a light laser, couldn't we do it in here?" inquired James, dissatisfied by Ajax's previous explanations.

"The truth is," began Ajax in a voice suggesting a previous crushing defeat, "I have been trying to create a laser for the past twenty years, but I have lacked a crucial piece of information: how to pack the energy into the smaller dimensions. All of my previous attempts failed, and that's why I decided to wait, and let Kronos do the work for me. After all, why do work when others can do it for you?" he chuckled.

"But you're right," said Ajax, straightening up. "The time for waiting has passed. Though I'm guessing that Adrian's use of light energy weakened Kronos, I'll bet that when he recovers, he'll try to find Adrian harder than ever. We need to try to save Adrian before that happens."

"Alright!" exclaimed James, excited that his arguments had finally made an impact on Ajax. " So, what are we gonna do?"

"I don't know if 'we' are going to do anything. I think that it might be better if you stayed behind. You haven't given me proof that I can trust you yet," mused Ajax.

"How can I win your trust if you won't let me do anything for you?" shouted James, losing his patience. "If you won't let me accompany you, maybe you'd be better off without me!"

"Oh come now, James. I'm not as agile as I used to be, and I need someone younger than myself to help me with this. And you need to find Adrian, because he's your only friend, even if you won't admit it," smirked Ajax, holding up a hand to stifle James' furious response. "You can come with me, but it won't be very interesting. All I plan to do is post video cameras around the city to keep tabs on the people, and try to find out where most of them work. Thankfully, the roads leading to Pilfershire have been blocked off, so the darkness contamination should remain repressed for a few weeks, before the deity — er, rather, Kronos' master, decides to focus his efforts on spreading it to the other people on this world."

"Wait, do you mean that there are other worlds in this universe, with people on them?" gasped James, fascinated.

"Yes. The human is the ultimate representation of intelligent life, and they, or we, have developed on other worlds. Most of them are at the same level of intelligence as us, with a few exceptions," explained Ajax, with a faraway look in his eye.

"I'll ask you again; how do you know so much?" exclaimed James.

"And I'll give you the same answer again: I'll tell you when you earn my trust. However, I will give you a hint; the story goes back to the creation of the multiverse. Now come on, we need to set up these cameras."

***

James looked around the corner of the building before sprinting into the street. Ajax followed him closely, glancing about as he ran through the road. James quickly ran into an abandoned building, overlooking the skate park, which had been just outside of the district that had been attacked by darkness, and thrown into the air. The skate park was composed of a large cement bowl stuck in the ground, and several objects inside the bowl that allowed skate-boarders to perform various tricks. It had not seen a good deal of usage in recent years, as it was just a little too close to the abandoned district for comfort. There were vines crawling up several of the railings, and some of the cement had begun to disintegrate. James took a camera out of his bag, and affixed it to the windowsill, so it was facing the skate park. He flipped the switch, activating the portable battery pack. It wirelessly began to feed the image of the skate park to a computer in the lab. Ajax glanced around; making sure that nobody was lurking outside the door. He gave the all-clear signal, and they snuck out of the doorway. They crept down the cracked street, for fear of the tendrils of darkness. They had contaminated the entire town with the darkness virus, and now everyone within city limits was working towards the same goal: to spread the contamination to the rest of the universe.

"Where to next?" whispered James, pressing up against a wall.

"Well, we've got most of the northeastern side of town covered, but I propose that we head back. We're running low on cameras, and I'm tired of running away from everything," answered Ajax.

"So, we're heading back to the lab?" inquired James.

"Right you are," answered Ajax

***

James stepped back into the ruined building, and Ajax walked over to the steel dome. He opened the hidden door with a touch of his hand, and they both stepped inside.

A few moments later, Ajax and James stepped out of the elevator, and walked into the recreation room Ajax had somewhat recently added to the lab. James threw himself down on the couch, and Ajax followed suit. Ajax flipped on the T.V, and changed the channel to the news.

"And now, reporting to you from Washington D.C, this is news reporter Jim Johnson," said the newscaster. "Congress is debating how to respond to the strange goings on in the small New England town of Pilfershire. Rumors have been flying about, and most theories involve some sort of mind control. Paranoia seems to be striking deep even into the hearts of even the politicians. The general theory of congress is that this was a test of a new terrorist weapon, with which they could control the entire country."

"Ridiculous!" scoffed Ajax. "No human could ever pull off a stunt like this."

"Then what did cause this?" inquired James, his curiosity piqued.

"Well, suffice it to say not a human," muttered Ajax, the faraway look returning to his eyes. "No, this was caused by something much greater than a human. One might even go as far as to call it a god. But enough of that! Let's see what our friend the newscaster has to say."

"This just in: Congress has decided to send a SWAT team to investigate the town, and see if it's safe to open the roads back up," said Jim. "Keep watching CNN for more details. Until next time, this is Jim Johnson, signing off."

"Well, that complicates things," sighed Ajax. "We'd better keep an eye on the SWAT team members, since I doubt they'll resist darkness contamination for long. Swat team members would make a very dangerous enemy, so we'd best get going. Come on, lazy, get up!" With that, James and Ajax got up off of the couch, and Ajax went off into the next room to fetch more cameras. James glanced around, really examining the recreation room for the first time. He saw innumerable video game systems, along with foosball tables, and dozens of computers littering the walls. He saw many other things lying around, and wondered again how much money Ajax had.

Ajax returned from the one room that he had forbidden James to go into, carrying several more cameras. He dumped them onto the couch and said, "Take five, and put them in your bag. We're heading to the southeastern section of town." James complied, and he and Ajax walked back to the elevator. James made the interesting observation that though many passages led from the elevator room, they had only ever followed one. That one led to the generator room, which led to the recreation room, which led to the forbidden room. James was starting to sketch a map of the lab, since he had nothing better to do, so he took note of this kind of thing. He and Ajax ascended the elevator, and stepped out into the ruined building. They looked about to make sure no one was around, and then they stepped into the street.

They raced down the street, slipping into buildings whenever they saw someone coming. After a half-hour of running, they began to periodically set up the cameras in some of the houses. They saw a bunch of people clustered around a certain building.

"We'll have to keep a close eye on this place," muttered Ajax, hiding in one of the surrounding houses. He and James set up two cameras to keep an eye on that building, lest one of them malfunction.

As they stepped out of their hiding place, James let out a gasp. In the street, he saw Mr. Cantor, Adrian's father, walking towards the building. He seemed to hear James gasp, and swirled around in his direction. Ajax pulled him back into the building, and slapped him in the face.

"Are you *trying* to give us away?" he hissed, glaring at James.

"That's Adrian's father. How can you expect me not to react?" snapped James, irritated by the rough treatment of Ajax. "If he's been possessed, that's a problem. He looks like he was quite the athlete in college. Do you think he saw me?"

"I don't know, but I'd bet my life that he heard you," grumbled Ajax. "We'd better get back to the lab, before he returns with reinforcements."

***

"KRONOS! Listen to me!" raged the dark voice, infuriated by his servant.

"Sorry, my lord, but after we were attacked by Adrian, my thoughts have begun to wander," said Kronos, through his weakened mental link with his master. "Anyhow, I w—l n-w repo-t..."

"KRONOS! Focus on me! Keep those filthy thoughts of rebellion out of your head, and tell me what's going on!" shouted the dark voice, struggling to maintain his mental link with his servant.

"Very well. You were right, fate does seem to be leaning towards the side of light," began Kronos. "Somehow Adrian managed to force me to crash-land on Maltesque, and then he manages to escape from me, due to the actions of some eco-terrorists. Then, I sent the necrossis after him, and he summons up light energy to destroy it with. Thankfully, things are going as planned in the other universe."

"Are you sure about that?" inquired the dark voice, and Kronos cringed. "There seems to have been a little... complication... if you will. Is it not true that Ajax Lightseeker was spotted the other day?"

"It is true, my lord," murmured Kronos. "But I was going to tell you, please believe me!"

"Enough pleading, Kronos! We shall do nothing for the present, since Adrian seems intent on getting to us, which is right where we want him," commanded Kronos' master. "Let Ajax be for a few days. When I say that, I mean don't directly confront him. Follow him for a day or two, and then strike when it seems appropriate."

"Yes, my lord."

***

The next day, Ajax and James set out for the northwest corner of town, bringing along several cameras. They saw rather quickly, however, that there would be no need for them. There was nothing one could conceivably call a building, just ruins everywhere. They had entered into the area that had closest to the devastation, short of the devastated area itself.

"Well, there's nothing to see around here," remarked James, looking about.

"Wrong, boy," snapped Ajax. "Look over to the southwest, and you'll see what I see." James did that, and saw a giant bubble of darkness, which all of the tendrils converged upon.

"The heart of darkness," James whispered, inching backwards.

"More or less," responded Ajax, with the faraway look returning to his eyes. "One might more accurately call it the dark miniverse, created by Kronos for the sole purpose of contaminating this world with darkness. It is that very target at which we will fire the light laser, once it is completed. But that isn't the thing that interests me the most. Look just next to the bubble."

"There's a woman there!" exclaimed James, closely scrutinizing the space around the bubble. "It's Mrs. Cantor!"

"Yes, that makes sense. Serena is feeding the darkness, so those who love her most are most affected," mused Ajax.

"So Kronos' master is using them to keep the others in order?" wondered James. Suddenly, he became aware of a presence behind him. He whirled about, but saw nothing. However, he thought that he saw someone slip behind a ruined building. "Let's go," he whispered to Ajax. Ajax nodded in agreement, and they ran back to his hideout without further incident.

***

The day after, James had a feeling of dread in the pit of his stomach as he woke up. He rolled out of bed and stretched, seeing that Ajax was still asleep. He was still curious about the room that Ajax had forbidden him to enter. He began to walk down the passageway leading to the room, and he saw pictures of books lining the wall. He took a closer look, and saw that they weren't pictures; they were the actual books. Also, they seemed to be drafts of the same book, but the title seemed to have been erased. He stepped towards the wall, when suddenly...

"STEP AWAY FROM THE BOOKS!" James whirled around to see Ajax angrily glaring at him. "I told you to *stay away* from this hallway!" he shouted, stalking towards James. "Did you go into the room?" he asked, staring James down.

"N-no, sir," stammered James, frightened by Ajax's violent reaction.

"Good," grunted Ajax. "Let's go. We've got cameras to set up."

"Where?" asked James, figuring that they had already covered the entire town. Granted, they hadn't covered the southwestern part of Pilfershire, but there was nothing but ruins there.

"The area around the dark miniverse. We need to keep an eye on it," grunted Ajax.

"If you say so," sighed James.

"I do."

***

James stepped out of the abandoned building that concealed the lab with Ajax close behind. They walked westwards, towards the abandoned observatory. Though it seemed innocent enough, James saw several guards hiding inside the building. They turned south, and began to walk towards the skate park. It seemed desolate, and James was pretty sure he was right about that one. When they reached the skate park, they took a right onto the shattered road that led to Main Street. The pavement was cracked by all of the earthquakes, which had stopped, since the dark miniverse had finally assimilated itself fully into our universe.

James saw the aquarium to his left, which didn't look nearly as bad as he thought it did. In fact, it seemed like the possessed people had rebuilt it, though James couldn't for the life of him figure out why. Though the sun was shining right on it, it seemed like it was shrouded in darkness.

"Enough loafing!" shouted Ajax, turning to glare at James. Without further ado, they proceeded onto Main Street.

They walked onto the street, and James saw exactly how much the town had changed in the past few weeks. Though it had never really been clean, per se, it had always been at least passable. However, it was now a total wreck. Debris from buildings littered the street, which was now broken into fragments. Water poured from sewage pipes, which now were piercing the skin of the street, spilling their waste for all to see. Worse yet, there were now more people on it than there had ever been before. The dark voice seemed to have sent all of the people he could muster to guard the street, and James was at a loss as to how they could possibly pass the crowd.

"We need a distraction," whispered Ajax. "Perhaps you could serve as a distraction, and draw them away, and then you could head back to the hideout, and I'd meet you there."

"Ajax, I don't know how to get into the hideout," responded James. "Could you tell me?"

"Actually, it's activated by my handprint. Maybe I could serve as a distraction, and you could set up the cameras. However, they'd see the entrance, and we wouldn't be able to use it again," pondered Ajax.

"Well, do you have a back entrance?" asked James, curious.

"Do you suggest that we use it now?" suggested Ajax, cutting off James' response. "That wouldn't work. It's not as well guarded. Still, if we use it later, that could work. So to answer your question, yes, I do have a back entrance. It's in the basement of the store just north of the skate park. Let's stick with me being the distraction, so you can set up the cameras."

James nodded in agreement, and they walked in different directions.

***

Ajax ran up the street, keeping out of the sight of the possessed people. He was nearly seen once, but he ducked out of sight just in time. He avoided the aquarium, as it was crawling with the taint of darkness. He thought he spotted several tendrils inside, and though the sun was shining directly upon it, Ajax couldn't see it totally clearly, as it was still shrouded in shadow. Just north of the aquarium, the building he had noticed two days ago was still infested with people. He had to keep to the shadows to avoid being seen, but he thought that he still felt a presence from behind him. Though he looked over his shoulder numerous times, he was never able to actually catch his mysterious stalker.

After ten or so minutes, Ajax reached the alley that led back to Main Street. He quickly looked about, and rushed down the alley as quickly as he could. The first part of the back street was blocked off by a toppled building. This was no true obstacle for Ajax; he bounded over it in a matter of seconds. He crept down the street silently, and he prepared himself for his mad race back to the lab.

"Shadius!" he shouted, using the hidden name of Kronos' master. "It is I, Ajax Lightseeker. You failed to vanquish me ten years ago, and you shall fail to vanquish me today! Come, and fight me, if you dare!"

"That was very foolish of you, Lightseeker," chuckled the dark voice of Shadius, speaking through the possessed people that lined the street. "What need could be so great to force yourself to reveal yourself to me? While I do not doubt that this is a distraction, I cannot resist such tempting bait. The only person in the multiverse who is possibly more dangerous than you is stranded on Maltesque. So, whoever you are diverting attention away from has nothing on you. Now run, Ajax Lightseeker, for I will be chasing you."

Ajax darted away from Main Street, and headed towards the lab. The possessed men and women began to catch up with him, so he ran into a building, and was quickly followed. He climbed out of a window, but this was not seen by the servants of Shadius. He hid just out of sight, and then people began to search the building. Quietly, he slipped away.

He stayed out of sight, and slipped away to head back to the lab, hoping idly that he had bought James enough time. He crept into the abandoned building, and pressed his hand against the steel dome.

The hidden door slid open, and Ajax slipped inside.

***

James waited, crouched, in the alley that led to Main Street. He heard Ajax shout a strange name, and then all of the possessed people ran towards him. After he was sure the street was deserted, he crossed quickly. He could have sworn, however, that someone just out of sight was watching him. He rapidly dismissed this notion as idle daydreaming, but he could not help looking over his shoulder once in a while.

James left Main Street, and entered the ruined territory. He could see the dark miniverse off in the distance, and headed for that. Ajax had given him only two cameras, so he decided to save them for when he needed them.

Suddenly, James saw something that he had not for a while: two tendrils of darkness, crawling away from him. They seemed intent upon wrapping themselves around broken building, presumably to destroy it further. James crept away, staying out of sight of the tendrils.

James stepped inside the foundation of one of the ruined buildings. He saw steps leading to what appeared to be a basement, and, out of curiosity, followed them. At the bottom, he two people crouched in the shadow. They seemed not to notice him at first, but suddenly, one of the people swiftly spun around in James' direction.

"Stay back!" he shouted, holding up a fist. "Stay back and don't you try none o' that mind control stuff on me!" James saw that it was the gunman that had threatened Adrian outside of the orphanage.

"Relax! I'm not with the darkness," said James, trying to calm him down.

"So you're not gonna mind control me?" inquired the gunman, skeptical. His hand reached to his gun holster, and then remembered that he seemed to have lost it.

"No. In fact, I'm actually rebelling against the darkness," explained James. "You might say that I'm part of a rebellion of two," he chuckled.

"So the mind control thing is called darkness, huh?" asked the gunman, glad to have a name for it. "Well, I'm with you."

"Who's your friend?" asked James, eyeing the person sitting next to the gunman.

"My old buddy. He's takin' a nap now. We didn't get any sleep last night, since we were lookin' out fer the darkness. It was gonna give us the mind control crap," answered the gunman.

Suddenly, two tendrils of darkness shot down the staircase, and went for the gunman.

"GET BACK!" he shouted, holding up his fists. The tendrils of darkness, however, were not deterred by his show of physical might. They entered his body, and the gunman slumped over, sighing.

"So, you're the person Ajax was trying divert attention away from," chuckled the dark voice, speaking through the possessed gunman. James was out of ideas, so he threw his camera at the gunman. It hit him square on the head, and he, along with the tendrils of darkness, hesitated for a moment. James seized the opportunity to rush up the stairs, and away from the building.

***

As he only had one camera left, James hurried towards the dark miniverse. He stuck to the shadows, and hid in the ruins whenever possible. He found a well-hidden spot, with a good view of the darkness bubble, and it was there that he set up the camera. As he was setting it up, he took a good look at the dark miniverse. It was about the size of the orphanage that had previously stood in its spot, but it was perfectly spherical, hovering two or so feet off of the ground. It also extended vertically for a few seconds periodically, immediately followed by a horizontal expansion. Though it appeared at first glance to be completely black, James observed multiple fluctuations of purple and a deep navy blue as well. Tendrils of darkness extended from the miniverse in all directions, and James noticed a couple of the tendrils seemed to have noticed that he was there, and were flowing towards him, slowly, as not to draw his attention, though they already unknowingly had.

James realized that he had to get out of there quickly. He made a dash for the door, but two tendrils smashed through it, and flowed into the room. James looked about frantically for another escape route, and saw one in the window. He turned his back to the tendrils, squeezed his eyes shut, and leapt at the window with as much force as he could muster. It appeared that the window had been weakened by all of the earthquakes, and shattered upon contact. James tumbled out onto the street, and sprinted away from the tendrils as fast as possible.

The tendrils seemed intent on following James, so he decided that his best bet was to try to lose them. He ducked into an alley that seemed to be outside the range of the cataclysm that had stricken the abandoned district a while back. He also saw a dumpster at the edge of the alley, and gulped as he realized that hiding in the dumpster was the best way to lose the tendrils. He climbed in quickly, and lost his balance at the top. He fell in head first, and deemed it best not to think about what he had just landed in.

James heard the tendrils slither by, and then heard them look around in the alley. They didn't think to check the dumpster, and James climbed out as soon as the danger was past.

***

After achieving that task, he ran back to Main Street. He looked about, and saw that there were less people about than before, so he decided to take his chances, and run across. When saw no one around, he booked it across, unseen by Shadius. He opted not to actually walk in the alleys, and just stuck to the almost-streets between the abandoned buildings.

Once he was past the aquarium, he turned and headed for the store north of the skate park. Nothing of consequence happened on the way, including when he passed the building he and Ajax had noticed a few days ago, which seemed to be the base of operations for the possessed people. He found the store north of the skate park, and went in. He found the basement, and located the hidden door. He opened it up, and went in. He walked down a long hallway, and was followed by security cameras all the way. Eventually, he came to door, which seemed to be locked. He heard a mechanized voice far away inform Ajax of his presence. He heard Ajax slowly stomp over to the door, and he heard the latch click as Ajax slid the bolt back to let him through.

"What took you?" he grunted, staring disapprovingly at James. "And why, pray tell, are we only getting the feed from one of the cameras?"

"I was attacked by tendrils of darkness, and had to throw one of my cameras at the possessed person," answered James.

"Well done," grinned Ajax. "You didn't actually need to set up the second one. I gave it to you for self-defense, and I'm glad to see you picked up on that. You're back in my good graces."

James was rather surprised by this exchange.

***

Throughout the next day, Ajax was in the forbidden room, watching the different camera feeds, or so James assumed. James spent the day playing video games and watching T.V, something he never would have gotten to do before the catastrophe, as he was now calling the time when Adrian had been kidnapped. And so the day passed, without much of anything happening.

***

"Wake up, James!" shouted Ajax, shaking him thoroughly. "We've got things to do today!"

"Wha- Oh, g'morning Ajax," sleepily muttered James. "So, are we actually going to do anything today?"

"That's right," smiled Ajax, despite the fact that he was irritated at James for being so blunt with him. "I spent yesterday looking at the video feeds, and I think that building we noticed on the first day is definitely their headquarters. I've analyzed it thoroughly, and I think I've found its weakness. It has a very brittle wall, and a slight concussive blast should be enough to take it out."

"And then everyone sees us, and we get attacked," pointed out James, still groggy from sleep.

"Yes, I know," scowled Ajax. "And that's precisely why I gave you the extra camera yesterday. As you proved, since all of the people are possessed, and thus controlled, by one powerful intelligence, if just one of them is injured, it shocks everyone. Yesterday, when I wasn't observing the town, I finished a prototype light laser. If we blast just one person, everyone else will be just a little stunned, allowing us to nail them."

"Do you know where to go once we get inside the building?" asked James. Ajax nodded, and James was satisfied.

Ajax went into the forbidden room, and returned with two small bombs, which he gave to James to hold, and some sort of gun-like weapon that James assumed was the prototype light laser. The bombs were perfectly spherical globed of metal, each with five lights in a ring around the middle of the spheres. There was what appeared to be some kind of a small red button on the very top of each of the bombs, which appeared to be the detonator. He and James, headed for the elevator, and were soon on the streets. There seemed to be an unusually large number of villainous figures around, and, as a result, Ajax and James had to work even harder than before to keep out of sight.

After scurrying around for a few minutes, they found themselves at the skate park. "We'll need to be even more careful around here," whispered Ajax. James quickly saw that Ajax was right; even more people were clustered around the buildings.

Ajax and James hid inside an abandoned building, preparing for the attack on the tech center, as Ajax had mentally begun to call it, after seeing how much technological work was being done there. The building in which they hid was right across the street from their target.

"How do we get the bomb over there?" asked James, assuming Ajax had a plan, while handing him one of the bombs.

"We throw it," answered Ajax, flipping the switch on the bomb. He tossed the bomb out the window, and it landed next to the building's weak spot. After a few seconds, it exploded, shattering the wall. Ajax jumped out the window, quickly followed by James. Ajax leapt into the building, and fired the light laser prototype at a bystander. A flare of intense light blasted out of the end of the laser, and quickly hit Ajax's target. As light moves at much too fast a pace for the human mind to comprehend, James did not see it fire, instead, he saw the bystander suddenly light up and fall backwards. This sent a current of light throughout the building, stunning everyone under the control of darkness. He then fired it at the rest of the people standing nearby, stunning every one of them. He then led James upstairs, dragging him by the arm.

Ajax and James burst out into a room upstairs and saw everyone dizzily staring into space. Ajax raced over to a table in the center of the room, upon which was a small shard of what appeared to be glass.

"I guess that that's their power source," remarked Ajax. James wandered over to a computer against the wall. On the screen was a file on the plans of the darkness. Since everyone else was till groggy, James printed a copy of the file, as there was indeed a printer in the room, and gave it to Ajax. "Thank you, James," said Ajax distractedly, putting the sheet of paper in his pocket. He picked up the shard of glass, and saw that it was not glass, but instead was a small piece of crystal. It was an orange color, with tinges of black, blue and white. "The color of twilight," mused Ajax. "James, do me a favor and hold the twilight crystal. I think that's what we should call this thing.'

James complied, and put the crystal in his pocket. They hurried out of the building, and headed back towards the skate park.

***

Ajax and James were even more pressed to stay hidden than before. The streets around the skate park were too crowded for them to pass through. Instead they opted to pass through the skate park itself. The way in was totally unguarded, so they passed through the entrance unhindered.

When they were about halfway through the skate park, a voice from behind them whispered, "Turn around and meet your death, fools." Ajax and James whirled around to find themselves staring into the eyes of the old lady that had mocked Adrian for his blue eyes weeks ago. Her voice was similar to how it had been before, but it was twisted by the darkness, as was her appearance. She wore a slight sneer, and had a faint aura of darkness about her. "Come with me, you two, or do I need to persuade you with... force?!" chuckled the old lady, as if preparing to strike.

"We'll fight you if need be," answered James, drawing a reproachful look from Ajax. However, he took out the light laser prototype, preparing to fight. The old crone seemed to become still, and suddenly, at least fifty possessed people jumped over the walls of the skate park, and rushed towards Ajax and James. They very quickly found themselves surrounded. Though the people were possessed by Shadius, only one thing differentiated them from normal humans: their eyes. Their eyes were completely black, with no whites or retinas. They also appeared to slump over a little, and their arms dangled uselessly at their sides.

"Surrender!" cackled the old crone.

"Never," snarled Ajax, firing the light laser. It hit the old lady squarely in the chest, knocking her off her feet. The rest of the crowd surged forward, creating a ring around Ajax and James. "James, we need a strategy, and I think I've got one," said Ajax. "You stay behind me. I blast with the light laser, and if anyone comes up behind us, you can stab them with the twilight crystal." With that Ajax began blasting with the light laser, and James covered the rear. Ajax scurried ahead, catching the surrounding people off-guard. They charged forward, with James covering the rear. However, James saw one person who Ajax had missed with the light laser, and attacked him with the crystal. Ajax, on the other hand kept advancing, and the two became separated.

"Ajax, help!" Ajax whirled around to see James being held captive by one of Shadius' men. Ajax had made it past the crowd, and was in a position to escape, but James had been captured.

"Ajax," began Shadius, speaking through the old crone, who was rising to her feet. "Surrender yourself to me, or else your friend shall be... disposed of. The lab is under my control, for I've been following you for a few days with this old lady. She knows who you are, for she's seen you before, ten years ago, on Halloween."

"All right, Shadius. You win," sighed Ajax, walking over to James, with the crowd parting before him. "James," he whispered, "Take the twilight crystal, and run. And here, take the sheet you gave me. It's in my left hand, take it discreetly, or else Shadius will suspect something."

"Who is Shadius?" asked James, tears coming to his eyes as he secretively took the paper from Ajax.

"If you ever get back to the lab, go into the forbidden room, and you'll have your answer," answered Ajax. "Now run!" he shouted, and James ran as fast as he could: away from Ajax, away from the crowd, and into the night. Shadius did not send minions after him; he was too busy with Ajax, who was firing the prototype light laser to divert attention away from James.

7

Necropheus

How much farther?" groaned Rose, her legs aching from hours of walking. She and Adrian had been following Blaise for at least four hours, flocked by vine-men. He was supposedly leading them to meet this Necropheus person, but Rose was beginning to doubt his intentions. So far, they had encountered very few dangerous animals, and none of the big cats from before.

"Perhaps another two miles or so," estimated Blaise, trying to hide a smirk. Adrian was beginning to feel Virda's spell wearing off, as even with the spell, he could only walk for a few hours at a time before the memory of the fifth dimension began to plague him. His broken arm was no help either, as it prevented him from defending himself from the wild animals.

"Are you sure?" asked Adrian, for that was not the first time Blaise had told them they were getting close. Blaise seemed to be leading them in the right direction, at least according to Adrian's compass, but he wasn't sure how big the deadwood really was. He figured that though they had walked maybe half the distance of his walk to see Virda, the going was much slower, since they had to fight their way through the brambles and trees and such.

Suddenly, Vinetia, who was walking at Adrian's side, gave a shrill cry of alarm. He seemed to see something that the others did not, and they all froze and looked about. Adrian saw a figure coming through the trees behind them, stooped over and stumbling.

"Kill the nasty trees, yes I will! Find the son of the son of the son of the son of the son of the son of Germiac, yes I will!" Democritus burst out onto the path that Blaise had blazed, and ran towards Adrian. "Get the boy, yes!" he shouted. However, he ran past the group and into the dead foliage ahead. Rose saw that his legs were still wrapped in vines, and thus were still being healed.

"Do you know him?" sighed Blaise, seemingly bored with the conversation he had just started.

"You know I do," said Adrian, becoming irritated at Blaise's know it all demeanor. "He was in the conversation with the ambassador that you were spying on!"

"Oh, yes," shrugged Blaise. "I forgot. He's very boring, in my opinion."

"Really?" asked Rose, surprised. "He's a bit... unpredictable, shall we say."

"Exactly," smirked Blaise. "Unpredictability bores me. I like to talk to people that understand me, and I like to be able to predict their responses, so I can formulate my argument ahead of time. Now with Democritus, on the other hand, you couldn't have a discussion with him if you laid his argument out in front of him."

"Interesting take on people," mused Rose. "And how many people like that do you meet around here?"

"Very few, I'm afraid," sighed Blaise. "But, oh well. I'll manage, somehow." They party returned to silence, somewhat shaken by the incident. Nothing of consequence occurred for the next few minutes, and they continued to walk in silence.

Suddenly, a huge cat like the second one they had encountered pounced on Blaise, leaping over his vine escorts. The cat snarled, preparing to shatter Blaise's neck with one sharp bite. However, Blaise was not totally defenseless. He closed his eyes, and reached out with his mind to the vine men, and the suddenly attacked the cat, knocking him away from their master. The cat snarled, and began to circle the group. Adrian felt his fear of the cat begin to break through Virda's spell, and he felt a slight headache begin to accost his skull. His hand flew up to his head, and he felt himself losing his grip on things. Blaise, however, remained undaunted, and prepared his vine servants for another attack. They pounced on the cat, driving him back. After a few minutes of fighting, the cat ran away, yowling.

"Could we rest for a little?" panted Adrian, clutching his skull.

"Well, I suppose," mused Blaise. "We could take a break before the last leg of the journey. We've only got about an hour of walking left." Adrian nodded his thanks, and lay down. He fell asleep almost instantly.

***

When Adrian awoke, he felt completely refreshed. His headache was totally gone from his mind, and he was ready to keep going. "Shall we?" he asked, glancing at Blaise, who seemed to be meditating. Blaise stood up, and stretched.

"Yes, we should. It's nearly noon, and I wouldn't want to keep Necropheus waiting," answered Blaise, glancing about. Rose seemed to have been taking a nap as well, and she too stood up.

"Are we going?" she asked sleepily, glancing about.

"Yes," smirked Blaise. "It's time you met Necropheus."

***

Nothing of consequence happened on the rest of their journey, and in about an hour, they arrived at what Adrian took to be the heart of the deadwood. Dozens of giant petrified trees lined a clearing, in which three huge trees grew, blocking out the sky. The river ran through the center of the clearing. All of the trees were a bleached gray color, and drew Adrian's eyes away from the thing he should have noticed first: Necropheus.

"Before we go in," began Blaise, "you should know that there's a protective field in the circle that cancels out life magic. Is that going to affect either of you?"

"Not really," answered Adrian, forgetting, for the moment, about Virda's protective spell.

Adrian and Rose stepped into the clearing, and Adrian fell to his knees. Necropheus' powers cancelled out the spell keeping his headache in check, and his head was now wracked with pain.

"My lord, I have brought you the two traitors to your law," announced Blaise, his poorly hidden smirk finally consuming his face.

Rose looked at him with incredulity. "You said we were guests!" she exclaimed, her fears confirmed.

"I overheard your conversation, and know that you mean to tell the Great Sage about us," sneered Blaise. "You are now our prisoners."

"Well done, Blaise," said Necropheus, and Adrian and Rose looked at him for the first time. He saw sitting upon a throne of petrified wood, and he held a staff of wood of the same variety in his hand. He himself was a medium height, with a sharply angular face. He was thin, but not quite so much as Blaise. He had black hair streaked with grey, though he looked to be only twenty, or so. His eyes were a grayish color, and he wore a faded cape. Though it was now grayed with age, Rose was pretty sure it had originally been gold.

"Welcome, guests," he snickered, in a normal sounding voice. "I have heard from my good friend Blaise here that you plan to try to report me to the Great Sage. I cannot allow that."

"Adrian, get up!" whispered Rose. "We can still get away!" She prepared to run, but Adrian couldn't stand up.

"Can't ... move... have... headache," moaned Adrian, clutching his skull. "Rose, run... go without... me."

"And it's a good thing too," snickered Necropheus. "My name means death in the ancient druidic language, and it's not for nothing. Blaise, give me one of your vine men."

Blaise obliged, surrendering one of his vine men to his master. "Now watch, as I demonstrate my power!" laughed Necropheus, before beginning to meditate. A green aura surrounded the vine-man, and one also surrounded Necropheus. Without warning, Necropheus' eyes widened, and his back became rigid. The aura of the vine man began to turn black and grey, and the green began to disappear. The vine man fell to the ground, lifeless. "I have fiddled with the connection between Greenkeepers and plants, and have twisted it to my own purposes," cackled Necropheus.

"Necropheus, Adrian and I don't know what this connection is," said Rose, hoping that Necropheus would fill them in.

"My lord, perhaps it would be best *not* to give them too much information," suggested Blaise, a smirk sliding across his face.

"Now really, Blaise, what harm could it do? They're our prisoners! They can't fight me!" laughed Necropheus. "Now, Rose, all Greenkeepers have to go through a ritual, during which they open their mind and souls up to those of the plants. They form a deep bond with plants, and they begin to rely on them to support their own souls. They can then mentally interact with flora, and, should the need arise; they can use the plants for their own purposes."

"Like Vitalius did to the vines," murmered Rose.

"Now, I have opened up my soul and mind to plants, but then I found myself in the deadwood, where no plants can live," scowled Necropheus. "I was wracked by pain by the separation from plants, like the loss of a best friend. Having no plants to connect to, I retreated into my own soul, and twisted the connection to work with the non-living things. While I did not achieve that, I did achieve unparalleled mastery over my own soul. After my period meditation, however, I discovered that I could now steal the life force from anything, and put in into this petrified wooden staff." He held up his staff. "Of course, I could put the life force into anything non-living, but I need this staff. I need it for a spell, one that you two will help me cast."

"Is that what you intend to use them for?" asked Blaise, genuinely surprised. Necropheus nodded.

"I still don't really get it," said a confused Rose. "So you can suck the life from anything? Okay, I get that, but wouldn't the things that you steal the life from still sort of be alive? I mean, their life energy still exists, doesn't it?"

"Well, alternatively, I could just fling the life energy into the air, in which case it would eventually disperse. But the things that I take the life from are definitely dead, and my staff is most certainly alive," answered Necropheus, so sure in his power that he didn't see the risk of giving Adrian and Rose all of this information.

"So what's this spell?" asked Rose, soaking up the information.

"It is a spell that will complete my reign over all things in this world," cackled Necropheus. Rose gasped, appalled at the thought that this lunatic could somehow become ruler of the world. Though every instinct was telling her to run, she still wished to know more. "There are four ambassadors of the Sage in the four corners of the deadwood. This clearing here is in the exact center of the roots. I need you two to affix these four pieces of deadwood to the four roots."

"Define deadwood," mumbled Adrian, slowly standing up.

"Deadwood is a certain kind of wood from a tree that that used to grow around here, However, now all of the wood is petrified, hence the name dead-wood," explained Necropheus. "You will pierce each of the ambassadors with a shard of deadwood. Then, I shall cast my spell, and be ruler of all!"

"And why... should we... obey you?" panted Adrian, standing up.

"Well, if you don't, I'll strike you down where you stand," laughed Necropheus, his eyes widening. "And Blaise will be overseeing your journeys, to make sure you don't stray from your mission."

"Very well," said Rose, still pondering all that Necropheus had told her. She couldn't see an option but to obey Necropheus, if he was as powerful as he seemed to be. Adrian grimly nodded, but still harbored plans to disobey Necropheus, and escape, for he had no intention of letting him use the Great Sage's ambassadors.

"I can see that you still plot to turn against me, Adrian," mused Necropheus. "Well, DON'T EVEN THINK ABOUT IT!" he shouted, his calm face suddenly becoming twisted with anger, and his voice became twisted with impatience. "IF YOU DARE TO REPORT ME TO THE GREAT SAGE, I'LL HAVE NO CHOICE BUT TO- YEARGGH!"

Suddenly, a black and red aura blanketed the clearing, and the wind began to pick up, sending dead leaves everywhere. Lightning began to strike from nowhere, and Adrian and Rose cowered. They noticed that Necropheus' staff was glowing red, like the air, as was Necropheus himself. The wind suddenly died without a trace, and Necropheus returned to normal.

"I'm sorry, Adrian, that you had to see that. I sometimes lose control like that. However, I hope that this experience has crushed any thoughts of rebellion," he cackled. "Now go. I've got things to attend to."

***

Adrian stumbled through the dense foliage, followed by Blaise. Rose was in front of him, blazing the trail. He had offered to do that task, but Rose had put down that idea by pointing out that with his arm still healing, he would have little luck. His headache had vanished long ago, and he was now bitterly regretting not running from Necropheus when he had the chance. He refused to speak to Rose, since he had seen her curiosity get the better of her during their little meeting.

Rose seemed to have stopped, blocked by a fallen tree. Its sides were smoothed by age, and it was impossible to climb over.

"Um, Blaise, we're stuck," stammered Rose, glancing over her shoulder.

"Well, find away around it," sighed Blaise, bored by the whole venture. He had yet to do anything to help Adrian and Rose, and they had yet to see the point of him accompanying them.

Rose glanced around, and saw, to her dismay, that the tree stretched out of eyesight on both sides. "Maybe we could try to get through it," she suggested.

"That won't work," muttered Blaise. "It's deadwood. It's more or less stone, and you'd be hard pressed to get through that. Perhaps you could have Adrian try to summon lightning to destroy it."

"How'd you know about that?!" asked Adrian, caught off-guard.

"The ambassador was thinking about it," answered Blaise simply. "I over-heard his thoughts during your conversation."

"I don't think I can do that on a whim," mused Adrian. "I tried when we were attacked by the cat." He immediately regretted giving Blaise that infor-mation.

"Well, that's a pity," smirked Blaise. "Well, you could always try to tunnel under it."

Rose thought about it, and decided it was the best option. She crouched down on her knees, and began to try to tunnel away the dirt underneath.

"That'll take too long," sneered Adrian. "I think we should try to go around it."

"Fine," muttered Rose.

"Very well. You two go left, and I'll look to the right. And don't even think about trying to run," ordered Blaise.

Adrian nodded, and he and Rose went off to try to find a way around the tree.

"Rose, what were you thinking?" hissed Adrian, once they were finally out of earshot. "Why are you cooperating with them? I couldn't go anywhere myself because of my headache, but you should've run!"

"I needed to know about Necropheus," defended Rose in a hurt tone. "I was curious. I didn't realize that he was planning to manipulate the ambassa-dors. But still, I want to know more about him."

"Rose, we need to escape!" shouted Adrian, all thoughts of secrecy forgotten. "Who cares about Necropheus? If we run now, we won't ever see him again."

"You're right," sighed Rose, tears coming to her eyes, accompanying the slight feeling of shame she felt. "Let's go."

Rose and Adrian had barely run ten yards when they were lifted off their feet, and flung into a tree.

"I told you running was a bad idea," smirked Blaise, holding them up with some unknown force. His hand was extended, and a grey aura stretched from his palm to his captives. It seemed to press them into the tree, holding them up with sheer energy. "Yes, I too have a certain amount of hidden talents involving misused greenkeeping powers. Though I'm not very good with plants, I can still manipulate the energy, like so." He twisted his arm to the left a bit, and Adrian and Rose were flung to the ground. "I could crush you to a pulp right now, if I felt like it," he smirked, "but I'm not in the mood, and Necropheus needs you."

Adrian and Rose shakily got to their feet. Blaise turned around, and Adrian and Rose quickly walked after him. None of them spoke a word as Blaise led them around the tree blocking their way.

After walking in silence for a few minutes, they came to a stream, which seemed to be a branch of the larger river that flowed through Necropheus' clearing.

"Well, go ahead," smirked Blaise, motioning them onwards.

"How can we get across?" inquired Adrian, failing to notice the bridge just a few yards to the left.

"Over the bridge, silly," laughed Blaise, pointing to the left. Adrian and Rose followed his orders.

"What should we do?" asked Rose, clearly referring to Blaise's newly discovered ability to attack them with energy.

"We play along," whispered Adrian. "If we can gain his trust, we'll have a better chance of escape."

"I suppose you're right, but I think we should try to get Blaise to come over to our side," argued Rose.

"If you two are quite finished bickering, we have a bridge to cross," smirked Blaise, crossing the bridge. Adrian and Rose followed suit, and all three were across. After a few more minutes something quite unexpected happened.

Five or so cats dragged a helpless figure onto the path, and Rose saw that the figure was Democritus.

"Lemmego, lemmego!" he shouted, thrashing about. The cats seemed to be about to eat him, and Rose panicked.

"Blaise, do something!" she shouted hysterically. "Do that energy thing! Make the cats go away! Please, they're going to kill him."

"If they did, we'd be fortunate," scowled Blaise. "If you want to save Democritus, do it yourself."

Rose pleaded with him, but he remained unmoved.

"Rose, we can drive them away," whispered Adrian. "Come on! There's go to be a way to, ah, divert them! We could distract them, and then Blaise would be forced to help us."

"Do you really trust..." Rose's comment was cut off by a screech from Democritus as he stood up, and was pounced on by the cat. The largest cat of the bunch sank his teeth into Democritus' arm and he screamed in pain. Rose nodded, and they charged at the cats. Adrian lost track of his senses for a moment, and lost himself in the chaos of battle. He latched onto a cat in a stranglehold with his arm, and was flung onto the beast's back. He held on for his life as the cat twisted about, trying to throw him off. The cat smashed into another one, which turned on the first with a snarl. The two cats began to fight, and Adrian was finally flung off. He felt Virda's spell weakening, and his headache began to return.

Rose seemed to be having trouble with her cat, a striped orange one. She was backing away slowly, and suddenly help came from a most unexpected source. Democritus flung himself at the cat, shouting, "Beastie, bad beastie, burn you, yes!" He clawed at the cat with his fingers, trying to get a firm grip. He was flung away, but launched himself at the cat once again. He tripped over a rock, and reached out with his hands to break his fall. In his way, however was the cat. His long fingernails tore at the cat's face, and at its eyes. The cat yowled, and ran away, blinded. The two fighting cats had long since fell to the ground, both dead from the fighting. The remaining two cats backed away slowly, frightened by their brother's defeat. However, another cat, at least twice the size of the others, calmly walked out of the bushes. It was easily ten feet tall, and hummed softly as it advanced forwards. It yawned, showing foot-long canines of death, and Adrian, Rose, and Democritus backed away slowly.

"An adult Leocavia!" gasped Blaise, his face turning white. "Ignore him, Adrian! I'll handle him! You just focus on the juveniles."

Adrian wasn't quite sure what Blaise had just said, but he caught his drift: focus on the small cats. He, Rose and Democritus ran at the two cats, shouting various choice words at the top of their lungs. Democritus tackled the one on the left, and when the cat tried to chomp at him, Adrian wrapped his arm around the mouth to keep it shut. Democritus pushed the cat backwards, and the cat reared up on his hind legs. While the cat was still on his back legs,

Democritus tore at its weak stomach with his fingernails, which actually more resembled claws. The young Leocavia squealed in pain, and ran away into the forest. Rose seemed to handle her cat well, sending it howling after its brother.

The three turned to watch Blaise fight his adversary. He seemed to be sizing up the cat, and prepared to strike. The cat tensed its legs, preparing to pounce. It did just that, leaping at Blaise. Blaise held up his hand, and green energy flowed from his palm to hit the cat in the chest. The cat was knocked to the ground, but it fought Blaise's attack. It struggled to its feet, and then licked itself, as if to show that it was not intimidated by this display of power. Blaise was beginning to sweat, and was putting all of his power into the green ray of energy that was keeping the cat back. The cat, however, surged forwards, and broke through Blaise's energy stream. Blaise winced, closing one eye. He rested for a minute, and let the cat slowly pace towards him. Blaise closed the other eye as well, and held his hands out to the cat. Grey energy flowed between them, forming a rotating sphere. He pushed his hands out, and the sphere of energy flew towards the cat. It nailed its target dead on, and exploded. The cat vanished in a burst of grey energy, the color of stratus clouds a few hours before it rains. Blaise fell to his knees, exhausted.

"We should rest," he gasped, forcing out each word. "You two should be grateful that I helped you fight that cat." He couldn't resist adding a smirk to that last comment.

"Kill the beasties, yes I did!" shouted Democritus, dancing around. "Off to Twilight City, yes I am!" With that, he darted away.

"Ah well," shrugged Blaise, seemingly disappointed that Democritus had not thanked him.

Adrian, Rose, and Blaise, sat still for a few minutes, before Blaise summoned up the energy to move again. "Let's go," he said. "There's only a few minute's walk."

***

After those few minutes had passed, Adrian and company were at the edge of a lake. A small grassy island bloomed from the center of the lake, and from the small island protruded a root, which writhed in the wind.

"And there's your target," smirked Blaise, pointing to the root. It seemed completely unaware of their presence, just swaying in the breeze like that.

"Is the process going to hurt the root?" inquired Rose, staring the ambassador down.

"Probably. I mean, you're going to stab him with a shard of deadwood, right?" laughed Blaise. "And yes, *you* are going to stab him with the shard of deadwood," he said, catching the surprised look in Rose's eyes.

"If we're the only ones who are actually going to attack the ambassador, then why are you here?" asked Adrian, confused.

"That's a good question," shrugged Blaise, "And it's one that I don't really know the answer to. I could have one of my vine men keep an eye on you, but I doubt that would fly with Necropheus the Great." Adrian detected just a hint of scorn in his voice when he spoke his master's name.

"Well, if we have no choice," sighed Adrian, "How do we get over there?"

"The lake really isn't deep, so I suppose you could swim across it without too much fear of drowning," mused Blaise. "But if you did that, the ambassador would see you coming, and that could prove too risky. Well, honestly, I'm not quite sure, so I'll leave that up to you two. After all, it's your life."

"What do you think we should do?" asked Rose, clearly at a loss.

"Well, we could swim. If we could get Blaise to act as a diversion, we should be able to get to the ambassador unnoticed," suggested Adrian. "Do you think that Blaise would go for that?"

"If it takes absolutely no effort, and poses absolutely no danger to him," laughed Rose. "Wait. You *can't* swim across! Your arm's still recovering!"

"You're right," gasped Adrian, having forgotten his injured arm. "I could help Blaise with the distraction, I suppose. You'd have to place the shard. Can you do that?"

"If I need to," sighed Rose.

"You do," decreed Adrian. "I'll go talk to Blaise."

***

"What's in it for me?" was the first question that came to Blaise's mind when Adrian proposed their plan to him.

"Necropheus will be happy with you," suggested Adrian.

"And who really cares about Necropheus?" sighed Blaise. "However, I'll do it, since I will admit that Necropheus would be a very dangerous enemy. So, how are we going to distract an omnipotent root?"

"By angering it, I suppose," mused Adrian. "If we throw stones at it or something, that might get its attention."

"I have a better idea," smirked of Blaise. "If you let me use your light powers, I could attack the root with energy. Work for you?"

"What do you think? Of course it does!" snapped Adrian, Blaise's snotty attitude irritating him. "Should I tell Rose?"

"Uh, I'm right here, Adrian." Adrian whirled around, and nearly tripped. He thought that Rose was still back where they had been talking. "So, I'll just slip back to the other side of the lake, and wait for your signal, then?"

"Yes, do that," sighed Blaise. After Rose had left, he turned to Adrian and said, "This could be hard on her. I saw how she reacted when she first saw what I did to the fifth ambassador. Keep an eye on her, or she could snap." He couldn't resist smirking as he put forth his last comment.

Blaise close his eyes, and extended a grey aura to Adrian. At first Adrian felt nothing, but then he felt a slight tingling everywhere, as if a thousand mosquitos were crawling over his skin. He started to squirm, but Blaise's grey energy continued to press in on him from all sides.

Suddenly, he felt his headache burst through Virda's spell, and he felt a crackling sensation replace the tingling. Blaise thrust his hands forwards, and Adrian's vision became obscured by a white glow emanating from himself. Blaise's grey energy pushed its way into Adrian's body, and Adrian's body reacted in kind. A cloud of white lightning formed around him, and it shot itself in a stream at the ambassador. Adrian lost consciousness, but Blaise continued to force lightning out of him.

Rose saw this, and swam towards the small island with the deadwood shard clutched tightly in her left hand.

She reached the island right as the lightning stream ceased. The ambassador failed to notice her as she slowly walked towards him. The root seemed to be using its powers to shield itself from the lightning barrage, and thus its powerful mind failed to notice a small girl climb onto its island. Though she regretted using the ambassador, she saw no other choice, since if she didn't, Blaise might kill her. Plus, she doubted that it would truly harm the ambassador. Rose gave up secrecy, and sprinted towards the root. She quickly jabbed the sharp end of the deadwood shard into the root.

In the last second before the deadwood pierced the skin of the root, it noticed Rose. When the deadwood shard pierced the ambassador, the root screamed in agony. Strange runes began to appear in white on the skin of the ambassador. "War be upon you, Rose Cores!" screamed the root. "War be upon you, daughter of Vr-" The ambassador stopped thrashing about, and came to a standstill. The wood of the ambassador became a much darker shade of brown, bordering on black. It took on the appearance of charred wood.

Rose felt sick. Her hand instinctively went to her stomach, and she suppressed vomit. She doubted that the deadwood would have a positive effect on the ambassador, but this was just not at all what she had wanted. She slumped to the ground, and started to cry. Rose sat there for minutes on end, just crying.

After she had run out of tears, she sat up, and then stood up. With her head down, she swam back to shore. She emerged onto the beach, and sat down next to Adrian.

And there she stayed.

***

Adrian awoke to find himself alone, as happened all too often these days. He glanced out to the island where the root was, and did a perfect double take. The root looked like it had been burnt to a crisp without any reduction in size, but there were odd white runes lining the sides of the root. It had stopped moving, and looked as if it had never been alive. Adrian couldn't really imagine what had done this to the ambassador, but then he saw the cause: the piece of deadwood, in the center of one of the runes. He was appalled that he had aided such a cause, and turned his sudden anger on the most obvious target: Blaise.

He leapt to his feet, and ran off towards the forest. He ignored the beaten trail, and followed a different one: the footsteps of Blaise and Rose. They had made no efforts to conceal their tracks; after all, whom were they going to hide from? After running for an hour, Adrian found them sitting on a log.

"Blaise, how dare you use us like that? I'll kill you for this!" stormed Adrian, losing his temper. He tried to call up white lightning, like he had done to the root, but the lightning no longer obeyed him.

"Let it go, Adrian," said Rose, her voice barely above a whisper. "It's not his fault for what we did. I was the one who killed the ambassador, not him. If you're going to kill anyone, it ought to be me."

Adrian saw that Blaise was right; Rose was taking this very hard. The incident seemed to have broken her spirit, and Adrian's anger was doing nothing to help.

"The ambassador is not dead, merely incapacitated," smirked Blaise in his superior manner. "However, Rose is right. I'm not the one to blame here. After all, I'm not the one who pierced the root with the deadwood shard, nor am I the one who attacked him with lightning."

Though Adrian disagreed with Blaise's last statement, his words seemed to have struck a nerve with Rose. She became even more withdrawn, and cast her eyes at the ground. Adrian was tempted to slap Blaise in the face for his last comment, but he felt that that would make Rose feel even worse. Instead, he tried to put his arm around Rose, but she pushed him away with a tear in her eyes.

"Well, what are we standing around for?" asked Blaise, hopping to his feet. "We still have three more roots to get!"

"Are you insane?" shouted Adrian. "We're not doing that again!"

"No, Adrian. We have to," murmured Rose. "If we don't, then Necropheus will do it himself. Either way, the roots get attacked, but this way, no one else has to suffer."

"What do you—" Adrian began to ask, but he was silenced by the look on

Rose's face. It was a look of desperation, anger, sadness, and barely controlled madness all wrapped into one. "So where do we go next?" he asked Blaise shakily.

8

The Tipping Point

Rose was on the verge of snapping. It had been painful enough to hear the ambassador scream in agony when she struck him with the deadwood shard, but the following few moments had crushed her spirit. Blaise had found exactly the right things to say to break her, and using those words, he played upon her weaknesses. He had reduced her to nothing, nothing but a drone who would follow his every command to atone for the sin that was truly his. For this, Blaise allowed himself a slight smile, and a brief feeling of satisfaction. He still needed to find the right words to break Adrian, for he was merely subdued, and not fully under his power. But he soon would be.

Rose shivered as she looked across the river, and to the stream on the other side. She knew that somewhere along that stream lay another ambassador of the Great Sage. Another target.

"Well, get ready to cross," said Blaise, with more than a bit of mocking in his voice. "We haven't got all day, you know. Once we take care of this ambassador, I need to report back to Necropheus. If I'm not back by the end of the day, he'll come looking for us, and I really don't want that. We need to get across that river," he concluded lamely.

Adrian nodded assent, and glanced across. "So, um, how do we do that? It's sort of, you know, deep. Plus, I can't swim."

"There's a boat around here somewhere," mused Blaise. "You two go look for it. I'll stay here. Get me once you find it."

Adrian and Rose walked away in silence. Rose was still reeling from having her spirit broken, observed Blaise, but why was Adrian so silent? The smirk returned to Blaise's lips as he came upon an intriguing idea: perhaps Adrian was afraid of what Rose would say? The smirk grew into a grin as he came upon yet another idea: why not use Rose's words to break Adrian, as opposed to his own? This idea pleased Blaise; he had to work hard to prevent a laugh from escaping his lips.

Adrian and Rose continued to walk in silence, until Adrian could take it no longer.

"Rose, what happened? The last thing I remember was a white light surrounding me, and then I fainted. As far as I can tell, you swam out to the ambassador's island, and impaled him with the piece of deadwood. But then..." Adrian trailed off, leaving the completion of the statement to Rose.

"There was a scream from the ambassador," said Rose quietly. "Then, it became black, and white runes started to appear on it. For the first few moments, I heard the thoughts of the ambassador, but then he became silent."

"Well, why do you still listen to Blaise?" asked Adrian, stating the nagging question. "It's his fault, not yours!"

"No, Adrian. He had no hold over me. I could have swum away, but I killed the ambassador nonetheless," whispered Rose.

"It's not your fault!" shouted Adrian, becoming exasperated.

"Yes it is!" screamed Rose, and Adrian took a few steps back. "Blaise told me that quite bluntly, and he's right! It's my fault and mine alone!" A crazed look came into her eyes, and she took a few steps towards Adrian. She reached out her hands, and suddenly leaped at Adrian, wrapping her hands around his neck. Adrian gasped for air, and tried to push Rose back.

Suddenly, Rose became herself once again, and let go of Adrian. She started to cry, and then returned to her previous melancholy state. Adrian backed away, frightened.

Meanwhile, Blaise was watching this from afar. He now saw that he had perhaps pushed her a bit too far, and any more pressure might put her over the edge. She was at a tipping point, and Blaise resolved to make sure she didn't go over. If she did, she could potentially become quite a threat. After all, a person with nothing to lose is a very dangerous person indeed.

***

Adrian and Rose had found the boat, and now brought it back, carried on their shoulders. They set it down in front of Blaise, and stepped back.

"Well done, you two. Now, let's get to that next root! Put the boat into the river," Blaise ordered. "Now hold it steady. Get in. I'll get in after you."

Adrian and Rose followed orders, though Blaise could see the anger in Adrian's eyes as he looked at him. Blaise suppressed a smile as he pictured the look on Adrian's face once he made Rose say the words that would shatter Adrian's spirit. He imagined that look would come in only an hour, once he orchestrated the attack on the next root. This time, however, Adrian would be the one to deliver the blow, and then come the words. Blaise wouldn't lie to himself; Adrian's healing arm was a definite hindrance. No matter, he would find a way to work around that.

Adrian and Rose rowed the boat across the river with the paddles they had found near the boat. Blaise sat in the back, watching them do the work for him. Within a minute, they were on the other side.

Blaise got off the boat first, stepping onto the muddy ground. The wet sediment gave way beneath his boot, clutching it for a moment, and he walked off of the mud, and stepped onto the hard dirt that lined the forest. He was followed by Adrian and Rose, both giving each other the silent treatment.

The trio entered what once might have been a grassy field, but it was now just a mass of dirt. They could see deadwood trees on the far side of the clearing. In the middle of the dead field was a small hill, on top of which was another ambassador.

"There he is," breathed Blaise. "Our next victim. All right, we need an attack plan. Any ideas?"

"Well, I could climb the hill," suggested Adrian. "And you two could try to distract it."

"Actually, I've got a better idea," smirked Blaise. "Perhaps I could propel Adrian up to the root very quickly, and he could stab it. Rose could wait with me."

Adrian nodded, though it churned his stomach to think of petrifying another root. He tried to screw up the courage to run away with Rose, forget Blaise. Then he saw the look on Rose's face, and thought better of it. Rose wouldn't be able to summon up the bravery to run, and then Blaise would probably kill them both. He could see no other way but to follow Blaise's orders for now.

"Get ready, Adrian," smiled Blaise, as he handed Adrian the deadwood shards.

Adrian braced himself, and Blaise closed his eyes. A grey cloud of energy formed around Adrian, and he was suddenly shot forwards. In less than a second, he landed on top of the small hill, and fell forwards, piercing the ambassador with the piece of deadwood. The root had no idea what hit him, and there was a small flash of dark grey light. The ambassador's skin suddenly became a much darker black, and the same strange white runes appeared on the other parts of the skin. A chill came over Adrian as he watched the root shrivel up, and he slowly backed away. He tripped on a rock at the edge of the hill's summit, and fell off. He closed his eyes as he fell, and when he hit the ground, he lay there, still, for a few moments. He took a deep breath, and pushed himself off the ground.

"Well, it's done," he said shakily. "Two down, two to go. God, I feel awful." Adrian's hand suddenly shot up to his head, and he fell the ground. Virda's protective spell was gone, and his headache immediately returned.

"Well, Adrian, now you know how I felt." Rose's words felt like cold knives in Adrian's soul. "You are no different than me, so don't act like this is hurting you any more than it did me!"

"Rose—" started Adrian, only to be cut off.

"Don't act like you don't get it, Adrian! It's your fault, and now it's mine too!" Adrian hung his head, feeling the same way he had felt before his venture into Light's End.

Once again, Blaise fought a grin of triumph. Rose had found just the right words to push Adrian's soul past its limits. Blaise could see that Rose was nearly at the breaking point herself, so he intervened.

"Oh come now, neither one of you is more at fault than the other." Blaise could see that this statement helped to achieve both goals of his: Adrian looked more dejected than before, and Rose seemed calmer.

The three walked in silence away from the hill.

***

"Where are we going?" sighed Adrian, as they seemed to be following the stream to the north, as opposed to heading west to attack the next root.

"I've decided that I've got better things to do than baby-sit you, so I'll be keeping an eye on you with one of my vine men for a while," answered Blaise. "We're meeting up with him about halfway to Necropheus' clearing."

"Okay," murmured Rose. Blaise detected the large amount of dejection in her voice, and that solidified his opinion that it was okay to leave them be for the time being. After all, Necropheus was not the only one he served.

A few minutes later, they came to a particularly tight cluster of trees, and in the center of the clump was a vine man. It wasn't Vinetia, but a different one, one with thorns growing out of its shoulders. It bowed once it saw Blaise, and walked over to Adrian and Rose, and held out its hand in gesture of respect, unlike Vinetia, who had seemed to offer friendship. Adrian shook the new vine person's hand, as did Rose.

"He goes by Thorner, due to the, ah, thorns growing out of his back," explained Blaise. "He's a bit more aggressive than Vinetia. Speaking of Vinetia, all she's been thinking about is you, Adrian. You saved her twice, by her reckoning, and she wishes she could be with you. I think you've found yourself a new lover, Adrian."

Adrian would normally have taken the bait, but he remained silent. Blaise walked away from the group, but then he turned around.

"I'll be keeping an eye on you two, so don't try to run," he smirked, before turning away. He knew his words were wasted; with their spirits broken, they couldn't run away if they tried.

"Well, let's go," muttered Adrian, walking south.

"Adrian, we could try to run," suggested Rose, with a slight laugh. "Of course, Thorner here would catch us, Blaise would come back, and we'd both die."

"Maybe that would be better," sighed Adrian. "No more petrified ambassadors, and no more Blaise. Just us, in heaven."

"Or hell," chuckled Rose. "No, that won't help. If we do what Blaise tells us, we won't be at fault any more."

Adrian disagreed, but he was too depressed to voice his opinion. However, without Blaise around, the mood began to lighten.

After walking for hours, Rose couldn't hold back a statement that had been bothering her. "Adrian, I'm hungry. I haven't eaten since yesterday, and I have some food in my pocket."

They sat down, and Thorner kept a close watch over them while they gorged themselves on the few pieces of dried fruit that Rose had stuffed into her pocket days ago. A mist began to settle over the group, and a light rain began to descend upon them.

Suddenly, three men leaped out of the surrounding bushes, and charged at the group. Adrian put up his hands to shield himself, and he was tackled by one of the men. In the confusion, he saw that two of them wore loosely tied loincloths, and the third wore nothing at all.

"Aaaaggghhhh!" shouted one of them, punching Rose in the gut. Adrian felt something hard contact his skull, and then the world went black.

***

Adrian opened his eyes to see nothing, and for a moment he worried that he had gone blind. Then, he realized that it was night, and he seemed to be inside some sort of sack. He tried to move his hands, but he found that they were tied. He had nothing to do, so he closed his eyes again.

He woke up in some sort of tent, along with Rose and Thorner. He glanced around, and saw that though they appeared alone at first glance, there was a figure standing outside the tent. He seemed to be holding a spear. He was visible only because a lit fire outside cast his shadow against the side of the tent.

Rose seemed to be asleep, and he wasn't sure about Thorner. He didn't really have a face, *per se*, so Adrian didn't know if his eyes were open, or if he was asleep. Adrian didn't even know, for that matter, if he could sleep.

Suddenly, another man stepped into the tent. He wore a loosely tied loincloth, like two of the men that had attacked Adrian had, but he was thoroughly tattooed. His upper torso had two red wings tattooed on it, with yellow stripes down the middle. A red tattoo of a serpent crawled along his stomach, and crept up his arms. His head was shaved, and he had hard green eyes that pierced through the dimly lit tent like a lone star on a dark night. A scowl graced his lips, and he flexed his muscles, which were very formidable, at least to Adrian's eyes.

"Heellow, mun and gurl," he said, his speech halting and oftentimes incorrect. "I not speak langwage good, su I good if you not liaff. I Barbados, King of Barbarians. You on my lund. Why?"

"Please, sir, we were just," started Adrian.

"Talk slowerer. I not oonderstanding," interrupted the barbarian.

"We... were... just... passing... through..." said Adrian, pausing after each word.

"You on I land!" shouted Barbados. "We roast you, and eat you! That your punishment."

Adrian gulped. "Is... is that really necessary?" he asked, drops of sweat running down his face. "We didn't really do anything wrong, so I really think that you could just let us go."

"SILENCE!" he shouted, and Adrian tucked away the little bit of information that he had at least mastered one word. "I speak English okay, and I get that you trying to argoo! You are burn at stake!"

Adrian nodded his head, and asked himself if it really mattered if he died at the hands of these barbarians, since the alternative would be to serve Necropheus. He exhaled a sigh of acceptance, and Barbados took it as such, and left the tent.

Adrian returned to the previous argument: did it really matter? His life had always been miserable, and he thought that it might truly be better if it ended. He asked himself what he lived for, and found no answers, though he plumbed the depths of his mind. He had often read about suicides in the newspaper, the only thing his parents let him read, and he always wondered how they felt when they willingly condemned themselves to death, or what happened once they passed on.

Adrian wrenched his mind away from thoughts of suicide, and looked at the good things in life. At first, he had trouble finding any; after all, his life was very hard. He wished Rose was awake, so he'd have someone to share his thoughts with. Then he did a mental double take, and thought, "Rose!" He had forgotten all about her; Rose, his only friend, at least in this world. The thought of her made him smile, as she herself always seemed to be full of them, at least she used to be. She had become secluded, ever since the attack on the ambassador. Though he did not know it consciously, his mind was beginning to point the finger of blame at the one who deserved it: Blaise.

Adrian made a quiet resolution to himself: when they were being led out to the stake, he would use his lightning powers to break free, and nothing could stop him. After he freed himself, he resolved to speak with the Great Sage, even if that meant leaving Thorner behind for the time being. All this he resolved to do, all in the name of one cause: returning a smile to Rose's face. And so Blaise's plan met failure; without Blaise, Adrian's spirit had reversed itself, found a purpose, and was now past the tipping point, and no longer under Blaise's power.

***

Adrian awoke inside the tent, and the memories of his previous meeting with Barbados came back to him. To his dismay, Thorner and Rose were both gone, having been taken away while he unknowingly slept. He immediately feared for Rose's safety, but not so much about Thorner's. The thought passed into his mind that they had been burnt on the stake before him, but, in reality, they had just been moved to different tents. Rose was with the women, and Thorner was in the vegetable hut.

He felt a certain loneliness without Rose, but he was actually somewhat glad to be rid of Thorner, at least for the time being. Not having Thorner around meant that Blaise could no longer monitor his activities. This realization gave him a large amount of relief. A small smile graced his face, and he sat up. Though his hands were still tied, he tried to stand up. He realized that they had tied up his legs too, and he then suddenly did a double take. A small shiver ran down his back as he recognized the rope that bound him. It was very old, and somewhat yellowed. It was the same kind of rope that had bound him while he sat on top of Democritus' woodpile, waiting to be burned.

Suddenly, the flap to his tent opened. Barbados walked in, holding his head high.

"You see rupe?" he asked, gesturing to Adrian's bonds. "I get it from old man, vines on legs." Adrian suddenly sat up, for he was positive that Barbados had just mentioned Democritus. "He came into camp, tried to kill me. I stop him, and take rupe. That what he call it."

Adrian's mind was at the point of disbelief. Democritus had come into the camp, and he hadn't noticed? He mentally assailed himself for his stupidity.

"We not ready to burn you at stake yet, so you stay here," ordered Barbados. "We still have food for day, und yu not good for preserving." Adrian nearly wretched at the last comment, as cannibalism was the one most disgusting and revolting thing he could imagine.

"Look, sir, do you really need to eat me?" he asked, figuring that if he could easily worm his way out of it without having to resort to his lightning powers, that would be good.

"Yes. We need make guds happy!" he shouted, raising his hands up above his head. "You will be guud sacrifice!" And with that, he marched out of the room.

After he left, Adrian's mind began to wander. He could see why the barbarian wanted to keep his land protected, but he considered the methods he was using to be a bit extreme. The thought of cannibalism to appease some random god was extremely stupid, in his opinion; after all, two healthy, fit, slaves could undoubtedly be put to work. A though occurred to him; perhaps Barbados had not yet thought of that. If it would get him out of being burned at the stake, it couldn't be too bad of an idea. He mentally tucked away that thought, and resolved to mention it to Barbados the next day.

As he had nothing better to do with his time, Adrian began to meditate. He tried to summon up lightning, but every time he tried, he ran into some sort of mental wall. It took him a few moments before realizing that that mental blockade was Virda's spell.

Adrian's head began to nod, and he soon fell back into sleep. He dreamed about fire and darkness, and began to writhe about. Then, his dreams turned to Rose, and he returned to calmness. Then, with some reluctance, his mind focused on James, and he wondered what had become of him. He missed having him around. Then, slowly, the dreams stopped.

***

The next morning, Adrian was roused from sleep by a thorough shaking. He rolled over, and found the chief barbarian staring down at him. He flinched as the barbarian's rancid breath assaulted his nose.

"Up," he growled. "I untied rupe. Up!"

Adrian obliged, finding that his feet were indeed untied, though his hands remained in bonds.

"Time to burn at stake!" growled the barbarian.

Adrian quickly tried to summon up lightning, but found that Virda's spell was keeping him from achieving that end. He recalled that the only two times he had called up lightning before, he had been besieged by a headache, which only followed physical labor. He desperately hoped that the barbarian would not suspect the motive for his nest suggestion.

"Sir," began Adrian timidly, "isn't it a bit of a waste just to burn me? For instance, couldn't we, that is, me and the girl, do some work around here."

"You could work," mused the barbarian, "but I have other thing for gurl."

Adrian didn't like at all the smile on Barbados' lips as he said that last sentence, so he desperately appealed, "Please, sir, she could weave!"

"Yes, I think she could," thought the barbarian out loud. "Okay. You and girl work, and we burn you at end of day."

"Why settle for the end of the day?" Adrian knew that he was pushing his luck with his next proposal. "We could work for week, months, even years! After all, wouldn't it be better to have two living slaves than two dead former captives?"

"Maybe I could let gurl live," he thought, with the unpleasant smile returning to his face. "But I not make her weave."

Adrian really didn't want to know that Barbados was planning to do with Rose, as he knew that the barbarians were motivated by very primitive desires. "Very well, sir," he said. You shall burn us at the end of the day." An undercurrent of mockery marred his futile attempt at formality.

***

Adrian hauled a bucket of dung into the woods, and flung the contents a far away from him as possible. Though it was unpleasant work, he put as much effort as he could into it. A slight irony occurred to him: now that he once again promised himself to fight for Virda and the Great Sage, Virda's spell worked again. This was making it harder to achieve the very goal that the spell had been intended to aid. He made yet another promise to himself, and this one was to get rid of the spell as soon as he could. He then thought better of it, as it had helped him more often than not.

Adrian hurried back to the camp ground as fast as possible. He could feel Virda's spell wearing down, and he started to walk a bit slower, he didn't want to be hit by the headache too soon. He came back to the animal pen, ready to carry another bucket of dung to the forest, only to be intercepted by Barbados.

"You done carrying poop," he said, jerking his fist at the pen. "I have other job for yu. You not big enough to hunt, and yu have hurt ahm, so you help in field." A sneer fastened itself on his face as he gave that order. Adrian assumed that working in the field was some sort of humiliation for men, as so far he had only seen women harvesting crops. However, he nodded assent, as working in the field seemed like just the right amount of exertion to wear down Virda's spell.

"Follow me!" commanded Barbados, and turned around and walked away. Adrian followed him into the thin layer of trees separating the field from the rest of the encampment. Though you could see either side from the other, Barbados seemed to think that Adrian needed accompaniment to the other side. They emerged into what Adrian supposed could be called a "field", if one used the term rather lightly. There were thinly spread, unhealthy looking plants that Adrian assumed were the crops. They were well grown, considering that the soil probably held little to no nutrition. It was a light gray in color, and when Adrian pressed his foot to the ground, it would not give way. He wondered what kind of plant could possibly survive in the barren environment. Adrian saw the women harvesting the crops, and then putting the crops into wheelbarrows.

"It get culd soon, su yoo help havest," ordered the barbarian. "GO!"

Adrian hurried over to the women, and began to pick the plants, and when he pulled his first plant totally out of the ground, a harsh lecture in an unknown language from one of the women taught him that he was only supposed to pick the actual food. He stared at his second plant for a while, being watched by the lady. He reached out his hand, and picked what looked somewhat like a pepper. The woman slapped his hand away, so he assumed that wasn't it. He reached out for a round shape, and was rewarded with a smile from his supervisor. He picked the first plant clean, and then deposited the spoils into the wheelbarrow. He moved on to the next row of plants, and continued to work.

Adrian found working in the field to be incredibly tedious and repetitive work, but he eventually became aware of a dull, throbbing pain at the base of his skull. For this, he allowed himself a small smile.

After hours of tedious work, Adrian was taken away once again by Barbados, this time to help build spears out of wood, to replace the ones they had lost hunting. It was difficult without the use of both arms, but not overwhelmingly. He put his all into the work, and his headache evolved from a dull pain to a sharp one. More than once he had to rest, so as to avoid fainting.

At what he guessed was about five o' clock or so, Barbados made an announcement in their crude language to the entire tribe. Adrian was lead off, and tied onto a wooden pole. He was then carried out, and headed towards the fire.

He saw Rose being carried on a different pole, but she had her eyes closed, and Adrian was unable to discern any emotion from her face. Adrian frantically began to meditate, retreating inwards with his mind. Once again, he encountered the barrier of Virda's spell, but this time, with a huge mental push, it fell away. Adrian then writhed in agony as the pain of his memory of the fifth dimension permeated his body. He struggled to master it, and suddenly, he lost control. As he fell into unconsciousness, he thought, "It's over." His hand shot out, and by chance, found Rose's.

Suddenly, Adrian was jolted back awake as lightning exploded from his body, scorching everything around him. He saw Barbados' shocked expression, the fear in the little one's eyes, the wonder in the eyes of the women, and the hatred in the eyes of the men. His bonds vanished in a burst of flame, and the barbarians screamed as their bodies were disintegrated by lightning. He frantically tried to stop it, but it was beyond his control. He watched a baby, not past one year, vanish in the lightning storm. Somehow, he had managed to keep hold of Rose's hand, and shockingly, she had been untouched. Adrian, however, could not see this, as he could not see anything but a veil of white.

Without warning, he was pulled away from the clearing, and into the woods. Once again, he lost consciousness.

***

Rose was in shock, but thankfully not literally. Adrian's sudden explosion of lightning had been the last thing she had expected, as was finding herself still alive. She dragged Adrian into the forest, as he seemed quite incapable of moving on his own. She had laid him down on the softest patch of land she could find, and she had clung to his hand until the lightning stopped. He seemed to sleep peacefully, so she let him be.

A few hours later, Adrian awoke in a cold sweat. Rose was sitting next to him, staring at the moon, which had only just risen.

"Rose, what happened?" he asked sleepily, as he sat up.

"You summoned up lightning, like at Light's End. It killed everyone in the tribe, except for us," she answered distantly. Then, with sudden ferocity, she shouted, "Why did you do it Adrian. All my problems were about to end, and you ruined it. No more guilt, no more pain, all that would have been mine, but you took it away."

Adrian felt a feeling of shame creep over him, but then his instincts took hold. "Rose, I saved our lives. You have so much to live for, as do I! You just need to find it, and I have. Have you?"

Rose looked at the ground before answering. "Yes Adrian, I think I have. But I was afraid that what I lived for didn't live for me."

Adrian took a moment to interpret that comment. "And what is it that you live for?" he asked tentatively.

"You," she said, almost imperceptibly. "Adrian, I love you. You're my only friend, and my only family. I thought that after what I said to you, and after what I did to the ambassador, that you would hate me. I didn't think that I had anything to live for."

Adrian quite visibly blushed at those words, and put his arm around Rose's shoulder. "Rose, you should have known that I, er, felt the same way."

Rose nodded, and she put her head on his shoulder, and a single tear rolled down her cheek. A strange urge overcame Adrian, and he kissed her on the forehead.

After a few minutes, a smile came over Rose's face, and Adrian made a check mark on his mental to-do list.

"Rose, there's something that we need to do," he said. "We need to find the nearest ambassador, and clear things up with the Great Sage."

"A very good idea," smiled Rose.

***

After wandering aimlessly for a few minutes, Adrian had an idea. "Rose, maybe the next ambassador is like the first one: in a stream. We just need to find the river again."

The two of them were perfectly silent for a few moments, and Adrian heard the faint sound of trickling water. He swiftly pointed it out to Rose, and the two of them ran after the sound. In less than a minute, the two of them found their target. They followed the stream, and sure enough, they found an island with a root in the middle.

"How do we approach him?" asked Rose, motioning to the root. "If we just expose ourselves, he'll attack us!"

"And if we don't, we deserve to be attacked," pointed out Adrian. "Ambassador," he shouted, "It's me, Adrian Cantor!"

"ADRIAN CANTOR, YOU AND YOUR FRIEND HAVE ATTACKED TWO OTHER AMBASSADORS!" raged the root, thrashing about. "YOU WILL DIE!" Suddenly, the surrounding tree's branches picked up Adrian and Rose, and prepared to drop them to the ground.

"Wait, ambassador!" pleaded Rose. "Listen to us! We had no choice! If we refused, we would be killed!"

"THERE IS NO EVEIDENCE TO PROVE YOU RIGHT, SO- Wait, what's this?" The ambassador suddenly became much quieter. "Another being approaches. Perhaps he can prove you right."

Sure enough, Thorner came out from the trees, only to be caught by a branch, and then hit in the head by another. He slumped in the branch, unconscious.

"I have glanced through this creature's mind, and I concede. You are not the true threat, merely a slave of the real danger, Necropheus," sighed the ambassador. "I see what Blaise threatened you with, and no mortal would have chosen otherwise. You are forgiven."

Adrian and Rose smiled at each other, as the trees set them back on the ground. "Will you help us escape from Necropheus?" asked Adrian.

"I have a better idea," mused the root. "If you produce a hairline crack in the piece of deadwood, it would explode when Necropheus attempts to activate his spell. If you could just- Wait, there's no time! Thorner's coming to! Blaise is going to have you attack Light's End next, and when you do, make sure there's a hairline crack in the deadwood! Now petrify me!"

Though Adrian felt guilty, he obliged, and forded the few feet separating him from the root to run the ambassador through with the piece of deadwood. There was the familiar blackening of the wood, the familiar white runes appearing, but this time, Adrian felt a clear conscience, as, in his last sentient moments, the root thanked him.

9

Assault on Light's End

Adrian stepped out of the woods, and looked around. He was at the riverbank, with Rose and Thorner behind him. Initially, Thorner had objected when Adrian started to lead the party, but after Adrian proved he knew where he was going, Thorner became content to be led. They had followed the sound of flowing water for some time now, and they had finally found the river. Thorner seemed uneasy, so Adrian decided to use that to his advantage.

"Thorner, do you think that you should scout ahead?" he inquired, hoping for a chance to talk to Rose alone. Thorner nodded, and walked away.

"Rose, do you think that the ambassador knows we're coming?" he asked. "I don't know if the other one had time to communicate with the one in Light's End."

"Well, we'll just explain ourselves if we need to," shrugged Rose. "And we'll have Thorner with us, if he needs proof."

"We should try to put the hairline crack in the deadwood shard now," suggested Adrian. He checked his pockets for it, only to discover that he did not have it. "Do you have it?" he asked Rose.

"No. Shoot, Thorner's carrying them. I guess we'll have to wait," she answered.

A few moments, Thorner returned to them, and motioned for them to continue. The three of them walked along the riverbank as fast as they could without slipping. Suddenly, a large wave crashed on the beach, and water lapped at their feet. As a result of this, Rose slipped, and fell into the river with a scream.

"Rose!" shouted Adrian, jumping in after her. Thorner was dancing about wildly on the beach, clearly trying to communicate something to them. Rose seemed to have taken in a mouthful of water due to her scream, and was thrashing about. Adrian reached out an arm to grab her, but he was forced to wrench himself away when he himself was nearly pulled under. He looked about frantically, and saw a long branch lying on the beach. He swam back to shore and pulled himself out of the water, and rushed over to the branch. He picked it up tentatively, as if he was afraid it would rip his arm out. However, he quickly discovered that though it was very long, it was also very light. He reached it out to Rose, and Thorner picked up the far end, and helped to keep it balanced. Rose reached out, and grabbed the other end, and they began to pull her to shore.

Suddenly, something started to pull Rose back. Adrian dropped the log, startled. What he saw chilled him to the core. A man like thing in the middle of the river was pulling on Rose's legs, trying to get her to let go of the log. The thing was a foot or so taller than Adrian, or so he thought, since he couldn't really see the monster from the distance he was at. It was totally covered in mud, and it had weeds growing out of its shoulders. Adrian thought fast, and the idea that struck him both amused and sickened him at the same time. He was about to think it over, but he saw that Rose had lost consciousness, and had let go of the log. He could see that the river monster was about to drag her under, and he couldn't allow that.

Acting fast, he seized Thorner by the scruff of his neck, and threw him at the river thing. Thorner screamed as he hurtled through the air, and he collided with the river demon hard. He began to thrash about, clawing at the monster's face. The monster attempted to swat Thorner off, and while he did not succeed in that respect, he did manage to catch Thorner in his left hand. In the process, he dropped Rose.

Adrian saw this, and he jumped back into the river, and he swam out to get her. While he was swimming, Thorner took action of his own. He reached out with his mind to the weeds growing on the monster's shoulders, and brought them to life. They writhed uselessly for a moment, but they then wrapped themselves around the demon's head, blinding him. While he did this, Adrian managed to swim out to Rose, and grabbed her hair with his arm, and paddled back to shore using his legs. As she was unconscious, she was able to offer no resistance.

Thorner chose that moment to deal the final blow. He used the shoulder weeds to force the river monster back underwater, and then pushed off of the top of its head with his legs to launch himself into the air, and then he landed on the demon's head with a thud. The thing sank to the bottom, unconscious.

Back on the beach, Adrian was pushing down on Rose's chest to try to force her to cough up the water. She did, but she remained unconscious. Adrian felt her heartbeat: it was faint. Having no other choice, he attempted to give her mouth-to-mouth. In third grade, his parents had forced him to take a class on CPR when Serena had begun to take swimming lessons. He felt Rose's heartbeat getting stronger, and he continued the mouth-to-mouth. Rose began to breathe normally again, and Adrian pulled away, if a bit reluctantly.

Rose sat up, and then she knelt on the beach, coughing up the remainder of the water. Adrian stayed by her side to make sure she was all right. After a few moments, she seemed to okay. She stood up, and then threw her arms around Adrian.

"Thanks," coughed Rose, expressing her thanks through her hug, also. Rose stood up, and the trio then continued to walk down the shore, and towards Light's End.

Adrian and Rose began to recognize some of the surrounding area from their initial voyage down the river. After a half hour or so, Adrian saw the fork in the river leading to the Verdant sanctuary, and Light's End.

"Adrian, let's not head to Light's End right away," suggested Rose. "I want to see the Verdant Sanctuary again. We haven't been there for... how long? A week or two, I'd guess."

Adrian also wanted to see the Verdant Sanctuary again, so he suggested it to Thorner. After some consideration, he nodded his approval. The three of them took the right path, and continued to walk for a few minutes. They came to the pool of water where they had last been before being found by Vitalius. In fact, Adrian saw that their makeshift raft was still there, albeit rotting. They made their way past the small dam, and found themselves once again in the Verdant Sanctuary. In the days after Vitalius had died, the plants had begun to wither, as there was no one to operate the machine that filtered the salt out of the water that they drank. Plants didn't do too well on salt water. Adrian and Rose saw this as they entered the clearing. They quickly hurried to the edge of the clearing, and figured out how to use the machine. They turned it on, and made it so the activation lever would stay in the on position for years to come using a piece of rope. They took a look around Vitalius' house, and Adrian once again admired the finely carved ceiling. After glancing around, Rose started to cry once again. Adrian put his arms around her, and the two of them stood there for a moment.

After the moment had passed, the two of them stepped out of the cabin, and Adrian could have sworn he saw a face in the window, and one that looked a lot like Vitalius'. Adrian and Rose walked over to Thorner, who led them back to the fork in the river. They walked down the riverbank, and suddenly, a barbarian stepped out of the woods.

"Aaauuugh!" he screamed, pointing at Adrian. He flung himself to the ground in the most intense bow Adrian had ever seen.

"Um, are you okay?" asked Adrian, reaching out to help him. The barbarian flinched away from Adrian's hand, and crawled backwards a few feet. "Rose, I think this guy has issues," said Adrian.

"He was in a hunting party. I saw them leave the camp, right before..." Rose's voice trailed off, and Adrian knew that she was talking about the lightning storm. "He and the other members of the hunting party fled when you summoned up lightning, and he managed to escape." Adrian took the barbarian's hand, and he passed out from fear. Adrian looked around, and saw two other men in the surrounding bushes, with looks of fear on their faces.

"We'll just ignore them for now," decided Adrian. "It doesn't look like they can do us much harm." Thorner, Rose, and Adrian continued down the shore. After they had left, the other two barbarians rushed out, and dragged their comrade into the dead foliage.

The trio progressed down the beach, and they came to the waterfall. Adrian saw cloudless skies a mile ahead, and wished he could feel the sun again. Much to his irritation, the Verdant Sanctuary had become subject to the cloud layer.

Without warning, Thorner stopped, and refused to be moved. Try as they might, Adrian and Rose could progress no further. The reason for the sudden change in behavior suddenly came stumbling through the bramble.

"Good to see you two again," smirked Blaise, walking over to them, another vine man in tow. "Thorner can't help you any more, as his temporary residence of the vegetable hut was too much for him. So, I'll switch guards. This one doesn't actually have a name, so just call it whatever you like."

Adrian's brain was struggling to absorb what just happened. The sudden reappearance of Blaise was a bit much for him to handle. "So you're ditching us again, and taking Thorner with you?"

"Well, I can't accompany you myself," mused Blaise, "and Thorner's too tired to keep an eye on you. So, yes, I suppose so."

"And you're not coming with us yourself because..." Rose left the statement hanging, in the hopes that Blaise would answer it.

"Oh, it's much too dark and scary in there," he smirked. "And, apparently, the ambassador knows you're coming, so it's a safe bet that he's prepared for us. No, I think I'll let you handle this alone." Adrian desperately tried to keep his relief from showing. "But don't think I won't be watching you," Blaise smirked.

Adrian and company left the riverbank, and entered the barren area in which the entrance to the cave was hidden. Adrian saw it immediately: a huge mouth of rock, jutting out from the surrounding stone.

"I'll just stay out here, thank you very much," said Blaise, sitting down on a rock.

Adrian, Rose, and the vine man walked in, and were immediately met with the last thing Adrian expected.

A necrossis stepped into their path, an odd grin on its face. Adrian jumped back a few feet, crashing into Rose, who screamed. Then Adrian noticed something funny: he didn't have a headache. The necrossis looked slightly different than before, and Adrian took his chances, and charged at it. He collided, and suddenly, the necrossis vanished in a burst of light, and Adrian saw through the illusion: what appeared to be the necrossis was in fact a luminescent plant figure. It vaguely resembled Thorner, but it was much lankier, and stood up straight, so it was taller than Adrian. Picture one long vine with four other vines sticking out from the spot where humans have limbs, and a rounded nub for a head, and you'll have a decent picture of the vine thing.

"ADRIAN CANTOR!" boomed a voice from the assailant. "I AM THE AMBASSADOR YOU FIRST MET, AND WHILE YOU ARE IN LIGHT'S END, IT WILL BE WAR BETWEEN US! YOUR CRIMES AGAINST MY BROTHERS WILL NOT BE FORGIVEN, NOT UNTIL YOU ARE LYING DEAD IN YOUR GRAVE!" Adrian and Rose took a few steps back, unnerved by this display of anger.

The outburst made Adrian realize something, however: for some reason, the ambassador still thought him guilty of the crimes he had been forced to commit by Blaise. It also occurred to him that the assault on Light's End was just one step in the plot to destroy Necropheus, but he couldn't let Blaise or the vine man know his true motives.

"Not quite," giggled a feminine voice in Adrian's head. "And don't call me a vine man, please. I have a name, you know, and I'm a girl."

"Who are you?" shouted Adrian in his mind.

"It's me, Vinetia!" Adrian looked at the vine man on the ground, and it waved to him. "I freed myself from Blaise's control without him realizing it, and I convinced him to send me to help you!"

"Wait, what?" asked Adrian, totally confused.

"All of Blaise's vine men are under his mental control from the moment they're created," explained Vinetia. "I, however, was able to take control of my own mind. See, because you saved me earlier, I felt that I owed you something. With that mentality, I took control of my own mind. Also, Thorner realized what the two of you were up to, but I managed to convince him not to tell Blaise, so I could help you. Then, I convinced him that he was too tired to work, so Blaise would send me as his replacement."

Adrian was duly impressed. "Okay. First, Vinetia, could you put a hairline crack in the deadwood shard?" Vinetia obliged, putting just enough pressure on both ends to make a tiny crack run straight down the middle.

The three of them walked down the tunnel in silence, in fear of whatever undeserved danger awaited them next. Their suspense was unanswered for some time, and they climbed downwards towards the lake without incident.

"Adrian, Rose, if the first attack was any indication, you're going to need something to defend yourselves with," thought Vinetia in their heads. "Wait a second. I'll make you both weapons." She meditated, and vines began to twist out of the ground, and tightly wove themselves into a rigid staff, which Vinetia gave to Rose. To Adrian, she gave a long piece of stone from the tunnel floor, sharpened to a fine point by the vines. "A spear and a staff," mused Vinetia. "Those should make good weapons." The three allies continued to walk for some time.

The temporary period of restfulness was broken by a demented laugh from up ahead. The trio came to the fork in the tunnel that Adrian had been in before, but this time, Adrian saw a glow from both tunnels. He couldn't remember which one led to the lake, but the left one seemed brighter, so he followed that one.

He immediately discovered that it did not lead to the lake, as the source of the glow was standing in the middle of the tunnel, blocking them from progressing any further, and the source of the glow was the member of the second order of druids that Democritus had killed during their first visit. Of course, Rose was the only one to realize it. Instead of just his limbs, now his entire body, except for his face, was covered in luminescent vines.

"Welcome back, Adrian, Rose!" cackled the man, his voice considerably higher. "I am X, the reanimated body of one of the members of the second order! Democritus killed me, but the Great Sage returned me to life. And I remember you, Rose! You just crawled away, and Democritus killed me! Now, as payment, you will diieeeee!" He shouted the last word, and he lunged at Adrian and Rose. Adrian put up his good hand to defend himself, without even thinking of his spear, and he was knocked back into the area where the tunnel forked. Adrian was quickly followed by Rose, and then by Vinetia. The three of them crowded into the tunnel leading outside, and then X slowly walked into the intersection of the three tunnels. He calmly held out his hand, and three vines shot out from it. Adrian swatted them away with his spear, as did Rose, but with her staff.

Vinetia, however, assumed a meditative stance, and suddenly, normal vines, that didn't glow, shot out from the tunnel walls, and assailed the other vines. Adrian used this distraction to his advantage, and stabbed X with his spear. X let out a grunt as he stepped back, reeling from the blow. A strange green fluid seeped from where the spear had torn the vines. With sudden ferocity, he screamed a war cry, and the vines surrounding his body reached out, and enveloped Adrian. He struggled his hardest, but the vines had a good grip on him, and he could not free himself.

Vinetia was quick to notice this, however, and diverted her attack force of vines to attack the glowing vines holding Adrian in place. They tore the vines loose, and Adrian stepped back, gasping for breath. However, X took the opportunity to reach out his three extended vines, and swat Vinetia back twenty yards or so.

"Vinetia!" shouted Rose, running over to her. Adrian tried to hold his ground, but was forced to retreat as X advanced. X sent out three more vines to attack the group, and Adrian tried to swat them away, but to no avail.

"Adrian, use your lightning powers!" screamed Rose, as X stepped even closer.

"I can't!" responded Adrian. "I can't control them. I might kill you by accident!" He was, however, running out of options. X kept advancing, and they didn't have room to fight in the tunnel. He stabbed out blindly with his spear, but to no avail, as X was able to leap back safely. Vinetia seemed to be running out of strength, holding up the defensive with the vines like she was. That gave him an idea. "Vinetia!" he shouted. "Bring the tunnel down on him! Then, we can get out to the lake!" Vinetia nodded, and the vines sticking out of the wall began to wildly thrash about, and cracks began to appear in the ceiling. Adrian and the others rushed away, and the roof of the tunnel collapsed on X.

Adrian ran through the open tunnel that was directly behind the flowing water, and had a strange feeling of déjà vu. Though he was no longer fleeing from the necrossis, he still felt it was similar enough to merit the term.

"Rose," he began, speaking the thought that had been annoying him. "I guess that the last ambassador wasn't able to communicate with the Great Sage after all, since this ambassador seems quite intent on killing us."

"Perhaps," mused Rose. "Or maybe he's just testing us."

Their discussion saw abruptly ended by the sound of footsteps from behind them. The trio sprinted away, and continued to run towards the lake. This time, Adrian was able to avoid bumping into the tunnel wall at the sharp turn, and he warned the others of the danger quietly.

The three of them left the tunnel, and stepped into the fog shrouded lakeside area. They wordlessly formed a perimeter around the opening, and braced themselves.

X calmly stepped out of the tunnel, though he looked worse for the wear. The three heroes, however, were ready, and launched their offensive immediately. Adrian punched X with his good arm, and Rose locked him in a headlock. Meanwhile, Vinetia summoned up vines that lashed out at X, with unintended results. Vinetia's vine tore off those of X, exposing him to be a very frail old man.

He crumpled to the ground, utterly defeated. He groaned as he fell, and then he was silent forevermore.

A few minutes later, the three victors were searching for another tunnel, having marked the first one with an X above the entrance, in honor of the fallen man.

Adrian took the left side of the lake, and Rose took the right, while Vinetia looked on the far side.

***

Adrian walked along calmly, as there seemed to be very little to worry about. So far, there had only been two threats, so he assumed there would not be another. He discovered he was wrong very quickly. He had found a cave, and entered, in hopes of finding the entrance to the abyss.

He walked in darkness for a few moments, but then he heard a mewling sound. He looked down, and saw three baby Leocavia. They looked so helpless, just sitting there, that Adrian wanted to hug them, and never let them go. However, he forced himself to look away, and keep walking. After a few minutes, he felt like something was watching him, and he turned around. Instead of the three small cats he remembered, he saw three medium sized cats, and he could see them growing larger with each passing second. They growled at him, and Adrian pointed his spear at them, in self-defense.

"Stay back!" he warned, stepping back.

"No," growled the cat, and Adrian did a mental double take. "We were bred by the ambassador to do this!" They pounced at him, and Adrian had no choice but to jab the nearest one with his stone spear. It howled, and then collapsed into a pile of vines. Adrian wondered if he was losing his sanity.

"Not exactly," purred the female cat. "We were created to destroy you, Adrian. We can grow at will, and talk to you." All the while, the female cat was slowly inching towards Adrian. With a vicious snarl, she suddenly pounced, becoming twice her former size as she jumped through the air. Adrian ducked under her lunge, and followed up with a jab to the rear. The female squealed, and whirled around, baring her teeth. Adrian struck out with the spear once again, and this time connected with the cat in the face. After another howl, she too collapsed into a pile of vines.

The third cat made no speech. It grew ridiculously, until if filled the entire tunnel. He let out a gut-wrenching roar, and Adrian quite literally had to step back a few feet. He glanced at his spear, and immediately compared the situation trying to cut down a redwood tree with a butter knife. He turned around, and ran for it. The giant cat, easily twelve feet tall now, struggled to force its way through the tunnel. After a few moments, Adrian came to a dead end. The cat opened its mouth once again for another roar, and that was its undoing. For when it opened its mouth, Adrian hurled his spear into the beast's mouth as hard as possible. It punctured some vital organ, and the cat collapsed into vines, like the others.

Adrian walked slowly out of the cave, and was suddenly pulled back in. He landed on his face, and was dragged in. He tried to get a grip on a stone jutting out of the ground, so as to hold himself in place. He dragged himself into an upright position, and saw that the vines from the remnants of the cats had woven themselves into one huge pile of vines, which had reached out, and was dragging Adrian back into the cave. Adrian reached for his spear, but the he remembered that it was still in the cave, where he had thrown it at the Leocavia. He squirmed about in a futile attempt to free himself, but he found that the mass of vines had too tight a grip on him. He bit at the vine, and clawed at it with his free arm, but it was incredibly resilient to his attacks, and, slowly, Adrian saw that some of the vines had thorns growing out of them, and two of them had raised themselves up high, and prepared to descend upon Adrian.

***

Meanwhile, Rose was having troubles of her own. She too had found a cave to investigate. She had entered it casually, not expecting anything to happen. When she had gotten not fifty feet into the cave, she was struck from behind, and she fell into unconsciousness.

A few moments later, she woke up with a throbbing headache. She was being carried by some huge monstrosity, made entirely out of vines. It was about ten feet tall, with bulging muscles. She bit back a scream when she gazed into its face. It was a giant clump of vines, but there was a jagged line where a mouth should have been, which opened and closed periodically, and it had one small, black eye, and one huge, green eye. But most frightening of all was that instead of hair, snakes protruded from its head, like Medusa of Greek mythology. She realized that in its other hand, it held her staff. She slowly, almost imperceptibly reached out for it. She succeeded in not drawing the monster's attention when she grabbed it. Then, with surprising quickness, she bashed the staff into the monster's head, and her target dropped her onto the ground with a thud. She stood up quickly, and held her staff in what she thought was a satisfactory defense position.

However, the monster let out an angry bellow from its slit of a mouth, and he charged at Rose. Rose, all thoughts of holding her ground forgotten, darted away as fast as possible. After a few moments, though, she skidded to a halt in front of a chasm, as deep as she could see. The monster, however, failed to see the chasm until it saw too late. It skidded to a halt, but he and Rose were both pushed off the edge.

***

Adrian rolled to the side as the first of the thorn vines fell to the ground, nearly decapitating him. He rolled into the thorns, and succeeded in using them to break the vines that bound him in place. He stood up, rubbing his arms, and raced to the side just in time to avoid the second thorn vine. However, the second attack was so strong that the thorn vine broke off, and the very thin end rolled away, and onto Adrian's foot. It didn't hurt too much, and he absent mindedly picked it up in the heat of the moment, and flicked it at the mass of vines. It served quite well as a whip, he realized, and flicked it at the vine mass again. The vine mass retreated a few steps back, and Adrian pressed his advantage, delivering quite a few blows in rapid succession to the mass of vines.

The vine mass seemed to be defeated, so he turned around and walked away, leaving the whip on the floor. With his back turned, he failed to see a last ditch attack from the vine mass.

***

Rose screamed as she went over the edge, and mindlessly groped in the air for something to grab onto as she had dropped her staff moments ago. She found a vine, and clutched in as hard as possible. She slid a few feet, burning her hands, but then she ground to a halt.

When the monster had attempted to stop itself, a few of the vines that made up its body had snagged on some of the surrounding rocks, and had torn themselves away from their source. They had been caught tight, but the velocity at which they were previously moving caused them to dangle at the top of the chasm. It was one of these vines that Rose had caught herself on. With great effort, she climbed back up to the top, and walked out of the cave.

Meanwhile, Adrian was hit squarely in the back by the vine mass, which had hurtled itself at Adrian. He writhed desperately, trying to free himself. The vine mass pulled him back into the cave, and, much to Adrian's annoyance, dragged him over a thorny vine. That irritation turned to jubilation as he realized that the thorn vine he had been dragged over was his whip. He grabbed it with the closest hand, and viciously attacked the vine mass. The mass of vines collapsed into a useless pile after just three blows, and Adrian stood up, and walked away.

***

Adrian and Rose met back up with one another by the tunnel they had originally come out of.

"Rose, even though I found another tunnel, it doesn't go anywhere. It's a dead end," said Adrian, still holding his whip.

"Same here," said Rose. "I found one, too but it's a drop off. Democritus couldn't have survived the fall."

"Wait," Adrian suddenly said. "What if there doesn't need to be another tunnel? What if the other tunnel, the one that X was in, in fact led to Democritus' nest? It's the only significant fork in the tunnel."

The theory struck Rose as being incredibly plausible. "Yes. Yes! That has to be right!"

Without warning, Vinetia ran back to the group, apparently fleeing from some threat. Four vine creatures like the one that had greeted them when they first entered Light's End suddenly emerged from the fog.

Adrian, his patience at an end, mercilessly laid into them with his whip. After a few moments, the vine things fled, defeated.

"Well, that was interesting," murmured Rose, to no one in particular. "Well, let's go!" With that, she ran into the tunnel with the X above it.

"Rose, wait!" shouted Adrian as he ran off after her. Vinetia followed the two down the tunnel immediately. In a few moments, they all caught up with one another. They ran beside one another for a few minutes, passing through the open tunnel, and they finally came to the fork in the tunnel. This time, they took the alternate route. The tunnel looked just like the others, except the ground felt smoother to Adrian's battered feet. He assumed it was due to Democritus walking through the tunnel for millennia. Eventually, they saw a light coming from ahead. The tunnel came to an abrupt halt. It seemed to open up into a much larger room, but the floor was ten or so feet beneath the edge of the tunnel. Adrian was undeterred, and jumped out of the tunnel. He landed with a thud in Democritus' nest, which was illuminated by an oil lamp.

"Rose, the fall's not too bad! Just jump!" shouted Adrian up to Rose, who was still in the tunnel, paralyzed by fear.

"Adrian, I'm scared of heights!" she called down, clinging to the tunnel wall. "I can't do it!"

Adrian sighed. "Alright, fine. You don't need to jump. Vinetia, could you push her down?" Vinetia obliged, and Rose, startled, fell out of the tunnel at a shove from Vinetia.

"Adrian, you could've warned me!" she sputtered indignantly. "And I would've rather jumped than—"

"Calm down, Rose," he smiled. "We've got a root to find."

***

The three comrades walked down the tunnel hurriedly, on the verge of finding the ambassador. They came to the chasm, with the oddly placed pillar still sticking out of the middle.

"Do you have any rope?" Adrian asked Rose. She shook her head, and Adrian tried to think of an alternative. "Vinetia, could you make a rope of vines?"

"Sure thing," said Vinetia, projecting her words right into Adrian's head. She started to meditate, and vines tore themselves out of the ground, and wove themselves into a chain. It descended down into the abyss, and Adrian climbed down, a difficult task with only one arm fully healthy, as the other was still recovering, though it felt much better these days. Ironically, it was in this very place that he had injured his other arm in the first place. He set his foot down on the first step, and saw his own bloodstain from a week ago.

Rose climbed down with a strange feeling of déjà vu, a suddenly common feeling. She stepped down, and she too saw the week-old bloodstain. It was hard to imagine that so much had happened in just a week, though she wasn't sure if that was exactly how long it had been. Vinetia climbed down after all of them, and she was the only one not encountering a past memory, as this was the first time she had set foot in the abyss, or even Light's End, for that matter.

They descended down the step in silence, each absorbed in their own thoughts. They entered into what could best be called the antechamber of the abyss. The luminescent plants from before lined the walls of the tunnel leading to X's old room. The same living, glowing plants surrounded the chamber, and Adrian could feel the hostility exuded by all of them. Suddenly, the luminescent vines on the walls began to twist themselves together, and they formed more of the strange vine men impostors that had attacked the group when they first entered Light's End. They surrounded them, and suddenly, a strange figure emerged from the opposite door. It was like the vine impostors, but different, somehow. It was smaller, and even more disproportionate than the others. It seemed, however, much more powerful than the others. It seemed to be in control, and Adrian felt one of his friend's wills bending to it.

"Welcome, Adrian," laughed the vine impostor, speaking both out loud and in Adrian's head simultaneously. "I am the power behind the throne, as they say. Rose was right, at least initially. The ambassador was to spread these vine impostors out throughout Light's End, so as to test you, and in the end, he would have pitted you against X. I was a mutant, a deformed vine impostor. However, in the ambassador's attempts to salvage my body, he gave me a bit of his power over the plants here, and a will of my own. I overthrew him, and rearranged the tests to my liking. I hid most of the vine impostors in this room, to attack you when you came. I am Arbor, lord of Light's End!"

Without warning, Vinetia pounced on Adrian, attempting to tear him to shreds.

"I am also lord over all plants, due to the ambassador's foolishness," laughed Arbor. "Now, Vinetia serves me."

Adrian was in a panic. This was not going well at all. He pushed Vinetia away, and jumped back a few feet. He retreated back to the wall with Rose, and tried to batter away the horde of vine impostors. True to their name, they shape shifted into various things, including Kronos, Blaise, and Adrian's image of the Great Sage. He imagined his as an old yet fit man, wearing green robes.

"Adrian, summon up lightning!" begged Rose, as she slapped away a vine impostor, which was in the image of a boy that Adrian assumed was her brother from long ago.

"I can't!" cried Adrian. "It's too dangerous! I couldn't live with myself if I were to accidentally kill you."

"Adrian, hold my hand! I don't think that it can harm me if you hold my hand!" yelled Rose, desperately trying to ward off blows from the same vine impostor.

Adrian took her hand, and tried to summon up lightning. "I can't, Rose!" he admitted, after trying for a few seconds. "I can't do it unless I'm on the verge of collapse. It's because of Virda's spell."

"Then we're doomed," whispered Rose, her eyes cast to the floor. Before the vine impostors struck the final blow, she grabbed Adrian in a passionate embrace.

Suddenly, the tide turned. The vine impostors began to fight amongst themselves, driven by an unknown force. Adrian looked up to see Vinetia at the head, directing half of the vine impostors. Arbor, caught off-guard, ran into the ambassador's room.

"Thank you, Vinetia!" exclaimed Adrian, rushing over to her, pushing his way through the crowd.

"It was nothing, Adrian," said Vinetia. "When he took control of me, I was able to steal control of half of the impostors without him noticing. I just had to wait for the right moment."

Rose seemed to be hanging back. "Rose, are you *jealous* of Vinetia?" asked Adrian incredulously, looking at her. "Just because I'm paying her some attention doesn't mean I've forgotten about you!"

Rose flushed a deep crimson. "I'm not jealous!" she exclaimed, walking over to Adrian's side. "We'd better go catch Arbor before he causes even more trouble."

The trio walked through the tunnel leading out of the room, ignoring the fighting vine impostors. They progressed through the tunnel without interruption, and emerged into the open room with the pool. The bioluminescent fish swam about, unnerving Vinetia. She clung to Adrian's hand as they walked by, irritating Rose. This amused Adrian to no end.

The three of them entered the final tunnel, leading to the ambassador's room. They exited the tunnel to find themselves in the room that Adrian and Rose remembered, save one thing: Arbor, standing next to the root.

"Welcome, Adrian, Rose," his voiced boomed in the small chamber. "Welcome to the master's chamber. And above all, welcome to the land of the dead, for that's where you shall live soon!" With his last statement, he suddenly changed forms, becoming a large demon. It wore ebon armor, and wielded an obsidian sword. "Most vine impostors can merely change their appearance. Sadly, I, too, am limited to merely that." Adrian could've sworn that he was lying, however. The illusion was much more convincing than that of the other's. He felt as if he could reach out and touch him with his right arm. Suddenly, the demon/Arbor charged Adrian. Adrian put up his arm to defend himself, but was unnecessary. Vinetia threw herself in front of the attack, to shield Adrian.

In that instant, a life disappeared. One living being could never take another breath, nor speak another word. That being would never feel the warmth of sunlight, or feel love in her heart. And that being was Vinetia.

"Vinetia!" shouted Adrian and Rose simultaneously, rushing over to her. Adrian looked up with fury in his eyes at the form of Arbor. "You'll pay for this!"

However, Arbor seemed to have changed in the past instant. He seemed distant, and vaguely subdued. "No," he said. "No. No no. No no no! Nonononono! Don't take me! Please!" His voice changed without warning. "Well done, Adrian! You cost me one of my best vine men! Oh well, I guess I'll have to make do."

"Blaise!" gasped Adrian. "You took control of Arbor!"

"Yes. I was sort of watching you through Vinetia, though I couldn't really tell what you were saying. Well, anyways, I think I'll let you have some fun with Arbor for a little. Enjoy!" Even though Adrian couldn't see Blaise, he was pretty sure that he was smirking. Arbor was suddenly himself again, and tried to shape shift. Apparently, Blaise had removed that ability from him. Caught off-guard, it took Arbor a few seconds to realize that he could still control plants, but those few second cost him. The ambassador had managed to free himself from Arbor's control, and summoned the plants in the room to do his bidding. Arbor was torn back into the vines from which he was made by other vines, and the vines lay there on the floor.

"Adrian, Rose, come here," said the ambassador. "I deeply apologize for my carelessness, which resulted in the creation of that monstrosity. I also apologize for the death of Vinetia. She seems to have been very dear to you."

"I think we can call it even, ambassador," said Adrian. "We killed two other ambassadors, and though the third one gave us permission, I still feel bad about it."

"They are not dead," laughed the root. "They're just, ah, I believe petrified would be a good word. However, once Necropheus casts the spell, they'll return to normal. Have you put a hairline crack in the deadwood shard?"

"Yes, ambassador," responded Rose. "And I've been wondering, what exactly is Necropheus' spell going to do?"

"If it were properly cast, it would kill the Great Sage," answered the ambassador gravely. "However, as we've interfered with it, it should backfire on Necropheus."

His answer didn't really surprise Adrian, who had suspected it was something like that all along. "Well, since we've got the hairline crack in the shard, shall we..." he asked.

"Go ahead," said the ambassador. "I'll deal with it."

Adrian felt slightly ill as he thrust the deadwood shard into the ambassador. With a flash of light, his wood blackened, and the familiar white runes appeared. However, Adrian saw that one of the runes was slightly changed from before.

"Let's get out of here," said Adrian, walking away from the petrified ambassador, and through the chamber, towards the exit. Rose followed him.

They met Blaise right outside the entrance to the cave, which was very well concealed, realized Adrian, as he tried to find it again. It's not that it was hard to see, but there were hundreds of other, shallower caves that were indistinguishable from the one they had just stepped out of, also built into the rock cliff.

"We'd better get back to Necropheus," mused Blaise. "And I don't want him to know that I left you two on your own for a while, okay?" Adrian and Rose nodded, as they were not entirely blameless either.

***

After hours of walking without any incident to speak of, they came back to the river, near the center of the Deadwood. After a few moments, they came to the clearing where Necropheus made his residence. The river flowed through the middle, like before, but aside from that, the entire clearing had changed. White runes similar to the ones that littered the skin of the ambassadors covered the total are of the clearing, and one that was bigger that the rest was in the center of the island in the middle of the river. And on that rune stood Necropheus.

"Welcome back!" he cackled, seemingly excitable. "As a reward for the two of you, I got you a little gift!" he tossed Adrian his backpack from Vitalius' house. He couldn't quite recall when he had lost it, but he hadn't had it for a while. "Now, Adrian, Rose," began Necropheus, "I'd advise you to stand back. I'm about to cast the spell that will make me ruler of all!"

10

The Quest

Necropheus stepped into the middle of the island, his staff held high. He took a deep breath, readying himself, and stuck it into the center of the white rune that covered the island. There was a grey flash, and then...

Meanwhile, the first root that Rose had petrified was suddenly illuminated by a white brilliance, emerging from the runes. The white light focused itself through the deadwood shard, and shot towards the clearing where Necropheus stood. On a hill to the south, another ambassador suffered the same fate.

On an island to the east, the ambassador went through the same process, but in a few moments, he suddenly regained consciousness, finding himself in Necropheus' clearing.

In Light's End, the fourth ambassador met a slightly different fate. The deadwood shard shattered into a thousand pieces, which rained to the ground as dust, thus foiling Necropheus' plot. Also, as it shattered, a green, pulsating circular rift in space opened, and the Great Sage's viridian energy flowed through, and shot towards Necropheus' clearing, like the others.

Necropheus was holding his head high in triumph when suddenly everything went wrong. Three streams of white light met on his island, but the fourth was a brilliant green. The vast amount of energy necessary for the spell was gathered on the small island, but Necropheus found that he could not manipulate it, due to the Great Sage's energy, which mixed with that of the petrified ambassadors. The energy formed a sphere, and Necropheus felt his flesh being twisted every which way by the vast amounts of energy. He felt something split open, and part of him was converted into pure light.

"Necropheus!" boomed a voice as old as Maltesque itself. "I am the Great Sage, whom you attempted to kill! You have used two innocent children to petrify four of my best ambassadors, and your servant, at your request, turned the fifth into a tool! You shall now pay for your crimes, Necropheus!" Suddenly, four roots protruded from the ground, one for each ambassador. It took Adrian a minute to realize that they *were* the ambassadors. They each reached out, and pierced Necropheus' body. Suddenly, they, and the Great Sage, were all gone, leaving Necropheus alone with an incredible amount of energy which he could not control. A scream pierced the night as the energy exploded out, sweeping across the Deadwood, transforming into a veritable hell. Suddenly trees were alive and malicious, and the oversized cats were much fiercer looking, with scimitars instead of teeth, a casual observer might say. The river had turned red. The birds that had attacked Vinetia when Adrian had first met Blaise were suddenly much bigger, and dozens of other changes occurred. And the thing that had changed the most was the one responsible for the mess: Necropheus. Adrian and Rose, however, did not see the remarkable changes bestowed upon him, for they were running from a more immediate threat: Blaise.

As soon as Necropheus' spell had begun to go wrong, Blaise had turned on Adrian with a sad look in his eye. Adrian took that as a good sign to run, and he bolted. Blaise reached out with energy, but only succeeded in pushing Adrian farther ahead of him, though he caused him to trip in the process. He lay sprawled on the ground for a second before jumping to his feet, and sprinting away once again. He felt another hand grab his, and he looked to the side to see Rose running with him. A small smile crossed his face as the song *Born to Run* ran through his head.

Adrian looked behind him to see that Blaise seemed to have given up. He was standing perfectly still in the middle of the path. Adrian slowed down, and turned around to see that Blaise had assumed a meditative stance. An invisible wave of force rolled across the ground, emanating from Blaise. Though Adrian couldn't see the wave of force itself, the wave was creating a very visible disturbance in the dirt of the path. Suddenly, the wave was no longer a wave as it morphed into a sphere of energy, colored by the dirt it picked up as it rose into the air. It swirled around in the air for a moment, but then Blaise ordered it to do something further.

The sphere shrank, but from the shrinking sphere emerged a monster made of pure energy. It let out a deafening roar, and charged at Adrian and Rose. The two of them slowly backed away in shock.

It came to a halt right in front of Adrian, and it lifted its arm in preparation to flatten him with one powerful blow. Adrian rolled to the side, but he still felt the impact from the hit on the ground from the energy creature. Blaise seemed to become irritated, and poured even more of his power into the creature. It grew to twice its previous size, and charged towards Adrian again. Adrian saw that there was no chance of him defeating it man to man, so he bolted away, with Rose in tow. However, the creature was faster than Adrian, so he thought of something else. He skidded to a halt, and the creature overshot him, and crashed to the ground. Adrian whirled around, and rushed as fast as he could towards Blaise. Blaise failed to see him coming, as he had his eyes closed, as he was incredibly intent upon controlling the energy beast.

Adrian delivered a swift and incredibly satisfying uppercut to Blaise's chin, sending him flying back ten or so yards. His eyes snapped open, and he lost his focus on the energy beast, and he lost control of it. The energy creature exploded with a flash that could be seen for miles, and sent deadly rays of energy flying. Rose used a tree as her shield, but Adrian pushed Blaise in front of him, to take the blow for him. Blaise vanished in a flash of light at the same time as the ray of energy that was flying at him.

Adrian stood in place for a moment, absorbing what had just happened. "Rose, are you okay?" he shouted, glancing around.

"I'm fine," said a voice shakily, and Adrian saw Rose standing behind a tree. "Where's Blaise?"

"I used him as a shield," said Adrian, his voice wavering. "I pushed him in front of me when a ray of energy came at me. He and the ray vanished."

"So he's dead?" inquired Rose. Adrian nodded. "Well, I wouldn't count Blaise out just yet. He's too tricky for that." Adrian shrugged, mentally disregarding her words. "Well, come on, Adrian. The Deadwood seems even more dangerous than usual, after Necropheus' spell went wrong."

Adrian glanced about, and saw that she was right. The forest seemed more dangerous than before, though he couldn't quite put a finger on why.

One reason for the feeling of danger stumbled out of the trees behind them. Necropheus had grown to twice his normal size, but that wasn't why he looked a thousand times more threatening. He looked entirely different than before. His legs were a deep black, and very thick and muscular. His torso was also black, but much larger, and was lined by grey tattoos. His arms were similar to his legs, but they were tinged with red. As opposed to hands, he had what could best be described as claws, though that doesn't truly do them justice. Most frightening of all, however, was his new face. Half of it was the same as before, but the other half was that of a hideous beast. However, the face was not evenly divided. Rather, it was like parts of his old face had been stuck onto the head of a monster. Adrian could also see parts of his old body stuck onto his new one, giving the impression that his old body was unsuccessfully trying to keep the new body in check.

"Adrian," he wheezed, stumbling towards them. "Rose. Adrian. SABOTAGE! You ruined me! I underestimated you, and," he broke into a fit of coughing. "You took advantage of that. Well, CONGRATULATIONS!"

He was still for a moment, and power seemed to build up inside of him.

"YOU REMEMBER, DON'T YOU, ADRIAN? YOU REMEMBER WHEN I LOST CONTROL BEFORE?" He took a step forwards, casting the appearance of a demon of hell. "NOW YOU WILL PAY FOR WHAT YOU DID TO ME!" The air around him turned black, and whirled itself into a cyclone. The twister of air grew in size, and it then launched itself at Adrian and Rose. They ducked to the side, and ran away as fast as possible. "RUN, COWARDS! RUN FROM ME! RUN FROM me... Too exhausted... Can't handle... power" His voice faded away into nothingness, and Adrian and Rose saw him collapse behind them. They kept running, and didn't stop for a long time.

After a half hour or so, Adrian and Rose came to the red river again. They hadn't seen it turn red, as they had been running from Blaise. "I guess that's also from Necropheus' spell," mused Adrian, gesturing to the river. Rose nodded, and they followed the river for some time in peace. They were on the west side of Maltesque, though they did not realize it. After a few more minutes, Adrian sat down, hungry, and idly wished that he had his pack. When he mentioned this to Rose, she just laughed.

"Adrian, you do have your pack! Necropheus gave it to you when we came back!" Adrian flushed red, and realized that she was right. He took out a piece of dried fruit, and munched on it hungrily. After a few moments, he handed the pack over to Rose, and she helped herself. After she had finished eating, they got up, and kept walking.

They walked along talking about whatever topic came to their minds. It began to rain, sending droplets of water falling upon their heads. After an hour, Adrian saw that the river was bulging, and close to overflowing.

"Rose, we'd better get going," said Adrian. "Hey, you know, it's kind of funny. We're just now going on a quest that was given to us a week ago, the quest to get to Twilight City. I guess we've been a little sidetracked since we left Vitalius' house. But hey, at least we're following through on our promise!"

"That's true, I suppose," responded Rose. "But there was another promise. Remember Democritus? Remember how if he hasn't rid himself of his bad side by the time he get to Twilight City he dies?"

"Well, yes," muttered Adrian. "Wait. That's impossible! Democritus can only become sane if he isn't in pain, which isn't going to happen if he's in the wild!"

"I don't think that's the Great Sage's plan," argued Rose. "I think the idea is to overwhelm the insane side of him, so it's destroyed." Adrian figured her explanation had some merit, and abandoned the conversation.

After walking in silence for a while, they heard a sound from behind them. They swiftly turned around, but they didn't see anything. Suddenly, a huge bird flew overhead, casting a shadow upon both of them. They looked up, and saw the same sort of bird that had dive-bombed them when they had first arrived at Blaise's hut. This time, however, it was much bigger, and its talons could easily lift Adrian into the air. Its beak was serrated, and looked ready to tear Adrian to shreds. It let out a terrifying caw, and dived at Rose. Adrian pushed her out of the way, and just narrowly avoided being torn to shreds by the thing's beak. It seemed to get its beak stuck in the ground, and thrashed about wildly in an attempt to free itself. While it writhed, stuck in the ground, Adrian delivered a fatal blow to its neck. The bird slumped, defeated.

Rose was cowering on the beach. Adrian walked over to her, and helped her up. "Let's get out of here," he whispered.

***

After an hour, Adrian noticed that the trees had begun to thin out. The river seemed to be growing thicker, too. However the danger of the Deadwood forest had not yet passed. A Leocavia stood in their path, and Adrian and Rose were much too tired to fight it. Instead they feinted an attack, but then turned around and ran away. The Leocavia walked after them in a bored manner, but lost interest very quickly.

"Well, I guess we can't go back that way," mused Rose.

"Wait. I've got an idea. Do you remember the boat that we crossed the river in a few days ago? I think it's nearby!"

After searching for a few minutes, they found it, lying on the beach. Adrian and Rose hauled it into the river, and paddled it across to the east side. They walked for another few minutes, and then Adrian noticed that the river had begun to widen. After another minute or so, Adrian could no longer see the other side.

A few moments later, Adrian and Rose passed by the last tree, and were officially out of the Deadwood.

***

Adrian and Rose looked about. They hadn't really seen very much of Maltesque, other than the Deadwood forest, and the river. Also, the river was no longer red, so they had passed out of the reach of Necropheus' spell. However, there was another side effect to leaving the Deadwood.

Adrian's hand shot up to his skull, and he doubled over in pain. It seemed that Necropheus' spell had weakened Virda's, so Adrian was once again assaulted by his headache. He imagined that this would be a bit of a hindrance, since he didn't trust himself enough to use his lightning powers.

"Adrian, are you okay?" asked Rose, putting her hand on his shoulder. He nodded, and then stood back up. Adrian and Rose spent the rest of the day walking for a few minutes, and then resting. The scenery failed to change as they walked; it was just a barren desert all around, though it wasn't very hot. They imagined that it was because they were very near the river, which undoubtedly cooled it down a bit. Also, the sun barely penetrated the cloud cover.

When the sun set, Adrian and Rose discussed where to camp for the night.

"Do you see some sort of sand dune anywhere nearby?" inquired Adrian, glancing around. "I think we'd be safer if we stayed out of sight. Even though we haven't seen anything dangerous around lately, I still don't trust this planet, just as a general rule."

"I dunno, Adrian," thought Rose. "I haven't had a chance to sleep under the stars yet, and it's just something odd that I like to do."

After debating for a few minutes, they decided that Adrian's was the best idea, due to the fact that even though they were in the open, the stars were still hidden by the cloud layer. They curled up next to each other underneath a sand dune, and went to sleep.

The next morning, the two of them awoke to the same thing they had fallen asleep to: the cloud cover. Adrian supposed that since no sun ever shone on the land, it never heated up, which explained why it was the first cold desert Adrian had ever seen.

Adrian shook Rose, and she sat up sleepily, and blinked a few times before standing up. The two of them had slept in their clothes, so there was no delay other than a short breakfast before the two of them started to walk again. They had run out of things to talk about, so they walked in silence.

Suddenly, they discovered that the desert was no less hazardous than the Deadwood. A scorpion as tall as Adrian skittered out from behind a sand dune, and eyed Adrian hungrily. Adrian reached into his pack, and took out a piece of dried fruit, and tossed it at the scorpion lightly. The scorpion, however, took this as a threat, and ran at Adrian as fast as its legs could carry it, and that speed rivaled that of a cheetah's.

Adrian leaped to the side in time to avoid the blow, but Rose was not so fortunate. The scorpion's stinger pierced her stomach, and she let out a gut-wrenching scream. The scorpion was cowed by her scream, and scurried away. However, the damage was done.

"Rose!" cried Adrian, running over to her. "Rose, oh my god, are you okay?"

"Adrian, I'm... not... sure," her voice trailed away, but then she pulled herself together. "I don't think it was... poisonous." Each word was a struggle, and she was gasping for air. "The bigger ones usually... aren't. I... read that somewhere..."

Adrian believed her, and attempted to staunch her wound, but to no avail. He tore off the sleeve of his shirt, and wrapped that around her stomach as a makeshift bandage, but it was still bleeding. Rose had fainted, and Adrian picked her up, and ran as fast as he could towards the city. After a few minutes, he saw a lonely house in the distance, and he sprinted over to it as fast as possible, disregarding his headache.

In just a minute or so, he made it to the house. He stepped inside, and was hit in the back of the head with a sharp blow, which knocked him to the ground, and caused him to drop Rose.

"You know, it's proper manners to knock," chuckled a voice from behind Adrian. "Are you an ally, or an enemy?"

"Sir, please, I need your help," begged Adrian, standing up. "My friend here was attacked by a giant scorpion, and is in grave danger!"

"Very well," sighed Adrian's assailant. Adrian saw that he was man of about fifty, though more muscular than Adrian would have expected. However, his expression was kindly, and Adrian felt that he seemed trustworthy. "If it was a giant scorpion, odds are it wasn't very poisonous, though every scorpion has a bit of poison in its tail, and this attack looks like it was from the tail. Am I right?"

"Yes, sir," nodded Adrian.

"In that case, we'd better find an antidote right away, before the poison takes effect," mused the man. "Boy, you go out, and try to find a cactus. They grow around here, but they're somewhat rare. I seem to recall that there's one about a mile to the south. You need cactus juice to heal this kind of wound."

Adrian nodded, and went out the door. He took the compass out of his pack, only to find that it was broken. He sighed, and then looked at the sun. It was still in the morning, so he figured that it was still in the east. Then, with a groan, he remembered that he wasn't on earth anymore, so he really didn't have a clue where the sun rose. He walked back into the house, and asked, "Sir, where does the sun rise? I mean, is it north, or west, or..." He left the statement open.

"So I guess you're not from around here, are you? Are you a friend of the technology giver?" inquired the man. Adrian assumed that the technology giver he spoke of was Kronos. "However, right now you need to find the cactus juice. The sun rises in the south in Maltesque. Now fly!"

Adrian hastened out of the house, and ran towards the sun.

After a half hour approximately, he found the cactus plant. Unfortunately, it was guarded by another scorpion, though this one was a good deal smaller, and thus more deadly. Adrian stood in place for a moment, judging the distance very carefully. He faked right, and the scorpion lunged at him. He twirled to the side, and the scorpion got its claw stuck in the dirt. Adrian ran over to the cactus, and broke off one of its arms, for lack of a better term. Unfortunately, this meant that Adrian got several needles stuck in his hand. He took no notice of his, however, as he scurried away. The scorpion gave chase, but was unable to catch him.

He returned to the old man's house in another half hour or so, and he looked worse for the wear. He handed the old man the cactus arm, and the man squeezed the juice out of it, and applied it to Rose's wound.

"Very well, the poison has been stopped," said the man. "There's still more work to be done, though. I was trained as a surgeon, and I think I can stitch up her wound, though it's pretty bad."

In the next hour or so, the strange man sewed together Rose's wound, and left her to heal.

"Now, tell me about yourself," he said to Adrian.

"Well," began Adrian, "I'm from another world. My name is Adrian Cantor, and I was kidnapped."

"Oh? By who?"

"Well, by a man named Kronos. He seems to have it out for me, for some reason. He could control these things called tendrils of darkness, which have the power to possess people," explained Adrian.

"Well done, Adrian," said the man, catching Adrian off guard. "I am a member of the Third Order of druids, and our leader, Arrow, has been expecting you for some time. He is the son of Vitalius, and he has been waiting for you for a week or so now."

"Who are you?" asked Adrian suspiciously.

"I am Falcon, spy for the Third Order of druids!" said Falcon. "I've been assigned to watch the Deadwood, and I've been keeping an eye on you for the past week. We know all about Vitalius' death, so there's no need for you to look so morbid."

"So, should we head out to the city?" asked Adrian.

"Once the girl wakes up, yes, you should be on your way."

***

The next morning, Rose had finally awakened. She hopped up out of bed, seemingly fully recovered. She thanked Falcon, and then she and Adrian walked out the door. They were on the lookout for scorpions for the rest of the day, and the day passed rather quickly. Come night, they found a sand dune to curl up underneath, and they went to sleep.

The next morning, they awoke to yet another cloudy day. No rain fell, but it just felt wet to them. Absolutely nothing happened that day, or the next.

In the third day after leaving Falcon's hut, they came to a lone figure, sprawled in the sand. Racing over to it, they saw that it was Democritus, though the vines had disappeared from his legs.

They gently shook him, in an attempt to wake him. He blinked slowly, and then sat up.

"Rose? Where am I? The last thing I remember, we ran into my old associate from the second order of druids, and then— Where am I?" inquired Democritus, clearly sane.

"You're in the desert, near Twilight City," answered Adrian. "You've destroyed your dark side!"

"Have I really?" chuckled Democritus. "Oh, I doubt that! I've thought that a couple of times in the past, but he's always come back in the end."

Adrian and Rose decided it was best not to argue with him on this point, and they continued onwards. They walked a bit to the east, in hopes of running into the river, which Rose missed the sight of. In an hour, they came to what Rose had been looking forwards to seeing.

"The river!" she exclaimed joyously, racing over to it. She splashed around in the shallows for a few minutes, and got out.

As she was returning to dry land, however, a hand lunged out of the water, and grabbed her by her hair. Struggling in vain, she attempted to free herself. However, whatever her attacker was had a strong hold on her hair, and dragged her into the water.

Her assailant surfaced for a moment, and Adrian saw that it was the river monster they had seen while en route to Light's End.

Adrian remembered how Thorner had defeated it before, but, sadly, Thorner was no longer around. He saw the creature was getting away, and then he had an idea.

"Democritus!" he shouted. "Can you throw me onto that thing?" Democritus tried, but Adrian was too hefty for him to lift.

"I can't do it," he sighed. "Adrian, you stay here! I'll save our friend!" As Adrian opened his mouth to object, Democritus shoved Adrian to the ground, and swam at the river demon. The demon began to swim away with Rose, but Democritus latched onto the weeds that grew from the creature's shoulders. This sent a spasm of pain through the demon, forcing it to let go of Rose, who swiftly swam back to shore. Adrian met her on the beach.

"Rose! Are you all right?" he asked kneeling down next to her. She didn't respond; she just stared at him with a terrified look in her eyes. Adrian held her in his arms until she stopped trembling.

"Adrian, that was terrifying!" she squeaked,

Adrian, however, was fairly distracted by the fight between the river monster and Democritus. Democritus was putting up a good fight, but he seemed to holding back for some reason, signaling to Adrian that he was still in control of himself. The monster, however, had no such restrictions. It thrashed about, attempting to send Democritus flying. While it failed to achieve that, in its haste, it smashed Democritus' head with his arm. Democritus suddenly went berserk, and began to claw at the monster will all of his might, shouting:

"Die, beastie! Bad beastie, yes you are! Die die die!" Democritus seemed to strike one of the monster's nerves, literally. He and the creature fell into the river, and Adrian thought he saw a small figure swim away from the spot of the fight, and towards the city.

"What happened?" gasped Rose, glancing around.

"I think Democritus lost his mind again," sighed Adrian. "I saw him swim towards the city, even though that means he's swimming against the current. The sane Democritus is smarter than that, so I think we can assume that he lost his mind again."

Rose seemed somewhat disturbed by this bit of news. "Do you think he'll go back to normal? Before he reaches the city, I mean?"

"I'm not sure," mused Adrian. "I guess we'll find out."

After they walked for another hour, they saw two interesting landmarks in the distance. There were two mountains reaching into the air, one of which was shrouded in red, with lava flowing out of the top, while the top of the northern one was shrouded in ice. Adrian consulted Vitalius' map to see that they were named Vulco Mountain and Icecap Mountain, respectively. The second name seemed a little unimaginative to Adrian, but he figured that as he had never named a national landmark, he was not one to criticize.

To the south, he saw a shattered dam. It was made of a grey stone, but it was now tinged with green, due to the good deal of fungus growing upon it. The river flowed through the middle, where the damage seemed to have been the greatest. He also saw wooden beams, now rotted, signaling where there had once been attempts at repairs. He vaguely remembered Vitalius telling him that when the people noticed that the water was flowing away from their city, they had attempted to dam off the water flow, but they had been unsuccessful as far as Adrian could see, though the aforementioned wooden beams now signified the location of the attempted repairs. He also saw that the dam marked the entrance to the aptly named sludge lake.

Though Adrian couldn't see the lake yet, he could smell the pollution even from back where he stood. He slowly walked towards the lake, along with Rose. Even though the dam was shattered, it still posed a significant obstacle to overcome.

Adrian found himself blocked by a wall of stone, the only remnant of the dam. He spotted an ancient stairway leading up, and he walked over to it, carefully scrutinizing it. After forming his opinion, he tentatively put his foot down on the first step, in fear of it collapsing. It held, however, and he slowly ascended the ancient staircase, and, when he reached the top, waved down to Rose.

"Up here!" he shouted to her, waving with his right arm. She looked up in surprise, and he smiled. "The stairs still work! Come on up!" After just a few minutes, Rose was also standing atop the shattered dam, surveying the surrounding areas.

"Hey, you can see the city from up here!" she exclaimed, looking to the south. "And there's another forest to the southwest! I think that's where they get their resources from. I can see people working out there."

"Yeah, probably," agreed Adrian absentmindedly, absorbed in his map. "It looks like that's the Poisonsap Forest, and that's the Tree of Ages to the west of it."

After looking around for a few minutes, they descended back down the stairs, and headed towards the river. When they came to the bank, Rose clutched onto Adrian's arm, in fear of the river monster. However, the creature failed to appear, and they made their way through the remnants of the dam. They had to step over broken pieces of stone occasionally, but they found it easy to pass through the ruins, as when the dam had broken, the river had completely destroyed the part of the dam closest to the river.

They came out of the ruins to see that it had not been named Sludge Lake for nothing. The water was a deep brown from the pollution, and Adrian thought he saw a tinge of purple in some spots. It reeked horribly, but Adrian attempted his best not to pay too much attention to that. There were stones floating, probably due to the high salt content of the pollution, in various spots. They actually formed a pathway across the lake, but Adrian doubted that that was totally natural. On the other side of the lake, Adrian could just see the outskirts of the city. Laughing, he raced along the shore of the lake, headed in a generally southwards direction, elated that he had nearly completed his quest. After a few moments, Rose caught up with Adrian, laughing along with him.

After a minute or so, they were both out of breath, and they paused to rest on a rock sitting on the beach.

"Well Rose, we've almost made it!" laughed Adrian, really laughing for the first time in a while. "We got a little sidetracked, but we're almost there!" Rose joined in, relieved at finally seeing Adrian in a good mood. There was nothing for them to worry about for once, at least for right now.

Suddenly, a bedraggled form pulled himself out of the lake, and started towards Adrian and Rose. They immediately ceased to laugh, and jumped up. They were saved the suspense of wondering who the figure was by the first words out of his mouth.

"Made it to the city, yes I did!" cackled Democritus, stumbling as he continued to walk towards Adrian. "Burn, you will burn!" he shouted, searching for a torch. Failing to find one, he lunged at Adrian, knocking him back a few feet. Adrian was caught off guard by the sudden attack, and failed to retaliate in time. Democritus shoved him into the lake, and then turned on Rose.

Rose, however, anticipated Democritus' attack, and got him in a headlock before he could launch an attack of his own. She pushed him to the ground, and kicked him repeatedly with her feet before he could stand up again, and he finally cried:

"Give, I give! You win, yes you do!" he writhed pitifully on the ground, and Rose stopped, rushing over to pull Adrian out of the lake. He stumbled out, dazed, but Rose was that he was mainly okay. Her relief was shattered when Democritus used her own technique against her, and put her in a headlock before she could turn around.

Adrian refused to stand for this, and kicked Democritus as hard as he could in his shin, before throwing him a punch to the head. Democritus fainted, and fell to the ground with a thud.

"What should we do with him?" asked Rose, throwing a glance of pity at the figure sprawled on the ground, the same way that they had found him before. "We can't just leave him here! He's a lot of trouble if he's left alone. We should take him with us."

"What, and take him to the Great Sage? That's like murder!" protested Adrian.

"As is leaving him out here!" exclaimed Rose, glancing at him. "Maybe the Great Sage will be a good sport, and let him live! And even if he does kill him, it'll get rid of his evil side. I think that's what the sane Democritus would have wanted."

"Well, we'd never know, would we?" murmured Adrian, glancing at the ground. "Maybe it isn't. But you're right; we should take him with us."

Rose nodded, and Adrian picked up Democritus, and started to carry him off.

"That won't work," mused Rose. "If he wakes up, he'll attack you, and then he'd escape, and he always manages to find a way to make trouble. See if he has any rope."

As usual, Democritus had a coil of rope wrapped around his waist, which appeared to be very old, like all of his rope. Adrian bound Democritus' hands with it, and then attached something along the lines of a leash to his bound hands. He gagged his mouth, in the very likely case that Democritus decided to try to bite him.

As good as the plan was, Adrian figured out that it was severely flawed when Democritus awoke. He struggled violently, making it impossible for Adrian to carry him any further. He set Democritus down, and forced him to follow them by leading him with his leash.

After a few minutes, Adrian gave the leash to Rose, and took out the map. They seemed to have left the lakeside, and were now in what the map called the Polluted Delta. It was a marshy area, and retained the stench of the lake. What little water existed was brown, though the purple spots were gone. A couple of times, Adrian saw a few people working in the drier areas, apparently harvesting some unknown crop. The weed that grew irritated Adrian; they clung to his clothes, releasing their spores. Democritus had ceased his resistance, and was now obediently following Adrian and Rose.

After an hour or so, they exited the delta, and entered the foul outskirts of the city, where pipes poured waste from the city into the delta. They finally came to a gate, and they entered the city.

***

Adrian felt uncomfortable as he took his first step into the city, glancing around. He hadn't seen this many people in one place since he had been kidnapped by Kronos. The air was choked by smog, giving it an orangey tinge, the color of twilight, which gave the city its name. Adrian saw teenagers looking out from garages, and he saw clean skyscrapers reaching out to the heavens, above the pollution. The one thing that caught him by surprise was the conspicuous lack of cars. Everyone seemed to be walking on foot.

"Adrian, we've made it!" cried Rose, flinging her arms around Adrian, dropping Democritus' rope. However, he did not flee, as the presence of all of the people seemed to subdue him. Overjoyed to be back again in civilization, she kissed Adrian on the cheek, laughing. She picked up Democritus' rope again, and glanced around to see people staring at him. One person, specifically, seemed more interested in him than the rest. He looked to be a boy around Adrian's age, possibly a couple of years older. He was fairly well muscled, but he had an intelligent look about him.

"Are you perhaps Adrian Cantor?" asked the boy in a voice that Adrian vaguely recognized. It was the voice that had shouted "For Benevolaria!" when the strange blast of air had freed Adrian and Rose from the clutches of Kronos. "I'm Arrow Viridia, son of Vitalius."

11

A Rebellion of One

James stumbled away from the skate park, still in shock. The sudden loss of Ajax had left him confused, and a confused person is not one you should entrust a precious artifact to. As James wandered aimlessly away from the skate park, he accidentally dropped the twilight crystal on the ground. A lone tear dripped from his cheek, only to be followed by several more.

James lost track of his location after a while, and glanced around, uninterested. He observed that he was near the tech center, the building that he and Ajax had attacked, and stolen the twilight crystal from. Suddenly, two people stepped out from the shadows. They slowly advanced towards James, and he saw that one of them was the possessed gunman. He stepped towards James with a grin on his face.

"Well, look what the cat dragged in. Old Ajax's little lackey," he smirked, his voice mixed with that of Shadius. "Come here, boy, and I'll put you out of your misery." James saw that the gunman had a companion, but he no longer really cared. The gunman held up his revolver, and his finger tightened on the trigger, preparing to shoot as James walked towards him.

Without warning, a voice reached out to James. "Fight back, you fool!" it screamed in his ear, and James realized that it was the voice of Ajax. "Without you, our cause is finished! So fight back!"

James saw everything happen in slow motion: the gunman's finger muscles tightening, himself jumping to the side, and punching out with his left fist, catching the gunman in the chin, knocking him out. He saw the gunman's friend reach out with his hands to strangle him, but he twisted away. James dropped to the ground, and grabbed the gunman's revolver. He pushed himself up, and his finger closed on the trigger. A gunshot pierced the night, and then all was silent. The man who had attacked him fell to the ground, coughing blood. He seemed to have regained his senses.

"Thank... you..." he wheezed. "Thank you... for freeing... me..." He fell to the ground, dead. James felt numb, his mind unable to accept what had just happened. Without thinking, he reached into his pocket, and pulled out the sheet detailing Shadius' plot, and began to read. That lone sheet of paper held more information than James had gleaned from any book, even though he read it without truly noticing it.

Shadius seemed to be using the tech center to develop a laser, which would open a wormhole in space, spreading the darkness virus throughout the universe. As he read, he became aware that the fact that the plan involved other planets, it was a fair assumption that there was intelligent life elsewhere. He vaguely recalled Ajax mentioning that to him before, and once again wondered who Ajax really was. He recalled the words that Ajax had spoken to him not a half hour ago: "If you ever get back to the lab, go into the forbidden room, and you'll have your answer." He was determined to honor what may well have been Ajax's last wish, and was filled with newfound determination to return to the lab. A glance at the bleeding figure on the ground merely hardened his resolve, and he glanced about to get his bearings. He found once again that he was near the tech center, and he turned around, facing in a generally northward direction.

The stars were shining as he neared the skate park once again. The sight of it sent a chill down his spine but the congregation of darkness-controlled citizens had disappeared, along with Ajax. James was somewhat relieved by that, and he was also happy that he would not have to see Ajax again, for he figured that might have been too much for him. He found the street to the west of the skate park, the one that ran straight north from the aquarium. He didn't see anyone, and he then realized that he was still carrying the revolver, and though he had absolutely no intention of ever firing the wretched thing again, it felt comforting to have a weapon other that the dinky little crystal. He felt his pockets for it, and then, with a cold feeling creeping up his spine, he realized that the twilight crystal was no longer in his pocket. He mentally and literally kicked himself for dropping it. He had ruined Ajax's plans.

"Then again, maybe it isn't really that bad," he thought to himself. "After I find out what's in the forbidden room, I can go look for it. It should be right around the skate park." Satisfied with his reasoning, he continued walking, the revolver held out in front of him to ward off potential threats.

He came to the northern intersection, and decided to take a bit of a risk, and head left at first, just to see the observatory. He had never really paid much attention to it before, but it seemed that it was the location where Shadius planned to open the portal, and spread the darkness virus throughout the universe.

He hid behind the wall of a nearby building, and glanced around the corner. There seemed to be very little activity, as James imagined that they'd be busy trying to create another twilight crystal back at the tech center. He did, however, see a giant telescope sticking out of the roof. He also saw a few people inside, though he could not fathom their purpose.

He left the safety of the wall, and walked towards the lab. Even from a distance, he could see that he had been wrong: the people had not returned to the tech center to work, they had gathered at the lab should he come back.

He held up the revolver as he walked towards the lab, and noticed something interesting. The steel dome was gone, destroyed, along with the old abandoned building in which it had been hid. There were ten or so people possessed by darkness standing around the elevator.

"I don't want any trouble!" he shouted, calmly walking towards the lab, the revolver held high. The presence of a weapon had severely elevated his confidence level, almost to the point of cockiness. Though he knew that every second he was in the sight of the enemy, he put himself in mortal danger, but he thought that he would be able to easily defend himself.

He quickly discovered that he was wrong when a tendril of darkness reached out from behind him, and harshly struck him on the back. James crumpled over, reeling from the blow. He fell to the ground, and the tendril wrapped around him, and pulled him away. He pushed himself upright, and began randomly firing the gun at the tendril. He seemed to hit a weak point, and the tendril let go of him. However, it reached out, and grabbed the revolver. A spark of darkness ran down the tendril, and the revolver exploded into a dozen different pieces.

James scurried away, mentally lecturing himself for his cockiness. He noticed that the tendril wasn't following him, and then he focused on what he was running towards, and discovered why. Standing in front of him was a mob of possessed people. The ten that had been in the lab seemed to have gained backup, and were now standing his way. James desperately wished that he still had the twilight crystal, and was still mentally kicking himself for losing the revolver. The mob took a step towards James, and he suddenly had an idea. He looked around, and saw one particular building precariously leaning out over the street. He reached into his pocket, and found the other bomb Ajax had given him. He flipped the switch, threw it at the building, and then ran. The mob raced forwards, and were caught underneath the falling debris as the building collapsed, raining wreckage down upon them. James doubted that many of them were seriously hurt, but they could no longer pose a threat to him, and he ran around the wreckage, into the lab.

The elevator seemed to be in good order, and he descended down, as the steel dome had been destroyed. He came down to find himself nearly surrounded. The door leading to the forbidden room was the most heavily guarded, and James avoided that one, and ran into one of rooms that wasn't guarded, though it was one he had never been in, as he had only ever been in was the passageway that led to the forbidden room. He quickly discovered that the room hadn't been guarded for a good reason. Inside the room was an enormous pit, inside of which was the most hideous thing James had ever seen. It looked like a giant, but it was formed totally of vines. Its face was a mass of vines, and it had two horns growing out of its head. It glanced up at James, and bellowed.

James took a step back, and bumped into someone that had been standing inconspicuously behind him. He whirled around, and saw that it was one of the possessed people he had dropped the building on. With a vicious snarl and a merciless grin, he shoved James into the pit.

James screamed in terror as he plunged backwards, tumbling head over heels towards his doom. He thankfully landed feet first, and the monster set upon him. He lifted up his foot, and prepared to squish James. As the foot descended, James rolled to the side, just in time to avoid getting stomped flat. He sprang up, and desperately looked around for some sort of weapon for him to defend himself with. While he didn't see that, he was able to locate a door, located merely a few yards away from him. He made a mad dash for it, and made it, right before the giant's foot flattened him.

He breathed a sigh of relief as he leaned against the door, panting. He glanced around, and found that the room he was in was not really much safer than the other one. A suspended walkway without handrails was all that separated him from an untimely plunge into a giant vat of chemicals, which resided beneath him. He cautiously took a step forwards, and then another. Slowly, he made his way across the walkway in this manner.

He came to the door on the far end, and it opened when he approached. It led to a brightly lit room, and James gasped in surprise. Inside the room was a spaceship. It was neither large nor bulky; instead, it was a sleek black vessel, barely fifty meters long. It seemed to be fully operational, and James wondered why on earth Ajax had this masterpiece stashed away in his lair. The more he looked at it, the stronger he became convinced that the technology it possessed far surpassed anything the modern world could possibly produce. He could see this ship being built in perhaps a hundred years or so, but certainly not today, and not by an old man like Ajax.

James was filled with renewed curiosity, and walked up to the cockpit. He looked inside, and saw that the dashboard was lettered by strange runes, the likes of which he had never seen before. He wondered if Ajax had really built it, or if it was a piece of alien technology. James assumed that Ajax had somehow been to the alien planet that Shadius was trying to infect, as he had seemed to have a reflective look in his eyes when he had mentioned it, even though he had merely mentioned it in passing. Perhaps the aliens had given him a gift, and this spaceship was it.

He stepped inside, and found that he could not turn it on. He did, however, find something very interesting. It seemed to be a ray gun, as it looked somewhat like the pistol he had lost. He held it in his hands, and tried to find the trigger. After a moment of searching, he found it. Making sure it was pointed away from him, he pulled the trigger. A strange ray of energy shot out of the end, and wrapped itself on the first thing it came into contact with. It seemed to send a shockwave of electricity through the target. James would have liked to stay longer, but he was still very curious as the contents of the forbidden room, and the secrets it hid. He started towards the far doorway, and he turned to give the spaceship one final wistful look.

He exited out the far doorway, and found himself in a hallway that split into three, with one path leading forwards, and the other two leading back. Now that he had a weapon, he was determined to kick the possessed out of his lab. With Ajax gone, James did indeed consider it to be his lab. He took the path on the right, and was led into a room that seemed to be used for the construction of robots. Unfortunately, his entrance seemed to have activated the security system. The most modern looking of the robots seemed to turn, on, and stare in James' direction.

"Name?" it asked mechanically, taking two steps towards James. It looked somewhat like a man made of metal, but its arms were held stiffly, and wires stuck out of his body at various angles. James could see that touching it meant danger of electrocution, so he kept a safe distance.

"Name?" it asked again, taking one more step towards James.

"James," he said uncertainly, hoping that Ajax had included him on the non-intruders list.

"Intruder alert! Intruder alert!" shouted the robot, and James saw that he was not on the list. The robot took a step towards him, and reached out its arm to grab him. James imagined that it truly meant no harm, but he could see a live wire poking out of its palm.

"Stay back!" he warned, holding up his new weapon.

"You will stay here until I arrive!" said the robot in Ajax's voice, in what James assumed was a recording. "This robot will keep you in this place, and then I'll decide what to do with you." The robot took yet another step towards James, and he held up the gun for defense. The robot reached its arm out, and James had no choices other than fire the gun or electrocution. It didn't take him very long to decide.

An electric ray shot out of the end of the ray gun, and pierced the robot.

It began to go haywire, twisting around. The current of electricity seemed to have messed up the central computer. The robot's eyes began to flash red, and it madly charged towards James. James dodged to the side, and the robot crashed into a wall.

A red light on the wall lit up, and the other robots in the room came to life. One after another, they charged at James. Overwhelmed, James completely lost it, and began firing the ray gun every which way. When he came to his senses, he was surrounded by broken robot parts. He glanced around, appalled at what he had done. He knew that the robots had meant no harm, and then, suddenly, he saw a smaller robot hiding in the corner. He dropped the gun, and ran over to it, giving it a hug. The robot seemed to have not been preprogrammed, and hugged him back. James took the little robot's hand, and picked his ray gun back up.

He walked out the door, and entered into a different room. It seemed to be empty, but James no longer trusted Ajax's lab. He glanced around, and saw motion detectors on the wall. They seemed to be the kind that cast the invisible laser beam that alerted the security system when you went through it. He had none of the spray that made it visible, however, so he turned around to walk away, and try the left passage.

However, James' new friend seemed to have different ideas. It walked forwards, and seemed to avoid the invisible beams. It reached the other side, and James shouted, "Deactivate it!" Though he wasn't sure if the robot really understood what he had said, he entered a code onto a keypad attached to the wall. James trusted that it had done the trick, and he walked through the room without any trouble.

He opened the door to the next room, and, to his knowledge, it looked pretty harmless. It looked like a computer lab, and in the center was the largest computer James had ever seen. Most large computers were from the eighties or so, but this one looked both large and powerful. It was made of translucent plastic, and James saw a few of the circuit boards. It looked as if each one was significantly more powerful than the most modern computer. He shuddered to think what a computer that powerful could accomplish.

He saw others that he assumed were prototypes. James came to the exit, but he saw that the tiny robot he had spared was gazing at the large computer, as if hypnotized. James walked over, and dragged him away. The robot struggled at first, but he eventually ceased as the computer passed out of sight.

James was in another hallway, brightly lit. It seemed to lead into some sort of common room, in which seemed to be the elevator shaft. However, the common room that the hallway led to was guarded by one of the possessed, which is what James had begun to call the people under Shadius' control. James fired the ray gun at him, but, to his dismay, discovered that the ray gun only worked on electronic things.

James' target seemed irritated at the attack, and, with a snarl, charged towards him. James took the blow, and was sent sprawling backwards a couple of feet. However, James' robotic friend immediately stepped up to James' defense, and punched his assailant in the gut. The possessed man stepped back a foot or two, reeling from the blow. The robot followed up his punch with an attack James knew not that it possessed. A flash of light exploded out of its eyes, and it blinded the mind-controlled man. He stumbled backwards a few feet, and fell into the elevator shaft that he had been guarding with a scream.

James felt very ill as he saw the man tumble into the shaft. He looked up to see the robot peering expectedly at him.

"Why don't you just stay here, and guard the elevator?" suggested James to the small robot. "I'll head down, and see what's on the next level. Could you get the elevator down here?" The robot nodded, and plodded over to another keypad, and typed in a code. The elevator came down the shaft very quickly, and James heard confused screaming from up above him. He imagined the look on the faces of the possessed when the guarded elevator descended away from down. They had focused all of their security on the upstairs, not figuring that anyone would be able to get down easily.

The elevator came to a steady halt right in front of James, and he stepped in. The door slid shut, and the elevator descended towards the floor below. The door opened noiselessly, and James stepped out. He glanced around, and saw that there were four passages leading out of the room, each at right angles to each other. He randomly decided upon the one on the left. The passageway was dimly lit, and rust coated the walls. James wondered when the last time anyone had ever been down here was. Also, considering how dangerous the supervised floor above him was, he had a bad feeling about what was down on this floor.

His fears were justified when he passed through a door, and entered into room with the walls painted a bright red. It hurt his eyes a bit to look at them, but he got over that fairly quickly. What he found infinitely more interesting was a metallic suit of armor in the middle of the room. In the suit of armor was a man. However, it wasn't really a man, per se, it was more of a cyborg. The thing looked like a man, namely, it had four limbs, and was humanoid in shape. However, its face was infused with metal plates, and its eyes were covered with glass, and were a bright red, reflecting the color of the walls.

James walked over to it, and it failed to notice him. He tapped the cyborg on the shoulder, and it suddenly flared to life. Its red eyes glanced down, and saw James. It raised its arm, and a beam of energy fired out of the end. James just managed to dodge the blast, and immediately looked around the room to try to find something to defend himself with. However, the room was empty, except for him and the cyborg. James roll dodged another laser blast from the cyborg. He stood up straight, and sprinted out of the room, swerving to avoid more blasts from the thing. He came back to the elevator room, and he slid into a different passage. He ran through a door, and he hit the jackpot. The walls were lined with a thousand different weapons, and he picked up the one that looked the most effective. It looked somewhat like a gun, but there were different tubes with chemicals lining the sides.

The cyborg stepped into the room, and James fired the unknown weapon. The suit of armor shook, and the cyborg within was violently ejected. It sprawled on the ground, and James was that it was actually a fairly pitiful looking thing. Its limbs were replaced by thin metallic ones. It didn't seem to be able to stand, as its body was really just a thin stick of metal, which didn't look able to support any amount of weight whatsoever. In fact, the only human part to it was its head. James was surprised that it had actually filled up the suit. He touched the thing's face, but it was actually made of plastic.

James glanced around at the assortment of weapons in the room, but decided that he didn't need them for the time being. He walked over to the suit of armor, and got in. it fit him fairly well, and it made him a foot or so taller. He walked back into the elevator. As he got in, he thought, "It's time for the rebellion of one to begin."

***

James rode up two stories in the elevator, and stepped out only to find himself surrounded by the possessed. He didn't really care, however, as while he was in he elevator, he had figured out how to use the laser cannon on the arm of the suit. If he closed his fist, a blast of energy shot out from his wrist, and flew towards wherever he pointed it.

He closed his fist, and a blast of energy fired at one of the surrounding people, blasting him backwards. Though he didn't appear seriously hurt, he was knocked out. Two other men took his place, but he blasted them back too. He surged forwards, barreling through the crowd. He had just made it to the doorway to the recreation room, when two tendrils of darkness emerged from the shadows, and attacked him. James was able to fend them off for a little, but eventually, they overpowered him. They drove him back towards the elevator, but he looked around to see that the elevator wasn't there, much to his dismay. One of the possessed had sent it back up.

James fought with renewed vigor, his strength increased by his terror of falling into an elevator shaft. However, the tendrils overpowered him, and he was sent screaming down towards the bottom of the lab.

James had been falling for maybe a minute when he finally hit the ground. The suit saved him from death, but he was knocked unconscious,

When he awoke, he discovered that he could no longer move inside his suit. It no longer worked, and he was able to dislodge himself without too much trouble. He glanced around, but he couldn't see a thing. There was no light whatsoever, save from above. A tiny ray of it came down, but it didn't really help at all. James didn't trust himself to move, as if the last few floor were any indication, he was probably on a thin bridge suspended over a giant pit of some fatal chemical. However, he couldn't bring himself just to stand there forever, so he took a tentative step forwards. He didn't plummet o his death, so he took another, and then another. He proceeded in this fashion until he stepped right into a wall.

He inched along the wall, hoping to find some sort of door. While he failed to do that, his hand chanced upon a switch of some kind, and he pulled down upon it. The space lit up, and he saw that he was not, in fact, poised precariously on the edge of a bridge overlooking a pit of chemicals. He was just at the bottom of the elevator shaft. It looked a good deal like the other elevator rooms, with four passageways leading off in different directions. He stepped into the one that he was closest to.

After a minute, he came to a door that slid open as he approached it. Inside this room was one of the most intricate devices that James had ever seen. A bunch of tubes, all filled with a red liquid, surrounded a small globe. The globe had hundreds of wires attached to it, all leading off in different directions.

James assumed that this was the main power source for the lab, but he turned out to be wrong. A sign next to the machine read, "Backup Power Source." James assumed that one of the other doors led to the main power source. Intrigued, he turned around, and went back the way he came. When he returned to the elevator room, he took the opposite passage, and James came to a door. He entered, and he was in a room that looked exactly like the one he had just come from, only a hundred times bigger. He stood on a small platform, below which a pit extended miles into the ground. There were once again tubes filled with the strange red liquid, but they were about twenty yards across in diameter. They did indeed circle around a globe, but this globe was about the size of a small house. Hundreds of thousands of wires were attached to that globe, and James was absolutely sure that this was the main power source for the lab. As a rough estimate, he would have to say that this lab was worth about as much as the rest of the United States combined.

However, James could see that he wasn't going to get anywhere by trying to cross the pit, so he turned around, and went back the other way. As he left, he could have sworn he heard a soft cackle.

He came back to the elevator room, and tried to remember if the backup power room had another door. He didn't think so, so he chose a different path. This time, the passage was about ten yards long. James opened the door, which didn't seem to be automatic, like the others, and stepped into an interesting room. It was nothing but shelves upon shelves upon shelves. And sitting upon those shelves were millions of different weapons. James saw bombs, scrapped light laser prototypes, and also, spears and guns of different designs. He tried out a bunch of the weapons, and found three to his liking: a very portable but powerful light laser prototype that seemed to use antimatter for power, in case of an emergency, some sort of electrified sword, to fend off the tendrils, and a gun that caused an extremely bright flash of light. He figured he would use that last one to blind the possessed, so he could run past them while they were blinded. That way, less people would be injured. He was about to continue to look for a way up, but suddenly, the elevator hurdled back down the shaft. James whirled around in surprise to see his small robot friend waving at him from the elevator.

Smiling, James stepped into the elevator. The robot punched another code into a keypad that James had failed to see, and then he hurried back into the elevator before it rose up. It was a bit slower going up. Than James had been falling down, so it took them maybe five minutes to get back up to the top.

If the possessed had been surprised when the elevator had gone down without any known reason to them twice, they were downright shocked when the boy they had pushed down before emerged once again.

James strode casually out of the elevator. He squeezed his eyes shut, and pulled the trigger on the flash gun. A brilliant ray of light exploded out of the end, and blinded all of the possessed. While they couldn't see, James raced past them, and had almost made it to the recreation room when two tendrils of darkness shot out from behind him, and attacked him. He had just enough of a warning to drop his flash gun, and pull the electronic sword that he had snatched from the room below. He slashed wildly at the tendrils, but though he severed their ends multiple times, they consistently grew back. He was backed up against a wall, and his hand suddenly found a button on the hilt of the sword. As he was about to be destroyed by the tendrils, he saw no alternative but to press it.

Electricity shot up the edge of the sword, and electrocuted the tendrils. They stood perfectly still for a moment, before dissolving into black dust. James felt elated that he had finally dealt a blow to the darkness.

The door to the recreation room opened as he approached it, and he saw that inside, there were hundreds of possessed. He groped for his flash gun, but quickly realized that he had dropped it in the corridor outside. Panicking, he turned around to go get it, but ten or so people blocked his way. He scurried away just in time to avoid being tackled by one of his attackers. He darted away from the T.V. mounted on the wall that he and Ajax had been watching. Though he wasn't really paying much attention, he did hear one announcement: "The SWAT team has yet to return from their investigative mission into the strange occurrences of Pilfershire. It's been rumored that they've been put under the mind control that seems to have overcome the town." Though James wasn't really paying all too much attention to it, the thought of fighting a SWAT team member sent a chill down his spine.

James tripped over a video game console, and was sent sprawling on the ground. He saw about five possessed about to pile drive him into nothingness, and he decided that there was nothing for it, and fired the light laser prototype.

A brilliant glow enveloped the room, and all of the possessed collapsed. James saw that most of them looked dead. He had a feeling of invulnerability as he had come up the elevator both times. That feeling had now passed, and he felt sick as he looked about at all of the unconscious form. He wasn't sure how badly they were hurt, but he thought that they didn't look too good. James stumbled over towards the corridor to the forbidden room. For some reason, the possessed had left the forbidden room untouched, he observed as he walked down the corridor. A thrill of excitement overcame his sick feeling as he looked at the books that lined the wall. It looked like that had been the main goal of Ajax, namely, to write that book. They looked more and more updated the closer he got to the door to the forbidden room.

He pushed the door open, and was enveloped by a white glow from the computer screen that seemed to dominate room.

/

12

Legend of Darkness

Arrow led Rose, Adrian, and Democritus through the streets, back towards his house. He explained that though neither he nor his brother, Joshua, possessed any talent for Greenkeeping, they had resolved to strike out against the businessmen whose factories had polluted Maltesque. They were a band of eco-terrorists, if you will, he explained. However, Adrian agreed that their cause was justified. All of this, however, was lost on Rose, who did nothing but stare at Arrow. She seemed quite taken with him, and this caused Adrian a twinge of annoyance.

"So, what's Kronos been doing these past few weeks?" he asked.

"Ah, yes. Kronos. He's managed to explain that he's from the same world as Ulysses, but he's attempted to portray Ulysses as a villain, and the evil force that stole him away as the hero," chuckled Arrow. "However, there's something that very few people realize. Namely, *Ulysses and Kronos are the same person!* I'll give you more of an explanation when we get to my house."

Adrian shrugged. However, he realized that meant that Kronos was thousands of years old. That realization meant little to Adrian, however.

Apparently, Kronos had repaired his tower where Arrow had detonated the air bomb that had saved their lives. Arrow explained that his brother, Joshua, had spent a good deal of time developing the air bomb, and it was their main weapon, as it did little damage to actual people if used correctly. However, Arrow had been so angered by the appearance of the new building that he had failed to do so.

After a half hour, they came to a small, one story building. Arrow proclaimed this as his home, and the four of them stepped inside. The house was dimly lit, but well enough for Adrian to see a table, and a stove, along with a few chairs, was all that really was in the house. He also noticed a flight of stairs, leading to the basement.

"Welcome to my home," said Arrow proudly, gesturing to the table. "Please, sit."

"It's very kind of you to take us in like this," blushed Rose.

"Oh, you're not here for free," laughed Arrow. "We've got a deal to make with you. As of right now, our group, the Third Order of druids, only has five members. Would you like to join?"

"Absolutely!" answered Rose, before Adrian could get a word in. "We'd be honored to be a part of your group, Arrow."

"Then that's settled!" exclaimed Arrow. "You'll stay here with us, and you'll be a part of our group!"

"Wait," began Adrian. "Aside from you, Joshua, and Falcon, who's in the group?"

"Well, there's our recruitment officer, Barge," thought Arrow aloud. "And then there's our spy, B—"

"Well, Arrow, you could have at least told me that we have guests!" interrupted a young man that Adrian took to be Joshua. "I presume that you are Adrian, Rose, and Democritus?"

Adrian quickly looked over Joshua. He looked a bit like James, except he had no glasses, and his hair was a darker brown, as opposed to light blond. He still had that air of bookishness about him, though.

"I'll show you downstairs, if you like" volunteered Joshua, motioning to the stairs. "And when I said 'if you like', I meant whether you like it or not," he said jokingly.

Adrian and Rose followed him down the stairs, and were greeted by the glow of a computer screen. Joshua seemed to be working on some sort of project.

"What's that?" inquired Rose, indicating that her question was about the computer screen.

"It's a schematic of Kronos' building," he answered. "We heard that before you two do anything else, you want to, ah, have a word with him." Adrian nodded in agreement. "We've devised a plan. You'll drop in from above on Arrow's glider, while I detonate an air bomb to produce a distraction. I'll manage that from here."

Adrian was impressed by his plan, but something he said struck him as odd. "Wait. Arrow has a glider?" Joshua nodded his agreement.

"He's also got a helmet with a built in transceiver, so we can communicate," said Joshua proudly. "I invented both of them. The earliest we can pull this plan off would be tonight, as they'd see us coming during the day. In the meantime we can relax."

***

During the rest of the day, Adrian and Rose told Arrow and Joshua their entire story, starting with Halloween ten years ago, when Rose had been taken over by the darkness. Though Joshua and Arrow remained silent throughout, they exchanged glances occasionally, especially when Blaise was mentioned.

Thankfully, night soon came, and it seemed that Arrow had already set up the air bomb, so they could depart. Arrow had his glider carefully hidden beneath the table, and seemed barely large enough to keep Arrow on alone, let alone two other people. It was agreed that Democritus would stay at the house, with Joshua.

They reviewed the plan one more time: Joshua would detonate the bomb as a distraction, and Arrow would drop Adrian and Rose off at the roof, where they would climb in. The phrase "drop off" made Adrian a bit nervous, as they were about to be riding a few hundred feet in the air on an unstable looking glider. However, he chose not to dwell too much on that, as he had more pressing problems, like how to stay balanced on the glider. Arrow assured him that it wouldn't be very hard; after all, he himself had one it countless times.

The three of them finally crowded onto the glider, with Adrian clutching onto Arrow, and Rose hanging onto Adrian. Rose had initially wanted Adrian's spot, but he had talked her out of it. She claimed that she wanted it to be safe, but Adrian had a suspicion that she just wanted it so that she could be closer to Arrow.

Arrow started the engine, and the glider rose up into the air. It was surprisingly stable, and Adrian didn't feel like he was about to fall off once. The three of them landed on the roof of Kronos' skyscraper, and Adrian and Rose stepped off.

"This is arrow to bow, do you copy?" inquired Arrow into his transceiver/helmet. They had codenames for each other, an unnecessary precaution, in Adrian's opinion. Arrow's codename was, well, arrow, and Joshua's was bow. Adrian supposed that it worked, in a way, as Joshua was the one who sent Arrow flying away on his glider to do the work.

Joshua seemed to respond, and Arrow nodded. "We're good," he said to Adrian and Rose. "You can probably break through the skylight over there, and once you're in, Joshua will detonate the bomb, and then you're free to find Kronos." Adrian nodded his understanding, and he smashed the skylight with his fist. At that moment, Joshua detonated the air bomb.

Adrian and Rose dropped into the building, and raced towards the stairs. They went down one flight, and found themselves in the throne room that had been destroyed by the air bomb. They thought that they saw a figure race out the door, and they followed it. Adrian had a slight headache, and he remembered Kronos saying that he controlled twelve other necrossis. He didn't see any nearby, but their presence seemed to be taking its toll.

As Adrian and Rose raced around the corner to follow the man, Adrian saw that it was indeed Kronos. "Kronos!" he shouted at the top of his lungs, and the figure stopped, and whirled around, sending a blast of darkness directly at Rose. She fell to the ground, unconscious.

"Rose!" shouted Adrian and Kronos, both rushing over to her. "Why are you here?" asked Kronos quietly, looking at Adrian. He suddenly stumbled backwards, his hand to his head. He seemed to be struggling with himself, and in the process, his mask flew off, and his black eye turned green, like his other.

"I recognize you!" shouted Adrian. "You're Rose's father!"

***

James stared in awe at the computer screen. It held a video recording of Ajax, which seemed to be on pause. In the center of the forbidden room was the final copy of the book of which drafts lined the hallway. The book was called *Legend of Darkness*. James walked over to it, but he was stopped by the video recording. Torn in two, he finally decided to watch the recording. He found the play button on the most intricate keyboard he had ever seen, and pressed it.

"James, if you're hearing this, it means something unfortunate has befallen me," said the recording of Ajax. "However, you must not lose hope! We may still prove victorious, if you fight hard. Do not, under any circumstance, attempt to free me. You must devote all of your energies to constructing the light laser. If you were to say, break the twilight crystal, or something like that, then you need to get another one. If you fail, the whole universe will perish."

Tears came to James' eyes as he heard Ajax speak again. "Our enemy if far more powerful than you can possibly imagine," continued the recording. "Shadius is an ancient god. When the universe was created, there were two deities assigned with the task of ruling over all of us, a god of light, and a god of darkness. Back then, there were two universes for the gods: Genesis, world of light, and Nightwake, world of darkness. However, the deity of darkness, Shadius, rose up against the deity of light, Photosia, with an incredible weapon, which he created by sacrificing his own world. This is the subject of my book, *Legend of Darkness*, which I devoted my life to writing. The universe that we live in now was part of a bigger universe of light. However, Shadius used his weapon to turn half of that larger universe into a universe of darkness before Photosia put a stop to it. She died in the great struggle, which took place on Genesis, but she destroyed Shadius' weapon, and reduced Shadius himself to nearly nothing. However, there is one more intriguing player in that final battle: Kronos."

***

"Yes," sighed Kronos. "I'm Rose's father."

"How?" asked Adrian, bewildered. "You're supposed to be thousands of years old! Rose's father vanished only ten years ago!"

"Actually, there's an interesting story to that," chuckled Kronos. "Ten years ago, on Halloween, Rose wandered off while we were trick-or-treating. She accidentally wound up in the dark district, as I believe it's called these days. Shadius, my master, sent one of his agents to kidnap me, and turn Rose into a spy, as a mission to prove his trustworthiness. However, here's the rub: that agent was me! I, serving Shadius, took myself back in time, about three thousand years into the past. However, I, the kidnapped one, struggled against myself, and we crash-landed on this world, much like what happened to you. I escaped, and accidentally introduced technology into the world. Then, Shadius sent a necrossis out to find me, and they took me to Genesis. Shadius turned me into his slave there. Back then Genesis was at war. Shadius was one of the two rulers of the universe, but he had rebelled against the other. He sacrificed his home world to make a weapon, which turned light into darkness. He tried to make Genesis his new home, but the other ruler of the universe fought with him. It was into this chaos that I was brought. Shadius turned me into Kronos, the shadow prince. It was I who struck the final blow against the ruler of light, and condemned Genesis to darkness."

"That's... confusing," said Adrian. "But I think that I get it. However, I think it's more important for us to figure out what you did to Rose!" Adrian and Kronos examined her, and Adrian found a shard of darkness lodged in her chest. It seemed to be spreading corruption throughout her body, but Adrian had no idea how to stop it. However, Adrian still had more questions for Kronos. "Okay, suppose your story is true, which I'm starting to think it is. Why do you need me? I'm just an ordinary kid. And why, if you serve Shadius, haven't you taken me to Genesis?"

"Can an ordinary kid summon up lightning?" smiled Kronos, choosing to answer Adrian's first question. "You are not who you think you are Adrian. Your parents are not Serena's. You were adopted."

***

"Kronos is a figure which little is known about, save that he was the one who struck down Photosia three thousand years ago or so," continued the recording of Ajax. "I did devote an entire chapter of my book to rumors about him, though. However, I do know this: Kronos is his own worst enemy. Ten years ago, on Halloween… Well, I'm sure you've heard the story. However, what you probably don't know is that the father who disappeared was Kronos, kidnapped by himself, and sent back in time. Also, I'd bet that you didn't know that I was also there. I had recently finished the final copy of my book, and was going to try to publicize it by spreading it to other worlds. See, I'm distantly descended from Photosia herself. She bore few children, for her marriage partner was supposed to be Shadius. However, she chose instead one of her human advisors about a hundred years or so before the war. This son had some of her powers. Adrian and I can trace our ancestry back to this son. He managed to escape Shadius' wrath, and he managed to bring along one of Photosia's advisors, whom he married on a distant world. The son's most powerful ability was this: teleportation. It was with this that he managed to escape. He dubbed himself 'Lightseeker', for he made it his goal to try to salvage the bit of life that remained. For though the universe was spatially divided in two, only two planets with life on them remained unaffected by the darkness. Earth is one of them, and the other one is a faraway world, called Alchema.

"However, I've sidetracked. I heard the commotion, and went over to investigate. I attacked the darkness with some of my light powers, but it fought back, and overpowered me. I lost the use of my abilities, and was forced to flee. That's more or less all I have to say, other than finish that damn light laser!"

***

"I'm adopted?" asked Adrian incredulously. That explained a ridiculous amount of his life.

"Yes, Adrian," said Kronos. "Your mother died in childbirth, and your father never recovered from that loss. Your true father was descended from Photosia, the other ruler of the universe. That's why you have such power, and that's why Shadius needs you. Since he was all but destroyed three thousand years ago, he's needed light energy to be revived. And you contain a good deal of light energy."

"So, returning to my other question," tread Adrian cautiously. "If you serve Shadius, why haven't you taken me back to Genesis?"

"Do you think I *want* to serve Shadius?!" roared Kronos with a sudden anger. "He put darkness into my brain, and he'd destroy me if I disobeyed him. However, he lost that connection, due to your intervention. When you attacked the necrossis with lightning, it almost broke his hold on me. Accidentally attacking my own daughter was the final shove I needed."

"So you can help me?" asked Adrian, figuring another addition to the team would be most welcome.

"I can't. Shadius is trying to overtake my mind as we speak. Run, Adrian! Run from me, before Shadius takes over my mind again!" howled Kronos. "And please, think of me as Ulysses, not Kronos."

Adrian hurriedly picked up Rose's unconscious body, and ran away with her. He turned to look at Ulysses, and saw that he was once again struggling with himself. He looked up, and Adrian saw that both of his eyes were now black. Before Kronos could do anything, Adrian was around the corner, and carried Rose up a flight of steps. He reached the top of the building, and Arrow picked him and Rose up on his glider, and carried them away.

***

"Do you think she'll be okay?" asked Adrian, bending over her. Joshua seemed to be carefully analyzing her wound, while Arrow had gone off to fetch something.

"Maybe. The wound doesn't seem fatal, but she seems infected. But really, I don't know," mused Joshua. "I think Arrow has another opinion, though. He's obsessed with that book of his."

"What book?" inquired Adrian, intrigued. Kronos, er, Ulysses, he mentally corrected himself, hadn't mentioned a book.

Arrow walked back into a room, holding a dusty book to his chest. It looked to be maybe twenty years old or so, Adrian guessed. He caught a glimpse of the cover, which read *Legend of Darkness*. The title seemed appropriate, if it had any relevance to the situation, Adrian thought.

"Ah ha!" exclaimed Arrow. "It mentions here some of the effects of darkness, one of which is a darkness virus. It says that if a small bit of darkness imbeds itself in a person, it could contaminate them with a virus which eats them from the inside out."

"Can I see that book?" asked Adrian, taking it. He looked at the cover more closely, and it said that it was written by someone named Ajax Lightseeker. That name intrigued him, for he had been called Adrian Lightseeker by the Great Sage's ambassador. He glanced inside the cover, but found that there was no 'about the author', or anything like that. He assumed that it must have been a distant relative of his or something. He took a glance through the book, and saw that it was about the rise of Shadius three thousand years ago. It seemed to detail fairly accurately the story of Kronos, though there were also other rumors. "May I keep this?" he asked to Arrow.

"Sure, I guess," he responded grudgingly. "It's pretty interesting, don't you think? I mean, the whole idea of there being two ancient gods and all."

"I suppose," mused Adrian. "However, I think we need to take Rose to the

Great Sage. When I spoke to Virda, she told me to go see him, and I think this seems like a good reason to."

"Well, we'd need to discuss it with the rest of the Third Order," thought Joshua aloud. "We should call a meeting."

"An excellent idea, Joshy!" cheerfully exclaimed Arrow. However, in the conversation, Rose had been forgotten. She reminded them of her existence with a terrible wail, while she thrashed about in the cot where they had laid her.

"What're the side effects of the virus?" asked Arrow worriedly. "Does it say?"

"I'm reading, I'm reading!" exclaimed Adrian impatiently. "It says that violent retching, high fevers, and random convulsions are all common effects, and the ultimate result is death. Also, the life expectancy for one with the virus is about a week." He looked up worriedly. "Can we have the meeting soon? Tomorrow?"

"I guess it's possible," mused Joshua. "But that might take work, and I hate work." He caught the horrified look in Adrian's eye, and quickly said, "Kidding! Just kidding. Of course we can have the meeting tomorrow. I'll contact Barge and Falcon, and Falcon'll just have to get the word out to our spy in the Deadwood."

Joshua activated a different application on his computer, and seemed to achieve communication with Barge. "Hey, Barge? This is Joshua. We're having a meeting tomorrow..."

***

It was noon the next day. Rose's fever had ridden higher, and Adrian was beginning to really worry about her. Falcon was the first to arrive, and he had done just that around ten in the morning. Maltesque's days were identical to those on Earth, which was very fortuitous for Adrian, who had never had to adjust himself to another time zone, let alone a different day length. Adrian and Falcon chatted about the new state of the Deadwood, and Falcon informed him that the only safe place was Light's End. Apparently, three of the four ambassadors had gone insane, due to the overload of power they themselves had caused.

At noon, Barge squeezed through the door, and Adrian could immediately see why he had been given that name. Adrian estimated him to be about six foot eleven, and he was nearly as large horizontally.

"Sorry I'm late," he muttered gruffly. "I got held up by some stupid salesman, who tried to sic a cop on me when I pushed him out of the way. Ah well, I guess we might as well start, even though *he* isn't here. Odds are, we're better off without him."

Barge squeezed into a chair at the small table that filled up most of the first floor of the small house. Adrian slid into one, as did Arrow, Joshua, and Falcon.

"I hereby call this meeting of the Third Order of druids to, well, order!" chuckled Arrow, mostly to himself. "Before we do anything else, I'd like to introduce our newest member, Adrian Lightseeker!"

Suddenly, the door slammed open. "Sorry I'm late," smirked an all too familiar voice on an all too familiar face.

Adrian was out of his chair immediately. "You!" he shouted, glaring at the new arrival. "What the hell are you doing here?"

"I'm part of the group," smirked Blaise, casually striding over to take his seat. "I told you I didn't only serve Necropheus. I'm their spy."

"Right," said Arrow with a worried look at Adrian. "Adrian," he started, "can you forgive Blaise for what he's put you through?"

"I didn't *want* to do any of those things to you," plead Blaise, with a look of false innocence on his face. "I was merely the victim of circumstance!"

Adrian had turned white with rage. This man standing in front of him had caused him unimaginable emotional pain, but his new so-called comrades were just letting him walk in on their meeting!

However, his blistering retort was cut off by a groan from Rose. He remembered that this was for her sake, so he decided that working with Blaise for now was tolerable. With a scowl on his face, he sat down.

"Okay, returning to the agenda, I'd like to introduce our newest member, Adrian Lightseeker," announced Arrow, looking at Adrian, troubled. "He's from the same world as Kronos, whom I mentioned at the last meeting. Kronos kidnapped him, and, uh, that's why he's here. As he's an enemy of Kronos, who's an enemy of ours, so he's joined our group. Any questions?"

"Yeah," rumbled Barge. "Y'mentioned sumthin 'bout yer dad. Didn't 'e know these two or sumthin?"

"Yeah," answered Joshua. "They saw our dad right before he died. Actually, they're more or less the *reason* he died. He was protecting them from a servant of Kronos."

"So I guess your dad loved Adrian and Rose more than he loved you, Arrow," smirked Blaise. "After all, he never did anything like that for you."

"Stop trying to stir up trouble," ordered Falcon softly. "You know that's not true, Blaise, so stop trying to pretend that it is."

"Right," answered Arrow, who seemed to be having little luck keeping the meeting on track. "Well, anyways, they confronted Kronos, but it didn't go too well. Rose, Adrian's companion, was infected by a darkness virus. We believe that only the Great Sage has the power to cure it."

"Good luck!" laughed Barge, a deep rumbling sound. "He doesn't talk much these days!"

"Well, I'm sure that a person as busy as the Great Sage—" began Adrian, only to be cut off by Joshua.

"The Great Sage isn't a person. He's a tree."

"Wait. *What*?" asked Adrian, totally caught off guard.

"Yeah, Adrian," answered Joshua. "He's a tree. Didn't you ever wonder why all of his ambassadors were roots?"

"You mean I went to all this trouble to meet a tree?!" bellowed Adrian, outraged. "All this time, I thought he was a person! How can he do anything at all if he's a tree?"

"Adrian, just calm down!" commanded Joshua. "Just sit down, and shut up."

"Sorry," muttered Adrian, dropping back into his tree. "But how can a tree help Rose?"

"It's kind of a sentient tree," explained Joshua. "It was the first living being on Maltesque, and he's at least ten thousand years old. Virda was his apprentice. He has powerful magic, and he can definitely help you heal your friend."

"Can we *please* keep this meeting civilized?" shouted Arrow, growing exasperated. "As I was saying, we believe that the Great Sage can cure the virus. I'll take Adrian and Rose on my glider, and Joshua can manage things here. I think we've done enough testing of the waters. We need more members. I'm putting Barge back in charge of recruitment, with supervision from Joshua. If we get ten members a week, I think we'll be in good shape. As we know, Maltesque isn't really ruled by anyone. The cops work for the companies. If we could set up some sort of new government, we could work on saving Maltesque, and turning it back into Benevolaria."

"To do that, we'd need an entire army," mused Blaise. "Then again, the corporations don't really have an army, so I suppose it wouldn't really need to be very big. I'll go with the plan."

"I'm in," rumbled Barge. "Or at least, I'm in as long as I get to beat someone up."

"I think I'd make a good general," mused Falcon. "Sure, I'll go with it."

"I'm in," said Adrian. "if we can attempt to take down Kronos. What exactly has he been doing? That tower of his is no factory, as far as I can tell."

"Well, Adrian, there's a bit of politics here on Maltesque," started Arrow. "The business leaders have formed sort of a board, which more or less runs the city, and therefore, the entire world. Kronos has taken one of the five seats on the board, which is called the corporate council. In doing such, he took over the businesses of the man whose position he now holds."

"That's... interesting," mused Adrian. "So the world is ruled by business-men? Who enforces their verdicts?"

"Well, Adrian, they do," frowned Arrow. "Everyone works for someone on the corporate council, if indirectly, so if anyone disobeys them, they get fired. If someone were to, say, open a different company, not on the council, the other businesses would team up to take them down."

"So they use business politics to rule the world?" wondered Adrian. "But then they're open to physical confrontation!"

"Exactly!" grinned Arrow. "As we don't hold jobs, they have no power over us."

"Wait," started Adrian. "If you have no jobs, then where do you get your money from?"

"Well, we don't," explained Arrow sheepishly. "We had jobs at one point, and then we found out exactly how badly the corporation's actions were hurt-ing the environment, so we quit. We get our food ourselves, from the Poison-sap forest."

"If you've got nothing to offer them in return, then how are you going to get others to join the group?" pondered Adrian.

"Well," started Arrow, and then he realized that he really didn't have an answer. "Um, guys, help me out here. What did I use to get all of you to join?"

"Well, I'm an environmentalist," smirked Blaise. Adrian thought back to the sight of the ambassador in Blaise's hut, and had to fight very hard against the urge to speak out against that comment.

"I was a friend of your father," answered Falcon.

"I got fired from my job," replied Barge.

"I'm your brother, and I helped start it," responded Joshua.

"So they all joined because they were either an enemy of the corporation, or, possibly, an ally of the environment?" asked Adrian.

"Well, yes," gulped Arrow.

"Then that's easy!" beamed Joshua. "If I could hack the computers of the companies, I could probably dig up some dirt, and then they'd be enemies of the corporate council! And maybe I could also, like, transfer some of the money from their online account to ours."

"Good idea!" rumbled Barge. "I'll spread the word, and I'll make signs and stuff."

"Plus, we could show people what really happened to the Poisonsap for-est," mused Arrow. "Everyone's been told that it was unaffected by the pollu-tion."

"Then what actually happened to it?" inquired Adrian, unfamiliar with Maltesque lore.

"The poison mutated it," shuddered Joshua. "It's pretty nasty now. The trees are, well, I don't know, *poisonous*? Hence the name 'Poisonsap'."

"To be more accurate, the tree's sap is poisonous," corrected Blaise. "The creatures there are a thousand times worse than what you would find in the Deadwood. I've heard rumors of a tiger with a poison stinger on its tail."

"Well, that's... um... interesting, shall we say?" commented Adrian.

"Well, returning to the *point*, I'm going to take Adrian and Rose there so the Great Sage can heal the girl. Any objections?" challenged Arrow.

No one had any arguments. "Good," smiled Arrow, satisfied that he had finally made his point. "Now, returning to recruitment strategies..."

***

Adrian didn't feel entirely comfortable attaching Rose's body to the underside of the glider, but he couldn't see any alternative. He had carried Rose when they had flown back from the meeting with Kronos, and it hadn't worked out too well. Arrow couldn't very well carry her, as he had to steer the glider. So, Adrian was securely binding Rose to the glider's underside, drawing strange looks from the pedestrians that flocked the streets, as the limited amount of space in the house forced him to work outside.

As he reluctantly carried out his task, he looked more carefully at the glider. It was pitch black, with a flat, five feet by two feet platform in the center. From this extended two thin wings, which served to keep the glider aloft. It was propelled by a small jet attached to the center platform. The glider steadily zipped along at a steady fifty miles per hour, bombarding Adrian's face with wind.

After Adrian had finished scrutinizing the glider, his thoughts turned to the meeting. It had been somewhat confusing, but three major facts stood out: Blaise was suddenly a supposed ally; while he was gone, the group was trying to recruit more members; and finally, that the Great Sage was a tree. That last bit of information irked him greatly, as he had imagined the sage to be some sort of wizened, yet physically fit, old man. The fact that his only hope for Rose's life rested upon an ancient tree disturbed him a bit; he wasn't going to lie.

He was reminded of the poor state of Rose's health by a terrible groan from her. He gently stroked her face with his hand, and found it to be drenched with sweat. He temporarily left his work behind to go and get a wet towel. It had been about four days since Adrian's meeting with Kronos, so he figured that he only had three days to get to the Great Sage before Rose was beyond saving.

A clatter from behind him caused him to whirl around, and he saw himself staring at Democritus who seemed to be viciously attacking an orange with his teeth. Ever since they had come to the city, Democritus had been subdued, and had taken it upon himself to remain out of sight. In fact, Adrian had nearly forgotten about him. He suddenly remembered Democritus' deal with the Great Sage: regain your sanity before you come to the city, or die. Democritus had most certainly not regained his sanity, and Adrian wondered if it would be best to bring him along too. He then wondered if that would be justifiable murder on his part, and decided that it would be best not to.

"What's up, Adrian?" smiled Arrow, emerging from the basement. Apparently, Joshua had wanted to show him something. "Did you finish tying Rose up to the glider? I'm just about done with preparations."

"No, not quite," replied Adrian, truthfully.

"Then what're you doing out here?" inquired Arrow, skeptically.

It took Adrian a second to remember, but the answer returned to him very quickly. "Rose's fever went up," he explained. "I came out here to get a wet towel."

"You really care about her, don't you," mused Arrow seriously. "From the few conscious hours that we spent together, I'd say she reciprocates. However, she seemed, well, a little bit obsessed with me. Maybe it's because I'm older."

That statement caused the smoldering spark of curiosity in Adrian's mind to flare. "Arrow," he asked, "how old *are* you?"

"Fifteen," he answered, pouring himself a glass of soda. It struck Adrian just how much Maltesque was like Earth. "Though he may not look it, Joshua's my twin. We're fraternal, though, so we don't look at all alike. Nor do we think alike. He's always been the more down to earth one."

"Arrow, why do you use that expression, 'down to earth'? You live in Maltesque," he reminded him gently.

"It's from the book," explained Arrow, picking up his copy of *Legend of Darkness*. "In the back, there's a whole section on Earth and Alchema, the other world in your universe."

"There's another world in our universe?" inquired Adrian incredulously.

"Yes!" exclaimed Arrow, surprised. "You didn't know? I figured that since you were from the same universe, you'd know."

"Are there aliens?" inquired Adrian excitedly.

"None to speak of," laughed Arrow. "Alchema is ruled by humans. Ajax, the author of *Legend of Darkness*, proved that humans are the only sentient race capable of sustained existence. They are, therefore, the only race capable of ruling a planet. Any other race would wipe itself out, for various reasons."

"Arrow, I don't mean to impose, but can I have the book?" asked Adrian carefully. "After all, if I'm descended from one of the ancient gods, like Kronos said, it'd be good to have more information on, well, everything."

"Sure," sighed Arrow. "Up until about two weeks ago, when my dad told me about you, it hasn't been of much use to me. I guess it would serve you better."

"Thanks, Arrow!" grinned Adrian, as he took the book from Arrow's hands. It was respectably heavy, not overly so, but just the right weight, in Adrian's opinion. He gazed at the cover, and saw that though it was now faded to a near brown, it had once been black. The letters that carefully spelled out the title still retained a bit of their original gold color.

Adrian felt an odd attraction to the book, and he felt as if its author was nearby. He visualized an old man, most likely in a wheelchair by now, sitting by a fire in his home somewhere. His visualization of Ajax was horribly off.

***

"How is it even *possible* for one boy to overcome an entire lab full of men?" raged the dark voice of Shadius, directed at his captive, Ajax. "Damn you, Ajax, your side has the luck of the lord himself. Sometimes I think that when Photosia fell, she gifted her descendants with good luck. Of course, her descendents were supposed to be mine, as well."

"Or perhaps the one who created Photosia gave her side all of the luck, or maybe luck just likes me," laughed Ajax weakly. He hadn't had anything to eat in days, and he was being held captive in the orphanage. Shadius gave him all of the news he needed, which was how he knew that James had retaken his hideout, or the lab, as James had taken to calling it. He had felt Adrian's presence approaching closer to the source of his link with him in the past few days, and wondered exactly what he was up to. For although he had told James that his link with Adrian was from relation alone, it was, in fact, from his book, which he had planted on Maltesque ten or so years ago.

***

Adrian suddenly remembered why he was in the main room in the first place. He hurried over to the sink (again, the similarity to his own world struck him), and he wet a towel with cool water. He hurried back out to Rose, and dabbed at her forehead. Now that he had finally finished that, he returned to his work.

In just another few minutes, Rose was securely attached to the glider. Adrian stepped back to admire his work. It didn't look like she would be coming loose anytime soon. He walked back inside, and walked back over to the table. He picked up his book, and put it into his pack, along with his compass and map, which he had unpacked onto the table days before. Arrow was bringing the food, so he felt no need to worry about that. He checked his bag to make sure that he had everything he needed, and he then walked down the stairs, and into the basement.

Arrow was looking at the computer over Joshua's shoulder, and Joshua seemed to be putting some secret access code into the computer. Arrow heard Adrian coming down the stairs, and turned to greet him.

"Hey, Adrian!" he exclaimed, motioning for Adrian to join him. "Joshy here is about to hack into the corporate council's bank account. Right now he's trying to disable the security system."

"Correction," said Joshua. "Joshy here has hacked into the account. I'm putting some of their money into our account right now!"

"Nice going, Josh!" exclaimed Adrian, thumping him on the back. "So, Arrow, are we ready to head off?"

"Yep," replied Arrow. "Just let me grab my helmet. You can head out to the glider. I'll meet you there in a second." Adrian followed his commands, and was quickly standing on the small platform that made up the center of the glider. Arrow came out from the house, and grabbed the two wing levers that allowed him to steer the device. "And we're off!" he shouted as he pushed down on the ignition pedal, and the glider rose into the air, to the astonishment of the bystanders on the street below.

***

Adrian and Arrow had been flying for about an hour or so when Adrian finally felt the need to say, "Arrow, my arms are tired! Can we land?"

"Sure!" shouted Arrow back, over the wind. They landed in the desert, on the outskirts of the Poisonsap forest. Adrian let go of Arrow, who he had been holding onto for dear life for the past hour.

"Are we getting close?" asked Adrian hopefully. "Doesn't the Great Sage live in the forest somewhere?"

"Not exactly," chuckled Arrow. "Do you see that branch of the river?" he asked. "That's the branch that feeds the Poisonsap, and the Great Sage. However, before the pollution reached him, the Great Sage used his roots to create a wall of stone between him, and the river. However, once the flow of the river was dammed off, he had nothing to drink. So, he created caverns in the stone wall, placed just right, so as to filter the poison out. Miraculously, it worked, and that's how the Great Sage has managed to stay unpolluted for so long."

Adrian visualized the stone wall of which he spoke. It probably looked more like a cliff of stone, and he took out his map, to see if anything like that was depicted. He found exactly what he was looking for: a sheer wall of stone, marked "Cavernous Cliffs". It didn't look particularly large or intimidating; in fact, Adrian saw that it looked like a lees dangerous Light's End.

"We should be going soon," yawned Arrow. "I want to make it to the Great Sage before dark. It's about noon, and it should take us about four or so hours to cross the Poisonsap."

Confused, Adrian looked at the map, and saw that the forest actually took up less space than what they had already traversed. Arrow caught the puzzled expression, and answered it by saying, "Not because of the physical size, since it's about a quarter of the size of the Deadwood. Do you recall the birds from the Deadwood? Here, they're much fiercer, and often attack other birds. As we'll be in the air, we'll just look like prey to them."

"So we have to avoid them?" inquired Adrian. Arrow nodded. "Well, we might as well start now."

Arrow and Adrian stepped back onto the glider, and Adrian wrapped his arms tightly around Arrow's waist. The position made him feel a bit uncomfortable, but that feeling was replaced by the sheer terror that consumed him when Arrow pushed down on the pedal, and the glider rose into the air again.

After they had finally entered the airspace over the forest, Adrian caught sight of an enormous pack of birds. They circled about, and it took some fancy flying from Arrow to get around them.

In this manner, they continued onwards, and after two hours of flying, Arrow and Adrian both needed a break. There was a giant nest on top of one of the trees, and they stopped there for a few moments.

Suddenly, the bird to which the nest belonged returned, and it dive-bombed Arrow and Adrian. It's body was about the size of Arrow and Adrian combined, and Adrian clanked at it with disbelief. The two of them rushed back to the glider, and Arrow swiftly stomped on the pedal, and the glider shot up into the air. They raced forwards, but the bird persisted. Adrian summoned up the courage to look behind him, and saw that the bird was but a yard away from them, and gaining.

"Arrow!" he shrieked hysterically. "Do something!"

"On it!" responded Arrow, who proceeded to lead the glider into the trees. His masterful flying led the glider through unscathed, but the bird got its wing stuck in one of the branches. Adrian and Arrow flew away, causing the bird to caw in distress at seeing its prey escape.

Another two hours later, Adrian saw the Cavernous Cliffs ahead. He laughed with happiness, and relief, for he was very tired of flying. He glanced behind him, and screamed in terror.

The bird that had chased them seemed to have acquired hundreds of normal sized followers, who were flying after the glider as fast as they could. Adrian and Arrow were very quickly surrounded, and Arrow had to maneuver the glider very carefully to avoid being torn to pieces by the birds' sharp beaks. However, by chance, the ropes holding Rose in place were torn, and she plummeted to the ground.

"Rose!" screamed Adrian, and he jumped after her.

"Adrian, don't do that!" groaned Arrow, sending the glider into a dive. Adrian weighed more than Rose, and caught her in his arms. Arrow, grabbed Adrian by the neck, and pulled up just in time to avoid crashing into the cliff. They rose just enough to avoid being smashed to pieces on the cliff, but as Arrow attempted to fly over it, a vine shot out of nowhere, and pulled the glider back to the top of the cliff, which they had now reached.

Adrian tumbled out of the glider, and landed on the ground with a thud. He crawled over to the edge of the cliff, and looked down. Far below, the river stretched into the cliff, upon which he now sat. He rolled over to look at the vine that had swatted them out of the air, and saw that it was really a root.

"Welcome, Adrian Lightseeker," said the root. "I am the Great Sage's last ambassador. However, I am afraid that I cannot let you pass. Your friend, Arrow Viridia, is holding someone who is wanted by my master the Great Sage. Arrow, correct me if I'm wrong, but you have taken under your wing one Democritus Deveridia, enemy of the Great Sage."

13

The Great Sage's Tests

Is Democritus really worth that much to you?" asked Arrow, giving the root an odd look. "Why do you need him?"

"Well," began the root, "the Great Sage needs to talk with Democritus' good side. So if you could please fetch him, Arrow, it would be greatly appreciated."

"He's back in the city!" exclaimed Arrow incredulously. "I'd need to fly back the way I came, and that's quite a journey, let me tell you."

"Unless you bring us Democritus Deveridia, we shall not let Adrian pass," ordained the ambassador solemnly. "Rose will most likely die, and Adrian will never work with you. You will have undone all that you have fought to do."

"Fine," scowled Arrow. "I'll get Democritus. But when I do, you'd better let Adrian pass." With that, Arrow stepped back onto his glider, for even though it had been swatted out of the air, it has sustained minimal damage. Arrow hit the pedal, and the glider propelled itself into the air.

"Now, with him gone, we can turn too much more important matters," said the root in a much more business-like tone. "Adrian, I apologize for lying to you."

Adrian, confused, tried to figure out how a root he had known for all of a minute could have lied to him.

"Ah, I see. You're confused as to how I lied. For me to explain that, let me first explain to you how the ambassador system works. As you know, the Great Sage is a tree. Thus, the ambassadors are his roots. Therefore, one might say that the ambassadors are part of the Great Sage himself. However, the farther away an ambassador is from the Great Sage, the more of a personality they develop. As I am but a mile away from the Sage, I have developed no personality. Thus, we come to my lie. If one stretched the definition, one could say that I am the Great Sage. Actually, I'm more of a telephone, allowing you to communicate with me, the Sage."

"Okay, so right now I'm talking to the Great Sage," mused Adrian. "Interesting. However, you said that you were moving onto more serious matters. What are they?"

"Rose," said the ambassador/ Great Sage simply. "I do not have the power to cure her. Only light can cure the disease that has infected her as it was caused by darkness. And right now, the only person on Maltesque with the ability to conjure up light is you, Adrian. However, due to the fact that you have not mastered your skill, you can only conjure light while in direct contact with darkness."

Adrian figured out what the Great Sage meant, and he touched the source of Rose's disease. Nothing happened. "Sadly, the small amount of darkness in Rose's body is not enough to trigger your light power, though it is enough to place her life in danger," sighed the ambassador. "You can also summon up light when under great physical stress, as you learned in the barbarian encampment. Therefore, I shall present you with a test to bring out your light powers."

"I can't summon up light; I can only summon up lightning!" protested Adrian. "While light may heal Rose's wound, I doubt that lightning would improve the situation very much!"

"You have been able to only summon up lightning so far because you have not had the proper guidance," remarked the ambassador. "If I were to lend you aid, you could most certainly heal Rose's wound. Now allow me to share with you the test. You must pass through the Cavernous Cliffs. I trust that Arrow will bring Democritus, so I can now allow you to pass. If I were to make you wait, it would needlessly put Rose's life in danger. On the other side of the cliffs, I will be waiting for you. The small cave you see over there will lead you to a path that should lead you through safely. Good luck, Adrian." The ambassador's voice faded, and the root became still. Adrian walked over to the tunnel, and stepped inside. He turned around, and saw three roots drag Rose away, towards the Great Sage.

The tunnel was not overly easy to see in, but a source of light seemed to be at the end. The tunnel was only about fifty yards long, much shorter than he had expected. He assumed that it had just seemed longer outside.

He came to the end of the tunnel, and saw that it did not, in fact, lead to the outside. It converged with dozens of other tunnels, and one other tunnel that seemed to have come from below. Water flowed through the intersection, and was filtered into various other tunnels, which then, Adrian assumed, connected with other intersections. Adrian took the nearest tunnel, and continued on. Though he assumed that all of the tunnels led to the outside, only one of them was lit. Adrian assumed that it was the Great Sage's work.

For hours, he struggled through the tunnel, and his headache began to reappear. The light was growing stronger, and consistently followed it. Finally, he came out, and ascended to the surface. Though it had been completely uneventful, Adrian was tired to the bone. He looked up, and saw that the tunnel had opened into a completely flat, but grassy, area. In the middle of the clearing was the Great Sage.

He was at least two hundred stories tall, with branches reaching in every direction. Roots poked out of the ground, and though none of them mentally spoke to Adrian the way the other ambassadors had done, they all exuded a certain sense of power.

"Adrian!" boomed the Great Sage, and Adrian wasn't sure if he was communicating mentally, or if he was actually speaking to him. The Sage had a low, resounding voice that seemed to come from all directions. Adrian then remembered that he was surrounded by roots, and so it probably did come from all directions. "I'm glad to finally speak to you in person, after communicating to you through my ambassadors, like I've been doing for so long! Your friend Rose is at my base, in case you wanted to see her. Though I'm not able to destroy the source of the virus, I am able to slow its progression. I'd guess that you still have about a week to learn the necessary techniques to save her."

"What do you mean?" asked Adrian, confused. "I thought that you said that once I got to you, you'd give me instructions as to how to heal Rose!"

"I can't do that, Adrian," sighed the Great Sage. "You don't yet have the power."

"Then what was the point of making me walk through the tunnel?" raged Adrian; annoyed that someone he had fought for so long to meet would mess around with him like that.

"You needed that to begin your training. The first step is for you to overcome the insanity that grips you, should you ever fully remember your sight of the fifth dimension," explained the Great Sage. "You see, usually your ancestors received their powers by natural means, around the age of sixteen. Your sight of the fifth dimension has considerably sped up that process. Your body and mind were not yet ready for it."

"So how do I conquer the insanity?" inquired Adrian curiously. "I mean, it's not like I can mess with my own mind." As he said those words, a feeling of nausea washed over him, and he began to lose his grip on reality.

"You will return to insanity, and then I shall enter your mind, and fix the problem," began the Great Sage. "I'd try to explain it to you, but you and I perceive the world differently, so I cannot. Suffice it to say that I'll reroute some of the neuronic pathways in your—well, I'm not quite sure what it's called—so as to drive you away from insanity."

Adrian failed to follow a word of what the Great Sage had just said, so he didn't proceed to ask any further questions. He tore himself away from sanity, and fully immersed himself in the image of the fifth dimension. He returned to the screaming world of unthinking chaos, but then he suddenly saw an image of a desert...

Without warning, the Great Sage intervened. He reached out with his mind into Adrian's own, and changed... something. Adrian suddenly became himself again, if just for a moment. His own mind felt vaguely unfamiliar to him, and he collapsed onto the ground. In his last conscious moments, a root reached out to him, and caught him as he fell...

***

Adrian dreamed once again of the strange desert he had seen in his few moments of insanity. There were numerous odd figures that walked about, though all of them had Adrian's face.

Adrian awoke in a cold sweat, and completely forgot about his dreams. He was lying at the base of a giant tree, which he then remembered was the Great Sage. He say up, and then looked around. He was Rose lying not a yard away from him. She was nearly completely covered by vines, with the exception of her face. She looked peaceful and serene, despite the illness that plagued her.

"Ah, young master Adrian! I'm very glad to see that you are once again awake," rumbled the laughter of the Great Sage. "I think yesterday went fairly well, don't you? You're now one step closer to healing Rose."

"Well, aside from the fact that I fainted dead away, I suppose yesterday went well," mused Adrian. "So I won't get any more headaches?"

"Ideally, you will not," sighed the Sage. "However, there's really no telling, as I was, after all, manipulating your mind. However, it should be much easier for you to cast light magic now. Try to recall the fifth dimension, please, Adrian."

"Um, okay," conceded Adrian. He returned to the depths of his memory, reliving his being kidnapped, his sudden near- realization of Kronos' identity, his quick sight of Rose, looking disheveled, and then- nothing. "Ah, Sage, I think something went wrong," said Adrian cautiously. "I can't remember the fifth dimension, like, at all. I can remember everything up to, and after, that point, but I can't remember it."

"Of course," mused the Sage. "I should have seen that coming. You don't nearly have the necessary mastery of your own mind to recall something that's been altered. Well, we've got a week, or, rather, six days, as of now, to change that."

"And if you can't?" inquired Adrian tentatively.

"Well, you won't be able to save Rose," mused the Sage seriously. "So, we'll need to do everything in our power to make sure that doesn't happen.

I've arranged six tests for you. The first is probably going to be deceptively simple. All you need to do is remain silent for the entire day."

"What's the— Mmpphgh!" Adrian was interrupted by a vine swiftly wrapping itself around his mouth.

"I said, you must remain silent for the entire day. Ideally, you'll learn the basics of meditation," thought the Great Sage in Adrian's head. "I, too, shall keep the silence. With this, I shall cease to speak." The Great Sage then lapsed into thought.

Adrian was somewhat annoyed by this task, and he was about to protest to the Sage when a moan froze him in his tracks. Rose was looking much more feverish today, and Adrian remembered that all of it was for her. To him, not talking seemed a bit easy, compared to all of the other things that he had been through. He walked over to Rose, and sat down beside her. All that was visible was her face, which was flushed a brilliant crimson. Perspiration littered her forehead, and a bead of sweat rolled down her cheek. Adrian reached out with his hand, and wiped the sweat off of her cheek, a motion which fluidly turned into a caress.

***

Barge sighed. As Arrow's home, the base of their operation, was a terrible place to hold a recruitment session, he instead had found another location. Sadly, this location was an old warehouse, which he had worked in when he was younger. Now, though, it was utterly destroyed. The company that it had belonged to was one of the few independent companies, and, like all of the others, it hadn't lasted very long. The destruction company had destroyed all of the machines that used to be inside and used the metal for building materials.

It was in this building, however, that Barge had forever become an enemy of the corporate council. His boss had been absolutely ruthless, and even beat him once. So, Barge led a riot with his fellow workers. However, it didn't end well, and he had been fired, and had to flee from a policeman, who had been bribed by the council. Worse, one of his fellow rioters had been killed by a different cop, which was the real reason why he despised the corporate council.

However, it was the only available open space that Falcon had been able to get. Barge forced himself not to think about the past as he set up the monitor through which Joshua would communicate with the mass that he had assembled. He looked out at the crowd of people, and saw that their idle chatting had died down to a mere whisper. They didn't know exactly why they were there, and were waiting in hushed anticipation for the answer. Well, Barge planned to give them their answer.

"Aright, lisen up!" he shouted at the crowd. "Y'all here fur a reason, in case yeh were wunderin'." Every single face in the crowd turned to look at him. "You've heard of the first and secund order of druids, right? And how they're ainchunt history, right!" Various faces in the crowd nodded at him. "Well, there's a Third Order, too. But, see, it's really small. We need yeh tu join."

"And what do we have to do to join?" asked a young man, listening seriously. "And what exactly does the group do?"

"Well, the group—" began Barge, but then he remembered that it was Joshua's job to explain it. "If you could please turn your attention to the monitor, all of your queeschuns'll be answered." He flipped the switch, and the monitor buzzed to life, revealing Joshua at his computer.

A red light flashed on his computer screen, so Joshua knew that he was being watched. He turned around to face the camera, and put on a smile. "Hello, my name is Joshua. I'm one of the two founding members of the Third Order. The other one is my brother, who, due to events beyond our control, was not able to be here." His face condensed into a frown. "On a more serious issue, I'm sure that you're all wondering exactly why we need to have a Third Order. Am I correct in my assumption that all of you hold jobs? Well, I have no way of knowing, but I'll assume that the answer is yes. Now, I'm sure that you're all aware that the war of the druids completely wrecked our world's environment. However, it could conceivably be restored. That is the goal of the Third Order. Barge, are there any questions?"

Joshua held up a transmitter, identical to the one that Barge now held in his hand. Barge spoke into his: "Uh, and what do they have to do tuh be in thu group?"

"Oh yeah," murmured Joshua. "Okay, first let me talk about what's preventing us from reaching our goal. Well, see, the factories are still polluting the world." There was hushed murmuring at this, for the corporate council had assured everyone that their new factories were completely environment friendly. "In the fine print of their assurances, there's one small comment that gives it away," resumed Joshua. "What it basically says is 'everything else on this paper is a lie'. So, yeah, the factories are still hurting the environment. So, in order for you to help us, you would have to quit your job." At this, there was angry whispering in the crowd. "I realize that the possibility doesn't sound all too inviting, but if you join our small army, we'll pay you. So, you don't do as much work, and you still get paid. I think that's a pretty good deal."

"Aright, all uh yeh sign this sheet if you want to join, and give us a way to contact you!" shouted Barge at the assembled crowd. "Just sign right here!"

176

***

Adrian was fairly near the end of his rope. He had been silent all day, and not a thing had happened. He had tried meditating at first but that had gotten him nowhere. And all the while, there had been a slight buzz in the back of his mind. Whenever he tried to focus on it, it disappeared. So, he had then tried to deliberately not focus on it, to try to bring it into focus, and though that worked fairly well, when he brought it into focus, he noticed it, which drove it away.

Exasperated, Adrian was saved from further monotony by the sound of Arrow's glider returning. He opened his mouth in greeting, but suddenly remembered that his sole task for the day was to keep silent.

The glider gently landed upon the ground, and Arrow stepped off, and untied Democritus, who had been tied to the bottom as Rose had been. Suddenly, Democritus caught sight of the Great Sage, and shouted, "Bad tree! Burn you, yes I will!" He charged at the tree, but was grabbed by the back of his shirt by Arrow.

"Ah yes. Welcome, Democritus," said the Great Sage in a soothing voice. "Arrow, just hold him there for a moment, please." Three vines wrapped themselves around Democritus, holding him tight. The Great Sage reached out with his mind, and brought out Democritus' good side. "Now then, Democritus, we had a deal, and you failed to keep your end. Sadly, this means your execution. However, allow me to search through your memories, just to make sure that you truly deserve your execution." Democritus stood perfectly still as the Great Sage went back into his mind, and sorted through his memories. "Hm. This seems to be more complicated than I thought," mused the Great Sage. "You actually did conquer your dark side, but a chance encounter with a river demon caused it to resurface. I leave the choice to you."

"Great Sage, first allow me to apologize for my actions three thousand years ago," begged Democritus. "However, if my death would mean the destruction of my dark side, then I would gladly accept. However, I would like you to do me one favor. I'll accept my execution if you swear to aid the Third Order in their war."

"Very well," sighed the Sage. "I shall join the Third Order. Now then, goodbye, Democritus." The Great Sage left Democritus' mind, and Democritus returned to insanity. "Arrow, could you please hold him still?"

"No. I don't want to see this," exclaimed a sickened Arrow. "I don't have anything to do with this."

"Very well," rumbled the Sage, and dozens of vines shot out, and twisted around Democritus. Adrian and Arrow turned away, and they heard a sharp crack from behind them. "It is done," murmured the Sage. "In all honesty, I never wanted to do it. I had hoped that he would overcome his dark side, but I guess that it was not to be."

"How can you be so nonchalant about?" screamed Arrow, suddenly enraged. "You just killed a man, and now you're casually saying that you didn't want to! Do you respect anyone? Can you even feel pain?"

"Human life is... temporary," explained the Great Sage. "After all, humans are very lucky if they make it to their one hundredth birthday. How much information can any life form amass in a mere one hundred years?"

"Democritus," began Adrian angrily, breaking his temporary vow of silence and siding with Arrow, "lived for about three thousand years. How old are you?"

"Well, I've been around for as long as Maltesque, so that's, what, ten thousand years or so," answered the Great Sage.

"Then he's been around for one third as long as you have!" shouted Adrian. "That's a very long time, thank you very much!"

"Well, I-" The Great Sage was at a loss for words. He hadn't really considered that Democritus had amassed about as much knowledge as he had. "I never really thought of that. I truly apologize."

"And that helps Democritus *how*?" inquired Arrow. "The best thing you could do would be to keep your promise to him, and help my organization."

"I will most certainly follow through on that," hurriedly agreed the Great Sage. "I think it would be best for all of us to go to sleep now, though. It's getting late. Oh, and Adrian, you pass. Even though you did break the silence, you were meditating for long enough. The main thing that I wanted you to notice was the faint buzzing in the back of your head. That's what we're going to try to bring out."

***

The next morning, Adrian was awakened by a piercing scream that he had heard twice before. Rose was wailing in her sleep, and Adrian rushed over to feel her forehead. He quickly pulled his arm back, as he felt as if her head was truly on fire.

"Is your friend well?" inquired the Great Sage. "It seems that her illness is progressing more speedily than I expected. However, she should still have five days left. We must resume your training."

"So what do I need to do today?" asked Adrian warily. "You said that the main goal is for me to bring out the buzzing noise."

"Yes," responded the Sage. "Today's task is designed to distract you so completely from it that it will emerge. As you most certainly discovered yesterday, if you focus on it, it goes away. But if you don't notice it, it comes out."

"Yes, I noticed that," said Adrian impatiently. "So what is the task, exactly?"

"You are to climb me," laughed the Great Sage. "However, I'll be sure to make things difficult for you. You may start whenever you feel ready."

"Um, I'm not sure that I'm entirely comfortable with this," stammered Adrian, feeling that the task was somewhat awkward. "I mean, climbing you? It seems a bit random, I guess. And kind of awkward."

"You will do as instructed," growled the Sage. "If you do not, your friend will die."

"Well, that's a cheery outlook on things," thought Adrian, but he thought that it would be wise to keep that statement to himself. "I guess I'm ready to start," he said, grabbing onto the Sage's lowest branch with his hand, and hoisting the rest of himself up. The first part was fairly easy, as all Adrian had to do was keep his balance.

Once he finally got to the area where the branches began to grow thicker, things began to get a bit trickier. Adrian reached out with his hand, and the branch that he was reaching for shifted just out of his reach. He reached for it, figuring that it had just been the wind. However, the branch shifted out his reach once again.

Adrian decided that it was the work of the Great Sage, so he reached out for a different branch. However, that one also moved out of his reach. Irritated, Adrian reached for a branch farther away from the trunk, and though that one too shifted away from him, it was just slightly slower, and Adrian was able to catch it. He pulled himself up onto the branch. He moved even farther out, and the branches took even longer to move out his reach.

Adrian smiled to himself, and climbed with relative ease, as even though the branches moved away from him, he was able to catch every one of them. However, one of the branches that he caught broke, and he had to act quickly to avoid plunging to the ground.

Adrian forced himself to move slightly inwards, to a point where the branches were still slow, but didn't break at the slightest amount of force. He climbed easily, but then things got a bit harder.

Adrian reached out for a branch, like he had done so many times before, but the branch that his feet rested on suddenly began to shake. Adrian quickly grabbed on to the branch above him, and pulled him onto that. That one also began to shake, but Adrian managed to retain his hold on it. He pulled himself onto that branch, and grabbed onto the one above him.

He continued climbing in this fashion for some time. He imagined that it was near noon, and he was a bit hungry. He forced himself to keep climbing, though. He saw that he was about two thirds to the top, and things became a bit more violent.

Adrian heard a faint swishing sound, and ducked just in time to avoid being decapitated by a wayward branch. He quickly discovered that the branch was not, in fact, wayward, as another one came swinging at him. The branch upon which he crouched was still shaking, but as a third branch swung at him, he grabbed onto it, and let go to find himself flying upwards. He began to fall again, but he caught himself on a branch.

The Great Sage had not expected that, and was slow to respond. By the time a branch flew at where Adrian had hung, he was already elsewhere. He could see light coming through the dense tangle of branches, and raced towards it. He suddenly emerged once again into the world, and was out of the foliage. Adrian suddenly became aware that the faint buzzing was now like a tidal wave of force, and Adrian let it flow. Lightning exploded out of him, and then he saw no more.

***

"Adrian! Adrian, wake up!" shouted the Great Sage. "Get up, Adrian! You're okay! I caught you on the way down."

"Are you okay?" inquired Adrian fuzzily. "The last thing I remember is conjuring up lightning..."

"Yes, yes, I'm fine," answered the Sage impatiently. "Do you have a headache?"

Adrian examined himself, and was surprised to find that the answer was no. He didn't have a headache, but as he probed his mind, he instead found an odd, well, the best he could do was to describe it as a cloud of light. It seemed that that's what the buzzing sound was if he brought into focus.

"I see that you've found the place in your mind that I redirected the memory of the fifth dimension to," smiled the Great Sage. "That is where the source of your power lies. You should now be able to focus on it without it disappearing. Try."

Adrian focused on it, and felt a bit of power growing. He didn't really try to use it, though. "You're right!" he happily exclaimed.

"Great. Do some tricks for me," yawned Arrow. Adrian whirled around with a start, as he had not expected Arrow to be there. "C'mon, Adrian! You mean that even after three days, you still can even, like, do a magic trick?"

"Sorry, Arrow," grinned Adrian. "I can't do that yet, but I'll let you know when I can."

"Well, with any luck, you'll be able to do that at the end of today," laughed the Great Sage. "My task, or, rather, test, for today is designed—"

"Yeah, yeah," waved Adrian impatiently. "Just tell me what the task is."

"Very well," sighed the Sage. "Today's task is this: create a stable ball made of lightning. It's actually a good deal harder than it sounds."

Adrian thought that the task sounded difficult in the first place, so he shuddered to think how difficult it really was. "Should I start now?" he asked the Sage. Though the Great Sage was a tree, Adrian could have sworn that he nodded. He wasn't quite sure how the Great Sage had managed to mentally convey a nod, so he ignored that, and began to focus on the task at hand. First, he reached into the cloud of light at the foreground of his mind, and attempted to pull out the required amount of energy. It was tedious work, but he eventually was able to pull lightning out of the cloud. However, he had to quickly suppress it, as it nearly rushed out dangerously. However, he tried again.

***

Joshua happily looked at the list of new recruits. It was about ten times the number of people they had expected to get, as nearly every single person in the audience of the lecture had joined. None of them had the faintest idea that the environment could be saved, or that the corporations were making it worse still. It had come as a shock to a bunch of them, and it had been enough to rouse them into action. There had been a brief announcement in the news about how a small number of workers had mysteriously quit. However, the reporter had assured them that it had been a mere coincidence that they had all chosen to quit at the same time.

"I'm not sure that one hundred workers quitting their job for no apparent reason could ever be a coincidence," thought Joshua. "Well, I guess that I'd better prepare for the next lecture. It is tonight, after all."

Joshua stared hard at his computer screen. Displayed upon it were various notes from the companies about developing parts of the Poisonsap, which was strictly against the law. However, Joshua had found the lost minutes from a meeting of the council, which had spoken of a quiet cancellation of that particular law. For some reason, this had not been announced on the news. He looked again at the screen, and thought, "How stupid do you have to be to destroy the only source of food? The Poisonsap has sustained the city for years, and they would just throw that away?"

As Joshua probed through the hidden documents, he failed to notice a small red light that flickered at the top of the screen for a moment.

***

As everyone assembled for the anxiously awaited next meeting, Joshua, who was actually at the meeting this time, reviewed the notes on his laptop. His laptop was hooked up to a projector, which displayed the companies' plans on a large screen, or at least it would. Joshua would turn on the projector when the time was right.

Barge had been trying to get the crowd to listen up for about ten minutes. Losing patience, he shouted, "SHUT UP! JOHSUA'S GONNA TALK!" Everyone quieted down, and looked expectantly at Joshua.

"Hello, everyone," he smiled. "Welcome to the second lecture. Were any of you here at the first one?" A few hands shot up, but not many. "Well, alright then. I'm Joshua, and I'm in charge of the Third Order of druids. Now I'm sure most of you have heard of the first two orders..." For a few minutes, the second lecture progressed much like the first one, including the shocked reactions when Joshua informed them of the council's destruction of the environment, and the fact that, if the proper actions were taken, it could actually be saved.

"Now, how many of you here have ever eaten food from the Poisonsap?" inquired Joshua. Everyone's hands shot up, as that was where all of the food came from. "And you all know that there is a law against development of it? Well, how many of you are aware that just recently, that law was revoked?" Total silence. "The corporate council is planning to develop parts of the Poisonsap."

"How do we know that you're not lying?" shouted an elderly gentleman from the back.

Joshua turned on the projector, and the wall of the abandoned factory lit up with the image of the hidden minutes from the council's meeting. Everyone recognized the council's official website, as most of them had used it before. There was a collective gasp in the audience. "There you go. Proof," shouted Joshua triumphantly. 'They're planning to destroy our only food source. We've got enough food in storage to supply us for maybe fifty more years, by which time all of the council members will have died nice and wealthy."

"Well, what about the ocean? Couldn't we fish for our food?" inquired the same old gentleman.

"We haven't caught anything in the harbor for about a hundred years," scowled Joshua. "Like I said, they're planning to destroy our only food source."

The lecture ended, and the entire crowd surged forwards to sign up to the Third Order.

***

Adrian had finally managed to figure out how to control the amount of lightning that he summoned. He was working on forming it into a ball, though it proved to be a somewhat difficult task. He tried to sort of arc the lightning around, but it didn't seem to work.

Suddenly, Adrian was struck by a new idea. He tried to force all of the lightning into the same space, and it started to pile up. Eventually, it formed a sphere.

"I did it!" he shouted excitedly, turning towards the Great Sage. However, that small action distracted him from maintaining the sphere. It exploded, sending lightning flying everywhere.

Arrow threw himself against the ground, and vines popped up to protect Rose. Adrian, however, was struck by the lightning, but he unintentionally tried to absorb it. Oddly enough, he succeeded. The lightning raced back through his body, and found a focus point: the cloud of light in his mind, where it had originated.

Adrian fell to the ground, unconscious.

***

"Adrian! Adrian, wake up! C'mon, Adrian!" Arrow shook Adrian vigorously, attempting to rouse him. After the fiasco of the day before, the Great Sage had not spoken a word, and Arrow wondered if he had given up on Adrian. For the last two hours, he had done nothing but attempt to rouse Adrian. Adrian, however, had remained stubbornly asleep. His patience growing thin, Arrow slapped Adrian in the face with a good deal of force.

Adrian suddenly awoke. "Arrow, are you okay? I don't know what happened! I just turned around, and then-"

"It's okay, Adrian!" hurriedly assured Arrow. "I know it was an accident, and I didn't get hit. Actually, I'm more worried about you. Are you okay?"

"I think so," mused Adrian, mentally checking himself. His body seemed to be fine, but when he examined his brain, he found that something was wrong. "The cloud! The light cloud in my mind! It's about half its size!"

"Yes, Adrian, and that could prove to be quite a problem," mused the Great Sage, awaking. "I now see no alternative. I will leave my body and enter your mind, so I can heal Rose."

14

Joshua

Joshua stood in the doorway of his house, debating whether to leave or not. Ever since his lectures had grown popular, he had been attracting some unwanted attention from the cops. Even though they didn't really do their job, namely, enforce the law, they had been issued special orders to attack Joshua. They didn't know where he lived, so as long as he stayed inside his house, he was fine.

However, he had promised Falcon that he would meet him to discuss the new security measures for the Third Order's new hideout. He considered using Barge to send a message to Falcon, saying that he would have to postpone the meeting. However, Barge was busy with promoting the Third Order, and Blaise was with Falcon.

Drawing a deep breath, Joshua stepped out the door, and quickly hurried down the street, keeping to the shadows. After a few minutes, he was at the door of Falcon's house. He knocked twice, waited four seconds, and then knocked three times. Falcon immediately recognized the secret knock, and opened up the door.

"Thanks," whispered Joshua, stepping in. He glanced about, and Falcon led him through the hallway to his sitting room. Blaise was waiting for them, and the two of them sat down. "Falcon, before we discuss the new hideout, can we talk about my house? I don't really feel comfortable in it. I mean, we don't even have a front door! It just opens into the street! Don't you think that's a little risky?"

"I suppose," mused Falcon, "but we can deal with your personal security later. It's more important for us to focus on the new hideout right now. I've found an ideal location."

"Really? Where is it?" eagerly inquired Joshua. "Is it another factory?"

"No. It's an old skyscraper," answered Blaise. 'One of the companies is thinking of selling it, and we want you to pretend to be another company that they can sell it to."

"That sounds like a good idea," responded Joshua. "I'll do it. Now what about the security measures?"

"Well, I think it would be good to have guards posted at all of the entrances," suggested Falcon. "It would also be a good idea to have surveillance cameras set up, so we can keep an eye on everything. And of course, there has to be an entrance password."

"I like most of those," mused Joshua, "but I think that the password is kind of unnecessary if we have guards posted at the door."

"Ah, yes. But how will the guards know who to let in?" smirked Blaise. "I think that the password is a good idea."

"Fine," conceded Joshua. "Is that all?"

"I think," answered Falcon. "It should do, don't you agree?"

Blaise and Joshua nodded. "Well, Joshy, it looks like you'd better get home," smirked Blaise. "After all, you still need it to get the skyscraper, right?"

"Yes, but what about the security measures for my house?" inquired Joshua.

"That can wait," ordered Falcon. "Right now, you need to get that skyscraper before someone else does."

"Fine," sighed Joshua. "I'll do it."

***

Joshua walked down the steps to his basement, and sat down. He flipped the switch on the computer, and it flared to life. He typed in his password, and, once he was in, set about finding the skyscraper that Falcon had mentioned. He found the "for sale" notice in the corporate council's website, and set about buying it.

First, he let one of the other companies start the purchase, but then he blocked them out. He then posed as the same company, and entered all of the correct information into the computer. Though he now owned the building, the company he had blocked out had paid for it.

Joshua congratulated himself on that, but he once again failed to notice the small red light that flashed in the upper corner of the screen. He then began to prepare himself for his next lecture. He was browsing through the corporate council's website, and found something else. It seemed as though the council was going to issue a statement regarding the development of the Poisonsap, however, it seemed like they were going to ignore some of the more important facts, like the loss of food, and were instead going to focus on only the positive aspects, such as the fact that the possibility of homelessness was far less due to the new houses.

Joshua chewed his lower lip, concerned that some of the members of the Third Order might actually believe that garbage. However, he had found enough data to prove the statement irrelevant, and, after all, the official statements were notoriously misleading anyways. He dismissed the issue, and returned to working on his speech.

***

Joshua woke up at his computer, and lazily glanced around. He figured that he had fallen asleep while working on his next lecture. He glanced at the screen, and double-checked his work. He mentally patted himself on the back, for the speech was finished.

Joshua yawned, and stood up. He glanced at the calendar on his wall, and saw that it was the day of his next lecture. He grabbed his laptop, stuffed it haphazardly into a backpack, and raced out the door. He stuck to the shadows as he walked, but suddenly he heard:

"Stop him! That's the boy we're looking for!" Joshua whirled around, and saw that a cop was running towards him at high speed. He ducked into an alley, and ran towards Falcon's house.

He left the alley, but saw three new policemen, plus the one he had seen before, making a beeline towards him. Joshua didn't want them to find out where Falcon lived, so he ducked into a different house. The residents, a married couple, screamed when he burst through the door, but he ignored them, and ran up the stairs. He found a window, and swiftly opened it. He heard the woman from below scream to the cops for help, but he still ignored her, and squeezed himself out the window. He balanced on the windowsill, and he jumped towards the house adjacent to the one he was in. He grabbed the windowsill of that house, but he lost his grip, and one of his hands fell to his side. He reached back up with that hand, and hoisted himself up onto the sill, and he then pulled himself onto the roof. He made for the skylight, and dropped in. He could hear the woman confusedly assuring the police that the strange boy had gone into the room, but had mysteriously vanished.

Smiling to himself, Joshua glanced around. He recognized some of the details of the house from his previous visits, and assured himself that he had picked the right house.

He walked down the stairs, and slowly crept up behind the sole resident of the house. He tapped the man on the back, and then ducked out of sight.

"Hello?" said the man cautiously, looking around. "I'm warning you, I'm armed!"

"I got you good!" laughed Joshua standing up. "Sorry about that, Falcon.

I just couldn't resist myself."

"Why are you here?" inquired Falcon. "You should be at the warehouse, setting up for the next lecture. Did you have anything to do with all of the shouting at the house next door?"

"Yeah, sorry about that," grinned Joshua. "I had to avoid the police. They saw me coming out of my house, and chased me all the way here. I faked them out by going into the neighbor's house, and the jumping to this house from the window. I had to sneak in through the skylight."

"Well, we'd better get going, hadn't we?" mused Falcon. "We'll take the back door. I don't think it would be particularly beneficial to our cause if we were arrested." Joshua nodded, and Falcon led him to the back door. They stepped out into the brightly lit street, illuminated by the freshly risen sun.

Joshua heard a knock at Falcon's front door, and whispered, "It's the cops! Let's run!" The two of them sprinted off towards the old warehouse where Joshua intended to give his next lecture.

***

"Well, gentlemen, it seems that we have a crisis on our hand," murmured a well-dressed man in a suit and tie. "No doubt that all of you have heard of Joshua Viridia. He's been gaining power as of this past week."

"He's no threat," laughed another man, sitting in a chair. "He's what, fifteen? My own daughter is older than that!"

"But what does your daughter think of Joshua?" asked the first man. "Well? We're all waiting."

"She's become a little obsessed with him, if you can believe that!" laughed the other man.

"I can believe that quite easily," growled the first man. "Being fifteen is not a weakness. He's assembled hundreds of followers in this past week. And the worst part is that all he's done is tell them the truth!"

"Well, why don't we make some changes in our system to placate him?" suggested a different man, this time sitting on a couch. "After all, all we need to do is add some new environmental laws."

"And do you really think he'll stop then?" asked the first men angrily. "No. I think that he'll keep on going, and we'll be thrown out of office."

"So what do you propose we do?" asked the second man.

"Gentlemen, allow me to reintroduce you to the newest member of our little council: Kronos," smirked the first man. "He first met all of you last meeting, and I seem to recall that you all hit it off very well."

"Nice to see you again, friends," smiled Kronos smoothly. "Our friend here has decided to place me in charge of taking care of this Joshua character. Our first act will be to strike tonight, during Joshua's next lecture."

***

Barge met Joshua and Falcon outside of the warehouse. He had been worried when Joshua had failed to show up at the appointed time, and he breathed a sigh of relief as he saw his two comrades rushing towards him.

"What took you?" he asked gruffly, patting Falcon on the back. "I was worried that the cops had gotten you!"

"They almost did," sighed Joshua. "Thankfully, I managed to avoid them. So, is the warehouse set up for the lecture?" Barge nodded. "Well, that's a start. Do we have watchmen posted?" Again, Barge nodded. "Glad to hear it. Why don't we head inside?"

The three of them found Blaise checking out the building. "It looks secure," he sneered, "but is it really? The cops could probably surround the building fairly easily, and I'm not sure that the watchmen are posted in the right spots." Blaise and Falcon began to argue about security measures, and Joshua and Barge began to rehearse the speech.

A few hours later, the warehouse was fully packed with people. Barge was attempting to get the crowd to quiet down, and Joshua was preparing to speak.

"SHUT UP! FOR THE LAST TIME, SHUT UP! DID YOU ALL COME HERE TO TALK, OR TO LISTEN TO JOSHUA SPEAK?" That quieted the crowd down fairly quickly. "Thank you!" shouted Barge.

"Very well, then. Let's begin, shall we?" began Joshua. "I recognize quite a few faces from my last few lectures, but I'll still give the opening speech. See, despite the fact that the corporate council has issued a statement saying that they will not attempt to harm the environment, they are, in fact, making the world worse by polluting it with waste from their factories. Also, they plan to develop the Poisonsap Forest. I'd imagine that some of you have read about that on their website." There was a nod of assent from a few of the members of the crowd. "However, in their short article, they failed to mention that it would destroy the only source of food left in the world! Sure, it'll open up new housing opportunities, but what good will that do if-"

"ATTENTION THIRD ORDER OF DRUIDS! THE BUILDING IS SURROUNDED! GIVE YOURSELVES UP NOW! THOSE WHO SURRENDER WILL BE FORGIVEN!" Joshua looked above him, and saw helicopters in the sky through the shattered windows.

The mass of people made for the doors, all thoughts of the lecture forgotten. In the chaos, Joshua was able to find Falcon and Barge.

"What's happening?" he wailed, wildly glancing around. "Why didn't the watchmen warn us? Falcon, what's going on?"

"We must have been betrayed!' exclaimed Falcon. "How else would they have found us?"

"Well, what do we do?" shouted Joshua. "C'mon, Falcon! We've gotta have a plan for this!"

"Barge, get everyone's attention!" ordered Falcon. Barge shouted at the top of his lungs, and everyone turned around. "Everyone, flee! But, if you get a chance, head to the skyscraper that was just bought by the farming company! Please, just find us there!" pleaded Falcon.

The crowd had stopped to listen, but they all returned to their charge towards the door. Joshua also made a dash for the door, but Falcon caught his hand.

"Josh! What're you doing?" shouted Falcon. "They'll let the citizens through, but they'll kill you on sight!"

"So what do you suggest I do?" inquired Joshua.

"There's a hidden passage out of here," explained Falcon. "It's hidden under one of the crates. Here, I'll show you." Falcon hurriedly led Joshua over to one of the boxes that littered the ground, and swiftly pulled it up, revealing a hidden passage. "Get in, quick!" ordered Falcon. Joshua immediately obeyed, and found himself sprinting down a flight of steps. He emerged into a dimly lit sewer. Falcon dropped to the ground behind him.

"What about Barge?" whispered Joshua, not wanting to be heard by the cops he assumed were searching right above him.

"It's too late!" responded Falcon. "He'll have to fend for himself. He's a big guy, and I think he'll be okay."

Falcon led Joshua through the sewer in silence. He came to another flight of steps, and he led Joshua up them. They emerged in a different warehouse, one that was still intact.

Falcon and Joshua stepped into the street, and Joshua immediately got his bearings. They were near Falcon's house, and Joshua suddenly remembered seeing the warehouse earlier, when he was running from the cops.

However, Falcon's house was crawling with policemen. "I guess we'll have to go to your house," mused Falcon. "I don't think that mine is particularly safe right now. Then again, there are probably still cops around yours, too. Well, I guess that yours is a better choice than mine right about now. Even so, I have a bad feeling about this."

Suddenly, Joshua threw himself to the ground as a shot rang out from behind him. "There they are!" shouted one of the policemen. "Get 'em! There's a big reward for them, dead or alive!"

"Run!" shouted Falcon, and he and Joshua scampered away. Two more shots came from behind Joshua, and he felt something graze his leg. Spasms of pain wracked his leg, but he ignored them, and kept running. Eventually, he could take it no longer.

"Falcon!" he gasped. "I need to rest! Please, just for a few minutes!"

"Fine," Falcon sighed through gritted teeth. "If you must, I think we can lose them in the alley network ahead."

Joshua smiled at the knowledge that they were nearing one of the infamous alley networks. In an online survey, they were voted 'easiest to get lost in'. Although no bigger than four blocks, they were incredibly complex. The alleys that led off of the road usually led to another road, but some of them led to a tangle of other alleys. The alley twisted into a terrible knot, and if you weren't familiar with the layout, they were extremely difficult to navigate. There were buildings, but they were mostly just small shops.

It was into one of these alley networks that Falcon led Joshua. They slipped into one of the buildings, and Joshua showed Falcon his wound. The two of them heard the cops rush past.

"It looks painful, but harmless," observed Falcon. "I think I have some painkillers in my backpack." He looked for a few moments, and found his quarry. "There we go! Now, just take two of these, and the pain'll go away in no time." Joshua swallowed the pills, and the pain began to ease. He tied a piece of cloth around the wound, and then stood up.

"I think I'm okay," he observed. "Let's go. You do know the way through the network, right?"

"Of course!" laughed Falcon. "Do you really think that I'd lead you into an alley network that I didn't know?" Joshua shook his head, and opened the door. Falcon stepped out first, and Joshua followed him closely.

Falcon carefully followed one street through the network, and they emerged onto a street in a matter of minutes. Joshua recognized it as one close to his own house, and, thankfully, not the one where he had been chased by the cop earlier. That street was on the other side of his house.

Two policemen were patrolling the street, and Joshua wondered how they were going to give them the slip.

"Stay here," ordered Falcon. "I'll get rid of the cops, and when I do, get inside the house."

Joshua stood in shadows while Falcon slipped back into the alley. Suddenly, Joshua heard him shout, from the other side of his house. "Here, Joshua! I don't think that there are any cops around here." Joshua saw an excited look come across the cops' faces, and they ran towards the voice, and away from Joshua. He darted into his house, and waited for Falcon to come. The two of them scurried down the stairs, and hid themselves underneath Joshua's desk.

"Okay, you're right," sighed Falcon. "This house does need some new security measures."

***

Joshua woke up, and shook Falcon. They had fallen asleep under the desk, and it was now morning.

Joshua pulled himself out from underneath the desk, and glanced around. He looked at his computer, and saw that it was about eight in the morning. Falcon also got off the floor, and stretched.

"Hey, Joshua, do you have a back door that we could sneak out of?" he asked.

"No, but we do have a back window," mused Joshua. "I think it's big enough to sneak out of. We could cover the doorway, so no one would see us."

"That sounds like a good plan," agreed Falcon. "I think we could pull it off. What should we cover the doorway with?"

"Well, I could project a hologram that looks like a door," suggested Joshua. "I think that'd work, don't you?" Falcon nodded, and Joshua set about programming a door into his holograph projector. That particular task took all of maybe five minutes, and Joshua crept up the stairs, and set the projector on the floor. He adjusted the range, and hit the activation switch. An exact image of a door appeared in the empty doorway, and Joshua signaled for Falcon to come up.

Joshua opened the back window, and squeezed himself through. Falcon followed suit, and the two of them walked quickly down the street. They didn't see any cops about, so they tried to avoid the alleys and blend in with the crowd of people heading to work.

Joshua could see their new skyscraper in the distance, and tried to walk towards it. However, he seemed to be fighting against the crowd, and he was separated from Falcon. The crowd forced him into a factory, and there was a man that seemed to be taking roll call. Joshua assumed that it was the foreman.

"Maxwell... Thomas... Williams... oh, and who have we here?" he asked, peering at Joshua.

"I'm sorry," hurriedly explained Joshua. "I'll just be going now. I mean, I've got a job to get to..."

"Do you really?" inquired the foreman skeptically. "Because I believe that you're Joshua, leader of the Third Order of Druids." Joshua's blood went cold. "Relax, son! You're welcome here!" Joshua was confused for a moment. "Oh yes, we know all about you, and we support your cause fully. I've been to two of your lectures, but I couldn't make it to the one last night. By the sound of things, that's probably good, am I right?"

"Yeah, things didn't go too well yesterday," sighed Joshua. "We got attacked by the cops. Wait. If you support my cause, how come you haven't quit your jobs?"

"You mean you don't know?" confusedly asked the foreman. "We explained it to that friend of yours, Blaise. See, when you hacked into the corporate council's bank account to take money, someone spotted you. However, they only confided in one person, but that person was one of the members of the council itself. He went to your first lecture as a spy, but you turned him to your point of view."

"Really?" asked Joshua. "I didn't know that we had an ally in the council!"

"Well, you do. He owns a bunch of factories, and he's using them to make supplies for the council," explained the foreman. "I could've sworn we told that Blaise fellow."

"He probably chose not to tell me," sighed Joshua. "If he did, that wouldn't surprise me at all. So, I suppose I owe you guys a thank you!"

"Think nothing of it," smiled one of the workers, the man named Maxwell. "If anything, we owe thanks to you."

"Well, either way, know that you've got a friend in the corporate council," smiled the foreman. "And a bunch of friends in the workforce. So, where are you headed?"

"To our new base of operations. I purchased a skyscraper in the name of one of the corporations," answered Joshua. "It should be pretty easy to defend, and I think that it'll serve its purpose well."

"Well, you'd better get a move on," smiled the foreman. "You should still be able to blend in with the crowd. Unless you want the cops on your tail, you should hurry up." Joshua nodded, and walked back outside.

A small portion of the crowd was surging towards the base, and he went along with them. He arrived at the new headquarters fairly quickly, and stepped inside.

Joshua figured he had about until the next corporate council meeting to set up the building. At the next meeting, they'd probably discuss the sale of the skyscraper, and then they'd find out that someone else had stolen it from their clutches. He resolved to tell Falcon to hurry up with the preparations.

He met Blaise inside the building, and they discussed the workers that Joshua had just met.

***

"I feel the need to apologize for last time. We didn't expect to be attacked by the police. How many of you were at that lecture?" Several hands in the crowd went up. Joshua estimated that it was about the same number of people that were at the next lecture. He continued his speech by asking, "Can one of you tell me what they did to you?"

Ten or so hands shot up in the crowd, and Joshua called on a boy in the back around his age. "They didn't really do anything to us. The police asked us if we knew where you lived, and none of us did. They also told us not to quit our jobs, but they let us go."

"Well, I'm glad that none of you got injured," assured Joshua. "It would have been a tragedy had anyone suffered because of this. If anything, this group is designed to help people. Well, allow me continue speaking about the topic I was addressing last time, before we were interrupted. The development of the Poisonsap cannot be allowed! It would destroy our only food source, and the only people that would benefit from it are the members of the corporate council!"

There was sudden applause from the crowd, and Joshua paused for a moment. "Continuing, we must speak out against this threat to all of us! If push comes to shove, we may have to take military action against this outrage. If we do, the attack would be lead by my brother, Arrow. Sadly, none of you have met him yet. He's helping another member to survive an attack from Kronos, one of the newer members of the corporate council. They required the help of the Great Sage, so he was unable to be here."

"On a different note, I need volunteers. This building that we're in right now is our new base. If the cops attack us again, we need to be able to defend ourselves. I need a few people to be guards for the building. If you're willing to take the job, sign the sheet that Falcon has after the lecture is over."

"On yet another different subject, I need information from all of you. When we were attacked by the cops, I lost track of Barge, the guy who yells at you to shut up." There was a bit of laughter at that last comment. "All comedy aside, have any of you seen him? It would be a pity to lose him."

The same boy from before raised his hand. "I saw two cops dragging him away. I'm sorry, Joshua."

"Oh. Well, will all of you excuse us for a moment while I speak to Falcon?" There was a general feeling of assent, and Falcon came up to the podium to consult with Joshua. "Falcon, this is terrible! What're we going to do?" inquired Joshua over the buzz of conversation from the audience. "I told you we should've gotten him!"

"We'll rescue him later," assured Falcon. "I'm not going to let good old Barge get away that easily. I'd bet that they've taken him to their secret prison in Cloudhall, atop Mount Ice Cap. Once we handle the development crisis here, we'll have to after him. Plus, Cloudhall is right near another great target: the magma re-router. It would take a while, but eventually the plant life would return to Maltesque if we destroy the re-router."

"All right," agreed Joshua. "Attention, everyone! Falcon and I have decided to go after Barge at a later time, after we have dealt with the housing development crisis. In the meantime, let us continue. I have one more interesting fact to share with all of you. Kronos, the newest addition to the council, the one who I mentioned earlier, is requesting permission to build an army to combat us. I don't doubt that he will succeed, but I believe that we can defeat any army that he pulls together, no matter how strong!"

There was a roar of assent, and Joshua ended by saying, "That will be all. Good night. And don't forget to sign up to guard the new base!"

***

Joshua snuck back in through the window into his house. He walked down the stairs, and began to hack the corporate council's website again. He transferred a huge sum of money (to his eyes, not to the eyes of the council) from the corporate council's account to his own.

Once again, a red light flashed in the upper corner of the screen, but this time he noticed it, and he clicked on it. A message appeared on the screen that read: "SECURITY BREACH. INVESTIGATING... FOUND SOURCE. CONTACTING AGENTS... AGENTS CONTACTED. DISPATCHING MEN TO INVESTIGATE."

Joshua read this with a feeling of horror. He grabbed the communication device that he used to contact Arrow, and shouted, "HELP! SOS! I've been found! They're coming after me!"

Joshua heard the two policemen outside shouting excitedly to each other, and Joshua dashed up the stairs, and attempted to squeeze out the window. On the other side, however, he saw a cop smiling at him.

He ran for the door, but two different cops ran through the hologram. Joshua struggled to suppress a laugh. It appeared that the two policemen had been fooled by the hologram, and had attempted to ram the door down.

Now, Joshua could have used that opportunity to sprint past the policemen, and escape to the new base, but that's not what he did. He was scared, and he ran back downstairs. He attempted to hide himself underneath the desk, but that didn't work too well. He barricaded the stairs with his desk, and looked for some kind of weapon. He grabbed a power cord, and swung it around like a ball and chain.

The three policemen jumped over the desk, and charged at Joshua. They stopped short when they saw his makeshift defense. "Come any closer, and you'll get a mouthful of power cord!"

"I can't get to him, Sarge!" exclaimed one of the policemen. "I don't think I'll be able to take him!"

"So?" asked Sarge, lifting up his gun. "Remember, Private, they'll give you the reward dead or alive."

15

Talents

"Prepare yourself, Adrian. My first attempt to enter your mind will begin in five minutes." Adrian wondered how to prepare himself for the voluntary surrendering of his mind. He tried once again to focus on the cloud of light, but it seemed to have been irrevocably damaged by his incident with the lightning sphere. He wished that there was an alternative to allowing someone else control over his mind, but he valued Rose's safety above all else.

"I'm ready when you are," responded Adrian to the Sage.

"Then let's begin," replied the Great Sage, and before Adrian had time to react, the Great Sage was inside his mind, and Adrian was pushed into a small corner at the very edge of his consciousness. Adrian became vaguely aware of what the Great Sage was doing with his mind.

The Great Sage quickly found the cloud of light in Adrian's mind, and began to access it. He discovered that when Adrian had been blasted by lightning, some of it had cancelled out with the cloud, and now about half of the cloud was missing. The Great Sage, however, believed that he could work around it. The process needed a very small amount of light energy, but a good deal of energy in general. Thus, the solution: the Great Sage planned to use his own life energy to power the spell.

The Great Sage had put just enough of himself into Adrian to power the spell. He summoned up the very minimum of light energy from the cloud, and sacrificed the portion of himself that he had put in Adrian.

Light blasted out of Adrian's hands, and entered Rose's wound. It purged the darkness out of the wound, and out of her body. The Great Sage then returned to his own body, and finished the job. He used some of his long forgotten life magic skills to heal Rose's body.

Adrian returned to full consciousness. He felt the Great Sage's presence still; however, it was much weaker. He seemed to have been worn out by the spell he cast. Adrian then remembered the purpose of the spell, and ran over to Rose.

She lay unconscious on the ground, and Adrian shook her thoroughly. One of her eyes flickered open, and then the other. She glanced around, and then she became aware of her surroundings. Rose sat up, and looked in wonder at the Great Sage. Her eyes then chanced upon Adrian, and her mouth formed a question.

"Adrian, where... what... Adrian, what happened?" she asked. "Where are we? The last thing I remember, we were going after Kronos, and then he attacked me with some sort of thing, and then... All I remember after that is a bunch of nightmares."

"Um, that's a question with a very long answer," replied Adrian. "Kronos hit you with a blast of darkness. It knocked you out, and infected you with a virus."

"Why didn't he attack you?" inquired Rose fuzzily.

"He only attacked you because he was possessed by his master, Shadius, an old god of darkness," explained Adrian. "In actuality, Kronos is... your father."

"What?" exclaimed Rose incredulously. "He's my father? I know my father always had a short temper, but how could he be Kronos?"

"It's... complicated," sighed Adrian. "The man that possessed you was Kronos, but he also kidnapped your dad, who tried to protect you, and he sent your dad back in time, to, ah, here. Then, Kronos sent necrossis after your dad, and then Kronos returned to the present. Here, your dad was captured by the necrossis, and brought to Genesis. He was then corrupted by the Deity of Darkness, Shadius. Then, in the present, your father, now, Kronos, kidnapped your dad. If you don't get it, I guess that's okay."

"I think I get it," whispered Rose. "I just can't believe that my dad turned evil."

"Well, that's just the thing," smiled Adrian. "He isn't, at least not anymore. Shadius had him under some sort of mind control, and when I blasted the necrossis with lightning, it broke that hold, but just partially. Your dad has been trying to resist, and he broke free when Shadius made him attack his own daughter, you."

"So he turned good?" asked Rose hopefully.

"Yes," happily replied Adrian. "But continuing with our story, Kronos let me escape, but Shadius repossessed him right as I was leaving. Arrow and I escaped just in time. We brought you back to his house, and we discussed what to do with you. We decided to bring you to the Great Sage. However, we first had a meeting of the entire Third Order of druids. It turns out that one of the members is, well, Blaise."

"No!" shouted Rose. "Not him! He's evil! Can't they tell that?"

"I think that when they accepted him in, they needed all of the help that they could get," explained Adrian. "Look, I don't like it either, but I was willing to put up with it, since your life was on the line."

"So this is the Great Sage's house?" asked Rose.

"No. This is the Great Sage. He's a tree," laughed Adrian.

"What? You mean we went through all of that work to meet a tree?" shouted Rose.

"Yeah, that's the same reaction that I had," grinned Adrian. "But he's a conscious tree. He can talk to us, like his ambassadors. However, after he cast the spell to cure you, he kind of, ah, fainted. It took a lot out of him."

"So how did you heal me? Does it have anything to do with your lightning powers?" inquired Rose.

"Well, let me tell you all about it..."

***

After Adrian had finished explaining about how his power stemmed from his unusual heritage, he and Rose snuggled up beneath the Great Sage, and went to sleep, as Rose was still recovering, and Adrian was tired from curing Rose.

The next morning, they were awakened by the thoughts of the Great Sage entering their minds.

"Adrian Lightseeker, Rose Cores, awaken. There is much I wish to discuss with you." Adrian sat up, and Rose blinked sleepily. "First and foremost, allow me to introduce myself to you, Rose. As Adrian explained, I am the Great Sage. With Adrian's help, I healed you from your darkness virus. However, and this is something I wish to discuss with both of you, in the process of healing you, Rose, I gave you some of my power over plants. I think that if you do some training, you could gain the ability to use this talent for whatever purpose you choose. Now that I've healed you, Rose, I'd like to ask both of you this: What do you want to do?"

"I believe I have an answer to that question," smirked Arrow, stepping down from his glider. "Sorry I wasn't here yesterday. I wanted to check up with Joshua in the city. He's doing fine, and we're way ahead in recruiting! We've got about a thousand new members!"

"That's great!" exclaimed Rose. "So, what's your answer that you claim to have for us?"

"Well, the two of you promised to help the Third Order of druids, right?" inquired Arrow. "Well, now you have an opportunity to do that. We're planning to launch an attack on the new housing developments in the Poisonsap

Forest, and I think a light mage and a Greenkeeper would be a great addition to the team. Therefore, I would like for you two to stay, and finish your training. Is that okay with you?"

"I suppose that works for me," mused Adrian.

"Absolutely!" agreed Rose, always eager to please Arrow.

"Very well then," rumbled the Great Sage. "You two shall stay here, with me, to continue honing your talents. I shall work hard to train you. Today, I shall attempt to figure out how best to train you two. You may take the day off."

"So, Adrian, how exactly how do you plan to help us?" asked Arrow. "You could be one of our best warriors, or you could be a healer in the back. Which do you choose?"

"Couldn't I be both?" inquired Adrian. "I mean, couldn't I, like heal people in the front row while I blast our enemies with lightning?"

"Sure, that would work," smiled Arrow. "And Rose, how about you?"

"I'd like to be with Adrian in the front row," she stated firmly. "I mean, if that's okay with you, Arrow."

"It's fine. Now, if you'll excuse me, I need to go and work out some battle plans for our attack on the housing developments." With that, Arrow walked away.

"Rose, why are you so anxious to get Arrow's approval?" inquired Adrian curiously. "I mean, sure, he's our host and all, but we're repaying him by helping the Third Order. So why the sucking up?"

Rose flushed a deep crimson, not unlike the color of the flower she was named after. "Well, I... y'know... he's sort of... well..."

"Rose, I get it," laughed Adrian. "He's an older guy, he's in good shape, he's relatively handsome, I suppose... Anyways, I understand."

"Well, it's not like that. I mean, I guess it is, well, sorta, but... Well, yeah. Yeah, you're right," sighed Rose. "I'm sorry, Adrian. I guess that it sort of upset you. But, Adrian, c'mon. I just met him. Whereas we've fought giant cats, braved dangerous waterfalls, and, well, grown up together. Adrian, I still love you. Believe me, I do. I just sort of got carried away by Arrow."

"I surmised as much," replied Adrian.

"But you were jealous?" inquired Rose. "Maybe I should keep acting like that, to try to get your attention more easily."

"Rose, I hope you're kidding," sighed Adrian. "Anyways, what do we do? I mean, like, what are the rest of our lives going to be like? Are we just going to help the Third Order for the rest of our lives? Is that it?"

Rose paused for a moment before replying. "No," she said. "I want to talk to Kronos, and I want to get back to our world. I want to meet your friend,

James. And, once we're ready, I want to go to Genesis, and destroy Shadius. But, no matter what, I want to be with you. Always."

"Me, too, Rose," responded Adrian. "Me, too." Adrian leaned towards Rose, and they kissed under the branches of the Great Sage.

***

Adrian and Rose were awakened by Arrow.

"Get up, sleepyheads," he said, shaking them. "It's morning, and I wouldn't want my two best warriors to miss their first day of training."

"Yeah, I guess not," yawned Adrian, sitting up. "C'mon, Rose. Get up."

"Jus five mur minutes," she mumbled sleepily. "Still tired."

"C'mon, Rose. We need you to get up," said Arrow more forcefully. "Adrian, could you help me out here?"

"Will do, Arrow," replied Adrian, and he shook Rose harder. "Rose, if you get up now, I'll give you a kiss, if that helps at all."

Rose jumped to her feet. "Okay, Adrian," she said.

Adrian smiled. "I lied," he laughed, and Rose threw a handful of dirt at him.

"Ah, good morning, you two," rumbled the Sage. "Today, I would like for Adrian to meditate and try to assess the damage from the lightning incident, and I'll work with Rose. How does that sound to you two?"

They both gave general answers of assent, but Arrow had an objection. "Actually, I would like to work with Adrian on our attack plan on the housing developments. What do you think of that?"

"Very well," rumbled the Great Sage. "Adrian can meditate for half of the day, and, after noon has passed, he may work with you, Arrow. Is that acceptable for all parties concerned?"There was assent from everyone, and Adrian sat down and probed his consciousness. He found the cloud, and focused on it.

"Now then, Rose. We shall begin your training. Specifically, we shall discuss exactly what your new talent is," began the Great Sage. "When I healed you, I implanted some of my power in you, power that I had forgotten about eons ago. Specifically, the power to control plants. I assigned that task to my ambassadors, and I forgot that I myself had that ability. Therefore, I know little more about it than you do."

"So you're teaching me something that you don't know yourself?" summarized Rose.

"More or less," laughed the Sage. "Anyhow, I must first enter your mind and discover what impact it had on you. I shall decide what the first step in your training is after that."

Rose wasn't sure what the Great Sage had meant by 'enter your mind', as she had never seen the full extent of his powers. However, she assumed it would display ignorance on her part were she to ask. As a result, she was totally unprepared when the Great Sage pushed her into a small corner at the edge of consciousness.

The Great Sage examined her mind very closely, and compared it to various other minds he had seen before. Most of hers was exactly the same, but she seemed to have some kind of an extra lobe, somewhat like Adrian. He probed this particular section, and found that it had control over the basic cells that make up plants. He assumed that it was this control over the cells that allowed for the control over the plants themselves.

The Great Sage exited from Rose's mind, and Rose returned to full consciousness.

"Don't... EVER... do that again," demanded Rose shakily. "I like to have control over my mind, thank you very much!"

"I apologize if the experience was frightening," assured the Great Sage. "However, it was necessary. I have found the source of your newfound control over plants. It seems that when I healed you, I added an extra part to your brain. This new part allows you to control basic plant cells. If you speed up the growth of plants and tell them to grow in a certain direction, it can seem almost as if you are making the plant move. That's how my ambassadors make plants move."

"Great!" exclaimed Rose, who had not absorbed a word of what the Sage had just said. "So, can you teach me to manipulate plants?"

"Yes," sighed the Sage. "You didn't get a word of what I just said, did you?"

"No, not really," admitted Rose. "So, what's my first lesson, Sage?"

"Well, I'd like to think that meditation would help, but I'm not sure it would," mused the Sage. "Still, if you could just mentally examine your mind for a moment, you'd be off to a good start."

"Right," agreed Rose. She squeezed her eyes shut, and wondered what do. She just let her mind wander, and it found exactly what the Great Sage had wanted it to. She found that she could now think about plants differently, and, by an extent of that, force them to think as well. She tried to implant a thought into the Great Sage's mind, but she was mentally swatted away like a fly.

"I would appreciate it if you did not attempt to place me under your control, Rose," chuckled the Great Sage. "However, think not of it. I was merely the nearest plant, and I imagine that you just wanted to test it out. Am I right?"

Rose nodded. "I'm sorry, Sage. I don't know what came over me. It must have just been a reflex of some kind. Really, I'm sorry."

"Apology accepted, but make sure it doesn't happen again," replied the Great Sage sternly. "However, I don't doubt that some good came of it. You encountered a good deal of resistance when you attempted to control me, right? Well, the same applies with all plants, though none of them are quite as resistant as I. However, if you are not trained at breaking through their resistance, you will be able to control naught."

"So how can I overcome that resistance?" inquired Rose eagerly.

"Well, you'll need an easier plant to practice on. It is nearing noon, and I'd like for you to take a break and eat lunch. In the meantime, I will attempt to find a flower of some kind for you to practice on," thought the Great Sage.

Rose nodded, and walked off to try to find something to eat.

***

Adrian had grown extremely tired of meditation by the time noon came around. He had found the cloud very quickly, and saw that the Sage was right: the cloud was about half its previous size. However, he did detect something in his mind where the other half of the cloud had been, he just wasn't sure what it was. He wondered if it was some other kind of cloud.

The Great Sage reached into Adrian's mind, and said, "It's noon. You may now work with Arrow on the attack plan. However, I suggest eating something first."

Adrian nodded, and stood up. He walked over to Arrow, who was sitting by his glider. "Hello, Arrow," smiled Adrian. "How're the plans coming along?"

"Not so good," frowned Arrow. "I'm having difficulty deciding what I should do with our weakest unit. The way the numbers are, at least according to Joshua, we have one unit that's smaller than the rest. I can't figure out where to put it, since it would be a weak point in our strategy."

"Well, why don't you put it in the middle of a bunch of stronger units?" suggested Adrian. "That way, they'll just add to the strength of the other units. I think that could work."

"Adrian, that's brilliant!" exclaimed Arrow. "That would absolutely work! So, can I show you the plans I've made so far?"

"Sure," shrugged Adrian. "Where are they?"

"Right here, on the ground," stated Arrow. "Go ahead, take a look. I think that I did a pretty good job on them."

Adrian sat down, and looked at the plans. They seemed to be a schematic of the housing developments copied over a same scale map of the Poisonsap. There were markings on the map depicting where the battalions of soldiers were to be located. Adrian looked carefully at it, and found a hole in the strategy. The battle plan seemed to mainly focus on the offensive perspective of battle, ignoring the possibility that the workers would launch some kind of resistance. The guards positioned to the side could take out the side guards very quickly.

Adrian pointed this out to Arrow, and he adjusted the plan so that he had two battalions of soldiers guarding them from both sides. Adrian saw no further flaws in the plans, so he and Arrow continued to work out the finer details. That activity took Adrian well into the evening.

***

Rose returned to the Great Sage after eating a few bites of a sandwich that Arrow had packed. He immediately explained, "Ironically, the only flower I could find for you to practice on was a rose. It's just a few feet to your left."

Rose suppressed a small chuckle as she sat down next to the small flower. She thought in her newly discovered way, and encountered a bit of resistance from the flower. However, the Great Sage reached out to her mind, and guided her.

"Now Rose, this particular flower should not be able to stand up to even an untrained mind such as yours. Just keep pushing, and it should give away." Rose obeyed, and she could feel the flower's resistance weakening. Eventually, after a few minutes, it broke, and Rose now had full control over the flower.

"What am I supposed to do now?" she asked, not entirely sure.

"Tell the flower to grow upwards," suggested the Sage. Rose thought those words in her mind, but nothing happened. "You need to think it using the new part of your brain," explained the Sage. Rose obeyed him, and the rose grew a millimeter or so taller. Rose was a bit dismayed, as she had wanted it to rise a bit more. However, she was proud of herself for making it move at all. She figuratively gave herself a pat on the back. "Well done, Rose," smiled the Great Sage. "I imagine it must have been a bit difficult, but you did well. Of course, you realize that there is much more to it than that."

"There is?" inquired Rose, who had been under the impression that if she just practiced that, she would be fine. "What else is there?"

"Well, with larger plants, like the vines you saw in Light's End, you might require more strength to manipulate the plant than you can muster," explained the Sage.

"I thought that if I just practiced, I would build up all of the strength that I need," frowned Rose. "Why isn't that the case?"

"Well, everyone has a limit to how much strength they can acquire," said the Great Sage. "If you reach your limit, which by all means you should, there is an alternative source from which you can draw the strength you need, and conserve your own in the process."

"So what's the other source?" asked Rose eagerly.

"You recall how the plant offered resistance?" began the Sage. "Well that resistance is the predetermined actions of the plant built into its genetic code. If you can reprogram it, if you will, you can then use that to order the plant around. It works much better, since it was what was ordering the plant around in the first place."

"Can you teach me how to do that?" inquired Rose with enthusiasm. "I think that's brilliant!"

"Of course I can teach you!" laughed the Sage. "After all, isn't that my goal right now?"

Rose nodded, and she began to focus on the rose again. She encountered the resistance she had felt before, but met an unexpected surprise: it was slightly different. She examined it more closely, and found that it was, in fact, the programming of the plant, just like the Great Sage had said. However, it was now different because she had changed it just moments ago!

"Sage, what do I do now?" she asked.

"Well, focus on the wall of resistance," ordered the Sage. "Now, search for the part of the resistance that's telling the plant what to do." Rose obeyed, and found it very quickly. "Now, tell that part its new objective with the new part of your brain." Rose did as she was asked, and told it to grow. It took a good deal of concentrated effort on her part to change the objective, but she succeeded. The plant grew about two inches, much more than before.

"Wow, you're right!" exclaimed Rose. "It does work a lot better that way! I mean, a *lot* better!"

"Your tone implies more surprise than I would like it to," laughed the Sage. "And yes, it does work a good deal better. I'm glad you noticed. Anyhow, I believe that will suffice for today."

***

Adrian and Rose sat down with Arrow to eat dinner and discuss the events of the day. Arrow had brought some fresh fruit from one of the few clean areas of the Poisonsap, and some beans grown at the outskirts of the city.

"So, Rose, how'd your training go?" inquired Adrian.

"It went well!" happily said Rose. "I made a rose grow about two inches in under a half hour!"

"Well, I guess that's a start," murmured Adrian thoughtfully.

"I hope that's not the full extent of your new powers," commented Arrow.

"I have a slightly bigger role planned for you in our upcoming battle."

"Arrow, could you stop reminding us that we owe you?" requested an irritated Adrian. "It's getting kinda old, and pretty annoying. We know we're indebted to you, believe me. But you're starting to act kind of like a jerk."

"Sorry," sighed Arrow. "It's just that the Third Order has been around for a few years, and now that it's finally taking off, I can't be there to see it. I apologize if I've been sort of obnoxious. Friends?"

"Friends," smiled Adrian, shaking Arrow's outstretched hand.

"Well, Arrow, *I* didn't think that you were being obnoxious," said Rose reproachfully. "Anyhow, I've been meaning to ask you this: what exactly is my role in the battle against the housing development? I mean, what exactly am I supposed to do? Heal others? Destroy the buildings with plants?"

"The latter," answered Arrow. "Adrian is supposed to take out the soldiers or guards, whichever we encounter, and you're to take out the empty buildings, and force the vegetation to return to the area. Does that answer your question?"

"Completely, utterly, thoroughly, and totally," affirmed Rose. "So, Adrian takes out the people, and I take out the buildings? What does everyone else do?"

"They take out the trash. Anything you guys miss, they get," explained Arrow. "That's basically our battle plan, right, Adrian?" Adrian nodded. "Also, the other guys are supposed to make sure that you two don't get hit. Also, Adrian provides cover for you. Any more questions?" Adrian and Rose shook their heads.

"Actually, I have one for you, Adrian," began Arrow. "Did you actually accomplish anything during your meditation, or was it just busywork?"

"It wasn't just busywork. I actually found something," answered Adrian. "The cloud of light in my brain, which got blasted by lightning. There seems to be a new, better-concealed cloud about the size of what I lost. I'm not quite sure what it is, so I think I'll ask the Great Sage about it tomorrow."

"Why don't you ask him now?" suggested Rose. "For all you know, it could be dangerous!"

"I'm too tired to ask him right now," yawned Adrian. "I think I'm gonna head to bed. After all, tomorrow it's my turn to work with the Sage."

Rose nodded, and Adrian walked away, towards his makeshift bed underneath the Great Sage. Rose and Arrow talked for a few minutes about Adrian, and then they both went to bed. Arrow walked over to his glider, and lay down underneath a blanket he had brought from home. Rose lay down next to Adrian, and they both fell asleep beneath a sheet given to them by Arrow.

***

Around midnight, Rose awoke with a start. She could sense that something wasn't right with Adrian. He was sweating, and he seemed to be elsewhere in his mind. At first Rose assumed that it was just a dream, but that thought was quickly expelled when Adrian's eyes snapped open, and he shakily breathed, "Rose... help me... Shadius has it... he has it... please, help me..."

"Don't worry, Adrian. I'll help you! What do you need me to do?" she quickly asked.

"Please... my father... only he can stop it... you must find my father..." Adrian's eyes drooped shut, and he fell asleep again. Rose decided to write down what Adrian had said. However, she didn't have any sort of paper, so she crept over to Arrow's bag, and looked around, repeating in her head what Adrian had said all the while. She found what she was looking for very quickly: a blank piece of paper, and a black pen.

Rose immediately wrote down what Adrian had said, and she then walked back to their makeshift bed. Adrian was now breathing normally, and seemed to be sleeping peacefully. Rose felt a wave of affection wash over her as she stared at his sleeping form, and she caressed his cheek. "Good night, Adrian," she whispered.

***

Adrian awoke the next morning with no memory of the events of the night. He gently shook Rose, and she too woke up.

"Adrian! Are you all right? What happened last night?" she asked worriedly.

"Rose, what are you talking about?" inquired Adrian fuzzily. "Did you have a bad dream?"

"No, Adrian! It wasn't a dream; it was real!" protested Rose. "You woke up, and said something about your father and Shadius!"

"Right," agreed Adrian sarcastically. "I think I'd remember something like that, Rose."

"No! It was real, and I'll prove it to you!" exclaimed Rose. She searched the area around her, and found the piece of paper, and showed it to Adrian. "See! I told you it wasn't a dream!"

Adrian's attitude changed instantly. He closely examined the piece of paper, and decided that Rose was telling the truth. He asked, "What does this mean? What does that mean, 'Shadius has it'? Has what?"

"I don't know, Adrian," frowned a troubled Rose. "We should ask the Great Sage."

"Good idea," agreed Adrian. "Yo, Sage! We've got a question for you!"

"What is it, Adrian?" inquired the Sage. "What is it you wish to discuss with me?"

"Rose tells me that last night I woke up, and whispered this," explained Adrian, holding up the piece of paper for the Great Sage to see.

"Adrian, I cannot see the paper. I have no eyes; instead, let me see it through your eyes. Look at the paper," commanded the Great Sage. Adrian obeyed, and the Sage saw the strange statements through his eyes.

"Very well," sighed the Sage. "I do not know what this thing is that Shadius seems to possess. In fact, I do not know who Shadius is, though the name rings a bell..."

"Shadius is an ancient god of darkness," explained Adrian. "You seemed to know all about the source of my light powers, and how to use them, though."

"That is because years ago, a man by the name of Ajax Lightseeker came to Maltesque, and attempted to spread around a book called *Legend of Darkness*. We had a conversation, and he told me all about the source of his strange powers," explained the Sage. "He also mentioned that a copy of his book had already been given away, and that it explained everything. A pity we do not have it."

"But we do," grinned Adrian. "Ajax sold it to Arrow and Joshua, and they gave it to us."

"Excellent!" grinned the Great Sage. "May I see the book?" Adrian nodded, picked it up, and turned to the table of contents. The Sage saw it through his eyes, and told Adrian what pages to turn to. Though the Great Sage scoured the book, he could find nothing. "I'm sorry, Adrian. I can't find anything that fits."

"Oh well," sighed Adrian. "We'll deal with that when we need to. Right now, though, don't you need to be training me?"

"Ah, yes. Of course," laughed the Sage. "Very well. Today, I shall work with Adrian, and I would like for you to find some plants to practice on, Rose." The two being addressed nodded. "Very well. Rose, move along. Adrian, come closer."

Rose walked away to find some sort of flower to practice manipulating on, and Adrian stepped towards the Sage. "Now, Adrian, tell me what you discovered during your meditation yesterday."

"Well, Sage, I found a hidden cloud about the size of what I lost. Do you have any suggestions as to what it might be?" inquired Adrian.

"Well, let me take a look," mused the Sage. He entered Adrian's mind. "Hm. Intriguing. I believe I know what the hidden cloud is. Odd though this may sound, I believe that the new cloud is not new at all, but it is the part of the cloud that we thought you lost. Apparently, the lightning and the light cloud did not cancel out, but the lightning pushed part of the cloud into a hidden part of your mind. Allow me to examine it, please."

The Sage looked carefully at the new location of the cloud, and found that it was not, in fact, in a true part of Adrian's brain. There was a tear in the space-time continuum inside Adrian's brain. The Great Sage assumed that it had been formed when Adrian had seen the fifth dimension, and Adrian's ordeal with the lightning ball must have widened it, and the lost half of the cloud must have been pushed in.

"Ah, Adrian, we have a slight dilemma. The hidden part of the cloud seems to be in... well, it seems to be in a reality fracture," explained the Sage worriedly.

"Define 'reality fracture'," frowned Adrian.

"A hole in space-time," replied the Sage. "It can't harm you, but it could be a bit difficult to get the other half of the cloud out. I think our best bet is to assume that there's still a link between the two sections of the cloud. If that's the case, if we can use the remaining half, then we should be able to pull the other half out of the reality fracture. So, I'd like for you to summon lightning."

"Hold on, Sage," began Adrian. "Does the reality fracture explain my vision last night?"

"Perhaps," replied the Sage. "Since it's a break in space-*time*, it's possible that you saw the future. Do you recall what you saw?"

"Not really," sighed Adrian. "Actually, wait... I remember something... there was a huge sphere of darkness... and I was standing in the middle of it, being held prisoner."

"Strange," mused the Sage. "Anyhow, regarding your training, I believe that if you just use your light powers, it will dislodge the other half of the cloud. So, just practice on these dummies I made for you out of wood last night."

Two of the Great Sage's branches lowered down a humanoid figure, and Adrian called up lightning, which attacked the dummy at Adrian's command. Adrian felt something in his mind come slightly loose.

***

And so the next few days passed, with Adrian and Rose taking turns to work with the Great Sage. When not working with the Great Sage, Adrian either honed his lightning talents by attacking the dummy, or helping Arrow with his battle plans. Rose ventured into the fields surrounding the Sage, and found various plants upon which she could practice. Rose seemed to have a knack for plant manipulation, and by the end of the week her talents rivaled those of Vitalius. Adrian was gradually dislodging the second half of the cloud during his practice sessions, and reported his progress to the Sage, who looked inside his mind to check.

This near ideal system was suddenly shattered on the first day of the third week since their departure from Twilight City. It was in the evening, and Adrian and Arrow were making some last-minute adjustments to the attack plan when a green light flashed on Arrow's helmet.

"Hm," mused Arrow. "That means that Joshua's trying to contact me. Must be important." Arrow quickly put the helmet on. By that time, the message was nearly over, but he still caught the words "-ing after me!"

Arrow frantically hit the replay button, and the entire message played out. "HELP! SOS! I've been found! They're coming after me!" shouted the voice of Joshua.

"Adrian, I need to go! Joshua's in trouble!" exclaimed Arrow, hopping on his glider. "Finish your training, but get back to the city as soon as possible!" Arrow shot up into the air on his glider, and flew away.

"Arrow, wait! We need to come with you! How else are we supposed to get back to the city?" yelled Adrian at Arrow's retreating form. Arrow did not look back.

Adrian raced over to Rose, and shook her violently. "Rose, wake up!" he shouted. "Joshua's in trouble! We need to get back to the city! Arrow flew away, but I think that we can still make it in time to help if we rush!"

"Adrian, it would be better for you if you did not go," proclaimed the Great Sage, awakening from his rest. "You still have training to do!"

"What about me?" asked Rose; leaping out from underneath the sole sheet she slept beneath. "You just said yesterday that you had no more to teach me!"

"Yes, you may go, Rose," answered the Sage. "However, Adrian, allow me one more look inside your mind to assess whether or not your talent is developed enough for it to be of any use to you."

The Great Sage probed Adrian's mind, and found what he was looking for. He had worked with Rose the day before, so he hadn't gotten a chance to see Adrian's progress. Surprisingly, the Sage found that the second half of the cloud was almost entirely dislodged. However, it appeared as if the rest would only come out all at once, and it would require a good deal of effort from Adrian to dislodge it. The Great Sage resolved to think of a final test for Adrian, as he did not believe that the attack on the housing development in the Poisonsap would cut it.

"Very well," sighed the Sage. "Adrian, you may go, as I promised to do everything in my power to help the Third Order, and they need you. Also, I need time to think of a final task for you, and I think that your time might be better spent helping the Third Order than accomplishing nothing here."

16

Adventurers Again

Adrian double-checked his bag, and put his compass in his pocket. He had everything he needed: food, blanket, extra layers, *Legend of Darkness*, and a pocketknife for self-defense. However, he figured he would not be using the last item much, as he could now adequately defend himself with his lightning powers. Nearby, Rose was looking at a map of the Cavernous Cliffs, and tracing the best route through.

Adrian decided that he was finished, and walked over to ask Rose if she had any suggestions about what to bring. She didn't, so Adrian decided to talk to the Sage one last time.

"Sage, should I come back here? I mean, when I can?" asked Adrian. "After the battle in the Poisonsap, should I check back in with you? You know, to get that last task you were talking about?"

"Yes, Adrian, I think checking back in with me after the attack on the housing developments would be a very wise idea," mused the Sage. "I'll do my best to have that last task ready by then, alright?" Adrian nodded.

"Rose, are you ready to go?" inquired Adrian, kneeling down next to her. "We should head out as soon as possible. After all, we have no way of knowing if Joshua's okay or not. *Man*, I wish cell phones existed in this world!"

"Okay, Adrian. I'm ready," proclaimed Rose. "You know, it sort of feels like we're heading back into Light's End. Let's hope we don't meet another Democritus."

Adrian laughed. "I doubt we will. After all, you don't meet insane old hermits condemned to a lake by some ancient super-being every day!"

"Well, let's hope you're right," sighed Rose. "It's such a pity about what happened to Democritus." The two of them lapsed into solemn silence. "Well, we should probably be going soon," murmured Rose.

Adrian nodded, and the two of them leapt to their feet. Rose took the map, and Adrian grabbed the bag. Adrian bade the Great Sage farewell, and then walked back into the tunnel he had come out of so many days before. He led Rose in, and soon they could no longer see the Great Sage. Adrian ceased to glance behind him, and focused on keeping his footing. It appeared that the tunnel in which they walked had been subject to some sort of flood.

Presently, they came to an intersection, not unlike the one Adrian had seen before. However, this time, all paths were lit, and Adrian could see no path that immediately seemed like the correct one. Therefore, he chose to consult with Rose, who was serving as their navigator.

"Say, Rose, you've got a map, right?" inquired Adrian rhetorically. "So, which way do we go from here?"

Rose consulted her map for a moment before replying, "Well, it looks like if we take the tunnel closest to us on our left, it should eventually lead us to the ground. That is where we want to end up, right?"

Adrian shook his head in agreement, and they took that tunnel. After a few minutes, they came to a different intersection. Rose again pointed Adrian in the right direction, and this repeated itself without incident a few times.

Rose looked at the map for a few moments. She then looked at it again, and turned to Adrian and murmured, "That's odd. There's a large blank spot on the map. If we had a choice, I'd recommend ignoring it, but our present route seems to be taking us right through the heart of it."

"So what do you think it is?" inquired Adrian. "If you have any idea at all, that is."

"Well, I hope it isn't a chasm," frowned Rose worriedly. "Maybe it's a lake or something. I guess anything but a chasm would be good."

"Well, we'll see," mused Adrian. "I guess we'd better continue on."

He and Rose walked down the passage in silence until they came to the blank spot on the map. It was, in fact, a giant pool, but the water seemed to be flowing into it from some of the surrounding tunnels. Therefore, the water in the pool was moving, so Adrian figured that it was not truly a pool, but more of a giant lake.

In the lake was a giant wall of some sort of porous stone. It seemed to be filtering the water. Adrian assumed that it was this wall of stone that filtered the water for the Great Sage. He therefore reasoned that the stone wall must be full of diseases and various pollutions.

Rose saw the same thing as Adrian, but she noticed something else: five people seemed to be taking care of the wall. "Adrian, do you see them?" she whispered, pointing at the people. "Who do you think they are?"

"I dunno," replied Adrian quietly. "They might be aides of the Sage. You'd think he'd have mentioned them though."

"Well, I hope they're friendly," sighed Rose. "Considering our luck, though, I'd say that's fairly unlikely. With any luck they'll just ignore us."

Adrian and Rose took a steep path down to the lakeshore, and walked over to the wall. According to Rose's directions, they needed to cross, and the easiest way to do that seemed to be to walk across on the wall. However, when Adrian attempted to put his foot on the wall, one of the five people they had noticed shouted out to him.

"Do you have a death wish? If you so much as touch that wall, there'll be so much bacteria on your foot your head will spin!" shouted the man, who Adrian estimated to be around twenty.

"How else can we get across?" asked Adrian. "And why can you stand on the wall without killing yourself?"

"I think I'm the one in the position to ask questions!" huffily replied the man. "Anyhow, why do you need to cross anyways? It's not like you'd make it through the Poisonsap alive!"

Adrian was about to reply when he saw that the man was walking towards him. When he was a few feet away, "Sir, could you please tell me your name?"

"Fine," shrugged the man. "My name is Incarcerus. Actually, my full name is John Williams Incarcerus, but I go by my surname."

"Doesn't 'incarcerate' mean to get, like, thrown in jail or something?" asked Rose.

"Technically, it means to be imprisoned," whispered Incarcerus. "Which makes it an appropriate surname for our family. Tell me, have you heard of the war of the druids?'

"Yes," answered Adrian, figuring that it was a somewhat ridiculous question for a friend of Democritus.

"Well, in the second order, a druid came upon the gift of foresight, and predicted what would happen to Maltesque," began Incarcerus. "He repented, and left the second order to rejoin the first. He shared his vision with the leader of the first order, Vistus, and Vistus decided that the Great Sage must be kept free of the influence of the pollution. He sealed him away in this place, along with his wife and a few of his followers. Virda used magic to seal them and their ancestors away in this place. He was charged with the job of keeping the Great Sage safe. I am one of his descendants."

"That's so sad!" frowned Rose. "So you can't leave here?"

"No," sighed Incarcerus. "Actually, I've never seen anyone else come here. I'm not sure what our policy is regarding visitors. Anyways, returning to your questions, I'm not sure if there is another way across. There are a couple of plants around here that I guess you could make a raft or something out of. Also, to answer your other question, I can stand on this wall without fear of pollution because of Virda's spell, which grants all of us immunity to the diseases that lurk in the pollution."

"On the topic of getting across," began Rose, "How about a bridge? How long would it take to build one of those?"

"By hand, a while," sighed Incarcerus.

"How about with magic?" asked Rose with a gleam in her eye.

"Seconds," laughed Incarcerus, not taking her seriously. "There are definitely enough plants, but I actually you'd be better off if you didn't try to cross at all."

His words were lost on Rose, who found the plants with her Greenkeeping powers very quickly. They were all small, but she reprogrammed each and every one of them. It took about five minutes, but suddenly all of the small growths on the wall began to grow larger, and twist themselves into a bridge. Incarcerus stared wide-eyed at the spectacle.

"Okay, now it's my turn to ask you guys a few questions. The first of them is this: how is that even possible?!" he shouted. "That was amazing! I knew that Greenkeepers could talk to plants and things like that, but that was amazing! Besides, I thought that the Greenkeepers died out years ago."

"Well, Incarcerus, that's a question with a very long answer," smiled Adrian, amused by the man's reaction. "Perhaps we should sit down."

"Sure," grinned Incarcerus. "Allow me to show you to our camp site. Y'know, where we live."

Adrian nodded, and the three of them walked across the bridge. The other four people gave Incarcerus and the two travelers some very strange looks. Incarcerus led them into a small cave.

The three of them sat down at a table, and Incarcerus began by asking them, "All right, where are you two from?"

"We're not from Maltesque," replied Adrian. "We're from a world named Earth. We were kidnapped by a man named Kronos, who can travel between worlds."

"I thought that Maltesque was the only world in this universe," mused Incarcerus.

"It is," assured Adrian. "Earth is in a different universe. You have, no doubt, heard of Ulysses?" Incarcerus nodded. "Well, we're from the same world as him. Anyhow, Kronos, our kidnapper, held us in his tower in Twilight City, but we were unintentionally rescued by a man named Arrow."

"The leader of the Third Order?" asked Incarcerus, surprised. "My great-great-great-great-great and then some grandfather saw him in his vision."

"Very well then," murmured Adrian, "continuing on with the story, Rose and I wound up clinging to a piece of driftwood in the river, which swept us to the Verdant Sanctuary. There we met Vitalius. However, we were soon besieged by one of Kronos' men, and Vitalius died in the act of saving us. We were forced to flee to Light's End, where we met Democritus, and I accidentally destroyed Kronos' man. We bargained with the ambassador in Light's End, and Democritus was given a deal. He then went off to Twilight City. Long story short, we eventually wound up back in the city, and we met back up with Arrow, whose dad is Vitalius. Anyhow, he let us join the Third Order, but Rose here became sick, so we had to fly out to the Great Sage to cure her. He then sent us back to the city, and here we are now."

"That's an incredible story, though I do not believe that it is the full tale," replied Incarcerus. "However, that does not explain how your friend here was able to manipulate the plants like that."

"That Great Sage taught me," answered Rose.

"Very well; however, I still have more questions. For instance, what's your name?" he asked Adrian. Adrian gave Incarcerus his name, and then Rose gave hers. "And, Adrian, do you have any talents like Rose does?"

"I can summon lightning," shrugged Adrian. Incarcerus gasped.

"Of course! Everything fits!" he shouted excitedly. "You're the Lightseeker! The champion of the Third Order! Maltesque's second favorite hero!"

"Was I in the vision too?" inquired Adrian. Incarcerus nodded. "Cool! So, I think that Rose and I should be going now."

"Yes, Lightseeker! Absolutely!" exclaimed Incarcerus, suddenly eager to please. "But first, do you have any more questions?"

"Well, just one," began Adrian. "How old are you?"

"Nineteen. I turn twenty in a few weeks," answered Incarcerus. "The other four people that you saw were my sister, my brother, and my parents, who are also brother and sister."

"Your parents are related?" inquired Rose, shocked.

"Well, since Virda only locked one family away in this cave, um, yes, they are," answered Incarcerus. "Is that not normal?"

"Above ground, that's kind of looked down upon," frowned Adrian. "But I guess that there's really no other option, is there?" Incarcerus nodded.

A few moments later, Adrian and Rose were back in the tunnel, and Incarcerus was out of sight.

"Wouldn't that be awkward? I mean, to be married to your sibling?" asked Rose.

"Yeah, especially since I don't have one," laughed Adrian. "But I guess that they have no other way to survive. Still, that's kinda creepy."

"Yeah. Hey, Adrian, what do you mean that you don't have a sibling? What about Serena?" asked Rose confusedly. A feeling of cold dread rolled over Adrian.

"Oh my god. Serena! I completely forgot about her! I could have asked Kronos to free her earlier!" cried Adrian. "What kind of a brother am I? She was the reason I got into this mess in the first place!"

"Well, um, that's kind of, well... um... awkward, shall we say?" mused Rose. "Still, once we help Arrow, you can save her!""What if it's too late? What if by the time we're done helping Arrow, she's already, well... y'know... dead?"

"Then you know you tried your hardest," assured Rose consolingly. "And you'll have helped save a world."

"I guess you're right," sighed Adrian. "Even so, I still feel kind of bad about not mentioning her to Ulysses earlier. I guess you've sort of replaced her in my mind."

"What, as a maniacal tyrant who makes your life miserable?" laughed Rose.

"No, as a girl that I love," replied Adrian quickly. "Anyhow, we should be going. We need to help Arrow, remember?" Rose nodded, and she pointed them onto the right path, and they kept walking.

Eventually, they came out of the tunnel, and into daylight. Actually, they were at the very edge of the cloud cover, so they really were in daylight. It seemed that the night was now over, and the sun was high in the sky.

However, the sunlight swiftly vanished as they stepped under the dense foliage of the Poisonsap. It hadn't looked particularly inviting to Adrian when he had flown over it in Arrow's glider, and it looked even less inviting now that he was actually in it. Adrian saw some sort of green liquid dripping down the tree's bark, and he assumed that it was the poisonous sap which Falcon had mentioned back at that meeting of the Third Order of druids which had taken place so long ago.

However, it wasn't the trees that he was worried about. A poisonous Leocavia stepped out from a dense collection of bushes. It had some kind of stinger on its tail off of which some kind of orange acid dripped. It let out a low growl, and took a step towards Adrian. Adrian counted his lucky stars that it was only a juvenile, and not an adult, like they had run into in the Deadwood.

Adrian and Rose held their ground, and they both began to meditate. Suddenly, a branch of one of the surrounding trees began to whip the Leocavia. However that was nothing compared to the bolt of lightning which shot out of Adrian's fingertips uncertainly. It kind of wavered on its way, but it connected solidly, sending a shock throughout the Leocavia's body. It let out an agonized yowl, and ran away.

Adrian and Rose high-fived. "Great Job!" exclaimed Rose. "It's nice not to have to run away any more!"

"Yeah! I like having powers!" laughed Adrian. "So, that's one enemy down! Shall we continue onwards?"

"Yes, we shall," agreed Rose, and they kept walking.

***

A few moments later, they came to a rather familiar sight: a root sticking out of the ground.

"An ambassador!" smiled Adrian. "I thought that there weren't any more! I thought that we met them all!"

"Apparently not," mused Rose. "I suppose that the Great Sage might have forgotten about this one." The two of them walked up to it, and were met with little response.

"Ambassador?" inquired Adrian, tapping the root. No response. "Ambassador?" asked Adrian again, a bit more forcefully. "He's not responding," sighed Adrian, turning to Rose. "I think that we'd best just go on."

"Do you really?" hissed a voice from the root. It echoed in Adrian's head, and he began to feel slightly drowsy. "I apologize for being a bit slow in my response. Forgive me. It was very ungracious of me. On behalf of the Great Sage, I welcome you to the Poisonsap forest."

Adrian took a wary step back from the root. It looked black and withered, and not unlike the ones they had petrified in the Deadwood. The green sap that oozed from the rest of the trees also seeped from this ambassador. Adrian felt that this particular root was not to be trusted.

"Now then, Adrian, I have business to conduct with you," began the ambassador. "You see, I was ordered by the Great Sage to dispose of you."

"The Great Sage is our ally!" exclaimed Rose. "I don't believe you."

"Well, regardless," sneered the root, "I must dispose of you. Adrian, prepare to feel the wrath of the Poisonsap!" Suddenly, Adrian felt some sort of sticky material wrapping around him. He looked down, and saw that he was now partially covered in cobwebs. He looked up, and, to his horror, found a giant spider staring back at him. However, there seemed to be a shadow covering its head, and Adrian was unable to look upon its facial features.

Rose screamed in terror as she too saw the creature. She was also covered in silk, and a slightly smaller spider was attaching her to its back. Adrian fell backwards, knocked onto a different spider's back. The two smaller spiders scuttled off with the larger spider while the corrupted root laughed in the background. Adrian attempted to call up lightning to attack the spider with, but he discovered that his fear of spiders, great ever since he was a boy, prevented him from concentrating properly.

For the first time since he had left the Great Sage, Adrian actually considered the possibility that he might not make it. It had been a possibility that had become a constant in the Deadwood, but it had more or less vanished when he had trained in safety with the Great Sage. The transition back to taking death into consideration was not an easy one to make, but Adrian tried his best.

However, a fresh wave of fear engulfed him when the large spiders dropped him off in what he assumed was their home. It was a large cave wrapped entirely in spider webs, and a putrid stench engulfed the entire cave. Adrian saw skeletons littering the side of the cave, some wrapped in cobwebs. Adrian's resolve finally cracked when he saw the spider king. It was easily the size of a small bus. Adrian thanked his lucky stars that there was a shadow covering the thing's head. He had seen a picture of a spider's head before, and it was not a pretty sight.

Adrian shuddered in revulsion when the king spider spoke in a deep whispery voice. "Adrian Lightseeker," it whispered, "welcome to our humble abode. I am Arachnis, king of the Shadowweb Spiders. We have chosen to hide our faces from the world with the blessing of shadow. This blessing was bestowed to our ancestors by Kronos thousands of years ago. It is now our turn to repay the favor by eliminating his biggest enemy."

"Arachnis," began Adrian in a shaky voice, "why are you helping the ambassador? He works for the Great Sage, who opposes Kronos."

"That ambassador no longer serves the Great Sage," laughed Arachnis. "He serves his own dark purposes. He is an infection, slowly destroying the Great Sage. In but a few hundred years, the Great Sage will become as the corrupted ambassador is. However, that is far off."

Listening to Arachnis had calmed Adrian down a bit, as he was able to communicate with the spider, making it less of an unknown. He now attempted to call up light energy, and found that it was slowly coming. He desperately attempted to stall for time.

"So, Arachnis, why does the ambassador want us dead?" inquired Adrian. "Does the Great Sage truly wish for us to die?"

"I do not know," whispered Arachnis. "However, I do know this: that ambassador is not to be trusted."

Adrian now had enough light energy stored up to unleash a lightning attack. He let loose his stored up attack, and the light immediately destroyed what light destroys best: darkness. The veil of shadow was immediately torn off of Arachnis' face. Adrian glimpsed the unthinkable in that moment; the face of Arachnis was more terrifying than Shadius' voice, all the horrors of the Deadwood, and the thought of death itself wrapped into one. Word cannot describe the sheer hideousness bestowed upon Arachnis' features, nor the fear and horrors Adrian felt upon seeing it. Adrian immediately lost consciousness.

***

Adrian awoke to find himself and Rose lying on more cobwebs. He attempted to stand up, and found that he was still thoroughly encased in cobwebs. He attempted to move, and found that he was unable to. He tried to remember why he had fainted, and then he recalled seeing Arachnis' face. However, he could not recall what that face looked like, and he thanked whomever was in charge of luck for that. It would have been like seeing the fifth dimension all over again.

Oddly enough, Adrian didn't see any spiders around. He then realized that not only was he wrapped in cobwebs, he was also lying upon an intricately designed web, the sort which he usually admired for a few moments.

However, he felt no motivation to admire this one. He was suspended god knows how many feet in the air, and wrapped in a sticky thread. This, thought Adrian, is a bad situation.

Adrian would like to say that his mind raced to try to figure a way out at that moment, but instead his mind went totally blank. Suddenly, a slight jostle in the web told him that a spider was approaching. He held perfectly still, hoping that the spider would not spot him. Rose was still unconscious, and the spider ignored both of them, and went to investigate some of the other prey he had available.

Adrian looked straight up, and saw that there was no opening above him like he had hoped for. Adrian decided that his best bet would be to blind the spiders with a flash of light, then free himself and Rose with lightning, and then make a run for it.

Adrian squeezed his eyes shut, and gathered up the energy he needed. When he felt that he had amassed a sufficient amount, he let it loose in a burst of light so strong it made his closed eyes throb. He then used the rest of the energy he had amassed to cut the cobwebs that bound him. He gathered more as he carefully walked over to Rose, and cut her loose with a very precise bolt of lightning.

Rose awoke, and screamed as she saw her hideous captor. The spider, permanently (though Adrian did not know it) blinded, heard the voice, and lunged at it. Adrian sent another lightning bolt at it, but it missed, and hit one of the individual strands that was holding the entire web up. However, the web remained intact, for there were a good number of strands. Adrian gathered up all of the energy he could muster as he dodged the spider's clumsy lunge, grabbed Rose's arm to keep her safe, and then let loose all of the lightning.

There was an explosion of energy, and quite a few of the other strands holding the web up broke as well. As a result, the entire web plummeted to the ground.

Adrian and Rose braced themselves for the impact with the ground. The impact was jarring, at best, but they immediately regained their composure, and raced forwards. Adrian periodically let loose blasts of lightning, blinding the spiders. After a moment or two, Adrian realized that he was in familiar territory. They were near Arachnis' chamber, and Adrian warned Rose of that.

However, as they darted into the spider king's throne room, they found it empty. Adrian thought that to be strangely ominous.

The same deeply rooted instinct that had saved Adrian and James in the alley so many weeks ago kicked up again, and Adrian dodged to the side. A strand of spider web shot by, and Adrian saw Arachnis hanging upside down on the ceiling. Adrian gasped, caught off guard, and readied a lightning bolt.

However, Arachnis had other ideas. He dropped from the ceiling, aiming to land on Adrian. Adrian dodged to the side just in time to avoid being flattened. Arachnis hissed at Adrian and Rose, and lunged. Adrian loosed the bolt of lightning he had been saving at Arachnis' face, tearing away the veil of shadow, but also blinding the spider, who fell to the ground.

"Please... Lightseeker..." begged Arachnis. "Have... mercy. I'll... tell you... what you wish to know. The ambassador... was hired... by the corporate council... to defend their new... houses... that they're building." Adrian listened intently, though he had never believed for a moment that the Great Sage had been the one who had told the corrupted ambassador to dispose of him.

"We... were given the job... of destroying you..." wheezed the spider king. "We needed... to destroy you... to repay our creator... Kronos. However... I now see... that he does not.... deserve to be repaid... if he has done such things to you."

"What things?" inquired Adrian, confused.

"In the moment... you saw my face..." began Arachnis unsteadily, "I glimpsed... what he had... put you through, via your... memories. He does not... deserve... to be... repaid..." Arachnis gasped once more, and then he was still.

"Great!" exclaimed Adrian, throwing his arms up in the air. "We get someone who could get these spiders off our backs, and then he dies! Now the spiders are going to be more determined to kill us than ever."

Adrian and Rose left the corpse of Arachnis, and scurried out of the cave. They discovered that they were at the base of the cavernous cliffs, and not very far from where they had first entered the Poisonsap.

"Rose, I have an idea," mused Adrian. "I don't think that it would be smart to challenge the ambassador directly, but if we could cut off his connection to the Great Sage, then he would eventually shrivel up and die. He's a root, right? In that case, there should be an extension of some kind connecting him to the Sage. I think that if we destroy that extension, it would work."

"Well, how are we supposed to figure out where he connects to the Sage?"

inquired Rose. Adrian gave her a small grin. "Adrian, you're considering the possibility that I could, like, scan him or something, I'm sorry to let you down, but that's not what I can do."

"Okay, then. How about this? I could create a sphere of lightning around him, and that way, we'd destroy his connection with the Great Sage even though we don't know where it is," suggested Adrian. "I sort of managed to create a ball of lightning before, right? So why not again?"

"Well, I guess it sounds like a good plan," mused Rose. "A little outlandish, though. Do you really think it'll work?"

"Dunno," shrugged Adrian. "Worth a shot, though. Oh, yeah! We need to think of something for you to do!"

"Adrian, I'd be more than happy to sit this one out," sighed Rose. "But what did you have in mind?"

"Why don't you provide a distraction?" suggested Adrian eagerly. "That way, the ambassador won't see my attack coming until it's too late!"

"Fine," groaned Rose. "But if I get hurt, it's on your conscience." Adrian nodded, and the two of them found the path that they had been following before they had run into the ambassador.

Within a few minutes, the two adventurers had found the ambassador, and were positioned on opposite sides of the clearing in which he sat. Adrian signaled to Rose, and the attack began.

Rose reprogrammed the surrounding trees to beat the ambassador with their roots. The roots followed their directions wonderfully, and the ambassador cried out, "Curse you Rose! And curse you, disloyal spiders!"

"We're not disloyal," hissed a giant spider, stepping out from behind a tree. Four other spiders followed it. "Our leader was killed by the two brats, but we have appointed a new one to take his place, and destroy the two who killed his predecessor." The five spiders lunged at Rose, who screamed in terror.

Adrian let loose his pent-up light energy, and a sphere of lightning formed around the root. Suddenly, Adrian lost control of it, and it disintegrated into bolts of lightning, which hurdled themselves at any and all available targets. Rose defended herself by making two trees into a shield.

Adrian flung himself to the ground, and avoided being shocked. The spiders were not so lucky. They were dissolved into wisps of smoke by the attack.

After the lightning sphere had fully disappeared, Adrian pushed himself onto his feet. He saw a circle of smoldering dirt around the ambassador, and, to his satisfaction, a broken root. Not the ambassador, but the link between the ambassador and the Great Sage. Adrian's plan had worked.

He sprinted over to Rose to see if she was all right. She seemed fine, and she pushed herself to her feet. Adrian took her hand, and helped her up.

"Are you all right?" he asked. "I didn't know that..." Suddenly Adrian let go of her hand and jumped back as a small spark of lightning jolted out of his body. It was followed by several others. "Rose, what's going on?" asked Adrian cautiously. "What's happening to me?"

"I don't know, Adrian," frowned Rose. "Whatever it is, I hope it goes away. It's kinda creepy. Plus, I have no desire to have a boyfriend that randomly shocks me."

Adrian nodded, and kept a safe distance from her as they walked towards their destination. The rest of the trip passed without incident, as all wild creatures were deterred by the electricity randomly shooting out of Adrian's body.

Adrian stepped out of the Poisonsap Forest with a similar feeling of accomplishment as when he had finally made it to Twilight City the first time, though on a smaller scale.

Adrian and Rose walked towards the city, and reached it in a matter of minutes. They were immediately found by Falcon, who escorted them to the Third Order's new hideout.

17

The New Leader

Arrow landed his glider outside of his house, and dismounted. He took a step inside, and was tackled by two of the cops from earlier. The three of them fought for a moment, and Arrow came out on top. The two cops scrambled away in fear, and Arrow quickly walked down to the basement.

He anticipated the third cop's attack, and dealt him a sharp blow in the head. The cop crumpled to the floor, unconscious. However, Arrow paid no attention to him, and dashed over to Joshua, who lay on the floor. Arrow saw three bullet holes, and his world crashed down around him.

Suddenly, Joshua's eyes snapped open, and he coughed up blood. "Arrow..." he croaked. "I'm past saving. Please... just focus on the Third Order..." Joshua coughed once again. "Please, just focus on... the Third Order... and... if you get a chance... tell everyone... that... there's a... traitor..." Joshua ceased to talk, and a still look came over his features.

***

"Falcon, what's happened?" asked Adrian, who was being pulled along with Rose to the Third Order's new headquarters. "Why won't you tell us anything?"

"Please, Adrian, shut up!" commanded Falcon in a pleading voice. "I'll tell you why I can't talk now when we get to headquarters. So just shut up and walk!"

A few minutes later, Adrian and Rose were led into a small building, and Falcon opened up a secret hatch in the ground, and Adrian and Rose crawled in. They walked in silence through a tunnel for a while, and Falcon finally led them up into a different shack. Adrian then followed Falcon into a large skyscraper, after passing through security.

The three of them went into a conference room, and sat down. Falcon then sat down as well, and Arrow finally came into the room.

"Well, Arrow?" asked Adrian anxiously. "What happened?"

"Joshua is..." started Arrow, but he found himself unable to finish the statement.

"We understand, Arrow," whispered Rose comfortingly, putting her arm around Arrow. This action provoked a twitch of jealousy from Adrian, which was quickly tempered by the gravity of the situation, and he was left feeling shallow.

"No, you don't," snarled Arrow angrily. "How could you? Has anything like this ever happened to you?! How dare you insinuate that this pain can be felt by others, and not just me alone!?"

Rose backed off, deciding that it would be best just to let Arrow be. Suddenly, Blaise barged in, accompanied by his ever-present smirk. "Well, now that we're all here, I think that it's time that we get over our little loss, and focus on attacking the Poisonsap!"

Adrian felt a wave of anger wash over him, and saw that Rose shared it, and Arrow looked absolutely furious. However, it was Falcon who spoke up.

"Blaise, I think that it's time that you gave up your little masquerade!" he shouted, pushed to his limit. "We all know that you're a traitor, so you might as well give yourself up!"

"Me? A traitor?" asked Blaise quietly, seemingly shocked to the core. "How could you say that?"

"I believe that Adrian here has some evidence," whispered Falcon.

Adrian wasn't entirely sure what Falcon was talking about, but he decided to go with Adrian's first encounter with Blaise. "Well, for starters, Blaise has been spying on the Great Sage by torturing an ambassador. He served Necropheus, and he forced us to aid him in casting a spell that would have destroyed the Sage."

"I believe that's enough," whispered Arrow quietly. "Blaise, though I do not believe that you are a traitor, I shall assign a guard to you. He shall report back to us on your activities, and if you truly have betrayed us, then we will know of it. Also, on the off chance that you have betrayed us, we shall ban you from this meeting."

"That is a wise solution," admitted Falcon, regaining his composure. "However, we must turn to more important matters. We have secretly checked your apartment, Arrow, and we have discovered how they managed to track your brother down. It turns out that he triggered a hidden security system, and it informed the guards stationed in the surrounding areas to investigate. Therefore, Joshua's death was not the result of betrayal, so we shall let the matter rest for now."

"So, should I go now, or what?" inquired an irritated Blaise. "I've got things to do, you know." Falcon nodded, and Blaise strode away.

"Moving on, we should now discuss the attack on the Poisonsap," suggested Arrow. "Last night, I saw something interesting while flying to the city." Adrian and Rose motioned for him to continue. "I saw five giant spiders departing the building site. Does this mean anything to any of you?"

Adrian spoke up. "Indeed. On our way through the Poisonsap, a corrupted ambassador of the Great Sage ordered a clan of giant spiders to kidnap us. We were taken to their cave, where we slew their king, Arachnis. The other spiders vowed to destroy us, and help the corrupted ambassador, who pledged his services to the corporate council. We'll have to fight them when we attack the housing development."

"Do you recall the name of the spider tribe?" inquired Falcon. "It is imperative that we know!"

"They were called the Shadowweb spiders," replied Rose. "Arachnis told us."

"Interesting. I had thought their existence to be a mere legend," mused Falcon. "Well, I have heard that there is but one source in the world that gives information on the Shadowwebs. Adrian, may we see *Legend of Darkness*?"

Adrian nodded, and looked around for his bag only to realize that he did not have it. "I'm sorry. When the spiders kidnapped us, they must have taken our bags."

"Falcon, how important is it that we have the information on the Shadowwebs?" inquired Arrow.

"Very," frowned Falcon. "I've heard terrible rumors about their strength and power. We should not progress with our planning until we have that book."

"Very well. Tomorrow, I'll fly to the Shadowweb's cave, and get it back for you," promised Arrow. "I mean, if it's that vital to the success of our cause."

"It is," assured Falcon. "Anyhow, It's late, and I don't think that any of us got any sleep last night. We should all turn in." Adrian nodded, and failed to stifle a yawn.

***

Adrian sat on his bed, unable to sleep. He couldn't stop thinking about Joshua, and he felt incredibly sorry for Arrow. He wondered what it was like to lose someone he cared about, and desperately hoped that it would never happen to him. He was also sorry that he didn't have anyone to express his thoughts to. Deep thoughts should not be left in the mind.

As if on cue, Rose knocked on the door. She was wearing a silvery nightgown, and it was the first time Adrian had seen her wear anything other than what she had on when Kronos had kidnapped the two of them.

"Adrian?" she asked, walking in cautiously. "I'm sorry if I woke you. I just couldn't get to sleep. So much has happened in the past few days, and it's difficult to absorb it."

"Yeah, I guess," sighed Adrian. "But Rose, we're two children from Earth who were kidnapped by the servant of an ancient evil god, and it turned out the servant was your father. We were brought here to Maltesque because I went insane due to something that doesn't normally exist, and a bomb of air exploded, sending us into a river. If that alone isn't difficult for you to absorb, then I fail to see why the last two days have shocked you."

"Yeah," laughed Rose. "Well, anyways, I guess what I mean is, I find it difficult to believe that... well... I'm not sure. I suppose I just wanted to talk to you to get my thoughts out."

"I know what you mean, Rose," smiled Adrian. "I was also up thinking. I can't help but feel sorry for Arrow. I mean, just when everything is going so well, to have your brother die..."

The two lapsed into an uncertain silence, when suddenly the wind began to howl, and Adrian and Rose both jumped. They laughed for a few minutes, but then the solemnity of Arrow's predicament returned them to their somber state.

Adrian cleared his throat, preparing to suggest that maybe the two of them should go to sleep, but Rose suddenly burst out, "Why, Adrian? Why is the world so cruel to the side of good? The evildoers seem to have it easy, I guess. Why is that?"

"Because the world isn't good, like us," suggested Adrian. "Not this world, at least. But if we can help the Third Order, then this world will promote good and order, as opposed to evil and chaos, like it does now."

"Of course, there are other evil worlds," mused Rose, an idea suddenly dawning upon her. "But Kronos can travel between them using darkness, right? Then maybe you can travel between them using light!"

"So what are you driving at here?" inquired Adrian. "Do you have some kind of an idea?"

"Well, what if, once we finish fixing Maltesque, we help other worlds like it?" suggested Rose eagerly. "I think that would be a great thing to do with our lives!"

"Well sure, but first I'd need to figure out how to travel between worlds," pointed out Adrian. "Well, I suppose we could ask Kronos, though I imagine that the discussion would go somewhat like this: 'Hi. I'm your worst enemy. Could you please tell me how to teleport?' And then Kronos would say something like, 'Curse you, Adrian! You have escaped my master for the last time!'

Then we'd fight, and I wouldn't get the information."

"I suppose," sighed Rose. "Well, maybe the Great Sage could teach you. Either way, don't you think that it's a great idea?"

"Yeah," admitted Adrian. "Well, we should probably get some sleep. See you tomorrow."

"Good night, Adrian," whispered Rose, kissing him on the lips. Rose walked out of the room, and then Adrian fell asleep with ease.

***

Arrow awoke the next morning from a fitful night's sleep. The events of his flight after finding Joshua dead had haunted his nightmares, and his mind suddenly flashed back to the worst version: what had actually happened.

***

Arrow turned on the policeman that had attempted to attack him earlier, and furiously beat him with his fists. After a few minutes, the policeman stopped resisting, and Arrow left him unconscious on the floor.

Arrow ran outside to his glider, and turned it on with the push of a pedal. He rose into the air, and flew towards the building of the men he knew to be responsible: the corporate council.

As he passed by on his glider, he activated one of his air bombs, and threw it in through a window. A few seconds later, it exploded, a councilman hurtling towards the street. Suddenly, Arrow saw something dark on the edge of his vision, and then—

***

No, thought Arrow. I can't think about that. I need to focus on my mission.

Arrow walked away from his bed, and realized that he had fallen asleep in his clothes. He walked out of his bedroom, and down a hallway. He stepped into an elevator, and rode down to the ground.

Arrow stepped out of the Third Order's new headquarters, and walked over to his glider. He kicked the ignition pedal, and the glider blasted off, rocketing into the atmosphere. Arrow directed it towards the Poisonsap.

He observed that the canopy was too thick for him to find the entrance to the cave from above, so he decided to fly closer to the ground. He flew out of the Poisonsap before reversing himself, and gliding back into the Poisonsap.

Arrow flew barely three feet off the ground, but going was slow, due to the fact that he couldn't always fit between the trees, and thus he needed to backtrack, and find a different route.

Without warning, a Poisonous Leocavia adult leapt at him, and had Arrow been flying just the smallest bit slower, the cat would have undoubtedly decimated him. Arrow was angered by the attempt on his life, and he swirled his glider around.

Arrow had never used some of the features that Joshua had insisted on adding to his glider, but he figured that this was as good a time as any to test them out. His glider had a very sleek control panel, and there were four buttons he had never pressed. They were dark shades of red, blue, green, and yellow.

Arrow pressed the blue button, and a small needle protruded from the front of the glider. Arrow then flew at the Leocavia, and electricity burst from the tip of the needle. The Leocavia's hairs stood on end, and it let out a stricken mewl. The cat stumbled away from Arrow in a daze.

Arrow felt vaguely sickened by the exchange, as he had always had a soft spot for cats. However, he pushed the matter from his mind, and continued onwards.

Suddenly, Arrow caught a movement from the corner of his eye. He pulled his glider in that direction, and looked carefully around. Once again, he saw a small movement just at the edge of the foliage.

Arrow cautiously edged his glider forwards, keeping an eye out. Without warning, a barbarian leaped at Arrow.

"Die! Diediedie!" he shouted, flailing his arms about. "Die! Kill you, yes I will!"

Arrow recognized the strange use of the phrase 'yes I will', and realized, with a start, that this was not the first time he had seen this man. He reeled back, but suddenly an idea dawned on him, and he pressed the dark yellow button on his control pad, and a gas billowed out of the front of his glider, enveloping the man. The old man fell to the ground, coughing, and Arrow picked up the body of Democritus, and tied it to the bottom his glider.

***

After ridding himself of his cargo, Arrow headed towards the Shadowweb Spider's cave. He flew inside, and his glider was immediately caught in a web. Arrow found himself unable to move, as he too was entangled in the web. However, Arrow was able to move his arm enough to press the green button on his glider.

Air exploded from the glider, tearing apart the web. Arrow pushed the glider to full speed, and flew towards the back of the cave.

***

"Has no one seen Arrow?!" exclaimed Falcon, at the end of his patience. "I can't take it! We just lost Joshua, and we can't afford to lose Arrow, as well!"

"Hey, at least we know where Blaise is," frowned Adrian. "And I told you, Arrow must have just left to go and get *Legend of Darkness*! What's the worst that could have happened?"

"He was terribly distraught yesterday," sighed Falcon. "I just hope he didn't decide to join Joshua."

"Even Arrow wasn't quite that upset," reassured Adrian. "Either way, he's not here right now, so we might as well start without him."

"I suppose you're right," replied Falcon. "But Arrow is the only one who knows the battle plan!"

"Not true!" protested Adrian. "I helped him work on it! I know it just as well as he does!"

"Regardless, we need to find the actual paper with the plan on it," pointed out Falcon. "I don't suppose you know where it is, do you?"

"I have a theory," proposed Rose. "I mean have you checked his room?"

"Yes, yes," waved Falcon impatiently. "I looked there first. So where else would it be?"

"The only place that Arrow considers safe," mused Adrian. "He must have kept it in his glider."

"Well that's gone, so we're no better off now!" exclaimed Falcon. "Let's face it, we need Arrow for this meeting!"

"And he's here," grinned Arrow, walking into the room. "I've got the battle plan right here, along with *Legend of Darkness*. So, do we start now?"

"Yes," nodded Falcon. "We've waited too long, anyhow. The next lecture is two days from now, and we need to have the battle plan ready. So, what does it say about the Shadowweb Spiders in the book?"

"Well, it says here that they can never be looked directly in the face, for it will drive any man mad," read Arrow aloud. "However, their faces are covered by a veil of shadow which cannot be penetrated, except by the power of the descendants of Photosia, like Adrian."

"So then they plan to use the spiders as shields!" exclaimed Arrow. "If the spider's masks of shadow can only be penetrated by Adrian's lightning, then we can't use lightning attacks because the spider's faces will drive the soldiers mad!"

"So what do you propose that we do?" inquired Adrian. "I mean, our strategy was heavily dependent upon me."

"I guess that we can't use you," sighed Arrow. "I dunno. Maybe we should just call the whole thing off..."

"Do you think that Joshua would have liked to have heard that?" inquired

Falcon sharply. "He gave his life for this cause, and you're just going to give up when we run into one complication? I think that if we're going to be led by you, you need to set a better example for everyone else!"

"There's no need to be so harsh!" exclaimed Adrian. "Arrow's a good guy, and he's been through a lot!"

"Actually, I have a confession to make," sighed Arrow. Arrow opened his mouth as if to speak, seemed to think better of it, but then burst out, "I haven't felt like myself since Joshua died, and I don't know if I should be in control of the group."

"Arrow, don't talk like that!" exclaimed Rose. "You should totally run the group! You helped found it!"

"Well, I suppose you're right," answered Arrow. "But, even so, I would like for you three to make the adjustments to the plan without me."

"But you need to present it to the other members the day after tomorrow!" exclaimed Falcon. "If anyone here needs to know the plan here, it's you!"

"So show it to me the day before the meeting, and then the following day we'll launch the attack," suggested Arrow. "I don't think I should be in charge of this!"

"Fine," muttered Adrian. "However, I don't believe that you're not yourself. You seem fine to me."

"Believe me, Adrian," whispered Arrow to himself as he left the room. "You're a lot better off without me knowing the plan."

***

"Is it just me, or was Arrow acting a tad, shall we say, unusual just now?" inquired Rose.

"He's not in his right mind," sighed Falcon. "He recognizes this, and doesn't trust himself as a result. That seems like the most reasonable solution to me."

"I suppose," mused Adrian. "So anyways, I guess we should be working on the battle plan, should we not?"

"Very well," said Falcon matter-of-factly. "If you can't use your light powers, then we'd need to completely redo the plan."

"Who says I don't have to use my powers?" inquired Adrian. "If we could take out the spiders first, then there'd be no problem."

"Well, how do we destroy the spiders?" asked Falcon. "From what you two told me, they sound very tough. I don't think that an ordinary soldier would be able to kill one of them, let alone an entire defense force."

"We don't need an ordinary soldier to do it," smiled Adrian. "We've got Rose. She can pick off the spiders from farther away, and then the rest of us rush in afterwards."

"Doesn't that kind of put me at high risk?" inquired Rose skeptically. "It's not that I'm afraid, I just think that it's a bad idea to put our key to victory right into the enemies clutches."

"You wouldn't be completely defenseless," protested Adrian. "According to Arrow, there's one battalion that's slightly smaller than the others. We could surround you with that battalion. What do you think?"

"Well, what was the small unit doing before?" asked Falcon.

"It was in the middle of a bunch of stronger units, adding to them," explained Adrian. "However, I think that there's no problem if we move it."

"I guess it wouldn't hurt too much," replied Falcon. "But doesn't that leave us a big hole in the middle?"

"Well, yeah," frowned Adrian. "Does that matter?"

"No," mused Falcon, a grin coming over his face. "In fact, it could help us! If we're being rushed by enemies, then we could split open, and they'd be trapped!"

"I like that idea!" exclaimed Rose. "It's unique! Plus, it means that I'm probably not going to die!"

"So that's settled!" smiled Falcon, clapping his hands together. "So moving on to the next topic, what are we going to do about the speech tomorrow? Everyone is used to Joshua talking to them, and I'm not sure they'd listen to Arrow."

"So we tell them what happened to Joshua, and hope that they'll listen," suggested Adrian. "Plus, we point out that we'll be avenging his memory."

"I suppose that is the best option," answered Falcon. "Well, that's all for today. I'll write Arrow's speech, and he'll give it the day after tomorrow. Then the next day, we attack the Poisonsap."

"So what should we do for the rest of the day?" asked Adrian confusedly. ""And what do we do tomorrow?"

"Whatever you want," replied Falcon nonchalantly. "It doesn't really matter, as long as you stay out of trouble."

"Yeah, because we're really good at staying out of trouble," laughed Rose. "Anyhow, maybe we could go sightseeing. I haven't really seen much of the city."

"That sounds like a good idea," agreed Falcon. "You two aren't on the wanted list, unlike me and Arrow, so you should be fine."

Adrian and Rose stood up, and walked away.

***

Rose sighed as she stepped out the door of the skyscraper. It had been so long since she'd had any sort of free time that she'd forgotten what it was like.

Adrian was having similar issues, though he'd had a good deal more spare time in his life than Rose. Plus, he certainly recalled what it was like, as opposed to Rose. After all, Rose had been under the control of Shadius since she was about two or three. So, for the first time in years, Rose finally had the opportunity to do whatever she chose, and she intended to use that to its full extent.

The two looked about them, trying to decide what to do first. Falcon had given them a couple of destinations to check out. The closest to the skyscraper seemed to be the library, and they decided to head off in that direction.

The two walked in silence, absorbing the sights and sounds of the city. A vendor seemed to be selling some kind of new transmitter device that seemed suspiciously like a cell phone. Adrian wondered if Kronos had something to do with the development of the device, as he was one of the three people on Maltesque who had knowledge of a cell phone.

He ignored the vendor, and continued onwards. A store was advertising its newest product, a portable computer the size of one's palm. It struck Adrian how the technology of Maltesque was about equal to that of Earth, which he found odd, as Maltesque had been given an extra three thousand years to improve upon the technology. Adrian figured that it had probably taken them about that much time to figure out how the technology that they already had worked.

Rose noticed the library first. It was old and somewhat run down, but not overly so. It looked like something Adrian would have expected to find in England. It had a rustic look, and that made it stand out from the buildings that surrounded it.

Adrian and Rose stepped into the library with looks of awe on their faces. It was essentially all one room, but it was divided by incredible tall shelves of books. Adrian estimated it to be about a quarter the height of the Empire State Building. There were immensely tall ladders that ascended the shelves, and chairs littered the floor. Adrian and Rose each climbed a different ladder, found a book they thought looked interesting, and read well into the afternoon.

*****

Around three, Adrian and Rose dragged themselves out of the library, and headed toward their next destination. They were headed for the Five Towers, which housed the corporate council. Adrian had thought that it would be interesting to see what their enemy's stronghold looked like. Adrian recalled that it had been the Four Towers up until Kronos had come, and then, once he had added himself to the council, they had changed the name to the Five Towers.

Adrian and Rose stood at the foot of the first tower, and started up at it. It was easily fifty stories tall, and Adrian thought that it looked a bit taller than any skyscraper he had ever seen. Scarily, it was the shortest one. Adrian thought that the prospect of launching an attack on any one of them would be a formidable task.

A tour guide led them through the bottom floor, and Adrian found it to be incredibly boring. All there was to see was a bunch of people working at desks. Adrian found it difficult to believe that these were the people who Arrow had sworn vengeance against.

By the time their tour was finished, Adrian and Rose were bored to the bone, and very tired. Adrian noticed that Kronos' building was the only one that did not offer tours.

***

The next morning, Arrow awoke from another bad night's sleep. He rolled out of bed, and changed clothes, as he had once again fallen asleep in them. Arrow stumbled sleepily towards the door, and took the elevator to the conference room. He recalled that it was the day when he would give his speech to the soldiers that he would lead into battle, and wondered what the battle plan was.

A few minutes later, Falcon walked into the room as well, and sat down next to Arrow. Falcon pulled the new battle plan out of his pocket, and laid it out on the table.

"Well, there you go, Arrow," smiled Falcon. "Our new battle plan. Rose takes out the spiders, and then Adrian sweeps up the rest of them. What do you think?"

"I like it," answered Arrow. "It's creative, and not something I would have thought up on my own. Thank you, Falcon."

"Well, it was mostly Adrian's ideas," replied Falcon modestly. "He seemed to know the plan about as well as you do. So, are you ready for your speech?"

"Yes I am," grinned Arrow. "But, just to clarify, where is it?"

"It's in a different old warehouse," sighed Falcon. "I didn't think it would be safe to tell you while you were still out of your mind with grief. However, you seem fine now."

"And I feel better too!" laughed Arrow, though he had barely gotten four hours of sleep that previous night. "So, I've got the final draft of my speech all finished, and I've practiced it as much as possible."

"Glad to hear it," smiled Falcon. "Anyhow, we'd best be going. Adrian and Rose can take care of themselves, and they didn't really feel it was necessary for them to come, so they're staying."

"Say, Falcon, are you sure this meeting is safe?" inquired Arrow. "So far your security measures have left a bit to be desired. Granted, you've kept this building pretty safe so far."

"That wasn't entirely my doing," admitted Falcon. "Most of our supplies come from a company under the control of the corporate council, and they helped keep this building secret from the council. You see, such a small thing like the sale of a building is handled by subordinates, and so our allies managed to fake it, so that both sides have an explanation."

"So they can't find us?" asked Arrow, just to clarify.

"Ideally," replied Falcon. "Just as long as Blaise doesn't get the chance to betray us again."

"Falcon, Blaise wasn't the traitor," responded Arrow slowly. "When Joshua was hacking the council's website, some of our information was accidentally transmitted to their account."

Falcon let those words sink in. They implied that Blaise was innocent, a conclusion that he had been reaching as well. "Very well," sighed Falcon. "I shall allow Blaise to fire his security guard, should he choose to do so."

***

Adrian and Rose strode up to their quarry's door, and knocked three times. After a few minutes, and a couple of "Be right there!"s, Blaise opened the door. "Oh, hello," he smiled, opening the door. "Would you two like to come in?"

"Yes," replied Adrian. "We would. By the way, what happened to your security guard?"

"Falcon let me fire him," smirked Blaise. "He was cramping my style." Adrian and Rose stepped inside, and Blaise shut the door. Adrian immediately prepared a lightning attack, and Rose searched the surrounding area for some kind of plant. When Blaise turned around, he held a knife in his hand.

"Now Blaise, no funny business," commanded Adrian, sending a few sparks flying from his palm as a warning. "We just want to talk to you."

"Very well," sighed Blaise, dropping the knife. "What do you wish to talk about?"

"Look, Blaise, it's just us. You don't need to keep up this phony act," stated Adrian firmly. "We just want to know why you're helping the Third Order. After all, you tried to kill the Great Sage, along with Necropheus."

"The truth is," began Blaise, "I never did work for Necropheus. I always was a spy for the Third Order."

"Then explain what you did to the ambassadors," demanded Adrian.

"Me? What did *you* do to them?" inquired Blaise. "I was just being a good spy. You two, on the other hand, destroyed the Deadwood."

"All right," began Rose. "We've heard enough. Let's go, Adrian" Adrian, confused, followed Rose out the door, keeping a watchful eye on Blaise as he did so.

"Why'd you make us leave?" he hissed. "We didn't find out anything!"

"That's because there's nothing to find out," shrugged Rose. "Do you really think he'd tell us? Plus, he was trying to turn us against ourselves, like he did in the Deadwood!"

"So, do you think he's really helping the Third Order?" inquired Adrian. "I mean, doesn't it seem a little unlikely to you?"

"I think the only person that Blaise cares about helping is himself," whispered Rose. "I don't trust him, but I think that it'll be all right if we ignore him."

***

Arrow waited for the crowd to quiet down before beginning his speech. However, the crowd seemed to have no desire to do that of its own accord, so Arrow resorted to shouting into the microphone at the top of his lungs.

"HEY! UP HERE, ALL OF YOU!" he shouted, and the crowd settled down. "As you all can see, I'm not Joshua." There was irritated murmuring from the crowd, and a couple of people got up to leave. "I am, however, his brother, Arrow. I believe that he mentioned me in one of his lectures."

"Why isn't Joshua giving the lecture?" demanded someone from the crowd.

"Joshua is not giving today's lecture because... because he can't," shouted Arrow. "He can't give the lecture because he's dead. The corporate council dispatched three policemen to kill him!" There was shocked murmuring from the crowd, and quite a few people (mostly girls, Arrow noticed) broke down in tears. "However, we must not lose hope! I myself nearly gave in to despair, but his death must not be in vain! This crime will not go unpunished, and rest assured, we *will* avenge his death!"

"Why should we listen to you!?" shouted a young woman from the crowd. "We're lost without Joshua! He was the only thing that held the group together! That kept our resolve strong!"

"Which is why we must not let his memory go to waste!" replied Arrow, his voice wavering. "We must strike back! We must defeat the corporate council!" There were yells of approval from the crowd. "We all know that Joshua had mentioned an assault on the housing development in the Poisonsap forest. Well, that assault is tomorrow, and we shall prevail! All of you who signed up shall report to our hideout on 777 Enterprise Lane. Thanks to some computer magic by Joshua, we acquired a skyscraper to use as a secret base. You should report there to receive a crash-course in army training."

There were roars of approval from the crowd. "That will be all," ended Arrow. "All members of our new army, come with me. Everyone else, there's nothing else for you to see. You should return home. The next lecture is Friday of next week, ten days from now."

Arrow left the warehouse, followed by about a thousand people. They were all directed by Falcon's men to different routes, and in ten or so minutes, they all converged back at the Third Order's new base. Arrow gave a description of the battle plan, and the men were assigned to their battalions. The training began.

18

The Second War Begins

The day broke clear and bright upon the first day of the Second War of the Druids. Everyone was awakened right on schedule by the buzz of an alarm clock from each room in the hideout.

Arrow had already been awake, and he jumped out of bed, and raced over to the elevator, and descended down to Falcon's room. Falcon greeted him in the doorway.

"Well, today's the day," he smiled. "Today, our war begins. Are all of the troops ready?"

"Yes," replied Arrow. "We squeezed in all of the training that we needed to yesterday. They're as ready as they'll ever be."

"Good," said Falcon. "However, our main priority right now is to get them out of the city. I believe that the best way would be to fall back on the underground tunnel network."

"Good idea," mused Arrow. "Do they lead outside the city?"

"They lead outside the city proper, yes," answered Falcon. "And I've heard that the people on the outskirts are very big supporters of our cause."

"So is there an entrance to the tunnel nearby?" inquired Arrow.

"There is," smiled Falcon. "And once everyone's ready, we should go. It's best to strike early in the morning."

***

Arrow glanced at the entrance to the tunnel that would spirit the army out to the outskirts of the city skeptically. The tunnel was old and run down, like the library that Adrian and Rose had visited a few days ago. However, there was no alternative. He ordered his battalions into it, and led them through.

It was a relatively short journey, but it was nerve-wracking for Arrow. He had always been slightly touched by claustrophobia, and he felt as if the walls were closing in on him. However, he couldn't display the slightest bit of fear in front of his army, for he had yet to prove his worth in some of their eyes, and Arrow knew this.

After a half hour or so, the tunnel opened into an open field. There were a couple of farmers, but they gave the army a wide berth. Soon, they were upon the Poisonsap Forest.

The housing development was still a ways off, so they continued their trek. Regardless, the men grew tense, and Arrow had to keep some of them in line using harsher methods than he would have liked to.

Adrian, Rose, and Falcon led the party. Arrow flew above them on his glider, swooping down to reprimand a soldier when necessary.

"How much farther is it?" inquired Rose, carefully attempting not to whine, for she didn't think that Falcon would appreciate it. "Well? How much farther?"

"About a mile or so," estimated Falcon. "I'm feeling a bit tense. What happens if we lose?"

"Then we tried our hardest, and we failed," shrugged Adrian. "But even if we do, our message is out. More people will rebel, and then we'll really have won. The people of Maltesque aren't going to stand for the only source of food in the world being destroyed."

"True," mused Falcon. "Anyhow, I'm glad Blaise isn't here."

"So are we," agreed Adrian. "He has a way of making one unsure of oneself, if you know what I mean."

"I suppose," sighed Falcon. "So, what exactly did he do to you in the Deadwood? I've been wondering since the first meeting that you were at."

"Well, he forced us to attack ambassadors of the Great Sage," began Rose. "But that's not what hurt us the most. He, well, I'm not sure how to put this, but he made us hate ourselves. He made us completely despise what we were, what we had been, and what we would be."

"So he emotionally destroyed you?" inquired Falcon. "I guess that's not the worst thing in the world."

"I suppose not," mused Adrian. "However, I doubt that it's ever been done to you, so you can't really say much about it."

"Well, that's all in the past," smiled Falcon. "Arrow and I have agreed to trust him for now. Do you two agree with that?"

"Well, I think that Blaise will always side with the strongest party," shrugged Adrian. "So if we win, yes, I believe that we can trust him for the time being. So, I suppose I should drop back into the ranks soon, right?"

"Yes, that's probably a good idea," replied Falcon. "After all, we can't have you in the front."

Adrian left the front, and Falcon turned to speak to Rose. "Y'know, Rose, we haven't really had a chance to chat one-on-one. I've been meaning to ask you, why were you kidnapped along with Adrian?"

"Well, Shadius, the deity of darkness, used me to spy on Adrian ever since I was two or so," explained Rose. "However, Adrian freed me from Shadius' control, and when Kronos grabbed Adrian, he also grabbed me by accident. He was then going to bring me to Genesis, but then Arrow saved both of us, and we wound up floating down the river on a piece of driftwood."

"Intriguing story," mused Falcon. "This Shadius sounds like a very shady character, no pun intended."

"He most certainly does," agreed Rose.

***

As Adrian allowed a good deal of the army pass him, Arrow flew down to talk to him.

"So, Adrian, it's all on your friend Rose," he smiled. "Do you think we've got a shot?"

"I trust Rose more than I trust myself," reassured Adrian. "If anyone can carry our offensive, it's her. You've got nothing to worry about, Arrow."

"Glad to hear it," grinned Arrow. "It's quite a plan that you guys cooked up. I like the circle plan that you guys came up with. So, just let me make sure I've got this straight. If an enemy unit charges us, we open up, and they find themselves surrounded?"

"Pretty much," nodded Adrian.

"Sounds good to me!" smiled Arrow. "So, I guess I'd better fly on ahead and check things out." Adrian nodded, and Arrow flew off. Adrian began to casually chat with the soldiers, but they seemed to patronize him a bit.

Arrow let out a shout signifying that he had found the clearing where they were working on building houses. The main body of soldiers fell back, but the small defense force and Rose kept on going forwards.

Arrow squinted ahead, and he thought his eyes detected a small shimmering strand of light, but then it was gone. He kept his glider moving slowly forwards, and kept his eyes open. Suddenly, Arrow lost his balance as his glider suddenly snagged on a thin yet strong strand of spider web. He plummeted to the ground, and looked up in horror to see five Shadowwebs rush towards Rose's small defense force.

***

Rose heard a small cry, and whirled around to see Arrow suddenly drop to the ground, his glider spinning helplessly in the air, caught on some strand of something. Without warning, her guards screamed, and she whirled around to see five Shadowwebs rushing the small party.

A scream tore itself from her lips as she saw the gigantic spiders overrunning the small group. One broke through, and flipped Rose onto its back. Another spider tied a thick cord around Rose, binding her to the spider. Rose screamed again as she felt the spider's hairs brush against he back, where they were tied together. The spider rushed forwards, carrying her away. She turned around, and saw the army fall into madness behind her,

Guards that had hidden themselves in the surrounding foliage burst out, and began attacking the army. Chaos decimated the ranks, and it became every man for himself.

***

Adrian fought his way through the chaos, warding off blows from friend and foe alike. He was attempting to use his light powers, but they seemed to be slow in coming. However, he managed to make his way over to Arrow. As he approached the fallen figure, a pain accosted his arm, and he looked down to see a knife mark. He sprang back, and saw his assailant. Suddenly, he encountered an obstacle he had not felt for weeks: a headache. His assailant was a necrossis.

Adrian backed away in terror, but some of the lightning he had been attempting to build finally broke through, and a small spark sent the necrossis flying backwards. Adrian darted away from the necrossis, and knelt by Arrow.

"Arrow!" shouted Adrian, shaking his comrade. "Please, wake up!"

"Wha... what happened?" asked Arrow, shaking his head. "What's going on?"

"They knew we were coming!" shouted Adrian angrily. "They attacked you, and captured Rose!"

"They've got Rose?!" exclaimed Arrow, leaping to his feet. "She was the key to our strategy! Without her, we're doomed!"

"I know," murmured Adrian. "We've got to get her. Is your glider okay?"

"I think so," mused Arrow, dodging a stray blow from a soldier. "It's still stuck in the spider web, though. We'd need to get it down."

Suddenly, Adrian's headache returned, causing light to surge to the surface. He let loose an unintentional blast of lightning which barely missed Arrow. Then, without warning the headache disappeared. Though Adrian would not realize this until later, it was due to the fact that the headache was not from the interaction between darkness and the fifth dimension, but rather from the darkness being forced to affect Adrian's brain differently due to the Great Sage's meddling.

Regardless, Adrian regained control of his senses. He saw that the necrossis was but two feet away, and tried to force some lightning out of his system. However, the lightning was slow in coming, so Adrian ducked behind a soldier fighting for the Third Order. The soldier was rapidly thrown aside by a tendril of darkness.

Adrian ran towards Arrow and the tree where the invisible spider web originated. However, he felt something behind him, and whirled around to see the necrossis standing in front of him. Adrian attempted to summon lightning, but it refused to come once again. Adrian began to lose patience, but turned and ran again.

Suddenly, a tendril of darkness entered his body, and Adrian felt the necrossis attempt to possess him. He suddenly found himself in the desert he had dreamed about and seen when the Great Sage fixed his mind.

Standing across from him was the necrossis. Adrian attempted to summon light, and found that he was now able to. The necrossis rushed him, and he let loose the blast of lightning he had been saving. However, the necrossis was not completely destroyed, and continued forwards.

Adrian wished that there was more distance between himself and the necrossis, and the necrossis was suddenly hurdled backwards. I must be dreaming, thought Adrian. This is probably all happening in my mind.

Though Adrian did not entirely realize it, he and the necrossis were both in his mind, with Adrian defending it, and the necrossis attempting to take it over. Somehow Adrian was actually now inside his own mind.

Adrian was now conscious that he controlled the battleground, and began to experiment. He created a huge fist of sand, which descended upon the necrossis, crushing it beneath the sheer volume. However, the necrossis seemed relatively unharmed.

Adrian began his attempt to figure out how to remove the necrossis from his mind. He tried launching him into the air, swallowing him into the ground, and destroying him with lightning, but he remained relatively unscathed.

Suddenly Adrian was hit with an idea, figuratively speaking, as opposed to the necrossis, who was quite literally being hit with ideas. Adrian charged at the necrossis, and attacked him with light at close range. Not lightning, but just light. The necrossis seemed unhurt, but Adrian continued his assault.

Adrian felt the scenery change, and was suddenly engulfed in darkness. He had succeeded in pushing the fight into the necrossis' mind. Adrian suddenly retreated, and returned to reality.

He did not know how long it had taken, but he certainly would not have guessed under a second, which was, in fact, the amount of time spent on the mental battle. However, it had been just enough time to build up the lightning to the critical point, and it now poured from Adrian's fingertips, blasting the necrossis. After a scream of pain, the necrossis vanished, disintegrated into a wisp of smoke.

Adrian stood there for a moment, regaining his bearings. Lightning was still jumping from his fingertips, but this did not present a problem for him. He ran over to the tree where Arrow's glider was caught, and sent a bolt of lightning at the thin spider web, tearing it apart. The glider fell to the ground, and Arrow quickly turned it right side up. He and Adrian jumped on, and it lifted off the ground.

They flew towards the small party of spiders departing with Rose. They were about three quarters of the way across the clearing, and moving fairly slowly. They saw Adrian and Arrow coming, and let out a message in the language of the Shadowwebs, which sounds like a jumble of clicking to human ears. However, the spiders understood it perfectly, and the ones hidden in the trees leapt at Adrian and Arrow.

Adrian shot bolts of lightning at every one of them, and the lightning bolts began to sort of accumulate into a cloud. Adrian found that he could direct this lightning cloud, not unlike the one in his mind, like he could direct the lightning bolts that they had previously been.

Adrian kept the spiders away from the glider in this manner. "Drop me off!" he shouted to Arrow, who nodded in agreement. Arrow lowered the glider, and Adrian poured all the strength he could spare into the lightning cloud. When they were directly over the spiders, Adrian jumped off the glider, and surrounded himself with the lightning cloud. Adrian plummeted to the ground, a meteor of lightning descending upon the unsuspecting Shadowwebs. He grabbed Rose's hand, so as to protect her, but the spiders had no such defense. Adrian squeezed his eyes shut so he would not have to gaze upon the spider's faces, and Rose, assuming that Adrian did it for a reason, closed her eyes as well. Encouraged by this act of heroism, the soldiers began to fight with renewed strength, and the guards began to second-guess themselves.

Rose was caught off guard by the unsuspected turn of events, but she reacted well. She reached out with her mind to the plants surrounding them, and commanded them to attack the spiders. Within a minute, the five spiders that had grabbed Rose were no more.

Rose and Adrian took it upon themselves to finish off the rest of the Shadowwebs. Rose found them, and destroyed them with the trees in which they lurked. Adrian defended Rose by blasting away any Shadowwebs that got too close. In under a half hour, all but one of the Shadowweb spiders was dead.

However, just as they were finishing the task, the last Shadowweb leaped at Adrian and Rose, and neither of them saw it coming. Thankfully, though, Arrow, who was circling the two, saw the spider lunge, and flew down, pressing the blue button on the front of his glider. He rammed into the spider, and the spider flew back a few feet, but was still standing.

"Adrian Lightseeker," it hissed, "you killed our king! I am his temporary replacement, and you must answer to me!'

"Your old king died because he was too blind to see the evil that you have become!" shouted Adrian, neglecting to mention that the king had actually sided with them previously. "Must you too suffer the same fate?"

"If it means your destruction, then yes," replied the spider. Adrian used the remainder of the light cloud to attack the Shadowweb. Rose attacked it with plants, and the spider died in a shriek of agony.

A cheer rose up from the army, and the guards lost their resolve, and they retreated back to the small base they had previously erected. "HOLD YOUR POSITION!" shouted Arrow to the army, which was preparing to chase after them. "WE NEED TO REGROUP!" There were murmurs of assent from the army, and they stood in place while Arrow picked up Adrian and Rose and flew back to the army.

The army waited expectantly for Arrow to speak. "Well done!" smiled Arrow. "I'm sorry about the unforeseen complication, but you all did very well without my guidance. Also, I noticed that a couple of you soldiers were not taking Adrian and Rose here seriously. Well, they fended off about two hundred Shadowweb spiders on their own. I doubt that many of you could hold off even three on your own."

There was muted whispering in the crowd. However, Arrow was not finished yet. "However, we have not won yet. We must now force them to surrender the land to us, and then Rose here will re-grow the vegetation that they destroyed in the process of creating the new houses. We must stick to our previous strategy, so if you could all find your previously assigned battalions, that would be a good first step."

The crowd bean to move, and Arrow gave them a few minutes to find their old companies. Once they succeeded in that, he continued with his instructions. "So, now that there are no more Shadowweb spiders, we have nothing to fight but men. Thus, a new priority: the houses themselves. We must destroy the foundations, and Rose will then return the plant life to the area. However, we will move forwards as a group, the entire army, that is. We will destroy the house foundations when we get a chance, but focus on taking out the guards. I estimate that we outnumber them about ten to one, so we should have no problem finishing them off. If they surrender, *let them live*. There's no point to

243

killing people who might potentially aid us."

There was a shout of approval from the crowd, and Arrow nodded. "We attack in a half hour. You may do whatever you choose with the remainder of your time. So, just relax for now."

Arrow flew to the ground, and Adrian and Rose dismounted the glider, though Arrow stayed on it. "So, how'd we do?" inquired Adrian eagerly.

"Very well," grinned Arrow. "That was a very impressive display of talent when you destroyed the Shadowwebs. I'm amazed."

"Glad to hear it," blushed Rose. "That was very kind of you to tell the soldiers to spare anyone who surrenders."

"It's what Joshua would have done," whispered Arrow, more to himself than to Adrian and Rose. "I don't see the point in unnecessary killing. I hold no grudge against these men. The only ones whom I have a score to settle with are the members of the corporate council themselves."

"I see," mused Adrian. "So, what should we do for the next half hour?"

"Well, I guess you could talk with the soldiers," shrugged Arrow. "You can do whatever you want. Just be ready in a half hour."

***

After the half hour had passed, Adrian realized that he now didn't mesh with the soldiers for a different reason. They no longer patronized him, but they held him with a sort of awe and reverence that made Adrian feel a bit uncomfortable. A couple of them were a bit jealous of the attention that Arrow had placed upon him, and they resorted to making snide remarks behind his back.

However, even the ones that respected Adrian kept their distance, for they seemed to be under the impression that he was some sort of higher being. They felt inferior in his presence, and avoided him for that very reason.

Thus, Adrian was glad when Arrow called out, "ALRIGHT! THE HALF HOUR BREAK IS OVER! RETURN TO YOUR PREVIOUS ASSIGNED UNITS, AND YOUR COMMANDERS WILL GIVE YOU YOUR NEXT ORDERS!"

There was a bit of a scramble, and after everyone was in his or her proper locations, Arrow continued with his talk. "WE ATTACK AS SOON AS YOU'RE READY! OUR STRATEGY REMAINS THE SAME, AND PROTECT ADRIAN AND ROSE AT ALL COSTS!"

There were cries of assent from the crowd, though some looked a bit sullen at the comment. "VERY WELL!" boomed Arrow. "YOUR COMMANDERS WILL ORGANIZE YOU, AND THEN WE ATTACK!" Arrow flew back to the ground on his glider, which he had been speaking from. "Falcon, what do you think? Of the whole attack so far?"

"They knew we were coming," whispered Falcon. "However, my guess is that they just saw us from a distance, like with a scout or something."

"I see you've picked up one of Rose and Adrian's speaking habits," laughed Arrow. "I've never heard you use 'like' in that context before. It's mildly amusing."

"Well, I think that we should push ahead," blushed Falcon, ignoring Arrow's comment. "It seems to be the strategically best move. They haven't attacked us yet, so I'm not sure if they're either preparing defensively, or just planning to try to run away. Considering how badly Adrian and Rose thrashed the spiders, I'd guess that they're planning to escape. Still, they might be looking for revenge."

"We should start now," mused Arrow, signaling each of the commanders to start. The cry of 'March!' went up throughout the army, and the mass of people began to move. Adrian and Rose marched in front with the smaller battalion, and as they approached, a defensive party emerged from the hideout. Adrian summoned the cloud of lightning with ease, and prepared for battle.

Arrow was right; they outnumbered the defense force about ten-to-one. Adrian and Rose plowed through easily, and found themselves at the entrance to the defensive stronghold. He opened the door, and he and Rose charged inside.

It was a rather bleak and metallic structure, though Adrian heard voices down the steel corridor down which he walked. It was brightly lit, though, and Adrian thought he detected a hidden door.

Adrian saw a faint outline in the wall, and pressed on the outline. The door did not open, and he grew impatient. Adrian loosed the lightning cloud, and the door was blasted down, revealing the hallway within. Rose gave Adrian a funny look, wondering how he had known there was a door there.

The two raced down the hallway, and stopped at a steel door. On the other side, Adrian heard voices talking.

"There's no other option!" protested one voice. "They've got us surrounded! We must surrender!"

"You will keep fighting!" snarled the other voice, one that Adrian recognized with a shiver. It was the voice of Kronos, though twisted by some unknown force. It now sounded deeper, and more malicious. "Do not lose hope! I will send my eleven remaining necrossis to fight for you, and you will win!"

"I can't!" whined the first voice. "They'll kill us all by that time! Kronos, it's over. The Third Order has won the first battle!" There was the sound of a TV screen being turned off, and Adrian and Rose burst into the room.

"Freeze!" thundered Adrian at his target, a man in his late forties, who seemed to be a little on the chubby side. He was balding, and had that corporate look about him. Adrian realized that this was one of the members of the corporate council. "Put your hands up, or you'll be fried to a crisp!"

"Relax, Adrian," laughed the man. "I surrender. I'm surrendering my position on the corporate council to Arrow." Adrian was completely caught off-guard by these words. If Arrow was now part of the council, what would that mean for the Third Order? "I'm trying to help the Third Order," explained the councilman. "I'm not alone, either. There are two others that want to hand over their positions to Arrow. However, Kronos has us intimidated enough so we automatically obey him."

"So Kronos is the real enemy?" clarified Adrian. "He's been forcing you to fight us?"

"Yes," sighed the councilman. "However, if you can offer me protection, then I can hand my position over to Arrow. Does that sound fair to you?"

Adrian and Rose nodded. "Good," smiled the councilman. He walked over to some kind of tele-communicator, and commanded, "Surrender. We've lost. Give yourselves up."

Adrian heard the sounds of battle die down from outside. He turned to the councilman and asked, "So two other councilmen side with Arrow?"

"Well, not exactly," frowned the councilman. "One of them does, and so do I. One's kind of impartial, and then there's Kronos."

"Interesting," mused Rose. "Well, I guess that throws the council in a whole new light. Anyhow, I've been wondering why you still fought us, even though you were on our side."

"Kronos can be... persuasive, shall we say," replied the councilman. "He had the corrupted ambassador keep an eye on me with the Shadowweb Spiders, and he threatened me with death should I turn against him."

"And I always keep my promises," hissed a voice from the ambassador's shadow, and suddenly three tendrils of darkness emerged from it, and tore apart the councilman. By the time that Adrian had readied the lightning cloud, the dark deed was done.

Adrian and Rose stared in shock at the spot where the councilman had stood moments ago. "Where are you, Kronos?" shouted Adrian, preparing to unleash a lightning attack.

"I'm right here," he whispered, stepping out of the councilman's shadow. "Now, Adrian, prepare to die!"

"Ulysses, what's happened to you?" yelled Adrian. "Why are you fighting for Shadius?"

"Ulysses is not here right now," chuckled Kronos. "I am Kronos, through and through."

"Then I believe we've got a score to settle!" shouted Adrian, unleashing his stored up lightning, blasting Kronos off his feet. "Release Serena right now, or I'll fry you to a crisp!"

"On the contrary," growled Kronos, summoning up tendrils of darkness to use as a shield. Adrian found his lightning attack being repelled, but persisted in his assault. Kronos seemed to waver, but used a final burst of strength to push the lightning away. "Don't you forget this, Adrian!" he shouted, and disappeared back into the councilman's shadow.

"Why'd he leave?" exclaimed Rose. "You two were evenly matched."

"He didn't expect that," replied Adrian. "When I last saw him, I couldn't summon up a bolt of lightning if my life depended on it. I guess that there's nothing for us to do. I feel bad for the councilman, but there was nothing we could've done." Adrian spoke that last sentence more to himself than to Rose.

They met Arrow in the middle of the field, where the defeated guards knelt on the ground.

"You're on the corporate council," whispered Adrian. "The councilman turned his position over to you, and Kronos killed him for mutiny."

"Great!" exclaimed Arrow. "So I now control one fifth of the economy? I can put it to use for the Third Order!"

"Plus, if you can get control over the rest of the council, then you've beaten the council," pointed out Adrian. "If you could accomplish that, then we'd have won the war."

"Hm," mused Arrow. "Anyhow, I suppose that we're done here. We should be heading back to the city. Are you two coming?"

"No," apologized Rose. "Adrian needs to get the final task from the Great Sage, so he can finish his training. Knowing the Great Sage, it could take a week or more."

"So, specifically, *I* can't come back with you," corrected Adrian. "Rose, I don't think that you should come with me. It won't be particularly safe, or so I'd imagine, and Arrow's going to need your help."

"But Adrian!" protested Rose. "C'mon, we've been with each other through everything! You can't leave me behind now!"

"Hey, I'll be back!" laughed Adrian. "Besides, Arrow needs you in the city, and you need to undo the damage done by the council here."

"Adrian's right," agreed Arrow. "I've got something pretty big planned, and I'm definitely going to need your help. So, I think it would probably be best if Adrian went alone."

"Fine," sighed Rose. "If that's the way it has to be, then so be it. Well, goodbye, Adrian." With that, she turned around and walked away. Adrian felt a little put off by the exchange. Suddenly, Rose whirled around, and tackled

Adrian in a tight hug. "Come back safely," she whispered before letting go. Adrian gave her a quick kiss on the cheek, and the two of them walked their separate ways.

***

Adrian still periodically sent sparks flying from his body unintentionally. He had figured out the exact effects the lightning cloud's partial incompleteness had on his powers. It delayed the emergence of the lightning, but caused it to linger once it was finally there.

He estimated that he was nearing the first of the two places he wanted to visit in the Poisonsap before he got the Great Sage's final test. He wished to visit the corrupted ambassador once, and he could see the clearing just a little way off.

He saw the rift in the ground where he had cut off the root's connection to the Sage. However, he could not see the root anywhere.

Without warning, Adrian crumpled to the ground when something dealt him a vicious blow in the lower back. He rolled onto his back to find a giant, adult, poisonous Leocavia snarling down at him, venom dripping from its slightly open mouth.

Adrian found that he still had a bit of light energy left, and unleashed it on the cat, which was about one and a half times the size of the one that Blaise had fought in the Deadwood. The Leocavia flew back ten or so yards, and struggled to its feet. Unlike the one in the Deadwood, this cat did not have a look of bored nonchalance. Instead, it looked fierce, and very eager to rip Adrian to pieces.

Adrian leaped to his feet in almost perfect synchronization with the Leocavia. They stared each other down for a moment, and while Adrian was building up enough energy for another attack on the Leocavia, the cat tensed its muscles preparing to pounce.

As the cat flew at Adrian, he unleashed the extra energy, and the cat flew through a veritable maelstrom of lightning. It did, however, make it through, and the cat's claws gouged Adrian's left shoulder. Adrian felt the sting of poison, and his arm went numb. The cat however, crumpled to the ground, dead.

"CURSE YOU, LIGHTSEEKER!" bellowed the corrupted ambassador. "I see that my bodyguard failed to kill you right away, so I must finish the job myself."

Adrian looked straight ahead, and saw that he had missed the root when he had glanced through the clearing the first time. The ambassador had been lying flat on the ground, and Adrian had not seen it, as it was very well camouflaged.

However, now the ambassador stood up, and Adrian saw that it was about half the size of when he had last seen it, and it also looked even more withered. The green sap that had oozed from it was still there, but it wasn't quite as bright as it had been before.

"DO YOU SEE WHAT YOU DID TO ME?!" screamed the ambassador. "THIS IS WHAT YOU DO TO ALL OF US! WE AMBASSADORS HAVE LIVES AS WELL!"

"Not for long," smiled Adrian grimly. He had not used all of his energy battling the Leocavia, and loosed the rest of it at the ambassador. The root seemed to have been preparing a spell, but Adrian was able to disrupt it before it was fully formed.

The ambassador screeched in pain as lightning ran up and down the course of its body. "C-C-CURSE YOU, ADRIAN LIGHTSEEKER!" it exclaimed once again. "Please, Adrian, stop!" he shouted, and Adrian considered his request for a moment. "Please, just let me die in peace. You've already given me my death sentence. If you leave me alone, I'll make it worth your while."

The ambassador's voice had grown considerably weaker, and Adrian realized that he would be a fool not to accept its request. He stopped the stream of lightning, and the ambassador gasped for breath, which Adrian found somewhat odd, as the ambassador was a tree root.

"Thank you, Adrian," gasped the root. "I told you I'd make it... worth your while, and I will. The corporate council knew... you were coming. There's... a... spy. I don't know who it is... but..." The root gave one last twitch, and then he was still.

Adrian wasn't sure whether or not to believe the corrupted ambassador. However, he considered the implications had he been telling the truth. He remembered Falcon accusing Blaise of being a traitor, but Blaise hadn't had an opportunity to slip the information out.

Adrian decided to move on, and headed not quite towards the entrance to the cavernous cliffs, but to the Shadowweb Spider's cave. He had figured out after fighting them that they would make incredible allies for the Third Order, and decided that since he had made them into enemies, then it fell upon his shoulders to make them into friends.

On his way, however, a wave ran through Adrian's vision. He felt weak, and he fell to the ground. The scrape on his shoulder started to burn, and Adrian looked at it with reluctance, and saw, to his revulsion, that it had turned green.

Adrian recalled that he could also heal with his light powers, though the Great Sage had never taught him how. However, he attempted to access the light cloud in his head, and succeeded in doing so.

He attempted not to summon lightning, but just pure light. He was successful in his attempt, and it flowed into his wound, cleansing it of poison. Adrian then focused a little extra energy into the blight, and the scratch closed.

Adrian felt exhausted by the attempt, but he forced himself to keep going. After a couple more minutes, Adrian was standing at the entrance to the Shadowwebs' cave. He forced himself to take one step after another, though his strength was slowly coming back.

However, the cave was strangely barren of spiders. Once or twice he thought that he saw them scuttling about at the edge of his vision, but there was nothing when he looked. Suddenly a small spider, relative speaking, crawled towards Adrian from the shadows. It did not have a veil of shadow over its face, but its face did not affect Adrian in any way.

"Hello, Adrian," it smiled shyly. Adrian noticed that it was about a foot long, and much smaller than all the others he had seen. "I'm Arrachnia, the princess of the Shadowwebs. My father was Arrachnis. I have told the tribe the truth about how he died, and that he decided that you were our friend."

"I'm sorry about your father," comforted Adrian. "However, I have a favor to ask of you. Could you tell the rest of the tribe to help Arrow? Go to the city, and tell Arrow that you'll help him, please, can you ask the tribe to do that?"

"No," replied Arrachnia. "I can *tell* the tribe to do that. As my father and my uncle are now both dead, I rule the colony. Farewell, Adrian." Arrachnia scuttled off, and Adrian decided that it was time to leave. He turned around, and left the small cave.

***

Adrian stepped into the first tunnel of the cavernous cliffs, and tried to recall the exact route he had taken before. He had a general sense of direction, but he almost took a wrong turn a couple of times, and was incredibly glad when he ran into Incarcerus.

"Hey, Adrian!" exclaimed Incarcerus, shaking Adrian's hand. "I haven't seen you for a long time! What have you been up to?"

"Well, I was just heading back to the Great Sage, so I can complete my training," explained Adrian. "I've been helping Arrow fight the Battle of the Poisonsap. We found the first member of the council, and he gave Arrow his spot."

"Intriguing," mused Incarcerus. "Anyhow, you look a bit lost. Maybe we could catch up as I show you the way out?" Adrian nodded, and the two of them began walking.

"You know, Adrian, it's been boring down here without you," sighed Incarcerus. "Nothing's really happened since you and Rose came to pass through.

By the way, where is Rose?"

"I had to leave her behind," replied Adrian. "Arrow needed her help, and I thought that it might be too dangerous for her."

"But wouldn't it also be too dangerous for you?" inquired Incarcerus. "I mean, weren't you two about equal, power wise?"

"I suppose," sighed Adrian. "However, I think that I need to face this last task alone. It's not going to be easy, I can assure you that."

"Well, I guess that you've got a point," answered Incarcerus. "Anyhow, I think that you probably made the right decision."

"Incarcerus, what exactly did the prophecy say would happen to me?" inquired Adrian.

"I'm not sure," frowned Incarcerus. "Not too much, but it did mention that you play a huge role in the Battle of Cloudhall."

"What's Cloudhall?" inquired Adrian.

"It's the name of an ancient town on top of mount Icecap," explained Incarcerus. "However, I don't know too much about it. Anyhow, we're here."

Adrian looked up, surprised. He hadn't expected to get out of the tunnel that soon. "How are we already here?" he asked. "We didn't cross the river!"

"I took a shortcut," smiled Incarcerus. "Anyhow, it was nice seeing you again, Adrian." Adrian waved goodbye to Incarcerus as he stepped out of the tunnel.

19

The Battle of the Five Towers

Adrian climbed out of the tunnel, and shielded his eyes from the light. His eyes had adjusted to being in the tunnel, and he stumbled a bit as he came out of it. However, his vision cleared almost immediately, and his eyes alit upon a very familiar sight,

Adrian walked towards the Great Sage with a smile on his face, as he had missed his instructor's kind words. "Hello, Sage!" he called. "I'm back!"

"And looking fit," chuckled the Sage. "I'm glad to see you again, Adrian. I saw that the attack on the Poisonsap went very well. By the way, good job fighting the Shadowwebs."

"Thanks, Sage," grinned Adrian. "So, do you have the last task ready for me?"

"Yes, Adrian, I have indeed thought of one," replied the Great Sage. "You and I are responsible for the creation of a monster. And though we haven't heard much of him lately, he's been on the move."

Adrian listened intently. "Also, I have decided that if you destroy him, the curse will be lifted off of the Deadwood Forest. Virda could be a very powerful ally in the war against the council, but she is unable to help us so long as the curse remains," explained the Sage. "Thus, we come to the final task: you must fight and defeat the demon known as Necropheus."

"Necropheus?" inquired Adrian. "Did you see what he looked like in his new form? It'd be suicide!"

"Adrian, I would not give you the task if I didn't think you were up to it," reprimanded the Great Sage. "And I saw Necropheus' new form when I was in your mind. He's probably learned to use it by now, but you're Adrian Lightseeker! I'd bet my life that you could defeat him."

"Yes, but you're betting *mine*," pointed out Adrian. "On the other hand, I trust your judgment. If that's what I have to do, then do it I will. Do you have any strategy tips?"

"Well, have you figured out how to heal using your light powers?" inquired the Sage. Adrian nodded. "If he hurts you badly, heal yourself. Aside from that, just blast him with lightning. Actually, I'd hold back at first, for a couple of reasons. If he thinks that you're using your full powers, he'll underestimate you. He might make a mistake, and you could take advantage of it. Also, try to get him to reveal what his new powers are, and re-evaluate your strategy based on that."

"Sounds like a solid strategy," agreed Adrian. "So, um, when should I go?"

"Well, as soon as possible," recommended the Sage. "Did you bring your pack with you?"

"No," sighed Adrian. "I must've forgotten it in the rush to get to the Poisonsap. Is that bad?"

"Not necessarily," frowned the Great Sage. "I prepared another pack for you, just in case." A branch lowered a sack made of tightly bound leaves down to the ground, and Adrian bent over and picked it up. He sorted through the contents, and found that there was just about everything that he'd need. Food, a map and compass, a bottle of water, and a seed were all included in the bag.

Adrian looked curiously at the last item. "It's a communication device," explained the Sage. "If you feel the need to talk to me, you can just release a little light into it, and it'll act as an ambassador."

"Handy!" exclaimed Adrian. "So I can just talk to you any time I want?"

"Precisely," smiled the Sage. "I spent most of my time working on it once I figured out exactly what your last task was. Please don't lose it, Adrian."

"Don't worry," replied Adrian. "Hey, I've got a question for you. Did you know that there was a corrupted ambassador in the Poisonsap?"

"I was aware that there used to be an ambassador in there, but I thought that he died a while back," frowned the Sage. "He's alive?"

"Not any more," smirked Adrian. "He tried to kill me three times, and assisted the council in the Battle of the Poisonsap."

"Did he really?" inquired the Sage. "What did he do, exactly?"

"Well, he told me that you wanted me dead, and he then summoned up a couple of Shadowwebs to kidnap Rose and me" explained Adrian. "He was the one who involved the spiders in the Poisonsap battle. However, Rose and I cut off his connection to you, so he began to wither and die. Then, when I came back to you, he set an adult Leocavia on me, and then after I defeated the cat, he tried to use a spell on me."

"But you were able to defeat him?" inquired the Sage. "Well done, and thank you."

"It was no big deal," shrugged Adrian. "He attacked me first, so I was acting in self-defense."

"Either way, I still owe you thanks," smiled the Sage. "He could have corrupted me, as well. I owe you my life."

"Sage, it was no big deal," insisted Adrian. "Anyhow, I should probably be going. I've got a demon to kill."

***

Rose held on to Arrow as they flew back to the city, looking back at the plants that now stood in place of the half-finished houses, courtesy of Rose. They zipped over the Poisonsap in a matter of minutes, and within another two or three, they were at the outskirts of the city. Rose enjoyed every minute of it, as Adrian wasn't there to make her feel guilty about clinging onto Arrow.

Once they reached the edge of the city, Arrow lowered the glider, and Rose jumped off. "Are we walking the rest of the way?" she inquired. "We're not near the tunnel, though."

"We're not going through the tunnel," replied Arrow. "There's another path. I think that it might be a better option. It's not quite as narrow as the tunnel."

"You're claustrophobic, aren't you!" laughed Rose. Arrow blushed, and started to make excuses. "Don't apologize, Arrow. It's cute!"

"If you say so," sighed Arrow. "But yes, I am claustrophobic. It traces back to a certain experience from my childhood, which I would prefer not to discuss."

"Suit yourself," shrugged Rose. "Anyways, what's this other path you mentioned?"

"Well, see, if we fly around to the western entrance to the city, then we can slip into the hideout without much chance of them spotting us."

"Then why'd we land?" inquired Rose. "I mean, if we're just going to fly again."

"Well, even though the council wouldn't see us actually enter the city, there's still the high chance that they'd see us flying around the city," explained Arrow. "If I, however, plant an air bomb here, they'd be significantly distracted."

"Sounds like a good idea," smiled Rose. "Let's do it."

Arrow reached into the side compartment of the glider, and pulled out a small round object. He quietly crept towards the city, and after a few minutes, was crouched outside a sort of security station. It was on the outside of that building that he planted the bomb.

Arrow swiftly darted away from the station, making sure not to be seen. He got back to his glider, and pressed a well-concealed button near the compartment from where he had gotten the bomb.

"Get on!" he shouted to Rose, and as she stepped onto the glider, he slammed his foot onto the pedal, causing the glider to jolt up into the air. Seconds later, the air bomb exploded in a burst of oxygen. The front wall of the security station was blown to bits, and nobody noticed a small glider with two passengers zipping away from the scene of the crime.

Within the minute, the full city had been alerted of the incident, and the surrounding grounds were being carefully searched. As the culprits had already absconded, the search amounted to nothing.

A couple of minutes later, Arrow and Rose were approaching the Third Order's hideout. Arrow lowered the glider, and he carried it the remaining distance, while Rose followed him. He gave the guard the password, and the two were permitted entry.

Arrow and Rose parted, and the two went to their different rooms. As Rose entered, she lay down on the bed. The events of the battle flashed before her eyes, and as she drifted off to sleep, they also began to affect her dreams.

***

The next morning, Falcon shook her awake. "Rose... It's time to get up... C'mon, wake up..." Rose blinked sleepily, and yawned.

"What time is it?" she inquired. "And do I really need to get up?"

"Rose, it's ten thirty. Get up!" Falcon began to shake her more thoroughly. Rose sat up, and stepped out of bed. "Rose, we're having another meeting," explained Falcon. "Unless you get up now, you'll miss it, and I don't think that's something you want to have happen."

"Fine," groaned Rose, and she ushered Falcon out the door before dressing herself. After a few minutes had passed, she pushed the door open, and Falcon strode back in. "Now, what was that you were saying about a meeting?" she asked.

"Well, the corporate council is making an announcement tomorrow," began Falcon. "See, there've been riots in the streets about Joshua's death. The council wants to put an end to these riots, but it, ah, probably isn't going to go as planned."

"Are we interfering?" inquired Rose.

"Indeed we are," smiled Falcon. "See, last night, while you were asleep, Arrow went in and asserted his control over the first of the Five Towers, the towers owned by the council. He plans to use that as a base for a battle in the city."

"So what does that have to do with the announcement?" wondered Rose.

"Well, Arrow was thinking that if we manage to lead a riot, we could take advantage of the distraction, and use the opportunity to strike," explained Falcon. "Of course, none of this is official yet. That is, however, the basic strategy."

"That's what we're discussing?" clarified Rose. Falcon nodded. "Well, I want in. What time does the meeting start?"

"In about ten minutes," shrugged Falcon. By the time he had finished answering the question, Rose was out the door, and headed for the elevator. "You don't even know what room it's in!" exclaimed Falcon, hurrying after her. He managed to catch the elevator before the door closed, and he pointed her in the right direction.

Moments later, the two stepped out of the elevator, and ambled towards the conference room. Arrow and Blaise were already sitting down, preparing for the meeting.

"Hi Arrow!" blushed Rose. "So, what's the plan?"

"Well, as Falcon has probably already told you, they're holding a service for Joshua tomorrow," explained Arrow. "They recognize that it would be foolish for them to deny that he died, for that's a very well-confirmed fact."

"So what do they plan to say?" inquired Rose.

"They plan to say that he was a friend of everyone's, and of the environment," chuckled Arrow. "They do, however, intend to make me out as the villain who corrupted him with my dirty thoughts of revolution."

"And his death?"

"An accident," replied Arrow. "They're planning to say that they were going for me, but he got killed in the skirmish, and I fled the scene."

"And will the public believe that?" inquired Falcon, unsure of the answer.

"I'm not sure," mused Arrow. "There is a chance that the public will, though, and even if they don't, the address will probably cause most of them to subconsciously portray me as a villain. Either way, there's a chance that it might damage our cause, and that's a risk we can't afford to take."

"Very fair reasoning, Arrow," smirked Blaise from his seat. "But on the other hand, what if your choice of attacking the council on Joshua's memorial day upsets some of the members of the Third Order?"

"Well, I suppose that's a valid point," sighed Arrow. "However, I'm still inclined to say that our members thinking of me as a villain would be somewhat more dangerous than those same members being annoyed that we're vindicating Joshua's death on the day that we were going to honor it on anyways."

"Valid point," conceded Blaise, who withdrew his argument.

"Are there any other questions?" challenged Arrow. No one spoke up. "Great!" he smiled, and turned to Falcon. "Blaise, you may go. Rose and Falcon, stay. We need to discuss strategy." Blaise nodded, and walked out. "So, our strategy is going to have to be somewhat different this time around. We don't have Adrian to rely on, and Rose can't really manipulate any plants because they're all gone."

"Besides, these guys aren't going to surrender as easily as the others," pointed out Rose. "On the other hand, we have that tower that Arrow now owns to use as a temporary base. That can't be a bad thing, can it?"

"No, I suppose not," shrugged Falcon. "Arrow, do we already have men in our tower?"

"I put most of the army in there last night," grinned Arrow. "Not easy work, let me tell you. Anyhow, our main priority is to capture the two towers on each side of Kronos'. He's the main enemy, and if we've got him surrounded, he'll be severely hampered."

"Yeah, I guess," conceded Falcon. "By the way, Arrow, have you assigned our new companies to their new tasks?"

"Yep," smiled Arrow. "They seem to have plans for some new kind of weapon designed by Kronos. They might be using them in the battle, so we'll have to watch out."

"What kind of a weapon is it?" wondered Rose.

"It's some kind of long distance thing," replied Arrow. "There's a trigger, and when you pull it, something comes out the end. I don't think it's particularly dangerous."

Rose tried to visualize what Arrow had just described, and came up with a very disturbing result. "Arrow," began Rose, "that's called a gun."

"Yeah, that's what it was called!" exclaimed Arrow. "Why? Do you know anything about them?"

"Well, if they have guns and we don't, we're dead," responded Rose. "And I mean literally. One shot from a gun, and you'll never see the light of day again."

"Are they that dangerous?" inquired Arrow. "How should we guard against them?"

"Well, on Earth, we used bullet-proof vests," mused Rose. "Or, we could just avoid being shot. Or, if we also use guns, it would even the playing field."

"Well, I suppose I could get the company to make guns for us as well," frowned Arrow. "Do you think that they'd be able to get them ready in time?"

"I wouldn't know," shrugged Rose. "But I think you'd better start now." Arrow got up, and walked out the door, and over to the elevator.

"Are guns really as dangerous as you made then out to be?" wondered Falcon. "I mean, can they really kill you in one shot? In the Battle of the Poisonsap, they just fought with their fists, and I can't imagine that whoever's in charge of making these things would forget to give them to the guards."

"Kronos must be in charge of the gun production," figured Rose. "After all, no one else in Maltesque seems to have the slightest idea as to what they are."

***

Arrow hopped onto his glider, and sped towards his newly acquired tower. He stopped to talk to the troops, and discuss the new strategy. After he had finished his brief lecture, he flew towards the factory of his new company, and gave them his orders for gun construction. They assured him that they would have it done by the end of the day. Arrow left, and returned to the tower.

At the end of the day, he flew back to the factory, and saw what they had accomplished over the course of the day. Hundreds of guns littered the store-room floor, and Arrow looked at them with pride. He picked one up, and fired an experimental shot at the wall. He was utterly shocked by the power of the blast.

With some help from the company, Arrow managed to move the guns to his new tower, and then returned to the secret base.

***

Day dawned bright on Arrow's sleepless eyes. He stood up, having been sitting the entire night, not even trying to sleep. He hadn't slept well since before Joshua had...

No, thought Arrow. I must focus. Everything depends on me.

He strode out the door, and took the elevator down to Rose's room. He knocked twice, and after getting no response, decided that he should probably go in.

Rose was still soundly asleep, undisturbed by the knocks. However, after a bit of jostling from Arrow, she finally woke up. "G'morning Arrow," she yawned. "Is it time?"

"In a few hours," replied Arrow. "But the reason I woke you up is that I wanted to talk to you."

Rose sat up attentively at these last few words, and asked, "Why me? Don't you want to discuss it with Falcon or something?"

"No, Rose, I wanted to talk to you," smiled Arrow. "Falcon's an old man, just like everyone else in the organization. I am not a man. I'm fifteen, but I've had to act like an adult for the past week."

"So you're feeling stressed out?" clarified Rose.

"Well, partially," shrugged Arrow. "But it's more that I'm lonely. With Joshua gone, I haven't really had anyone to talk to."

"I guess you're right," sighed Rose. "By the way, I'm sorry about what happened to Joshua. I know it happened a little while ago, but I don't think I ever actually got a chance to tell you that."

"Thanks, Rose," whispered Arrow. He leaned over, gave her a kiss on the cheek. Rose took Arrow in her arms, and held him for a few minutes. "Look, Rose, there's something I need to tell you," began Arrow tentatively. "You're not safe."

"What do you mean?" asked Rose. "I've got a security guard."

Arrow's courage seemed to fail him, and his face went a deathly pale. "Never mind, Rose. I appreciate the brief talk with you." He got up, and left the room. Rose was left alone with her thoughts, which were now considerably more numerous than before.

***

After the strange incident of the morning, Arrow and Rose kept a slight distance from each other while they prepared for the upcoming battle. They didn't outright ignore each other, but they just kept a respectful amount of space between each other.

After the two of them had a last minute strategy meeting with Falcon, Arrow left to speak with the troops in the new tower. Rose decided that it would be smart to share Arrow's warning with Falcon.

"Falcon," she began somewhat timidly, "earlier today, Arrow told me something. He said I wasn't safe. What do you think that he was trying to tell me?"

"Well, I think that he was probably just concerned for your well being," suggested Falcon. "Unless," he thought to himself, "Arrow knows something."

"Thanks, Falcon," smiled Rose. "I've been worried about that for most of the morning."

"Always glad to help," he smiled, feeling somewhat unsure of himself. However, he forced all doubts out of his head as Arrow came back up the elevator. "How'd it go?" asked Falcon cheerfully.

"It went well," smiled Arrow. "There's a small crowd gathering for the address already. I put some of our men in there to help start the riot."

"Do they know the danger they're putting themselves in?" asked Falcon doubtfully.

"I pray they do," frowned Arrow. "Either way, it's too late. If we want to get there in time, we should probably head out about now."

"Most likely," agreed Falcon. "Say, why don't you take Rose with you?"

"Good idea!" agreed Rose eagerly. "I'd be glad to help."

Various emotions flashed across Arrow's face, and one of the few that Rose was able to discern was fear. "I'm not sure that..." he began to protest, before being cut off by Falcon.

"Take her with you!" he ordered. "Arrow, you need someone to help you, and Rose is the perfect candidate! I need to order the troops from our new tower, and Rose is the only other eligible candidate."

"I suppose you're right," sighed Arrow, whose hand flew to his skull suddenly.

"Are you okay?" asked Rose.

"I'm fine," snarled Arrow. "Just a bit of the stress getting to me. Anyhow, we'd better get going."

"I'm coming with you," decided Falcon suddenly. "I need to get to the tower, and your glider is the fastest route."

"Sure," sighed Arrow. Rose thought that she caught a bit of relief in his eye. She assumed that it was from having someone to rely on.

"Well, we'd best get going," ordered Falcon. "The address starts in a half-hour, and we need to get ready for the battle."

"Alright. C'mon," said Arrow, motioning to the elevator. The three stepped in, and emerged at the bottom floor.

A few minutes later, they were in the sky, gliding towards their tower. Rose thought she recognized some of the faces in the crowd below them from the Battle of the Poisonsap.

Arrow dropped Rose off in the crowd, and then deposited Falcon at the tower. He then rejoined Rose in the crowd.

The corporate representative began to speak. "Friends, family, lovers of the environment... I am speaking to you today to inform you of a tragic accident." There was a great deal of booing from the crowd, led by Arrow. "We were attempting to capture to notorious criminal Arrow Viridia. However, his brother, acting in his defense, received the gunshot that was meant for Arrow." There was confused murmuring in the audience. "Ah, I see that you're all wondering what a 'gun' is," chuckled the speaker. "It is a weapon, newly designed by the newest member of the corporate council, Kronos. With the pull of a trigger, it sends a capsule of lead into the target's body at high velocity. It kills almost instantaneously."

"NOT TRUE!" shouted Arrow from the crowd. "MY BROTHER JOSHUA WAS BLEEDING TO DEATH ON THE FLOOR WHEN I FOUND HIM! He did not die quickly!"

The members of the Third Order dispersed in the crowd recognized the secret signal, and hoisted up their new guns, and opened fire on the speaker. The crowd dissolved into chaos.

Suddenly, a voice boomed, "YOU ARE NOT THE ONLY ONE ARMED!" Suddenly, cops poured out of the surrounding alleys, and attempted to single out the rioters. By this point, every face in crowd had decided whom to blame for Joshua's death: the corporate council. Everyone had seen through the speaker's lie, and ordinary citizens began to fight on the Third Order's side.

Rose and Arrow fought their way through the chaos to their tower. "I see you did your job well," smiled Falcon, meeting them on the ground floor. "I think what did it was the imagery you used. I don't think any of the citizens were pleased by the picture of Joshua bleeding to death."

"Yes, well, they seem vulnerable now," observed Arrow hurriedly. "Now is the time to strike."

"Indeed it is," nodded Falcon gravely. "We must act now. Rose, you stick with me. Arrow you command your section of the troops, and I'll take mine. Remember, we try to get the two towers on both sides of Kronos'."

"I know," nodded Arrow. "Let's do it." Through the intercom, he instructed all members of his portion of the army to meet on the right of the building, and all members of Falcon's section to meet at the left."

A few minutes later, the troops were assembled, and Arrow and Falcon parted. Rose went with Falcon, though she longed to be with Arrow.

"All right, boys," began Falcon. "Listen up now. This is important. Today, we don't have Adrian's light powers to rely on, and Rose can't summon up any plants as there are none in the city."

"So what's our strategy?" inquired one of the younger members of the army.

"We go in hard and fast. We get inside the building, take out anyone who tries to stop us, and let everyone be who doesn't," explained Falcon. "Use your guns. They are the pinnacle of weaponry. Are we all clear on this?"

"Yes sir!" was the general response from the crowd.

"March!" ordered Falcon, and the army followed him as he strode towards the second tower. As they neared the tower, cops swarmed towards them. The Third Order quickly began to gain a good deal of respect for their new weapons. After a few minutes, they surrounded the tower. Once they beat the defense force back, Falcon and Rose charged into the tower itself.

They raced through the front door, cutting down anyone who held them back. Falcon thought that it would be a good idea to send himself and Rose up to the top floor in the elevator to scout out the place, while the rest of the soldiers ascended the stairs.

Rose thought that it seemed a bit ridiculous that they should go up in an elevator, but she supposed that it was a good idea for them to scout ahead.

However, when the door slid open, she quickly began to reconsider.

About a hundred guards stood in front of them, guns raised. Falcon seemed not to have expected this, and looked as if he was out of ideas. Suddenly, the first wave of soldiers charged up the stairs, and provided ample distraction for Falcon and Rose to charge down the hallway that the elevator had deposited them in.

At the end of the hall they found a closed door. It took them a couple of seconds to bust the door down. They gazed in shock upon an intriguing sight inside.

A man in a suit slumped in his chair, apparently dead. Beside him stood none other than a necrossis. Rose detected a wave of horror emanating from the shadow soldier.

Without a second thought, Falcon fired his gun at the necrossis. A tendril of darkness swiftly reached out from the necrossis' body, and grabbed the bullet out of the air. A dark spark, like the one Adrian and James had seen oh so long ago slithered up the tendril, and shattered the bullet.

"I'm afraid that won't work, Falcon," sighed the necrossis. Rose cringed at the sound of the necrossis' voice, which was strikingly similar to that of Shadius. "You see, ordinary weapons won't work on me. I can control shadow, and I'm afraid that supercedes gunfire."

Falcon seemed taken aback that his gun had failed to do its job. He took a step back, and the necrossis took that as an invitation to inch forwards. Rose scoured the room to find some sort of weapon to use, but all she saw was a desk, a chair, a sofa, and a potted plant.

Rose realized immediately what she had to do, and reached out to the plant, and it sprung to life at a little encouragement from Rose. It was a flower, and it blasted out pollen at the necrossis. It seemed to fill his lungs, and he surrendered to a fit of coughing.

Falcon took this opportunity to fire another shot from his gun. The necrossis reacted just a bit too slowly, and the tendril of darkness came too late. The bullet sank into the shadow soldier's heart, and he suddenly fell to the floor.

Equally as suddenly, he sprang back up. Darkness began to pour from the wound, and the necrossis' body began to disintegrate. It his place stood a lurching mass of shadow.

Rose wondered if the mass of shadow was also going to disappear, but it seemed to have other plans. Tendrils of darkness poured from it, engulfing the room. Rose was suddenly lost in shadow, but she reached out with her mind to latch onto the consciousness of the plant. It was unaffected by the shadow, and Rose manipulated it so it struck into the heart of the tendrils.

She somehow felt it alight upon something solid, and she ordered the plant to tighten its grip. It did, and Rose though she heard a scream somewhere from within the darkness. For a moment she wondered if she had hit Falcon by accident, but the darkness began to evaporate.

Falcon was huddled in a corner of the room, his face pale. "Is that what you're up against?" he whispered. "Is that what you and Adrian are fighting?"

Rose nodded. Falcon stood up, and looked warily around. He saw nothing else of interest, and he walked over to the intercom. "Attention guards!" he shouted. "Your boss is now dead. You answer to me now, and I am Falcon, strategist of the Third Order of druids. Put down your weapons, and accompany the troops out. As of right now, you are all officially part of our group."

Falcon and Rose strode out of the office room. They were content, for they had won their battle.

For Arrow, however, things were not going so well. Kronos himself had seen fit to defend the building, and as soon as Arrow realized this, he figured out that he stood no chance of winning. He pulled his men out, but lost about half his force.

The two leaders met back at their tower at around three in the afternoon. By that time the riots had pretty much ceased. Rose retreated to her room, as her battle against the necrossis had burnt her out.

***

Arrow looked about him in distress. He didn't know how well Falcon was doing, but he hoped that Falcon was faring better than he. Kronos seemed to have anticipated the attack, and was himself guarding the tower. The constant assault of tendrils of darkness had waylaid the Third Order's forces, and they were unable to advance.

"Steady!" he ordered. "Hold your positions! We can outlast them!" Not only had Kronos called the tendrils of darkness to his aid, but he had assigned all remaining necrossis, save one, to the task of defending the tower as well.

Arrow knew that he lied to his troops. They stood no chance against the necrossis and Kronos combined. "Retreat!" he ordered, changing his mind. "Stay in formation, but retreat!"

Suddenly, three of the necrossis teleported behind the Third Order's army, and blocked their retreat. Arrow, looking down from his glider, saw that it was hopeless. "Attack them!" he shouted to the soldiers who could no longer retreat. "Keep at it! We'll break through eventually!"

Arrow searched the battlefield for a way out. There was a square in between the five towers, and it was in that square that they fought. They were surrounded in front, and in the back, but not from the sides.

"Escape to the sides!" commanded Arrow. "It's the only way out!" The soldiers hurried to fulfill his command, but several more necrossis warped to the side. Arrow was now genuinely worried. To his benefit, though, his soldiers fought like maniacs, forcing their way through. However, the necrossis were too powerful to be plowed through that easily.

Suddenly, Arrow saw something scuttle towards the battle through one of the surrounding alleys. He couldn't see it very clearly, but it looked almost like a very large spider. The spider jumped on one of the necrossis, and sank its fangs into the shadow soldier's neck. The necrossis screamed in pain, but he did not go down, this did however, provide ample distraction for some of the soldiers to escape.

Arrow looked down, and though he heard a noise to his left. He turned, and, to his surprise, saw a huge horde of the spiders charging towards the battlefield. They attacked Kronos and the necrossis, and Arrow and his troops were able to escape.

***

"So you were rescued by giant spiders?" clarified Falcon. "Did you talk to any of them?"

"No, but I'm pretty sure they were Shadowwebs," frowned Arrow. "I don't know why they would want to help us, though. It's a miracle that we got out virtually unscathed."

"If you're wondering why we saved you, perhaps I can help you," smiled Arrachnia, stepping out of the elevator. "We've joined your side, to repay for what we put Adrian and Rose through. We were sent to help you by Adrian."

"So you're fighting for us?" asked Arrow incredulously. "That's great news!"

"Arrow, I've got news for you!" exclaimed Blaise, racing into the room. "As Joshua's permanently out of commission, I've decided to take over his role, and scout out the council's website via hacking. The two remaining councilmen, aside from Kronos, are heading to their secret base in Cloudhall, so they can keep an eye on the magma re-router!"

"So Cloudhall exists?" inquired Arrow. "I thought it was just a myth!"

"Joshua and I knew about it," explained Falcon. "I've known about it for a while, and told him about it when we were running from the cops. I never got a chance to tell you."

"Then our next step is clear," mused Arrow. "Our next step is to attack Cloudhall!"

20

The Road to Hell

Adrian stared blankly ahead of him, thinking. *It's ironic*, he thought, *I spent about three weeks trying to escape from the Deadwood Forest, and now I'm voluntarily heading back.*

Adrian stood atop the broken dam where he and Rose had first seen the city, but this time, he was facing the other way. He gazed towards the veritable hell that the Deadwood had become as a result of Necropheus' spell.

The woods were shrouded in a red aura, and Adrian saw that there was a hulking shape moving between the trees. It was, without a doubt, Necropheus. He was only a blur from Adrian's perspective, but he looked menacing even so.

Adrian turned to the left, and looked at the two mountains. He thought he detected some kind of movement at the top of Mount Icecap, but dismissed it as his mind wandering. However, he once again directed his attention to the Deadwood. He saw that the river ran red as it neared the forest, and he wondered if it was merely an effect of the spell or if it truly had run red with blood.

He shook his head, clearing it of musings. He looked at the stairs, and made his way down. His hand steady on the railing, he calmly strode down the staircase. He had seen on his previous ascension that it was not much worse than when he had first climbed it. He looked forwards, and he discovered that he could no longer see Necropheus. He assumed that it was a result of his descent down the stairs.

Regardless, he calmly walked along the riverbank, not particularly concerned with anything. He felt the Great Sage's seed in his pocket, as he had deemed the bag to be too risky. He no longer really needed the map, since he was now very familiar with the layout of Maltesque.

Suddenly, there was a disturbance in the water to his left. He whirled around, and without warning, the river demon from before burst out of the water, and flopped onto land. It seemed to be in a fit of rage, and Adrian backed away. The river monster was too far away to do any damage to Adrian, and actually seemed to be trying to communicate with him.

Adrian wondered if he could use his light powers to look inside the creature's mind. He summoned up a bit of light, and thrust it from his mind into the monster's mind. A bridge between the two minds opened up, and Adrian was able to glance into the thing's head.

It possessed a human intelligence.

Adrian wondered what this could mean. As far as he knew, there were very few powers on Maltesque that could transform a man into a monster. In fact he had only seen it happen to X.

Adrian realized that the river demon was most likely one of the members of the second order, transformed by Virda. He took the Great Sage's seed out of his pocket, and used it to contact him.

"Um, Sage?" he began. "Ah, I'm being attacked by a member of the second order, who was transformed into a monster. He can't actually touch me, but he seems to be trying to slither towards me."

"Are you in any danger?" asked the Great Sage immediately. "Can you defeat him?"

"Yes, but I don't think I need to," replied Adrian slowly. "He doesn't seem dangerous."

"Wait. Did you say that he's a former member of the second order?" asked the Sage warily. "If that's the case, then you might be fighting Chronicle. He was one of Democritus' close friends, and there's a chance that he was the one who corrupted Democritus in the first place."

Adrian carefully considered the Sage's words, while he watched Chronicle flop around on the shore. He once again looked into Chronicle's mind, and was able to communicate, in a sense. "Chronicle?" asked Adrian through the mental link. "Is that who you are?"

"I am," was the gruff response. "Free me from this form! Please! I'll die on the shore if you don't!"

"Don't do it Adrian," warned the Sage. "If you free him, Virda will never join our cause. We've already freed Democritus, and we've killed him and X!"

"I have to," muttered Adrian. "He's dying, Sage! I've got no other choice!" Adrian found the traces of magic locked in his body by Virda's spell, and attempted to annul them with his own powers. However, his magic was slow in coming, as was always the case now.

Adrian finally summoned up the necessary energy. He attempted to use it to cancel out the spell, but there was one overlying curse that he could not overcome. Suddenly, he felt another presence creep into the monster's mind, and canceled out the stubborn curse. Adrian then used his own power to abolish the rest of the ancient spell.

"Thank you..." wheezed a man, who had taken the monster's place. He shivered from the water, though his naked body was warmed by the desert air. "I sensed great power in you... the two times we met before. However, I, in my haste, mistook the girl for the source of the power."

"Well, I'm glad I was able to help," smiled Adrian, though he was more concerned with whom the other presence belonged to.

He heard a laugh in his mind, and pulled the seed out of his pocket. "It was you?" asked Adrian to the Great Sage. "But I thought that you were against it!"

"I thought better of it," smiled the Sage. "Since you weren't going to be talked out of it, I figured you could use my help."

"Thank," replied Adrian gratefully.

"D-d-d-do you h-have any sp-sp-spare c-c-clothes?" stuttered Chronicle. "I wasn't wearing any as a river demon, so..."

"I think I have a change of clothes in my backpack,' mused Adrian, rustling through his bag. Sure enough, he found what he sought. "They might be a little small, but they'll do."

"Thank you, boy," whispered Chronicle. "I'm sorry if my appearance caused any sort of disturbance for you."

"Ah, it's no trouble," shrugged Adrian. "Anyhow, I guess that it'll be good to have you with me. I'll take all the help I can get."

"And you've got mine," smiled Chronicle. "Anyhow, what's your name?"

"I'm Adrian Cant- No, Adrian Lightseeker. Pleased to make your acquaintance," grinned Adrian extending his hand. Chronicle shook it.

"So what brings you along this path?" asked Chronicle. "You do not seem to be of this world, as no one but Virda and the Great Sage possessed the kind of power you've displayed."

"Thanks," smiled Adrian. "I'm not from this world. I hail from the distant world of Earth."

"So why are you here?" inquired Chronicle curiously. "I mean, it's not a place one would voluntarily choose to visit, at least in its current state."

"No it is not," answered Adrian. "I was kidnapped and brought here by a man named Kronos."

"Do you know of a man named Ulysses?" asked Chronicle.

"He is Kronos," explained Adrian. "Ulysses turned evil, corrupted by an ancient god."

"Adrian, do you imply that you are an enemy of Ulysses?" asked Chronicle angrily. "I worship Ulysses! He brought technology to Benevolaria!"

"It seems I've got a bit of explaining to do, Chronicle," sighed Adrian. "The war of the druids ruined the world! The druids were all but wiped out, and the other people have used the technology to pollute Maltesque. That's the world's new name."

"So Ulysses ruined the world?" asked Chronicle, shocked. "I can't believe that! He was our savior! He lifted us out of the dark ages! He gave us the gift of technology!"

"But it wasn't a gift you were ready for," replied Adrian gently. "A Third Order of druids has been formed, and they are trying to fix the world. However, Kronos, the new Ulysses, stands in their way. I am Kronos' mortal enemy, and trying to save the world."

"Then I shall help you," proclaimed Chronicle. "If the actions of the second order have reduced the world to this hell, then I will do everything in my power to save it."

"Our first task is to kill the demon Necropheus," began Adrian. "It's my fault he was created, and I will see to it that I will be his demise."

"How can I help?" asked Chronicle. "I'll do anything you ask of me."

"Well, we'd best keep going. We need to make it back to the Deadwood Forest, since that's where Necropheus lives."

"Where is the Deadwood?" inquired Chronicle. Adrian pointed north. "Is that what the forest's now called? Is it accurately named?"

Adrian nodded, and the two set out northwards.

***

At day's end, they pitched Adrian's tent underneath a sand dune, and slept as far away from each other as the situation allowed, for they found the close proximity to one another to be somewhat awkward.

The next morning, they got up at the crack of dawn. After preparing and consuming a small breakfast, Adrian encountered a small problem: there was only enough food packed for one person.

"So what do we do?" asked Chronicle. "I mean, we need to eat, don't we? How much food do we have?"

"Maybe enough to make it to the Deadwood, but once we get there, we're stuck," sighed Adrian. "Ah well. I guess it's not a big deal right now."

"You're probably right," smiled Chronicle. "It's not a big deal, is it? So, should we keep heading north?" Adrian gave a swift nod, and they strode along the bank of the river towards the cloud of red on the horizon.

In an hour or so, Adrian saw a familiar landmark in the distance. Falcon's hut, long abandoned, stood at the edge of the river. Adrian and Chronicle made their way to the hut.

"What is this place?" asked Adrian's partner, as the two stepped in the door. "Did someone use to live here?"

"Falcon did," answered Adrian. "He's one of the leaders of the Third Order. I first met him in this hut."

"Are those bloodstains on the floor?!" asked Chronicle incredulously. "I'm not sure I want to meet this man." Adrian looked carefully at the stains, and laughed.

"Those are mine," he laughed. "I sort of charged in, and Falcon hit me on the head. I didn't realize I was bleeding, but I guess he hit me harder than I realized."

"Hm," mused Chronicle. He and Adrian looked about the hut, and found about a day's supply of food. This eased Adrian's worry somewhat, but not entirely. After a few minutes, they were ready to continue on their journey.

Adrian and Chronicle made camp beneath a sand dune again, and fell asleep swiftly, as it had been a hard day's journey.

The next morning, Adrian awoke, and squeezed his eyes shut immediately, wishing he had remained asleep. A giant scorpion stood poised directly over him, looked curiously at him.

Adrian summoned lightning. He began to crackle with energy, and the scorpion leapt back. Adrian loosed the burst of lightning, sending the scorpion flying backwards. Chronicle was awakened by the clamor, and his beast instincts, which he still retained from his experience as a monster, took over. With a cry, he jumped on the fallen scorpion, finding all of its pressure points in his mad assault.

The scorpion was dead, slain by its own curiosity. Adrian and Chronicle stood huffing and puffing, regaining their strength. They were bent over, tired and still waking up.

"Interesting start to the day, eh?" coughed Adrian with a smile. "I guess we should keep our eyes open. Something doesn't seem quite right about the whole affair. I see no reason for a scorpion to try to investigate a camp of humans."

"They haven't seen humans for years and years," suggested Chronicle. "After all, no one, save you, has traversed this route for decades, if not centuries."

"Maybe it was an effect of Necropheus' spell," suggested Adrian. "Look carefully at the carcass. There seem to be red markings on it, almost like tattoos. Do you see them?"

"I see them, alright," frowned Chronicle. "But I've never seen them before. It seems that you're right."

"Then all the more reason for us to hurry," stated Adrian grimly. "We have no way of knowing if killing Necropheus will remove the spell from the Deadwood, but I'm sure if that doesn't, I can."

"Adrian, how is it that you are able to summon lightning?" asked Chronicle. "I've lived a long time, but I've never seen that particular kind of talent. Is it a miracle of the new technology?"

"No," laughed Adrian. "It's a power inherited from my ancient ancestor, Photosia. She was the goddess of light."

"Indeed!" exclaimed Chronicle, surprised. "That's quite a prestigious position, isn't it!?"

Adrian was about to respond, but something caught his eye. He turned to the side, and saw something moving in the water. There were bubbles rising to the surface, and he was a disturbance of the surface tension, indicating that something was moving beneath the waves.

Without warning, a root burst out of the river, towering at least twelve feet above Adrian. It lunged. He was able to roll to the side in time to avoid being hit, but Chronicle wasn't so lucky.

"Hello, Adrian," hissed the root. "Do you recognize me? You should, since you've seen me in Light's End twice. You see, with Necropheus' spell in place, we are free of the Great Sage's restraints, and we can move of our own accord, though it's a difficult process. In exchange for freeing us of the Sage, we have pledged our loyalty to Necropheus. His first task for us: eliminate you, Adrian!"

Adrian was at a loss, but he did know one thing: at heart, the ambassadors were good, and would never willingly serve Necropheus. "Listen to yourself!" shouted Adrian. "Do you hear what you're saying? Do you realize what you're doing?"

"I do, Adrian," cackled the ambassador. "But do you? You're opposing the world's new master. Not a smart thing to do!"

Adrian looked carefully at the ambassador, and saw red markings, similar to the ones on the scorpion, littering its body. The wood that the root was made of was also more of a mahogany hue than it had been before.

While Adrian was thinking, the root made another lunge at him, though it still held Chronicle in its grip. Adrian did not see it coming until it was too late, and he was sent flying backwards. The ambassador then seemed to realize that it still held Chronicle in its grip. He dropped Chronicle, and made a lunge for Adrian. Adrian dropped to the ground in time to avoid being hit, and began to summon light energy to fight with.

Thankfully, he still had energy residue left over from fighting the scorpion, and unleashed it upon the ambassador. It screamed at Adrian in some indiscernible language, and then regained its senses, and picked Chronicle back up.

"Very well," it growled. "For now I'll be satisfied with taking your friend. I'll be sure to take good care of him, but it might be in his best interests for you to surrender yourself."

"Don't do it Adrian!" shouted the Sage. "You've already gone to too much trouble on his account! Please, I'm begging you!"

"Adrian..." coughed Chronicle, "please... people are counting on you. Listen to the Sage."

"Take Chronicle!" shouted Adrian. "But know this: I'll get him back!"

"Yes, but not right now," smirked the ambassador. "I guess I'll be seeing you around, Adrian." The root plunged back into the water, and Adrian saw it slither away. He watched it retreat for a few moments, and then ran after it.

"Adrian, you did the right thing," comforted the Sage. "After all, Chronicle hasn't done anything to help us yet. You didn't owe him anything."

"Yes," replied Adrian. "But now I do. I have to free him! I owe it to the ambassadors, as well. I owe them freedom, after what I did to them while serving Necropheus."

"Then your task remains unchanged: kill Necropheus," grimly said the Sage. "But Adrian, don't wear yourself out. There's no need for you to run the entire way."

"I know, Sage," replied Adrian, slowing his pace to a walk. "I know."

***

Adrian saw the first traces of red in the river soon after. He dipped his hand in, and decided that merely the color had changed, not the contents. Adrian was slightly glad about that, for it would have deeply disturbed him otherwise.

Adrian thought he saw something moving in the water, but he did not examine any further, for fear that it might be the ambassador returning for him. Adrian saw the first distinct tree in the distance, and took to musing.

"I'm really going back," he sighed aloud, though no one could hear him. "I have no choice, but still... When I think about all that's happened here, I can't help but feel a certain unique resentment. Especially towards Blaise."

Adrian then wondered exactly how different the Deadwood was now. It was closer than before, but still too far for him to really see everything. "I wonder if there was anyone else in the Deadwood, aside from Necropheus, Vitalius, and Blaise. I doubt it. It's not able to sustain life." But then how did the Leocavia survive, he wondered in his mind. Maybe they fed off of dead wood, he mused.

"No one knows how the giant cats are able to survive," replied the Sage unhelpfully, who seemed to have been eavesdropping on Adrian' thoughts. "It's one of those mysteries that may never be solved."

"Intriguing," replied Adrian, though his thoughts were elsewhere. The

Great Sage could hear what he thought, but not what he said, reasoned Adrian. He had never felt more secure speaking his thoughts than keeping them in his mind before. "Interesting," he smiled aloud. "So the Sage can't hear what I say out loud."

"Yes, but I can hear you figuring out what you're going to say in your mind before you say it," replied the Sage. "I'm like your conscience." Adrian could now see the drawback of perpetual mental connectivity.

However, he turned his thoughts away from that, and focused instead on the rapidly approaching Deadwood Forest. The red hue was now much more apparent, and Adrian saw that it was a result of the trees' transformation. They too had the strange red symbols on them, and Adrian wondered if everything that was affected by the spell had the markings on it.

"Well, here I am," smiled Adrian grimly. He looked at the ground, and saw something that immediately caught his attention.

"Sage, there's something interesting here," frowned Adrian. "Can you look at it through my eyes?"

"Yes. What do you see?" inquired the Sage. "What is it? I don't see anything interesting."

"Look at the ground," replied Adrian. The Great Sage complied, and still didn't see anything.

"What is it?" he asked yet again. "I still don't see anything."

"The red path!" exclaimed Adrian. "It's just on the ground here. Don't tell me you can't see it!"

"No, not really," sighed the Sage. "Describe it to me."

"Wait. Now I don't see it either," sighed Adrian. "Did you do something to me? What happened?"

"You sure you can't see it?" asked the Sage. "Was it a vision of some kind?"

"Maybe," mused Adrian. "It kind of looked like it was heading to the north. I'd bet you that it's somewhere around here."

"Keep an eye out for it," ordered the Sage. "Now you've got me curious. I guess you should keep following the river. It should lead you to Necropheus' clearing."

"Doesn't one of your ambassadors live around here?" asked Adrian cautiously. "He's probably out to get me as well."

"He doesn't live particularly near the river," assured the Sage. "I think we've already passed him."

"Let's hope so," shuddered Adrian. He followed the red river further into the Deadwood.

Suddenly, a Juvenile Leocavia jumped into his path, snarling ferociously.

Adrian looked closely, and saw that it too had the mark of Necropheus' spell. He had no lightning left over, and jumped out of the way as the cat lunged at him. Adrian saw a sudden change come over the cat, and the red markings began to glow.

The cat transformed into a being of pure energy, and shed its old body. It was now a glowing red mass of energy, which flung itself upon Adrian.

Adrian was not fast enough to dodge, and screamed in agony as the energy burned his flesh. Thankfully, it used itself up very quickly, and Adrian was able to summon up energy to cure himself.

However, that action seemed to render the energy in his body unstable. Lightning poured out of his hands without warning, using up his strength. He tried to stop it, but to no avail.

Thankfully, the Great Sage stepped in, and stemmed the flow of energy. Adrian had to use all of his self-control to prevent the energy from pouring out again. He wasn't able to make much more progress that day.

Come night, he found an old tree, conspicuously lacking of red markings. Adrian figure it would be a safe place to sleep for the night, and laid the blanket he had packed over him, and fell asleep.

He dreamed of Necropheus defeating him in battle, and throwing his body into the river. Necropheus, who seemed to be the protagonist of the dream, then traveled to the Rocky Outcrop, and teleported to the Great Sage, and then-

Adrian woke up in a cold sweat. He glanced around worriedly, and quickly calmed himself down.

The next morning, Adrian got up quickly, and continued following the river. His dream tormented him, though he tried not to think of it. The Deadwood grew more sinister the further into it Adrian walked. He caught a glance of something moving in the trees, and walked over to investigate. He didn't see anything, and turned around to leave.

As his back was turned, something struck him from behind. He sprawled to the ground, and pushed himself back onto his feet. However, he did not see anything save the trees. He backed away slowly, keeping his eyes open. He heard a swishing sound from behind him, and whirled around. He didn't see anything.

Feeling in danger, he raced away. Again, he heard a swishing sound, and this time he dropped to the ground, and looked up. A branch sailed by overhead. Adrian turned to see who had thrown it, but there was nobody there. He looked to see where the branch had fallen on the ground, but the ground was clear.

Adrian suddenly had a sort of epiphany. He turned in time to see another branch hurtling at him, still fully attached to the tree. Adrian tried to summon lightning, and failed to do so. This is getting old, he thought, annoyed at how long it took him to summon lightning.

However, his annoyance was tempered by fear. He wondered who was controlling the trees, and if it was a druid or someone like Rose, who had learned how to use the powers given to her.

However, he did not see anyone controlling the trees. "Are you truly that dense?" laughed a voice from nearby. "There is no one controlling me! I act of my own free will!"

Adrian looked around to find who was talking, and suddenly realized that it had been the tree. Necropheus' spell had brought it to life, he realized with a start! He didn't have enough energy to summon lightning yet, so he decided his best bet was to run away. He hated it, for urge to fight surged within him, but he had no alternative.

After he was what he considered a safe distance away, he turned to look. The tree had uprooted itself, and was slowly making its way towards Adrian. A thrill ran through him, and he stood his ground, preparing to face his pursuer. He had enough lightning built up to take down the tree, and unleashed it in a blaze of white fury.

The tree burst into flames, and staggered around a bit, bumping into other trees, which in turn caught on fire. "Curse you!" shouted the initial tree with the remainder of his strength. "Curse you, Deathbringer!"

"Deathbringer," thought Adrian, as he watched the forest around burn with the flames of his own making. "How fitting."

"Adrian, move!" shouted the Great Sage. "You don't need to burn too!"

"Relax, Sage," smirked Adrian. "I have no intention of dying." Adrian let his instincts take over, and a strange rage seemed to overcome him. Adrian's eyes flashed a deep crimson, and he strode directly through the flames, emerging untouched.

A dark aura surrounded Adrian, and it grew in size as he strode through the forest fire. After a minute, he was back at the river shore. He turned, and had one last look at the fire. He held up his hands, and attempted to summon lightning. Instead, the dark aura extended from his hands, and wrapped around the trees. There was an explosion, and the flames doubled in size.

Adrian stepped into the water of the river, and his mind was cleared. "Sage, what happened?" he gasped. "What did I just do?"

"I think that Necropheus' spell had an unforeseen effect on you," mused the Sage. "If I may explore your mind, I think I'll be able to see exactly what it did." The Great Sage entered Adrian's mind, and looked at the light cloud first. There was a small speck of darkness in it, but it was very well suppressed by the surrounding light.

"Is there any permanent damage?" asked Adrian worriedly. "Is everything okay? That was one of the more frightening experiences I've ever had!"

"Relax Adrian," began the Sage. "You're fine. There's a small bit of darkness in the light cloud, but I think it'll disappear quickly."

"I guess that I'm fine then," shrugged Adrian. "No big deal right?"

"Adrian, take a look at the western bank of the river," commanded the Sage. "While you may be fine, the forest doesn't seem to be so." Adrian looked back the way he had come, and gasped in horror. The entire west side of the forest was ablaze, the dead trees consuming one another in a storm of flames. "This is what can happen if you use your powers without thinking!" exclaimed the Sage.

"How should I have known it was going to happen?" asked Adrian. "I mean, I guess I could've figured it out, if I'd thought about it…"

"And there you go. You didn't think," reprimanded the Sage sternly. "And now half a forest is dead. Is this what you want?"

"No," sighed Adrian. "I guess I'd better keep going, on the other side of the river."

"Well, since there's no way to put the fire out now, you definitely should keep going," ordered the Sage. "But keep your head about you! Another stunt like that could cost your life!"

"Is it really a bad thing, though?" asked Adrian. "There was nothing living in there, was there?"

"One of my ambassadors was over there!" raged the Sage. "He'll be able to save himself, but what if Chronicle is over there? What then?"

"Then he's dead," replied Adrian softly. "Is there any way to keep the fire from spreading?" he asked suddenly. "I know we can't put it out, but can we keep it from spreading?"

"I suppose there might be a way, but I don't think it's a good idea," frowned the Sage. "Go to the edge of the fire, and I'll give you further instructions then."

Adrian nodded, and swam to the other side of the river. He got out, and raced quickly northwards. The fire was spreading quickly, but Adrian could see that there was indeed a spot in the north where it ended.

He raced as fast as his legs would carry him towards the north, and after a while, he looked to the side, and saw that he was now near the edge of the fire, though it was spreading quickly.

After he was what he considered to be a safe distance ahead, he jumped back into the river, and swam across. He pulled himself out, and asked, "All right, Sage, what's next?"

"Talking to yourself, are we?" smirked Chronicle, slowly walking towards

Adrian. "Did you get lonely without me?"

"Chronicle! You're safe!" exclaimed Adrian. "How did you escape?"

"The ambassador let me go," shrugged Chronicle. "However, we had a nice conversation first. He told me his side of the story, and he was very persuasive." Suddenly, a red rune lit up on his head, and a smile came over his face. "Now, goodbye, Adrian."

Suddenly, the man's whole body was aglow with a dark red aura, much like the color that Adrian's eyes had turned a few minutes ago. He lifted up his hands, and red energy flowed forth, wrapping itself around Adrian.

"Chronicle, what are you doing?" cried Adrian. "There's a fire! I must put it out! Please, Chronicle, let me go!"

"Ah, I don't think so," smiled Adrian's former friend. "You see, I now have a debt to repay Necropheus for saving me."

"Saving you from what?!" shouted Adrian. "Himself?"

"He saved me from you!" roared Chronicle. "You, Lightseeker, Deathbringer, Adrian! These are but a few of the names you have earned yourself. Here are some more: double-crosser, egotist, back-stabber! You have no sense of honor!"

"I saved you, didn't I?" shot back Adrian. "I saved you from an eternity of life as a monster!"

"And you then let the ambassador kidnap me!" replied Chronicle. "Either way, I'm done with you!" He snapped his fingers, and the red energy bound itself around him. Adrian toppled over, and fell to the ground. He was completely unable to move.

"So you're just going to let me burn, is that it?!" shouted Adrian. "You're just going to let me die?"

"I'm sure you'll be able to free yourself," shrugged Chronicle. "Anyhow, I don't intend to let you get killed by the flames, certainly. However, I do wish to see you surrounded by them, so you may experience true fear." Chronicle snapped his fingers, and a red pathway extended before Adrian, perfectly matching the one he had seen earlier. "Once you're free, follow the path," advised Chronicle. "If you manage to free yourself. But I warn you, it's a road to hell, and the further in you get, the worse it gets. If I were you, I wouldn't even bother trying to free yourself."

Chronicle walked away, and Adrian immediately summoned up lightning, and attempted to push apart the red energy. However, that approach failed, and he asked, "Sage! What should I do?"

"Adrian, see if you can use lightning to widen the space between you and the energy," suggested the Sage.

Adrian obeyed, and was able to sort of lubricate himself. He wriggled about a bit, and was able to worm his way out of the energy prison. He stood up, and looked about. The red path extended behind him a ways, and the fire was rapidly approaching it. Adrian observed that the path seemed to deflect the fire, as Chronicle had said.

"Sage, what do I do?" he asked. "I'm at the fire's edge."

"Throw the seed into the fire," commanded the Sage. Adrian didn't respond for a few moments. "Please, Adrian! I know I won't be able to communicate with you, but you can manage on your own! I've got enough strength in this seed to stop the fire, so throw me in!"

Adrian sighed, and obeyed. The seed burst into green energy, and attempted to waylay the fire. However, the Great Sage shouted out to Adrian, "This is not natural fire! You must have done something to it! It's as if it comes from the gates of hell itself! I cannot stop it!"

The Great Sage pulled his mind out of the seed, so as to avoid being consumed by the flames, and Adrian was alone. He stood in that spot for a few moments, while the fire surrounded him, though it could not touch him, as he was on the red pathway.

Soon enough, he could see naught but flames. He slowly walked north, taking care not to step out of the path. With both the Sage and Chronicle gone, a sudden sense of loneliness overcame him.

He walked the road to hell, an uncertain future ahead of him, and flames closing in behind him.

21

To Kill A Demon

Adrian walked slowly down the red path, his mind clouded by confusion. He ignored the flames, the heat, the horror; he focused on just one thing: he was alone again. Though he had been in constant danger ever since he had come to Maltesque, he had been alone only twice, during his initial visit to Light's End. A sense of abandonment was ever-present, as he strode down the red road.

Up ahead, he saw a giant hulking shape, and he knew that he'd found his target: Necropheus. The demon towered twenty-odd feet high, with his back turned, and Adrian prepared for his attack. He still periodically sparked bits of lightning, since he had just used his powers on the red energy that had bound him.

Necropheus was covered in red runes, exactly alike to the numerous others that Adrian had seen so far. He was very well muscled, and still retained a somewhat humanoid shape. There were two scars on both of his shoulders, and the parts of his body that weren't red were a dark black. Adrian guessed that the runes made sense, since Necropheus had been the main recipient of his own spell.

Adrian readied the lightning attack. However, as he stepped forwards, Necropheus turned around.

"Ah, hello, Adrian!" he rumbled. "I've been expecting you. Since it's your fault, along with the ambassadors, that I'm in this monstrous form, I think it's fitting that I should annihilate all of you with it!"

Necropheus lunged at Adrian, who sidestepped the attack, and Necropheus was sent sprawling into the flames, which licked at his body. He stood up again, untouched. "Well done, Adrian," he snarled. "But you're not the only one who's learned a few new tricks."

Necropheus jumped into the air, coming down directly over Adrian. Adrian did not have enough light energy stored up to stop Necropheus, so he jumped to the side to avoid being hit. However, he was directly behind Necropheus, and the demon turned around, and his hand shot out at Adrian. Fortunately for Adrian, at that moment, one of the periodic bursts of lightning escaped his body, and burned Necropheus.

The demon wasn't completely sure what had just happened, but he assumed that the fire had somehow burned him, even though he was seemingly immune. Regardless, he lunged at Adrian yet again, and the boy was easily able to sidestep the attack. Necropheus decided that his current strategy wasn't working, and attempted a new one that stood a better chance of working.

Necropheus concentrated, as if willing for the world to bend to his command. It did not, but Adrian relaxed his guard just slightly. Necropheus took this opportunity, and his arm shot out to grab the boy. Adrian was suddenly imprisoned in Necropheus' unusually cold grasp, a slight relief from the all-consuming heat.

"Well, it looks like I've got you now," chuckled Necropheus. "And what're you going to do about it? I'm invulnerable to fire, and it looks like that's your only weapon right now."

"So, Chronicle didn't tell you?" smirked Adrian.

"Tell me what?" asked a confused Necropheus. Adrian decided that his best bet would be to demonstrate. He let all the stored up lightning fly out of his body, shocking Necropheus.

The demon was temporarily paralyzed by the outburst of lightning, and dropped Adrian. Adrian now had a slightly different issue he had to deal with: he was falling from a height that could easily kill him. Fear of imminent death consumed him, and he let his primal instincts take over again.

Once again, his eyes burned red, and some sort of dark spell emerged from his hands, and his fall slowed. He crouched on the ground, glaring up at Necropheus. "So you want to kill me?" asked Adrian. "Well, allow me to fix that!" Adrian thrust his hand forth, and shadow magic exploded from his fingertips, enveloping Necropheus.

The demon screamed. It was a soul-shattering scream, the kind that no one hears without it being permanently burned into his or her memory. Adrian however, was unaffected. He let loose another round of shadow energy, and Necropheus was knocked backwards again, and fell to his feet.

Necropheus screamed again, this time in rage. He too, it seemed, now possessed some kind of power, and unleashed a whirlwind of red energy at Adrian. The boy was knocked back, and he sprawled to his knees.

"Very well," declared Necropheus. "I'll see you later, Adrian. It's fatal folly to face you at full strength, so I think I'll weaken you up a bit first."

Necropheus concentrated again, and this time something did happen. Two wings appeared, filling the scars on his shoulders. "See you soon, Adrian!" he cackled as he lifted up off the ground.

Adrian, in the meantime, was locked in a vicious battle with himself. It was like there were two sides of him, both battling for supremacy: the normal Adrian, and his dark side, who had just been given freedom for the second time.

Adrian Lightseeker, the one fighting for good, prevailed over his alternate self. He stood up, and saw Necropheus flying away. "I'm not done with you yet!" exclaimed Adrian, chasing after him. Necropheus easily outdistanced him, but Adrian kept his eyes on his target.

However, merely a few minutes had passed before something unexpected happened. He realized that there were few trees around him, but his eyes were still totally focused on Necropheus. Without warning, something charged into him from the side, knocking him over.

"Take that, Adrian!" shouted a voice that Adrian immediately recognized, and his lips formed one word: "Chronicle". "That's right, Adrian," snarled Chronicle. "I'm back! This time, you're going down!"

"No," replied Adrian, getting to his feet. "This time, it's you who's going down! I've got a score to settle with you, on the behalf of all the Deadwood!"

"So be it," snarled Chronicle. "Bring it on! Do you know where we are?"

"Not really," shrugged Adrian. "Where?" He looked around, but all he saw was the all-consuming fire. "Fool!" bellowed Chronicle. "Are you truly that moronic? We're in Necropheus' clearing! The place where the spell was cast!"

Adrian looked about again, and observed that Chronicle was right: they were in the clearing where Adrian had first met Necropheus, and where he had cast the spell that obliterated the Deadwood.

"So we are," chuckled Adrian. "So, does this have any particular significance to you?"

"It most certainly does," replied Chronicle. "It means that I am now in the exact center of the Deadwood, standing in the very spot where Necropheus thrust his staff into the ground. And you know what? It's still here!"

Adrian realized too late what Chronicle meant by that. By the time he realized what was going to happen, Chronicle's hand had shot out, and grabbed the staff. With a tug, it was wrenched free of the ground. Nothing changed, but Chronicle now held one of the most deadly weapons in the world.

Chronicle held the staff aloft, and his eyes closed. He stood like that for a moment, and a grin spread across his face. "Adrian, do you know what's in this staff?" he asked. "Necropheus used it to store the spirits of the things that he killed. Even though the vast majority of the spirits in here were used to power the spell, his first spirit remains. Do you know what the first thing he killed was? Of course not! However, with this staff providing the soul, and his spell providing a new body, I would like to introduce you to one of the oldest residents of Maltesque: the last of the dragons!"

He thrust the staff into the air, and grey and black energy poured forth, assimilating into a useless mass. However, Chronicle closed his eyes, and his focus turned to Necropheus' spell. He toyed with it a bit, and eventually was able to conjure up a red form, which mixed with the black grey mass. Chronicle willed it into a shape, and Adrian stepped back in awe as the most magnificent animal he had ever laid eyes upon came into being.

The cloud of energy solidified into solid mass, and Adrian initially could only discern two wings and a vaguely serpentine body. However, as the energy began to condense, he saw two brilliant red eyes staring at him, and a dark green body, covered in the now-familiar red runes, began to appear, along with several other sets of wings.

The fully formed dragon loosed a ferocious roar, knocking Adrian back a few feet. He swiftly recovered his stance, and prepared to do battle with the beast. It towered at about ten feet, though he estimated it to be about thirty feet long. It looked remarkably like a snake, albeit one with legs, and one with wings lining its body.

The dragon's mouth opened, and a stream of liquid fire came pouring out, barely missing Adrian. Adrian summoned up some of his lightning, unleashing it on the dragon. The beast, however, merely rolled to the side, avoiding the blow.

The dragon flapped its wings, and it rose into the air. It flew at Adrian, who sidestepped the attack. However, one of the dragon's wings caught Adrian squarely in the chest, and he toppled to the ground.

The dragon again lunged, its jaws open wide. However, Adrian fell to the ground, and the dragon was just a bit too high to hit him. Adrian saw the dragon pause, confused, and decided it would be a good time to barrage it with lightning.

He felt the energy draining from his body, but the dragon was sent sprawling to the ground. It coughed feebly, and then was still. Adrian turned towards Chronicle with a grin on his lips.

"Well, it looks like your monster lost," smiled Adrian. "Now then, I believe that we have some unfinished business to take care of!"

"Yes, but you have some of your own first," sighed Chronicle. Every atom of Adrian's body screamed out in protest as the dragon opened its mouth, and summoned forth flames, scorching Adrian's turned back. Adrian's back was completely engulfed in flames, and he rolled about on the ground, screaming.

The flames were put out quickly, but Adrian's back was now a victim of multiple burns. Suddenly, lightning exploded from his body, searing the drag-on, which jumped onto its feet, and retreated to get away from the storm of burning light.

Adrian was able, after a minute or so of screaming, to regain his sanity. He used the last reserves of his energy to heal his back. He fell back down to the ground, exhausted.

Unfortunately, the dragon wasn't done with him yet. He jumped at Adrian, and prepared to bite down on his neck. Adrian, not being in full control of his light powers, still in fact had a bit of energy left, though he was unaware of it. It came pouring out into the mouth of the dragon, and that was the final straw for the ancient beast. It exploded in a flash of red energy, which surged into Adrian's body, replenishing his strength. It attempted to flow into the spot of darkness in his mind, but the light cloud deflected and absorbed it.

"NOOOO!!!!!" cried Chronicle. "I can't believe that summoning a dragon failed to dispose of you! Do you ever die, Adrian? Curse you!"

"Well, not yet," replied Adrian, a grin coming over his face. "Anyhow, like I said, we have unfinished business to take care of. Prepare yourself, Chroni-cle!"

Adrian attempted to call forth lightning, but apparently the red energy had not only replenished him, but totally brought him back to square one. He guessed that it would take at least a minute to summon lightning, and he did not have that time to spare.

Apparently Chronicle was not going to waste his opportunity. He thrust the staff into the air once more, but did not try the summoning trick again. Instead, he thought it would be a good idea to shoot bits of soul at Adrian.

Adrian dodged the vast majority of the blows from Chronicle, but not all of them. One of the energy blasts hit him on the arm, sending him sprawling to the side. Chronicle then seized the opportunity, and blasted him with numerous other blows.

By that point, Adrian had enough energy stored to fight with, and he un-leashed a bit of it at his assailant. Necropheus' staff was knocked from Chroni-cle's hand, and Chronicle himself was send flying backwards, out of the safety of the red path. He fell into the fire, which he himself had assisted in the cre-ation of, and shrieked in agony and horror at his own demise.

Adrian turned away from the sickening sight. He continued down the red path, safe from the flames. However, after a few steps, a smirk alit upon his lips, and he turned around and walked back.

Adrian stooped over, and picked up Necropheus' staff, which Chronicle had dropped in his last moments. A grin came over Adrian as he lifted it into the air.

He entered the staff with his mind, and was immediately assaulted by thousands of messages by the spirits of those who had been trapped in the staff for ages. They all had several different things to say, but they all had one particular message: they wanted to be free. Adrian promised that he would free the remaining spirits at the right moment, and they agreed that they would do whatever Adrian asked of them until the right time, and Adrian assumed that they would know when the time came for him to free them.

***

Adrian noted, with some dismay, that the flames showed no sign of dwindling. He was still surrounded by clouds of fire, and though they could not touch him, the sheer heat still scorched his senses.

Off in the distance, he could see Necropheus. The demon still flew away from him, but he could see that Necropheus seemed to be tiring. He was flying towards a familiar place: the rocky outcrop. He wondered what had happened to Virda, or if the spell had affected her at all.

Suddenly, a lone ember spilled onto the red road. Adrian assumed that it would quickly dwindle out, but it did not. Slowly but surely, the road caught fire, and Adrian stepped away from the small patch of flames.

He turned around, and saw that the same thing was occurring behind him. Apparently, with Chronicle gone, his spell had worn off, and the red road was now susceptible to flames.

Adrian panicked. He turned around, and saw that the path behind him was also engulfed in flame. The fire was thicker behind him, so he decided his best bet would be to continue forwards.

He leapt over the first patch of flames, and saw that the path was getting narrower ahead of him as the flames entered new territory. He raced forwards, but the Rocky outcrop seemed impossibly far away.

He yelped as the flames licked at his feet, and he quickened his pace accordingly. However, the flames were faster than he, and swiftly discovered that the bottoms of his pant legs were ablaze.

He screamed, and jumped into the air. Sadly, he rapidly returned to earth, and his feet were now burning as well. Adrian desperately wished that he still had the Great Sage to talk to, but that was not meant to be. A feeling of calmness washed over him as he realized that there was nothing to do.

***

However, the spirits within the staff thought otherwise. They had made a pact with Adrian, and if he died, they might never be set free, or so they reasoned. They collectively pooled their wills, and a circle of grey energy flowed out from the staff, and formed around Adrian's feet, shielding him from the blaze.

***

Adrian gasped as the flames disappeared, and a circle materialized around him. He used his light powers to heal his burnt feet and legs, and wondered if the circle would move with him. He decided that his best option would be to test it.

He tentatively took one step forwards, but the circle remained in its previous location. He stepped back, and realized that he had somehow dropped his staff. He picked it up, and tried stepping forwards again. This time, the circle of energy followed him.

Adrian strode forwards, staff in hand, to face the evil master of the hell he was in.

After an hour of so, he noted that the fire was beginning to dwindle, though it still burned fairly bright. He was closing in on the Rocky Outcrop.

"Necropheus! I wasn't done with you yet!" roared Adrian, racing towards him. "Do you realize what you did to Chronicle? He's dead, because of you!"

By that time, Adrian had reached the outcrop, and was but feet away from his hated rival. "Welcome, Adrian," snarled Necropheus. "I do not yet need to fight you, though, I have one last servant for you to face first."

Necropheus stepped to the very back of the outcrop, and suddenly there was a flash of grey, and the spirit of an old woman materialized in front of Adrian. Though she was covered by the red runes that seemed to rule the Deadwood now, he still recognized her easily. One word formed on his lips: Virda.

"Hello, Adrian," she hissed. "It's been a while since we've seen each other, hasn't it. I'm glad to hear that you've taken my advice, and stuck to it faithfully. However, along the way you meddled in things that I never wished for anyone to meddle in. You've cancelled out the judgments I dealt out three thousand years ago!"

"You too, Virda!" cried out Adrian in exasperation. "Really? Very well, then. If I must fight you, then so be it!"

"Yes, you must," hissed Virda. "You must pay for the death of Democritus, who I promised eternal life, and for the freedom of Chronicle, who was meant to remain in his monstrous shell for all eternity!"

"Virda, I don't want to fight you!" plead Adrian. "You're a symbol of hope for this forsaken world! Please, the world needs your help!"

"Your pleas for mercy fall upon deaf ears," laughed Necropheus. "She is under my control now, and shall do as I command. And I think I'll command her to fight!" Necropheus snapped his fingers, and Virda assumed a battle stance.

Adrian began pooling his energy for a blast at Virda. His new enemy rose up into the air, as she was a spirit, and flew down at Adrian. The boy dove to the side to avoid being hit. Virda did not seem deterred, and swooped back down for another round. Adrian was unable to avoid it, but Virda just passed through him.

Adrian and Virda both seemed confused by the turn of events, and then they both seemed to realize that as Virda was a spirit, she had no physical mass, and, as such, was unable to touch Adrian.

Virda flew up high, away from Adrian, to contemplate a new strategy, and Adrian readied a bolt of lightning. Virda dropped back to ground level, and Adrian let the lightning fly from his hands. However, what goes around comes around, and since Virda was a spirit, the lightning passed harmlessly through her.

Now Adrian was stymied. He had never met a foe that lightning could not touch, and wasn't quite sure how to deal with it. However, Virda seemed to decide to press her opportunity, and reached out to the burning plants near the outcrop. They uprooted themselves, and flung themselves at Adrian.

Adrian was knocked onto his side, and the staff rolled out of his hand. He had nearly forgotten that he'd had it, and he quickly realized that since Virda was a spirit, other spirits were the only things that might be able to affect her, and the staff contained hundreds of spirits.

He recalled that Chronicle had managed to shoot bits of spirits at him, and they'd had quite an impact. He wondered, then, what would happen if he launched entire souls at Virda.

He thrust the staff forwards, and willed for a spirit to shoot out the end. That attempt did not work, and Virda used the opportunity to assault Adrian with burning foliage. Adrian then recalled how he had communicated with the spirits of the staff the first time, and entered it with his mind.

Adrian stood back up, and thrust the staff forwards once again. This time a spirit emerged from the end, and blasted itself towards Virda. It hit her in the stomach, and she fell to the ground, though the fall did not harm her.

Adrian took the opportunity to decimate the trees under Virda's control, which had ceased to move when their master crashed to the ground. They fell apart under the impact of the lightning strike.

"I'm sorry, Virda," whispered Adrian, firing another soul out of the end of the staff. Virda screeched, and slowly, the red runes began to disappear. Virda sat shivering on the ground.

"Well done, Adrian," she laughed softly, and she faded.

"She's dead," whispered Adrian, looking up at Necropheus. "You killed her!"

"She was already dead," sighed Necropheus exasperatedly. "She'll be back once you remove the curse from the Deadwood, which you'll only be able to do if you kill me, and that won't happen."

"Well, I don't know, Necropheus," smiled Adrian. "It looks like it's just you and me. No more servants to take the blow for you. No more tricks."

"No servants? Maybe," smirked Necropheus. "No tricks? I don't think so." Without warning, he lashed out, and the staff was knocked from Adrian's hands, and rolled just off of the rocky outcrop. It was just a couple of feet from Adrian, and he raced over to get it.

Necropheus concentrated, and a circular wall of energy surrounded the outcrop. Adrian tried to force his way through it, but the wall was too strong. He looked up, and saw that it did not cover the top of the outcrop. He wished that he could fly like Necropheus.

The demon seemed to have planned for the moment of confusion that Adrian had encountered. He rushed Adrian, slamming him into the wall of energy. Adrian felt something snap, and a sharp pain shot up his arm.

Adrian screamed in agony, and Necropheus picked him up, and flew into the air. He let go, planning to send Adrian falling to is death, but Adrian had other plans. He immediately used his light powers to heal his arm wound as he flew into the air, and then clung onto Necropheus' arm with all his strength. Necropheus shook him, but Adrian did not let go.

Necropheus brought Adrian up to his mouth, and prepared to bite the boy's head off. Adrian still had a lot of lightning left over, and he emptied it into Necropheus' mouth.

Necropheus crashed to the ground, and Adrian jumped out of his palm. Necropheus quickly regained his senses, and stood back up. He attempted to pummel Adrian with his fist, but Adrian was too fast.

Necropheus was growing impatient, and Adrian saw a cunning gleam in his eye, as he seemed to come upon a new idea. He flapped his wings, and rose into the air. Adrian kept a close eye on him, but he flew beyond Adrian's vision within half a minute.

Adrian turned his attention to the wall of energy that locked him in the Rocky Outcrop. He summoned the easily available lightning energy, and blasted the wall as hard as he could, but it refused to budge.

Adrian looked up again, and saw a giant meteor plummeting to earth. It took him a few seconds to realize that the meteor was Necropheus. The demon was planning to crush Adrian upon impact.

Adrian's mind raced with possible solutions, all of them outlandish. He definitely couldn't jump high enough to clear the energy barrier, and he knew this. He also knew that his light powers weren't strong enough to redirect Necropheus away from him. He decided that his best option was to just try to avoid Necropheus, and make sure that he didn't quite land on him.

Adrian kept a close eye on the demon as he plummeted. Necropheus seemed to be drifting a little to the left, so Adrian moved to the right. As Necropheus neared the ground, Adrian saw that he had calculated correctly.

Necropheus hit the ground with a huge amount of force, and the Rocky Outcrop was shattered. Adrian was caught up in the avalanche that ensued, and he realized that it had been Necropheus' plan all along.

Adrian still had an inordinate amount of light energy left. He and Necropheus both were nearly buried in the rubble from what had formerly been the outcrop, and Adrian saw that Necropheus had managed to embed himself in the ground. He recalled hearing somewhere that lightning hurts less if you're in contact with the ground, so he waited for Necropheus to pull himself out.

"You're still alive?!" he roared, seeing Adrian staring at him. "What does it take to kill you? Well, I'll do it again, it I have to!" He flapped his wings, and rose back into the air.

Adrian figured he had about a minute, so once he had built up the right amount of light energy, he looked at what had formerly been the Rocky Outcrop. The smooth portion, where Virda had lived, had only taken up a little bit of the full outcrop, which had now sort of formed a hill leading into the sea. He and Necropheus were on the beach, albeit a beach covered in rocks.

Adrian looked up, and saw that Necropheus was coming back down. He prepared the lightning barrage, and waited for him to come close enough, and then unleashed his attack. Necropheus was blasted back into the air, and Adrian used the rest of his strength to make sure he didn't come down again.

However, Necropheus was still alive, but just barely. He slumped to the ground, lying but thirty feet from Adrian. He attempted to stand up, but his legs were unable to perform that basic function. He loosed a roar of rage, and Adrian stepped back a few feet.

"ADRIAN!" he screamed. "CURSE YOU!" The red runes on his body glowed, and a whirlwind began to whip up at his feet. It directed itself straight at Adrian, who jumped to the side to avoid being hit.

Necropheus was lifted into the air by his own power, and another whirlwind brewed beneath him. He howled, and a dark sphere of energy began to appear in front of him

Adrian didn't like the look of the energy ball, and stepped backwards. Necropheus howled again, and a beam of black energy exploded from the sphere, and connected squarely with Adrian, who was lost in the swirling vortex of darkness.

Adrian was confused by the sudden turn of events, and he tried to summon light but the swirling darkness was too strong. He tried to run, but his legs were frozen in place. He felt his body begin to disappear, the darkness beam consuming it.

Adrian screamed, and lost his consciousness.

***

Necropheus weakly laughed in triumph, his nemesis vanquished. He figured that it would take a bit of time for him to recuperate, but not too long. The darkness beam faded, and, much to his horror, there was a boy standing there.

He looked immensely similar to Adrian, but there were a few things that set him apart. His eyes were a deep crimson, whereas Adrian's eyes had been a brilliant blue. Also, an aura of evil emanated from him, and Adrian had reeked of heroism.

"Hello, Necropheus," smirked the Adrian doppel-ganger. "I see that you weren't expecting to see me. Well, here I am."

"Who are you?" asked Necropheus. "Where is Adrian? Is he dead?"

"I am Adrian," sneered the look-alike. "I'm what your spell did to him. Well, both of your spells, actually. I'm Adrian's dark side."

"And do you support him?" asked Necropheus. "Or are you willing to join me? I could always use a new servant."

"I don't think so," sighed the dark Adrian. "You see, you, Necropheus, are too a slave. The spell that you cast on the Deadwood has gained a will of its own, and it has been using you. That spell created me, but Adrian locked me away. However, your darkness spell brought me out again."

"Then why are you siding against me? I created you!" shouted Necropheus. "You owe me! You should bow down before me!"

"No, I should bow down before Shadius, for he created me," cackled the evil Adrian. "And he wants Adrian alive. Yes, that's right. Shadius, the deity of darkness, is the one who took control of your feeble spell, and he is your master. If anything, you should bow down to me!"

"I WILL NOT!" roared the demon. "You will die for that!" Necropheus' runes glowed again, and he summoned another sphere of darkness. Instead of turning it into a ray, he chose to lob the ball at evil Adrian. Adrian's look-alike took it, and grew stronger from the hit.

Necropheus raged, and a red sphere instead appeared. It grew in size, but the dark Adrian ignored it, and shot bolts of black lightning at Necropheus, who ignored Adrian. Neither seemed to take the other seriously.

Adrian seemed to decided to wait out Necropheus' attack. The red sphere was now twice the size of the black ones, and Necropheus realized that it was not made out of darkness, so Adrian's dark side wouldn't be able to absorb it.

Adrian's eyes widened, and Necropheus assumed that he too had thought of that. It was too late for him now, though. A beam of red energy, not unlike the black ones from before, exploded from the sphere, and nearly reached the dark Adrian before he counterattacked.

The evil Adrian shot a beam of darkness into the incoming red blast, and there was a flash as energy erupted from the spot of contact, and both parties were obliterated by the attack.

***

Adrian stood up weakly. He didn't have any idea what had happened, but a giant skeleton lay on the ground in the spot where Necropheus had stood moments ago. He realized that something beyond the control of both him and Necropheus must have occurred. A grin spread across his features as he realized that his enemy was vanquished. He looked back at the Deadwood, and the grin turned to a look of confusion as he noticed that the red runes still covered the trees.

Also, the wall of energy locking him in the remnants of the Rocky Outcrop was still there, though slightly weakened. He blasted it with lightning, and though a strange feeling coursed through his body, he still was able to shatter the barrier in a certain spot, and grab Necropheus' staff.

Adrian turned around, and saw a cloud of darkness, tainted with red, rising from Necropheus' skeleton. "Greetings, Adrian," whispered the cloud, and Adrian fell to the ground clutching his head in agony, for he was listening to the voice of Shadius, undiluted and unfiltered. "I am Shadius, the deity of darkness. I have seized control of the curse upon the Deadwood, and this is the physical manifestation of that curse, infused with my own darkness energy. I require you for my regeneration, so if you will just kindly come with me..."

"I'll never help you!" cried Adrian, his anger overcoming the hold that Shadius' voice had on his mind. "Not after what you've done to Rose and Kronos! Not after what you've done to Photosia! And not after what you've done to me!"

"Oh, I've done more to you than you think!" cackled Shadius. "I infused you with a bit of... corruption. Sadly, your dark side was obliterated in his clash with Necropheus, which I arranged."

"Then I have even further reason not to go with you!" shouted Adrian.

"Ah, but you've got no choice," sneered Shadius. There was a pause, and tendrils of darkness erupted from the cloud, and swarmed at Adrian. Adrian, however, still had enough light energy to fight the tendrils. Lightning poured out of his hands, engulfing the storm of darkness in a sea of light.

Shadius fought back much more fiercely, however. "FOOL!" he bellowed. "Mere lightning is not enough to vanquish my tendrils of darkness! One would need pure light!"

The funny feeling that Adrian had gotten while blasting the energy barrier apart returned, and in his mind, the last part of the light cloud slid into place.

Pure light erupted from Adrian, burning the tendrils away. Shadius screamed in surprise and rage as he was banished from the curse on the Dead-wood. "Curse you, Adrian!" he shouted. "No longer do I wish to capture you! Even should I somehow regenerate, you'd still be much too big a threat! As of this moment, Adrian, I will do nothing but see that you are dead, killed in some way shape or form!"

Then Shadius was gone, and Adrian was still facing down the cloud of red energy from the Deadwood curse. However, he heard the voices of the spirits in the staff calling out to him, and they all knew that this was the time. Adrian ran up to the cloud, and stabbed it with the staff, which shattered upon contact with the energy.

Spirits long imprisoned flowed out of the staff, barraging the red energy cloud with thousands of blows. The cloud began to shrink in size, and it suddenly exploded in a flash of red.

Adrian felt a sense of relief as the curse was lifted from the Deadwood. However, the explosion of red energy had knocked him off his feet, and he fell to the ground with a thud as the sun rose over the horizon.

***

Adrian awoke, and looked around sleepily. He still lay upon the ruins of the Rocky Outcrop, but Virda stood over him, looking down.

"Did you sleep well, child?" she asked kindly. "I'm sure that you're wondering how I'm still alive, after my home, the Rocky Outcrop, was shattered. The truth is, the Outcrop was like a prison for me. Now that it's gone, destroyed by Necropheus, I'm free to move about."

"Virda, will you help me?" asked Adrian. "Will you lend your aid to the Third Order of druids?"

"Absolutely," smiled Virda, and Adrian fell back into a contented sleep.

***

Adrian woke up later, and looked about. Virda was gone, and he wondered how he was going to get back to the city, since all of his possessions had been in the bag, which had been destroyed in the numerous calamities that had ensued ever since he left the safety of the city.

A ghostly hand reached out to him, and a voice said, "Ah, master Adrian! It's been too long, hasn't it?"

"Vitalius!?" exclaimed Adrian.

22

The Traitor Revealed

Rose sighed. Ever since the Battle of the Five Towers, nothing interesting had happened. Arrow and Falcon had been working on plans for the attack on Cloudhall, and even when they hadn't been busy, both had seemed distant. Rose had been hoping to spend some time with Arrow, but they'd both been too distracted by the challenge of moving the entire Third Order out of the city.

Rose was glad for one thing, though. She had privacy, which was something that had not been hers ever since the night when Kronos had turned her into a slave. It hadn't been hers in the Deadwood, when she was with Adrian, and it hadn't been hers when she was constantly needed for meetings.

On the other hand, she got bored being alone all the time. She'd taken a couple of books out of the library, and read them, but none of them particularly interested her. She'd spent a good deal of her spare time sleeping, so at least she was well rested.

***

On the fifth morning since Adrian had left the order, Rose awoke with a strange feeling of anxiety. She'd had a nightmare about Adrian, and it still remained vividly in her mind, though most dreams faded very quickly.

Adrian had been surrounded by flames, and he'd looked scared and alone. She wondered how long it usually took a person to complete a difficult task from the Sage, as she had no further information about Adrian's task. Rose resolved to ask Arrow about it.

She rolled out of bed, and dressed herself. The feeling of apprehension did not disappear, and she felt a strange vibe coming off of the other members of the Third Order that she passed on her way to the elevator, and she assumed that she was not the only one perturbed by Adrian's absence.

She stepped into the elevator without really thinking, and pressed the first button that her hand reached. The doors slid shut, and the elevator rose up. This interested Rose, as she had never visited a higher floor of the tower before.

The elevator proceeded to rise for about a minute, and Rose realized that she must be headed towards the top floor of the tower. The doors opened, and she gasped in surprise. She was in standing in a room with walls of glass, overlooking the entire city. A smile spread across her face, and she realized that she had finally found something interesting.

She looked out the wall to her right, and discovered that it presented a view of the Great Sage, and the Poisonsap Forest. Straight ahead of her, there was a view of the sea. It was one of the few parts of Maltesque that she had not really seen, aside from when Vitalius had sent her to fetch Adrian.

To her left, the two great mountains loomed in the distance. Lava poured from the top of one, while the other was coated in ice. She looked at Mount Icecap and shivered. Though she looked forwards to having the boredom shattered, she did not savor the prospect of having to scale the icy peak. At the foot of the mountain, she saw a huge construct of machinery, and recognized it as the magma re-router. The device was thousands of years old, but yet it still performed its job magnificently. Rose almost felt a little sad that they'd have to tear it down, to both give the land a chance to heal and send a message to the corporate council.

Rose looked behind her, and saw the northern part of Maltesque. The Deadwood was alit with a red glow, and Rose wondered if it had anything to do with Necropheus' spell. She did not know that it was towards that very forest that Adrian was headed, nor did she know that the forest was going to be a much brighter red, before all was said and done.

Rose looked down from the windows, and saw something strange. There was a good deal of movement, more so than usual, in the streets. Various people seemed to be heading towards the base. Rose knew that the base was secret, so she dismissed it as a strange coincidence.

She turned towards the elevator, and jumped in surprise as the red light above the door suddenly began to glow, and a siren sounded throughout the building. The elevator refused to respond, and Rose realized that she was trapped.

She sprinted over to one of the windows, and looked down, in an attempt to see what had triggered the alarm. She saw that the soldiers she'd spotted moments ago were attacking the base. They threw bombs, and fired their guns, and rushed it with their men.

Rose doubted that anyone had seen it coming, and doubted that there would be much resistance at first. She desperately wished that she could help, but she was trapped in the glass room.

Suddenly, a helicopter floated up to the window. Rose was completely shocked, as she'd though that walking was the only means of transportation on Maltesque. Her father, she realized, must be behind the sudden advance in technology.

A man in the helicopter lifted up his gun, and shot the window of the room. Glass was strewn across the floor, and Rose ducked behind the pillar, which contained the elevator shaft.

The side door of the helicopter slid open, and a man looked into the room, and smiled. It took Rose a moment to realize that the man was none other than her father. "Hello, Rose," smiled Kronos, stepping out of the helicopter, and jumping into the room. "It's been too long, hasn't it?"

"Kronos," hissed Rose. "It has been too long. So, what do you plan to do with me?"

"Well, my dear, dear daughter, I think it's time that we took you to Genesis," sneered Kronos. "You see, I owe my master for allowing you to escape twice, and I wish to return to his good graces."

"Alright, Shadius, you can drop the façade," growled Rose. "I trust my dad, and know that he'd never take me to Genesis."

"Was I that obvious?" sighed Kronos. "You're right, of course. Ulysses has been locked far away, and I doubt that he'll ever be seen from again. Kronos is now just a tool for me, Shadius, to manipulate. Even so, though, he still retains a bit of Ulysses in him. It's more that I'm dominating his personality than his body."

"Intriguing," smiled Rose warily. "So tell me, Kronos, what do you expect to gain by taking me to Genesis?"

"You're right," frowned Kronos/Shadius. "Well, the primary purpose would be to lure Adrian, for I require his light energy for my reincarnation, which is, after all, my main goal. However, Adrian is currently walking right into my trap, in the Deadwood."

"And do you expect that Adrian will just turn himself in to you?" asked Rose with gritted teeth. "After all, I think that he'd value the fate of the universe over me. I know Adrian pretty well, and I'm sorry to say that your plan is going to fail."

"Then I'm taking you because you're in my way," growled Kronos. "After all, I have plans for Maltesque. I can't have a rebellion threatening it."

"Then you've got another thing coming!" shouted Falcon, jumping off of Arrow's glider, and landing on the floor in front of Kronos before firing the shotgun, which he clutched in his hand.

***

Falcon had found Arrow immediately after the building had been attacked, and they'd then ventured up to Rose's room, but they'd failed to locate her. They'd resorted to checking the security cameras. It took a few minutes, but they'd found her in the former lookout room.

There were no stairs, just the elevator, leading up to the room, so they'd assumed she was safe. That is, until Kronos crashed in through the windows. They'd then decided to come up in the glider, and save Rose. And they thought that they were doing a pretty good job of it.

***

Kronos fell to the floor with a thud, and lay there for a moment. The elevator flew off, and Rose felt numerous emotions pour over her, and she rushed over to her father's body. She felt his pulse, and realized that it was still beating.

She attempted to jump away, but Kronos was too fast for her. He grabbed her hand, and she looked into his eyes. They were no longer black, but a brilliant green. "Rose," he whispered. "Please. Forgive me."

"Dad," whispered Rose. "I do."

"Rose, I'm sorry. He's too powerful for me," begged Kronos. "I can't resist his power. Please, I'm sorry. I have to do what he tells me, but only because I have no power to resist with."

One of his eyes was suddenly transformed into a midnight black, and he screamed. His hand flew up to his head, and he staggered backwards. There was nothing to stop his fall to the ground.

Rose ran over to the window, and watched her father plummet to his death. Before he hit the ground, though, his body disappeared in a flash of darkness.

***

"So, Ulysses, you've come around?" chuckled Shadius. "Once again, you're willing to help me?"

"I have no choice," growled Ulysses. "You're just living through me, and I've really got no choice, like I said."

"Well, you do realize that you've always been halfway under my control," smirked Shadius. "So, welcome back, Kronos."

***

Rose stood atop the tower with Falcon, waiting for Arrow to return with the glider. Falcon was bursting with questions about the entire exchange, and he was not shy about asking them.

"So Kronos is really your father?" he asked again. "I'm sure that I knew that, but I guess I never really considered the full implications of that fact. You know, my respect continues to grow."

"Thank you," smiled Rose. "I appreciate it."

"So what exactly is Kronos?" asked Falcon. "It seems like he's a blend of two people."

"That's exactly what he is," sighed Rose. "He used to be my father, but he was transformed into an agent of evil by Shadius."

"It all leads back to this Shadius guy, doesn't it?" replied Falcon, shaking his head. "I wonder what made him so evil."

"Um, he's the god of darkness," laughed Rose. "But he initially was there to help maintain the balance between light and darkness, for if one, even light, gets out of whack, the universe will deteriorate."

"How do you know so much?" asked Falcon.

"I read *Legend of Darkness*," shrugged Rose. "The book that Arrow gave us."

"Speaking of Arrow, what's taking him so long?" impatiently asked Falcon. "He's been acting even stranger lately."

"Returning to the subject of Shadius," began Rose, "he truly became evil when he was refused by Photosia, the goddess of light. She was meant to be his wife, but she chose one of her advisors over Shadius. It seems a bit ridiculous to me, but I guess if someone I loved chose someone else over me, I'd be a bit angered."

"So what happened to Photosia?" asked Falcon.

"Kronos killed her," sighed Rose. "He was manipulated into the deed by Shadius. It was the culmination of the war that erupted between the forces of good and evil. It did to the universe what the war of the druids did to Maltesque."

"Wow," replied Falcon. "It must have been pretty devastating, then."

"Hey, you two! Are you coming, or what?" called out Arrow from his glider, and he flew towards the shattered window.

"What took you so long?!" exclaimed Falcon. "We need to get down to give orders to the troops!"

"What do you think I was doing?" retorted Arrow sulkily. "I was telling the troops what to do. Thanks to me, we've gained the upper hand."

"Glad to hear it," smiled Falcon hurriedly, stepping onto the glider. Rose followed him, and the glider dropped to the ground with all of the passengers aboard.

Rose braced herself for the fall, assuming that Arrow's flying would maneuver them out of harm's way. As the glider neared the ground, Arrow pulled up, and they swooped over the heads of their soldiers on the ground, who were pushing the antagonists back.

"Keep pushing forward!" commanded Arrow confidently. "Come on! Keep moving!" Suddenly, there was a whooshing sound above, and Arrow looked up. Rose thought she saw a small smile flash across his face.

She too looked up, and saw that Kronos' helicopter had returned without him. There were however numerous gun turrets which Rose had failed to notice previously, and they were in full use. The helicopter swept low to the ground, the guns blazing away. The soldier ducked for cover, and the offensive was shattered.

"Arrow, do something!" shouted Falcon. Arrow, however, seemed to have been shocked into a state of non-action. Suddenly, Falcon seemed to think of an idea, and he pushed Arrow behind him, and took control of the glider. He steered it back towards the building, and shattered another building with his gun, and flew in. He grabbed a potted plant, and tossed it back to Rose. "Work some of your magic on that helicopter!" he shouted to Rose, and the glider flew back into the air under Falcon's command.

Falcon plotted it towards the helicopter, and Rose prepared to jump, carefully holding the plant in her hand. As they reached the helicopter, Falcon flew slightly above it, keeping just above the line of gunfire.

Once they reached a good position, Rose clutched the plant tightly, and leapt from the glider, landing in the helicopter, for the sides were open, so that the guns could fire from the copter.

No one in the helicopter saw it coming. It took everyone a few seconds to react, and those were seconds that they didn't have to spare. Rose was already fiddling with the plant's genetic code, and the plant suddenly doubled, then tripled, and then quadrupled in size.

Rose wrapped the vines that grew from the plant around the helicopter around the propellers, and the helicopter suddenly began to fall towards the ground, preparing to crush the army that it had just been supporting.

Arrow had taken control of the glider, and flew back towards Rose, who jumped out of the helicopter and miraculously landed on the glider due to some impressive flying by Arrow.

Rose watched the helicopter fall with a feeling of revulsion at what she had done. Everyone had cleared out from under the falling copter, but the men who had been flying it had most certainly met their death.

"Well done, Rose," smiled Arrow, though it seemed forced to Rose. Regardless, the morale had shifted. The defending forces were revitalized, and they quickly beat the opposing army back.

***

Rose sat worriedly at the conference table. Falcon had called an emergency meeting, and Rose didn't know what it was about, but he'd seemed angry, almost, when he'd called it.

She looked around the table at her companions: Arrow, the security guards, and a couple of other people that Falcon had invited, seemingly randomly. Suddenly, the doors burst open, and Falcon stormed in.

"Where's Blaise?" he asked softly. "Has anyone seen Blaise lately? I doubt it. Do you know why? Does any one of you know why I doubt that Blaise has been seen lately? Well, I'll tell you why. Because I would bet my life that he's spent all day today in the company of a corporate councilman!"

"And why would he be in the company of the enemy?" asked Arrow cautiously.

"BECAUSE BLAISE IS A TRAITOR!" thundered Falcon. "THERE MUST BE A TRAITOR, FOR THEY FOUND OUR BASE!"

"Well, then the traitor could be anyone," frowned Rose. "Hey, maybe it's me!" Everyone turned to look at her. "Kidding, kidding," she assured hurriedly. "Seriously though, anyone could be the traitor. Plus maybe they found our base through computer hacking, like Joshua did."

"Possibly," mused Falcon. "But I stick by what I said. The way I see it, there's really no other option. After all, I've kept a close eye on Rose, and Arrow's our leader. And I'm pretty sure that I'm not the traitor."

"Sorry I'm late," sighed Blaise, walking in. "I had an appointment."

"Oh? And with whom?" asked Falcon casually, in the same manner he had used at the start of the meeting.

"I'm not aware that my personal life concerns you," smirked Blaise. "After all, is it really any of your business?"

"It is most certainly my business," growled Falcon. "Blaise, I never liked you. I've heard what you did to Adrian and Rose in the Deadwood, but that actually *isn't* any of my business. But your being a traitor is definitely my business."

For the first time that Rose had ever seen, Blaise exhibited true emotion in his response. "A traitor? Me? Why would I betray the Third Order?" he asked confusedly. "I stick with the winning side, and that seems to be you."

"The reason for your treachery does not concern me," replied Falcon coolly.

"I'm not a traitor!" exclaimed Blaise, growing concerned by the situation. "Come on, Arrow. Back me up here."

"I don't know what to think," sighed Arrow. "However, I do agree that some course of action must be taken. What it is I will leave up to Falcon."

"Then I vote we expel you from the order!" shouted Falcon. "Or better yet, we'll keep you as a prisoner. We can't risk your secrets getting out."

"Fine!" snarled Blaise. "If that's how you want it, then so be it."

"I assure you, it's exactly what I want," smiled Falcon. "Welcome to the cellblock, Blaise."

***

Falcon returned happily from his jaunt down to the prison room. He wasn't entirely sure why a former office building had a prison cell, but he was glad it did. Now, he thought, with Blaise finally out of my hair, I can get back to work.

Falcon strode over to the elevator, and waited for it to come down. As the door slid open, he gladly stepped inside. He looked behind him as he doors shut, and he was glad to see the guards standing in front of Blaise's cell.

The elevator rose slowly, playing some of his old favorite songs. He wondered how elevator music had come to be, but he liked it. The elevator came to a stop too soon for his liking.

He walked calmly down a hallway to the planning room. He and Arrow still had to get the plans finished for moving hundreds of soldiers out of the base and the city without being seen, for they could not afford any casualties.

Falcon walked into the planning room, and sat down at the small desk with Arrow. He looked at the list of ideas, and they began to talk.

"Arrow, I've been thinking. I'm fairly sure that our best bet is to get them out through the tunnels," began Falcon. "Granted, your idea of flying them out on your glider has some merit, but it would take forever. We'd need a larger aircraft."

"And now we've got one!" grinned Arrow. "What do you call the helicopter?"

"Brilliant!" exclaimed Falcon. "We can repair the helicopter! How many soldiers do you think it would hold?"

"Maybe about twenty?" estimated Arrow. "I mean, we don't need to get all of them out using the helicopter, just our best guys. There's just no point in risking a cave-in."

"I concede," grinned Falcon. "Great idea, though! I guess that we could ride out in the helicopter too."

"Nah, we'd be better off in the glider," suggested Arrow. "It's smaller, harder to target, and safer, if you hold on tight."

"I suppose," mused Falcon. "Is Rose coming with us in the glider?"

"She should," nodded Arrow.

"Then it's settled!" exclaimed Falcon, clapping his hands together. "We'll

302

start repairing the helicopter tomorrow."

***

Rose sighed, perturbed by the day's events. She believed whole-heartedly that Blaise deserved what he got, but she thought that Falcon's conclusion had been a little fast, and it had caused her to begin to question his character.

She decided that it was not really her concern, and she undressed herself, and prepared to sleep.

***

The next day, Falcon's alarm went off early, and he sighed as he got out of bed. He wondered if Arrow was up, but he doubted it. He deemed it unnecessary to check, and proceeded to wake up a few of the more technologically gifted soldiers.

The group then proceeded outside, and began to work on the helicopter. As their base was no longer a secret, it was unnecessary to work in private.

As the sun rose, Falcon surveyed the morning's work, and a grin spread across his face. He had greatly overestimated the amount of time it would take to repair the helicopter, and he now had the men roll it right side up, as it had landed sideways.

Before the clock struck seven Falcon's work was finished. He returned to the building, and proceeded up to Arrow's room. He knocked on the door, and heard a sort of scuffling noise. Arrow opened the door, and Falcon walked in, bursting with pride.

"Well, I did it," he beamed proudly. "I repaired the helicopter. We can start moving the troops out today."

"Excellent," beamed Arrow. "So, have you decided which troops we're going to move in the copter?"

"No. I thought that we could work on that together," frowned Falcon. "Plus, we need to pick a location to move them to. I know that we've picked a rendezvous point, but didn't we agree that the copter should land elsewhere?"

"True, true," mused Arrow. "Will you leave that to me? I'll tell everyone where the spot is, but I'd like to pick it myself. Will you permit that?"

"Sure," shrugged Falcon.

"Great," grinned Arrow. "I'll get to work right away."

***

Rose awoke around ten to hear a great clamor from outside her room. Everyone seemed to be on the move, or so she observed as she looked through her window. She closed it, dressed herself, and left the room.

All of the soldiers were hustling about, and they ignored Rose as she attempted to discover what was going on. Bemused, Rose walked over to the elevator, and went down to Arrow's room, only to find it abandoned.

However, she quickly located him, along with Falcon. They turned to greet her as she approached. "Good morning!" exclaimed Falcon cheerfully as she drew near. "We're moving the soldiers out. We're sending most of them through the tunnels, but we've repaired the helicopter, so about twenty more can get out that way."

"So are you going to send the helicopter at night?" asked Rose. Falcon looked at her in confusion. "I mean, you'd probably get spotted during the day, right? I think it's safer to send them out at night."

"That's a very valid point," mused Arrow. "I guess we should wait for the night. Besides, I still need to find a spot for them to land."

"Then you should go," pointed out Falcon. Arrow nodded, and he left the group. "So, Rose, you think it'd be wiser to send them out at night? Why?" inquired Falcon.

"Well, like I said, they'd probably get caught during the day, and we don't want the copter to get shot down," replied Rose. "It's better to be safe than sorry, right? Plus, you've gotta give Arrow time to find a good spot."

"Yeah," agreed Falcon. "So, I guess that you can just relax for the rest of the day, then. Tomorrow, the three of us head to the rendezvous point on Arrow's glider."

"See you later, then," smiled Rose as she walked off.

***

"They knew we were coming!" stormed Falcon, bursting into Rose's room. "Wake up! We've got an emergency on our hands!"

"Why? What happened?" muttered Rose sleepily. She looked at the clock, and saw that it was around midnight.

"There was a mine planted right where our helicopter landed! A *mine!*" screamed Arrow. "There's no other possible explanation!"

"Well, maybe it was left over from the war of the druids," suggested Rose.

"They didn't have mines back then," waved Falcon impatiently. "No, it's a recent mine. Someone must have told the council. I think we need to have a talk with our friend Blaise."

A few minutes later, Arrow, who had joined the group, left the elevator along with Falcon and Rose. They walked towards Blaise's cell, preparing for the worst.

"Hello, Blaise," smiled Falcon maliciously as he opened the door. "I suppose you've heard the news? The helicopter with our men in it was blown up the second it touched the ground. I don't suppose that you had anything to do with this?"

"Falcon, I've been sitting here all day," growled Blaise. "I haven't done anything. Granted, I heard the announcement that you were sending a group of soldiers to the bank of the river in a helicopter, but that's because you announced it over the loudspeaker. I haven't communicated with anyone."

"Thank you, Blaise," frowned Falcon. "Very well. I'll talk to you later."

Rose followed Falcon back into the elevator, and they rose up one floor. They were in the security center. Falcon ran over to the section that contained the tapes from the cameras, and hurriedly glanced at the one from that day.

He played it through in fast-forward, and Blaise had been telling the truth. He had not communicated with anyone all day, save for when he got his food. Falcon reluctantly walked out of the room, and took the elevator down to Blaise's cell again.

"Very well, Blaise," Falcon said shakily. "You are free to go. I'm sorry I accused you of treachery."

"All's well that ends well," smiled Blaise, returning to his normal nonchalant state. "No harm done. I'll see you around later." With that, he left the cell.

"So then who's the traitor?" asked Rose, turning to her companions.

"I don't know," sighed Falcon. "We don't have any leads to go on. I guess we should all just go to bed. There's nothing else to do tonight."

"Actually, Falcon, why don't you stay up to move the rest of the soldiers out?" suggested Arrow. "I'll take Rose up to her room. I'd like to talk to her."

"Very well," nodded Falcon, who turned and left. Rose and Arrow walked over to the elevator, and rode in silence up to Rose's room. Rose walked in, quickly followed by Arrow.

"So what did you want to talk to me about?" asked Rose, turning to Arrow. "Do you have a theory about the traitor?"

"Actually, I wanted to talk to you some more about what I said last week," replied Arrow. "When I said you weren't safe, I meant it. There's someone very dangerous to you in the order."

"Who is it?" asked Rose eagerly.

"Me," shouted Arrow, and the next thing Rose knew, she was pinned against the floor.

"Arrow, what are you doing?" she cried as he took a length of rope from his pocket, and tied Rose tight, before moving to shut the door. "Let me go!"

"Relax, Rose," smiled Arrow. "I'm not going to do anything harmful to you, if that's what you were thinking about."

Rose was a little relieved. "So then what are you doing?" she asked.

"Rose, it's me. I'm the traitor," laughed Arrow.

***

Arrow ran outside to his glider, and turned it on with the push of a pedal. He rose into the air, and flew towards the buildings of the men he knew to be responsible: the corporate council.

As he passed by on his glider, he activated one of his air bombs, and threw it in through a window. A few seconds later, it exploded, a councilman hurtling towards the street. Suddenly, Arrow saw something dark on the edge of his vision, and then a tendril of darkness reached out, and wrapped itself around him, and dragged him down off of is glider onto a rooftop.

"Hello, Arrow," cackled Kronos from the roof of his building. "Now, I can't just let you pick off my associates, can I?" Another tendril reached out, wrapping itself around the plummeting councilman, saving his life. "You see, Arrow, I've got plans for you. I need you to work for me."

"And why would I work for you?!" cried Arrow. "You killed my brother! I'll never obey you!"

"If you knew that Joshua was the very traitor that he spoke of, would you still stand by your side?" asked Kronos. Arrow was confused for a moment, and in that time period, he put a small bit of darkness in Arrow's brain. "Now, Arrow, if you choose to disobey me, I'm afraid your sanity will have to go."

"Joshua wasn't the traitor!" shouted Arrow. "I'm sorry, but I can't believe that."

***

"So you see, Rose, I really have no choice," sighed Arrow. "He gave me one task: capture you and Adrian. He doesn't care about the council in the slightest. I don't need to disband the order, or surrender to the council, but I do need to capture you. However, I was requested by him to plant the mine."

"So that's it? Just because he says you have to do what he says, you do?" asked Rose furiously. "Even if all you need to do is capture me, to be used as bait, I'm sure, that's still treachery. I'm one of the strongest members of the order! I used to look up to you, Arrow! I thought you were reliable, trustworthy, and great! But I guess I was wrong."

"Quiet, Rose!" shouted Arrow. "Please! I'm sorry! I just can't... I guess...

I didn't know what to do! And he didn't lie. If I ever try to disobey, I get these splitting headaches, and I start to lose my grip on reality!" Suddenly, Arrow went rigid, and his hand went up to his skull. "But enough. It's time for you to go."

Arrow stood Rose up, and forced her to walk over to the window, where Arrow's glider was stationed. As they were about to climb on, there was a gunshot, and Arrow fell to the ground clutching his arm.

"Good thing I got here in time," smirked Blaise, holding the smoking gun.

***

Falcon, Rose, and Blaise looked at Arrow in the prison cell. "So let me get this straight," began Falcon. "He was working for Kronos, and only Kronos. Not the council, but Kronos."

"Right," replied Blaise. "I was listening outside the door for a few seconds, and I caught that much. However, Kronos needs to do something once in a while to keep the council's trust."

Rose was silent, looking at the floor. She seemed to be in shock, as she had trusted Arrow completely.

"So what do we do?" asked Falcon, confused. "I mean, should we pretend that nothing's happened?"

"I think that's a wise move," frowned Blaise. "I suppose that you should be the one to lead the order in the meantime."

"Until Adrian returns," replied Falcon. "He's the natural next choice. Rose, do you have any idea when he should be getting back."

"He should be back by now," whispered Rose. "He's going to the Deadwood for his task, and I think he should be getting back soon."

"Probably," mused Falcon. "Anyhow, I guess I should keep moving the soldiers out. I'll just tell them that Arrow's gone to bed."

"I'll see you in the morning," yawned Blaise. "I'm going to bed. You should too."

"Maybe," laughed Falcon ruefully. "If we can get-"

Falcon was prevented from finishing his statement from an explosion from behind him. They had their backs turned to Arrow, and he had been keeping an air bomb in his pocket. He'd chucked it at the wall before turning to shield himself from the blow.

Arrow raced out, and raced over to the elevator. Moments later, he was flying away from his base on his glider.

"He escaped!" screamed Falcon. "How could he escape? How could we be so stupid? Now he'll be at Kronos' tower, and he'll help them strategize for the battle of Cloudhall, which they now know is coming!"

"Well, it doesn't really matter," shrugged Blaise. "You should still get the troops out. I'll just head up to bed. Where's Rose?"

"Right here," she whispered. Rose had been sitting on the ground, holding her legs to her body in a fetal-like position, though she was still sitting up.

"Are you okay?" asked Falcon, putter his hand on her shoulder.

"I'm fine," she replied softly, standing up. "I think I'll head off to bed now."

Thus ended the day.

***

The next morning, Rose refused to get up, even after being pushed and prodded by Falcon.

"I'm staying here until Adrian gets back," she stubbornly replied to any and all attempts to awake her. "Someone's got to tell him where to go."

"That's why we're leaving guards behind," replied Falcon. "Come on, Rose, just waiting for him isn't going to get him back any sooner."

"Are the spiders coming?" asked Rose suddenly. "Are they coming to help us?"

"Indeed they are," smiled Falcon. "We need all the help we can get. Cloudhall is even more heavily guarded than their own towers."

"Interesting," whispered Rose. "Fine. I'll come. It looks like I've got no choice. I guess you're right, and I see no point in staying."

"Glad to hear it!" exclaimed Falcon, "Well, get up! Dress yourself! We've got places to be!"

"Did you get all of the soldiers out?" asked Rose.

"Yes, I did," grinned Falcon. "They're all at the rendezvous point. We just need to meet them, so I can tell them what happened to Arrow."

"Then let's go," whispered Rose, getting out of bed.

23

Sir Adrian

"Vitalius!" exclaimed Adrian. "What happened to you? I thought you were dead!"

"Oh, I am," smiled Vitalius. "However, when a Greenkeeper dies, they pass into a certain world of spirits, linked to the others, in which Virda has a good deal of say. Normally, it is forbidden for a spirit to pass into the mortal world, but Virda has begun to build a spirit army, with which she hopes to aid the Third Order. Since the curse on the Deadwood was broken, she's free to do as she chooses."

"And are you a part of the army?" asked Adrian excitedly. "Wait. Was Joshua a Greenkeeper?"

"Sadly, he is not," sighed Vitalius. "I'm afraid that Arrow is still on his own. Anyhow, you should probably be getting back to the Third Order."

"Wait! I want to talk to you!" grinned Adrian. "I'm just so glad to see you again! I've felt terrible about your death ever since we left your house! Do you blame Rose and I for it?"

"I do not," smiled Vitalius. "You can hardly help the fact that you've got an evil god out to kill you, right?"

"I suppose not," chuckled Adrian. "So, how am I supposed to get back? Do I need to walk all the way back to the city?"

"Fortunately, you do not," reassured Vitalius. "We of the spirit world possess a couple of useful talents. Teleportation is one of them."

"Excellent!" exclaimed Adrian. "So, when do we go?"

"Right now," replied Vitalius, reaching out his ghostly hand to Adrian. There was a flash of light green, and they disappeared.

***

It took Adrian a moment to regain his head after the teleportation. It had thrown him off-kilter, and it took a moment for him to re-adjust to his new surroundings. He was in the Third Order's hideout, and for the first time it seemed to be deserted.

Adrian's immediate reaction was to assume that there had been some sort of casualty. He quickly turned to Vitalius, the question evident in his eyes.

"They're on the move," answered Vitalius before the question had even been asked. "I don't know where to, or why, but they're on the move. There are other people left, though. They seem to be guards, and I think it'd be wise to speak with them."

Adrian wondered how Vitalius knew all this, but he decided it was unnecessary to ask. "Where are they?" he asked instead. "Are they nearby?"

"There's one just down the hallway," answered Vitalius. "Go on. I'll come with you." The two walked, or, in Vitalius' case, floated, down the hallway. Soon, Adrian spotted the guard with his back turned.

"Hey!" he shouted, running towards the guard, who swung around, and prepared to fight. His posture eased as he saw that it was Adrian.

"Ah, Sir Adrian! So good to see you!" exclaimed the guard. "What's your girlfriend's name?"

Adrian was taken aback by the seemingly random question. "Um, why do you care?" he asked suspiciously.

"Security. Everyone has a specific personal question, per orders of Falcon, and that's yours," replied the guard. "I'm sorry. I know it's a little personal."

"Fine," scowled Adrian. "Rose. There. Happy?"

"Yep," smiled the guard.

"Now it's my turn to ask you a few questions," smirked Adrian. "First of all, what's up with the 'sir'?"

"Well, you see, while you were away, a small, ah, complication arose," began the guard. "For some reason, Arrow hasn't been seen lately. The general consensus amongst the soldiers is that you should take his place as leader. The 'sir' is meant to acknowledge that."

"Really?" exclaimed Adrian. "They want me to lead them? I thought they didn't like me!"

"Well, they've come to rely on you," smiled the guard. "While you were gone, we launched an attack on the corporate council's headquarters, the five towers. Had you been there, it would have gone much more smoothly."

"Well, I'm glad I'm appreciated," laughed Adrian. "So, where am I supposed to head to?"

"Well, everyone is headed to Mount Icecap," explained the guard. "But they should be organizing themselves at the rendezvous point."

"And where's that?" inquired Adrian.

"In the eastern portion of the desert, there's an abandoned factory," explained the guard. "It's at the edge of the lava bed, in the middle of which lies the volcano."

"When did everyone leave?" asked Adrian. "I don't want to miss them, after all."

"Falcon and Rose left this morning," replied the guard. "They'll probably be at the rendezvous point for a couple of days, at the very least."

"That's great!" exclaimed Adrian. "So I guess I'll be going then?"

"Looks that way," shrugged the guard. "Good luck! Say, how did you get into the building? No one came in through the doors."

"I'm afraid that's a secret," replied Adrian. "Say, you never told me your name. What is it?"

"My name is Richard," smiled the guard. "I was one of the soldiers you talked with at the Battle of the Poisonsap."

"Ah! I thought you looked familiar!" exclaimed Adrian. "Well, I'll see you later." Adrian returned to Vitalius in the perpendicular hallway. "So, we're heading off to the lava bed!"

"Adrian, why didn't you ask any further about Arrow?" asked Vitalius with furrowed brow. "I don't know anything about that, so it must have happened fairly recently, while everyone from the spirit world was watching you."

"Yeah. That's a good point," frowned Adrian. "Well, I dunno. I'll ask Falcon. I'm sure he'd know."

"Well, we'd best hurry, then" replied Vitalius. "I can teleport you near the lava bed, but I don't think that you want me to teleport you onto it."

"Why?" asked Adrian.

"Well, for one thing, it's made of cooled lava," frowned Vitalius. "But flowing, hot lava looks virtually identical to the cooled stuff, so you can't tell if you're stepping on hot lava or cold lava."

"I guess that would be a problem," laughed Adrian. "So, can you teleport me to the desert, then?"

"Absolutely," smiled Vitalius. "Let's go, then." There was a flash of greenish-white, and Adrian and Vitalius disappeared.

***

Rose lay on her bed, with the door locked. With Arrow gone, there was nothing to shield her from the pool of loneliness that only Adrian could fill. A tear slid down her cheek as she thought of Arrow. She couldn't believe that he had nearly betrayed her to Kronos.

Rose had always thought of Arrow as incorruptible, and the fact that Kronos had been able to take control over him shattered her image of him. She had relied on him, and now that he was no longer reliable, or there, for that matter, she did not know whom to trust.

Rose put her hand to her heart, and another tear dripped off her face. The bottom line was this: Arrow had broken her heart. She had loved him, though not as much as Adrian, and his betrayal had left her heart in pieces.

Worst of all, she now had no one to share her feelings with. Not only did she not have Arrow, but also she now had no friends. Falcon was an associate, and Blaise was beyond categorization. None of them were friends.

Suddenly, there was a knock on the door. She slowly slid off the bed, and walked over to open it. Falcon stood in the doorway, looking frantic. "Rose, come here!" he exclaimed, shouting over his shoulder as he raced away.

Rose quickly followed him, but a small nagging doubt crept into her mind as she raced after him. She had unquestioningly followed Arrow, but he had nearly brought her to Kronos. She prepared herself for anything that Falcon might attempt.

Rose quickly realized that she had nothing to fear as they raced into the security room. Falcon led her over to a monitor, and turned to speak.

"Rose, I've got something to show you," he began, chewing worriedly on his lower lip. "This is the tape of yesterday, with a view of the Deadwood Forest, where I believe you said Adrian was heading."

Falcon pressed the play button, and an image flashed upon the screen of flames engulfing the forest. It seemed that the entire west half of the forest had been engulfed in a raging inferno.

"Oh no," whispered Rose as Falcon paused the tape. "Is there any chance that Adrian might've- well, you know..."

"I think there is a high chance," sighed Falcon. Panic came over Rose, but she quickly pulled it under control. "Now, Rose, you have to realize that the Third Order is counting on you. Even without Adrian, we still…"

"Don't say that," whispered Rose. "Adrian lived. He always does. He finds a way, he pulls through. Adrian isn't dead."

"Rose, if he hadn't been hurt, he should be getting back about now from the Deadwood," shrugged Falcon. "We'll give him two days to come back, and then we'll address the troops. If Adrian isn't back by then, I guess I'll have to assume command."

"That's what this is about, isn't it!" shouted Rose suddenly. "You figure that with Arrow gone, you should be leader, even if someone else is better equipped for the job! That's all you care about."

"Don't be ridiculous, Rose!" exclaimed Falcon, but he did look as if he felt awkward to Rose. "Well, I guess that I do want to lead a bit, but that isn't my prime concern."

"A trip to and back from the Deadwood would take longer than a week, which is the time you're giving him!" exclaimed Rose.

"Fine, fine!" hurriedly agreed Falcon. "I'll give him five days. If he's not back, we move on. If he is, he takes command. Is that fair?"

"Yes," nodded Rose. "That's perfect."

***

Adrian looked about helplessly. He had no idea where this so-called abandoned factory was, and he was worried that Arrow and Falcon might continue without him. He quickly did a count in his head, and figured that he had spent at least eight days on the journey to and back from the Deadwood, since it had taken him three days to get out of the Poisonsap and to the dam.

He had spent three days with Vitalius looking for the factory, and he was getting concerned.

"Vitalius," began Adrian. "Do you think you could teleport around a bit, to see if you can find the base?"

"Well, I suppose I could," mused Vitalius. "However, my absence from the spirit world has taken a little bit of a toll on me. I can't teleport you. However, I'll find the base, come back, tell you where it is, and then we can walk there. How does that sound to you?"

"Excellent," smiled Adrian. "Should I pitch a tent, or just sit here?"

"I'd pitch the tent," shrugged Vitalius. "We're in no hurry." Adrian nodded, and as he got to work, Vitalius vanished.

***

Adrian was very bored. He'd been waiting over two hours for Vitalius to come back, and he figured that if Vitalius wasn't back by the end of the day, he would move on.

Suddenly Vitalius appeared directly in front of him. "I found it!" he exclaimed. "But leave the tent! It's too far away, and we need to get there by the end of tomorrow!"

"Why?" inquired Adrian confusedly.

"I overheard Falcon talking!" hurriedly explained Vitalius. "He and Rose made a deal three days ago. If you're no there in two more days, they deem you dead, and they'll move on without you!"

"Great!" exclaimed Adrian sarcastically, throwing his hands in the air. "And how far do we have to travel in these two days, exactly?"

"About twenty miles," estimated Vitalius. "Most people walk at about two miles per hour, so that's ten hours of walking."

"Then let's go!" exclaimed Adrian. "Yeah, we should probably leave the tent."

***

Rose was growing desperate. She kept telling herself not to lose hope, that he might've gotten lost or something, but the facts were staring her in the face.

It was the last day before Falcon assumed command and would leave. Rose knew that even if Adrian were still alive, he would still never find her. They would be separated forever.

However, it did not look remotely likely that Adrian was still alive. Rose had seen the tape of the fire, and knew that Adrian had been in the Deadwood at that time. A feeling of loss had overridden her mind, and she stayed in her room for most of the days.

Rose began to cry as she thought of the little time that she and Adrian had spent together, even though that time seemed like a lifetime. She recalled how conspicuous she had been with her affection at first, and how much she had matured since then. Looking back, she realized that she had been very naive and trusting at first, due to her total lack of exposure to the world. She had spent almost all of her life behind a veil of darkness, and she had really still just been a small girl at first.

She smiled ruefully as she thought about how much the month or so in Maltesque had changed her. Now, more than anything else, she just wanted Adrian back.

***

Adrian and Vitalius kept a steady pace as they moved towards the base. It was the last day before Falcon moved the troops, and Adrian still couldn't see the base. It was nearing noon, and Adrian was really getting nervous that he might not make it.

Suddenly, Adrian caught a glimpse of black on the horizon, and he made it out to be some kind of building. He looked up at the cloud layer, and sighed dejectedly at the lack of sun.

"Hey Vitalius, am I correct in assuming that the black speck on the horizon isn't the base?" asked Adrian.

"You would be incorrect, master Adrian," smiled Vitalius. "That in indeed the abandoned factory in which the Third Order currently makes its residence."

A grin spread across Adrian's face, and he quickened his pace, breaking into a run as it came ever closer. He ran as fast as he could, and the grin widened at the thought of seeing Rose again.

Vitalius followed close behind. After about a half-hour of running, the base was only about a mile away. Adrian called upon the last reserves of his strength, and dashed towards the building.

***

"Falcon, you were right," cried Rose. "Adrian's dead. There's just no other explanation."

"I'm sorry, Rose," replied Falcon consolingly, patting her on the back. They were sitting upon her bed, after Rose had called Falcon in to talk. "Rose, come with me. We should get ready for the announcement."

"Well, fine," muttered Rose. She went rigid as anger at Falcon overwhelmed her, but she quickly staunched it, and the feeling was replaced by depression.

As they walked past the hallway leading to the front door, it burst open, and Adrian rushed in.

"Adrian!" exclaimed Rose, and she flung herself into his arms, and held on tight. "God, I was so worried about you! I thought you died in the fire! Thank god you're okay!"

"Well, I think you just bruised my rib cage, but other than that, I'm great," smiled Adrian, hugging Rose back. "I was worried about you too. I was afraid you'd move on without me."

"Actually, Falcon was trying to make us do just that," frowned Rose. "However, I was about to go along with it. Please forgive me."

"Well, I'm sorry for making you wait," replied Adrian. Falcon cleared his throat, as if about to speak, but Adrian's expression seemed to silence him. It was an expression of happiness equal to the one on Rose's face.

Tears of happiness streamed down Rose's face, and she held Adrian even tighter. For a moment they stood just like that. No words were spoken, yet they achieved a state of total understanding.

Falcon cleared his throat again, and Adrian turned to speak.

***

Adrian had been completely caught off-guard by Rose's assault, for it was, in a sense, an assault. He could tell that Falcon wished to speak with him, no doubt to justify himself, but he ignored him for a few minutes.

Finally Adrian realized that Falcon would not be ignored, and turned away from the embrace to speak with him.

"Adrian, first let me say that I was entirely sure that you were dead, or else I would have never moved on," smiled Falcon sheepishly. "Anyhow, in case you haven't heard, you are now the leader of the Third Order. The troops have begun to call you Sir for all of your ventures, and I will gladly allow you to have the command position,"

"Excellent," smiled Vitalius, gliding into the room. Everyone stared in shock.

***

Rose was the first to speak. "Vitalius!" she exclaimed as yet another wave of relief consumed her. "How... What... I thought you were dead!"

"Yes, that's the same way that Adrian reacted," smiled Vitalius. "So, Rose, as you can see, I'm now a ghost. Virda has decided to lend all of the spirits under her command to the Third Order.

"On a different matter, where is Arrow? The guard told us that he hasn't been seen for a couple of days."

"Well, you see..." began Rose awkwardly, before deciding that Falcon could explain better, however, Falcon seemed to have the same opinion about her. Rose figured that since she could give a first-person account, Falcon was probably right. "After we condemned Blaise as a traitor, since he was the most obvious candidate—"

"What made you realize that there was a traitor?" asked Adrian.

"The council launched an attack on the hideout," explained Rose. "Anyhow, after we condemned Blaise, Arrow took me up to my room, and then tried to kidnap me! Right after Joshua died, Kronos took control over Arrow's mind. He's been scheming to kidnap me ever since."

"So *Arrow* betrayed the order?" exclaimed Adrian. "But he was the leader! Why didn't the council just make him disband it or something?"

"He wasn't under the council's control, he was under Kronos'," explained Rose. "Kronos doesn't care about the council, he just cares about getting to you, Adrian. He was going to use me as bait."

"Well, I'm glad you're okay!" exclaimed Adrian. "Did anything else happen?"

"Well, I saved her," shrugged Blaise walking in to the room. "I knew something was fishy about Arrow, so I follow him and Rose up to Rose's room, and I attacked Arrow as he was about to abscond with your girlfriend."

"I never thought I'd say this, but thank you, Blaise," smiled Adrian. "Well, it sounds like you had nearly as exciting a time as I did."

"Yeah, so what were doing in the Deadwood?" asked Rose. "I mean, everyone hates that place."

"I had to fight Necropheus," explained Adrian. There was a shocked silence. "And I won."

***

Adrian had to describe his exploits to the order, but his mind was elsewhere. He hadn't realized how much he'd missed Rose until he'd seen her again. His best guess as to why that had happened was that he had missed her so much that his mind had no choice but to block it out.

His hand reached out, and met Rose's. He held it tight, and she gripped it back. As Adrian finished telling the story, he looked in satisfaction at the awed look on everyone's face. Now there could be no question; Adrian was fit to lead the order.

Falcon led Adrian, along with everyone else, to the room where he and Rose had been heading when Adrian had arrived. It was filled with the entire army, and there was a small podium from where one could make a speech. He motioned for Adrian to step up onto the podium.

"Everyone, may I have your attention?" began Falcon. "I have a couple of announcements to make. First of all, Arrow is no longer with us. He defected to the other side, due to threats against his sanity. I'll explain that bit later, but right now, I just thought you might like to know that the man to replace Arrow is none other than Adrian!"

A chant rose up from the crowd. "SIR ADRIAN! SIR ADRIAN!" Falcon motioned for Adrian to take his place, and a cheer exploded from the crowd.

"Hello," began Adrian. The noise level dropped, and he started to speak. "So, apparently you all want me to assume command of the Third Order." Another cheer came from the audience. "So, I will do just that. Falcon will take the position of second in command, and Rose and Blaise will be my advisors, while Vitalius and Virda will be my strategists." More cheers. "The first thing for us all to do is to continue with the plan laid out for us by Arrow. Namely, tomorrow morning, we march to Mount Icecap."

***

Adrian woke up early, and woke up Rose and Falcon. Vitalius never seemed to sleep, so he was already awake. "All right, guys, are all the preparations ready?" asked Adrian.

"Not yet," answered Falcon. "We need to organize the troops into new units, but I think that can wait until we actually get to Icecap. We also need to prepare all of the supplies. I think that Rose and I should take care of that, while you plan out route."

"No, you should plan the route," replied Adrian. "I've never been to the eastern side of Maltesque before, so you've got more experience in that regard. Vitalius will help you."

"Very well," smiled Falcon. "You two should move along, and waking up maybe a hundred or so soldiers wouldn't hurt a bit. You'll need the help."

"Thanks for the advice," smiled Adrian. He and Rose walked away, and, instead of making for the supply room, they instead darted towards the room in which the soldiers slept.

Adrian and Rose proceeded to wake up all the soldiers that they needed, and they brought all of them to the supply room, and began to separate the supplies, and sort them into bags.

Soon, they had all of the supplies they needed, and Adrian and Rose checked back with Falcon and Vitalius.

"Have you guys finished planning the route?" asked Adrian.

"Pretty much," mused Vitalius. "We still need to double-check it, though. Our reference map might be outdated, but I'm pretty sure they're still fairly accurate. We're planning to cross the lava bed, keeping a safe distance from the volcano. It should be all hard, so there's no problem."

"Good," smiled Adrian. "So should I address the troops, or what?"

"Well, you're in charge," shrugged Falcon. "But if I were you, I'd probably at least wake them up. After all, we should be leaving in about an hour."

"All right," nodded Adrian, and he left Rose with the two men.

***

Adrian stepped up to the podium, and was very glad that microphones existed in Maltesque. "Good morning!" he smiled, and all of the soldiers woke up immediately. Adrian gave them a few minutes to get their wits about them, and once they all looked reasonably awake, he continued speaking. "We should be leaving for Mount Icecap in about an hour, so eat breakfast, which is in the room down the hall to the right, and then get ready for the march."

There was a general murmur of agreement, and the soldiers all began to get up. Adrian turned, and walked towards his room. He realized that Rose still had his copy of *Legend of Darkness*, and changed his direction towards Rose's room.

He stepped inside, and saw that Rose was still packing. "Rose," he began softly. "You've still got our copy of *Legend of Darkness*, right?"

"Yep," smiled Rose. "It's in my bag. I almost forgot I had it."

318

"Well, it's a good thing I remembered, then," smiled Adrian. "So can I have it? I think that it'd be best if I kept it with me."

"Very well," replied Rose, handing him the book. "It is written by your ancestor, after all. So, are we heading off now?"

"Yep," answered Adrian. "We're heading to Mount Icecap."

"You know, there's a chance that we might not get back," mused Rose. "Even with our powers, it's still risky."

"Oh really?" smiled Adrian, closing his eyes. He summoned up energy, and instead of lightning, pure light raced out of his hands, and blasted a hole in the wall. "The Great Sage picked a good task. I'm now even more powerful than before."

"Excellent!" exclaimed Rose. "Well, I guess that we should be going, then. After all, it's a long walk."

***

As Rose was walking behind Adrian, Falcon caught up with them, and pulled Rose aside.

"I'm glad I caught you!" he exclaimed happily. "I just finished designing something I think you'll find useful. I spent half the night trying to make it work, and it finally does!" Falcon proudly held up a glass tube filled with dirt.

"So what does it do?" asked Rose suspiciously. "It looks pretty useless to me. Unless the enemy is weak to dirt, how is that going to help anyone?"

"Ah, I forgot to demonstrate!" laughed Falcon. He hit a small metal switch, and a small speck of dirt flew out the end of the tube.

"Am I missing something?" asked Rose.

"Focus on the dirt with your mind," commanded Falcon. Rose immediately obeyed, and was surprised to discover that there was incredibly potent plant life contained in the speck of dirt.

Rose commanded it to grow, and it did. It grew at Falcon, who took a wary step back. "That's incredible!" exclaimed Rose. "It's like I can always use my powers now!"

"Exactly," smiled Falcon. "I felt bad about nearly leaving Adrian behind, and I wanted to make it up to you. Consider it a gift from a friend."

"Well, thanks," smiled Rose. "Anyhow, I think that Adrian's probably done prepping the troops. We should be able to head out now."

***

Adrian led the troops out of the hideout with enthusiasm. It was nice to have a lot of company, as opposed to having to solo, like in the Deadwood. Rose quickly caught up to him, and they began to talk.

"So Adrian, what was it like being surrounded by fire?" asked Rose. "I'd have been terrified. Was it scary?"

"Fairly so," replied Adrian. "It wasn't too bad. I had protection from the flames, though, so it wasn't quite as nerve-wracking as it could have been. When it got really scary was when the path began to disappear. The flames were closing in, and if I hadn't grabbed the staff, I would have died."

"And I'm glad you didn't," smiled Rose. "You did have me worried, though. I find it interesting that we both set out for the hideout on the same day, even though you got there five days after me. How did you know you had to hurry?"

"Vitalius scouted ahead, and found the hideout," explained Adrian. "He overheard Falcon talking about the five-day-deal that he had with you. We realized that it was the next to last day, so we bolted."

"I'm happy you made it," grinned Rose. "So, how far is it to Mount Ice-cap?"

"We've only been walking for a half-hour," sighed Adrian. "We're only about halfway through the lava bed. Anyhow, I'm glad there haven't been any mishaps yet." Adrian's words were eerily prophetic.

Barely five minutes after he had said that, Rose's foot became stuck in some sort of substance. It took Adrian and Rose a second that her foot was stuck in hot lava. Thankfully the boots kept her feet safe.

"Hold still, Rose," commanded Adrian. "Just... just stay there, and I'll find Falcon. He'll know what to do!"

Adrian quickly found Falcon conversing with a bunch of soldiers while walking. "HALT!" commanded Adrian, and the army came to a dead stop. Adrian looked behind him, and saw that he and Rose had been considerably ahead of the group.

"Falcon, we've got a major problem!" exclaimed Adrian. "Rose just stepped in hot lava!"

"Well, did you get her out?!" Inquired Falcon hurriedly. Adrian shook his head. "Well, pull her out, you idiot! She'll probably lose her shoe, but that doesn't really matter that much."

Adrian ran back, and lifted Rose out of the lava, though the shoe stayed behind. Rose asked Adrian to carry her, since she now had one bare foot. Adrian obliged, and they ran back to Falcon.

"So what do we do?" asked Adrian. "I don't want to lose any troops in the lava!"

"Well, there shouldn't be any hot lava," frowned Falcon. "Maybe there was a small eruption recently, or something. You pose a good question, though. I vote we send a small regimen ahead to test."

"Sounds good," agreed Adrian. "HEY!" he exclaimed. "EVERYONE! I NEED VOLUNTEERS TO TEST THE LAVA TO MAKE SURE IT'S SAFE!" A couple of hands shot up, and Adrian motioned for them to come forwards. They swiftly obliged.

"So, you all realize that you're putting yourself at risk here?" asked Adrian to the men. They all nodded, and Adrian sent them ahead. The rest of the army followed closely behind.

Suddenly, the group of soldiers that had been sent ahead stopped moving. A faint beeping noise could be heard, and suddenly there was an explosion of pressurized air. The group of soldiers was scattered, and a couple of them looked injured.

"It was an air bomb!" exclaimed Falcon. "They must've seen us coming!" Adrian listened to Falcon, but he thought he caught a glimpse of movement in the sky, and looked up.

Arrow's glider swiftly shot towards the ground, just pulling to a stop about ten feet above Adrian's head. "Hello, Third Order," smiled Arrow. "As you've probably heard, I've seen the light, or darkness, if you prefer, and I've defected to the other side. However, I am still your leader! Thus, I have an ultimatum: continue to follow me, your leader, and be safe, or, follow Adrian, and suffer like the soldiers who I just dealt with."

There was silence in the crowd. Suddenly, though, a voice piped up. "Long live Sir Adrian!" shouted the voice, and Adrian turned around. To his surprise, the source of the voice was none other than Falcon. "Arrow, you've been replaced! Face it, these men respect Adrian more than they respect you. We deny you! Do your worst, Arrow, for we follow Sir Adrian!"

"LONG LIVE SIR ADRIAN! LONG LIVE SIR ADRIAN!" was the chant that erupted from the crowd. "Long live our lord!"

"Fools!" bellowed Arrow. "You are nothing compared to the might of Kronos, the enemy that you will soon face! But here, let me show you that I too am a threat!"

Arrow dropped two more air bombs into the crowd, and the soldiers scattered to avoid being hit. Adrian summoned light energy, and unleashed it at Arrow's glider. It struck the glider on the wing, and Arrow was nearly knocked off.

"Arrow, you will not harm my troops!" shouted Adrian at Arrow. "Now run, and we will settle this later!"

"Very well," scowled Arrow. "But know this, Adrian: you are now my enemy, and will continue to be so."

"We do not fear you, Arrow!" shouted Falcon. "Not as long as we have Adrian!"

"I'll be seeing all of you later!' shouted Arrow as he flew away.

Adrian turned to the crowd. "Thank you for your support!" he began. "Take a short break. I need to make sure that the soldiers are okay."

Adrian, Falcon, Rose, and Vitalius, who had vanished when Arrow appeared, all walked around to the fallen soldiers to check if they were all okay. They were all in reasonable condition, since it had just been air, but they didn't look like they would be fighting any time soon.

Adrian resumed the march shortly. After another couple of hours, Adrian saw that the temperature was beginning to drop. He looked behind him at the lava, but barely a mile away from him the snow began.

Off in the distance, a huge mountain rose out of the frozen wasteland. Adrian recalled that his map had referred to the area surrounding the mountain as the Frozen Lake, and wondered if there was any accuracy to that name. As he stepped onto snow, he scraped some away, and discovered that he was standing on ice.

After another hour, the army was nearing Mount Icecap. Adrian saw the magma re router at the bottom of the mountain, and the sheer size of the thing struck him. It took up an entire half of the mountain's foot, and it extended for miles underground. However, as he recalled Falcon's plan, he was sure they could take it down.

"Hey! Does anyone have a shoe I can borrow?"

24

The Twilight Crystal

James continued to stare at the screen though it had long been blank. He no longer shed tears for the loss of Ajax, but the sight had filled him with determination to build the light laser, destroy the darkness, and save Adrian.

James turned around, and walked out of Ajax's lair. He walked down the hallway lined with copies of *Legend of Darkness*, and walked towards the elevator. He stepped in, and it rose up.

James was glad that he had picked up the light laser prototype, at the very least. It was a pity that his suit had been destroyed in the battle, and he still missed the security of having another person to work with.

The elevator rose up another story as James prepared to step into the dark-infested world. He recalled that he had dropped the twilight crystal near the skate park, so he struck out in that general direction.

Nobody was out on the streets, since about half the population of the town had been in the recreation room when he had fired the prototype. He was glad that there would be little interference.

As James ran east, he noticed an unusual amount of activity in the observatory. He had no idea what it was about, but he ignored it, and turned south.

He neared the skate park, and looked about. There was a little bit of moonlight, but he imagined that there would be some kind of a reflection from the crystal. After looking around for a half hour, though, he began to lose a bit of his faith.

He looked into a dimly lit alley, but he saw a speck of twilight light coming form something in the street. He scurried over to it, and saw that it was indeed the twilight crystal. Smiling, he bent down to pick it up.

Without warning, a hand reached out of the darkness, and grabbed at the crystal right as James' fingers closed around it. James jumped back, clutching the crystal, and found the eyes of a SWAT team member looking at him.

"Well, the trap worked," sneered the SWAT guy, shoving James backwards. "We've caught you, and I'm sure that you'll comply and hand me the twilight crystal."

"We?" asked James worriedly.

"Yeah," smirked the SWAT team member. "We." Suddenly, three other men jumped in James' way, forcing him further back into the alley.

"How do you guys know about the twilight crystal?" asked James suspiciously.

"Well, we're under the control of Shadius," replied the first SWAT member. James wasn't particularly surprised by that response. "Our job is to get the crystal from you and deliver it to the observatory. Shadius' plans are close to fruition."

"Well, I plan to make sure his plans will fail!" shouted James, firing the light laser prototype into the first SWAT member. The light seemed to spread through the members, and they stumbled backwards, temporarily incapacitated.

James bulldozed his way through the members, and saw that there was a small crowd heading towards the location from the north, so he instead ran south, towards the aquarium.

James ducked in through the doorway, and looked about frantically for a place to hide. The building was in fairly good condition, considering the many earthquakes that had wracked the town. In addition, some of the tanks were still full of water, and James could have sworn he saw something swimming around in a few of them.

There was no light in the entire building, so James realized that he really couldn't hide very well, as he was running from someone who controlled darkness. James wondered if there were any luminescent fish, like an anglerfish or something. He walked towards what seemed to be stairs, and crept down silently.

Suddenly, James realized that a slight light shone ahead of him. Rarely had he ever thought that hiding in light was better than hiding in darkness, but this was one of those times. He could already feel Shadius' prying eyes attempting to find him.

James raced towards the small patch of light as he heard the SWAT team barge into the aquarium. He wondered how long it would take them to find him with Shadius' powers, and ran even faster to the small light patch.

As James neared the light, he realized that he was running down a hallway. The stairs had led into a narrow corridor, which James was sure would be normally filled with all sorts of uninteresting posters and whatnot. James recalled being in an aquarium with his parents once, a very long time ago. They had forced him to stop and read the posters, though the only things that had really interested him were the fish.

The hallway led into a large domed room. It was filled with two pillars of glass that extended to the ceiling. Surprisingly enough, the glass tubes were undamaged by the quakes, and they were completely filled with water. Inside the water tubes were various forms of marine life. James saw an anglerfish; the source of the glow, swimming rapidly away from a shark that seemed to decide that the anglerfish would be its next meal.

James had read in a book that anglerfish are actually very slow fish, and the shark seemed to have nearly caught it. That posed a problem, as the scant light from the anglerfish was the only thing protecting James from the darkness.

James had little time. As long as the anglerfish provided him with light, he was safe for the darkness. There were lights along where the glass tube met the floor, though they seemed to be broken. James took it upon himself to fix that.

He crouched down, frantically attempting to find out if the lights were actually turned off, or if they were broken. He had no way of knowing, so he decided that the most likely solution was the possibility that the earthquakes had broken them. James wondered if there was any possibility that some of the light bulbs were still unbroken. He looked around, and saw, to his satisfaction, that very few of them were shattered. However, the one or two that had shattered had negatively affected the wiring. James decided that if he could find some spare wire, he could fix it.

Suddenly, the shark caught up with the anglerfish, and the slight glow disappeared, and James was in the dark again. He now realized that there was no way that he could fix the wires, so he instead looked desperately around for another anglerfish. Sadly it looked as if the shark had eaten the only one.

Above him, there was a sudden shout of triumph, and James immediately got up, and ran for the far exit of the room. The SWAT team was now on the lookout for him again. James didn't know if he would be able to hold all of them off with the light laser prototype, as this time they would see it coming.

The door out of the room with the water pillars led James into another hallway. This one split at the end, one passageway leading slightly downwards, while the other seemed to lead back up to the surface. James had no idea which path would be the better choice, so he went in the one that led downwards.

There was nothing but darkness ahead of him, and he heard the feet of the agents of Shadius pounding against the ground. He felt the atmosphere change, and though he could not see, he knew that he was in another open room.

There was no glow to direct him, but James felt a strange force pulling him towards the right of the room. He was now aware that a dim light emanated from a small tank. Inside the tank were bioluminescent jellyfish. James huddled behind the small tank, bathing in the dim light that blossomed from it.

The SWAT team barged into the room. They spread out, looking around, but they all stayed a reasonable distance from the place where James hid.

As one of the members neared James, he held up the light laser. As the member turned to look at him, James pulled the trigger, and the agent of darkness was blasted backwards.

The brilliant flash of light attracted attention, needless to say, and James picked up the light laser prototype and ran. He fired blasts of light over his shoulder periodically. However, the SWAT team was undeterred, and they kept chasing him.

James raced out of the room, as the blasts of light revealed the way for him. The path led even further down, and James was beginning to see some damage from the quakes. The floor was covered with water, and James was forced to slow his pace a bit.

After a few minutes of running down the wet tunnel, James became aware that not only was the floor covered in water, but also bits of the ceiling were strewn in his path. He was forced to slow down to a walk, and he kept blasting the light laser so he could find his way.

The deteriorating tunnel led into a room, as seemed to be the pattern, and it was a complete disaster area. The water was about ankle deep, and the chunks of the ceiling had increased in size.

James turned around, and the three remaining pursuers raced in. James fired the light laser, but the beam of light was deflected by a tendril of darkness that sprang up, shielding the SWAT team from the blast.

James ducked behind an unusually large piece of debris as he realized that one SWAT team member had a machine gun. Bullets ricocheted off of the debris, and the SWAT team also had to duck for cover. Slowly, each and every one of the bullets dropped into the water with a splash.

James waited for the SWAT team to come towards him before leaping out from behind the debris, and fired the prototype. One of the members was caught head on, and sprawled to the ground, and the others were stunned.

Now, James considered rushing through the team, but they seemed to be quickly recovering, so he chose to run away from them, further into the disaster room. His foot plunged through the three inches of water between him and the ground, but suddenly there was no ground beneath the water. James discovered too late that concealed at the end of the room, a large pool covered the entire corner. James had reached a dead end.

The SWAT team of two seemed to observe that James was trapped, and the one that he had knocked down had not been the one with the machine gun.

"Now, James, I suggest that you make this easy on yourself, and surrender the twilight crystal," smirked the voice of Shadius through the mouth of the team member. "I'll let you go if you give me the crystal. So be a good boy, and give it up to me!"

"NO!" shouted James, firing the prototype. Like the time before, a tendril of darkness reached up to intercept the blast. James backed away slowly, but he knew that the pool was right behind him, and that there was no escape. He fired again and again with the prototype, but a constant stream of tendrils of darkness blocked the blasts.

However, James had no such defense for the blast of bullets that erupted from the barrel of the machine gun, pelting his arm. James screamed, and fell back into the water.

***

Shadius' minions stared at the water for a moment, while Shadius decided what to make them do. The most obvious solution was to dive in after him, but Shadius thought he saw something moving through the water. He didn't want to know, but he didn't want to risk his two best servants on earth.

A smile crossed the lips of both SWAT team members as Shadius thought of a solution. Two tendrils of darkness reached out, engulfing the strange creature swimming about in the pool. Shadius could suddenly see through the creature's eyes, and he saw a few other fish swimming about. He possessed them too, and sent the SWAT team in.

***

James drifted in a state of half-consciousness, not breathing, letting the pain in his arm overwhelm him. He slowly realized that there was something else in the pool, but that did not concern him.

His eyes drifted upwards, and he saw that the two remaining members of the team were swimming down to meet him. James was too far past caring to truly notice. They were level with him, and searched his pockets, and found the twilight crystal.

A thought punctured James' lethargy: I need that crystal. However, James was painfully aware of the other thing in the water with him: the giant squid. He had no desire to tangle with the creature of the deep, so he played dead. Plus, he felt some kind of evil intelligence emanating from the squid, and he wouldn't put it past Shadius to possess it.

James returned to his lethargic state, and thought: well, playing dead shouldn't be too hard. However, like all humans, he needed to breathe. He waited until the

SWAT team had left, and he was sure that Shadius' focus was elsewhere.

Swimming towards the surface with but his feet, James attracted some unwanted attention from the squid. James swam even faster, using his good arm to propel himself as well, but he was unable to outdistance the tentacle that the squid reached out with. His lungs were screaming for air, but the tentacle held him back.

James was close enough to the surface, though, so that if he craned his neck, he was able to snatch a quick breath of air, which quickly transformed into a mouthful of water as the squid pulled him back down.

James whirled around, and viciously attacked the tentacle with his good arm, and the squid let him go. He swam faster than he would have imagined possible back up to the surface, and gasped for breath as he broke the surface.

Before the squid could get another try at him, James dragged himself out. He lay in place for a few minutes, trembling with both pain and relief. Eventually, though, James realized that he had to get up, so he forced himself to his feet.

James began the long walk out of the aquarium, and suddenly realized that he no longer held the light laser. He cried out in frustration as he realized his most potent weapon was gone.

After a few minutes, James walked out of the last tunnel and up the stairs into the large room where he had first entered the aquarium. He staggered out the door, and back into the street.

He saw an empty building to the east, and meandered in that direction. Since it didn't look dangerous, James assumed that it would be safe to take a good rest there. He entered the building and saw, to his delight, that it had been a food store, at least before the earthquakes.

James looked at the shelves, and helped himself to a few of the tastier-looking foods, and gorged himself. He thought that he would take care of his arm once he got back to the lab, and went to sleep.

***

Shadius cackled in delight to his captive. "Well, Ajax, it looks like you've finally been beaten!" he laughed. "I've got the crystal, and now I can spread the darkness to Alchema as well!"

"Shadius, I hate to point this out, but a very small portion of this world alone is under your control," coughed Ajax with the smallest hint of a smile. "And the wormhole won't fix that."

"I know that!" shouted Shadius impatiently. "What do you think I possessed the SWAT team for?"

"So you're planning to use them to spread the corruption?" asked Ajax, a look of partial admiration for the brilliant scheme spreading across his face. However, the admiration was tempered by the look of horror, which competed for dominance over his features.

"More or less," laughed Shadius. "Well, it looks like you've figured my little scheme out. Once I use Adrian to resurrect myself, I'll be master of the entire multiverse! And I've heard that there are more beyond this one, so why not move onto them next?"

"You'd need the weapon for that," laughed Ajax. "I don't think you'll be able to get the Deathstone back any time soon. But moving that aside, I still have one final question for you: why am I still alive?"

"As an extra precaution," cackled Shadius, and Ajax figured out what he meant with a look of shock.

***

James awoke from his uncomfortable position on the floor with a cry of pain. He had fallen asleep lying on his arm, which now felt even worse. He thought that it might be broken, but he didn't have time to think about that.

He rose to his feet, and prepared a small breakfast for himself from the assorted foods in the store. After that was finished, James struck out for the lab again. He avoided all paths that might have been home to any possessed people. After nearly ten minutes had passed, James had the lab in sight.

He rode the elevator down, and shouted: "Robby!" He had come up with a name for the small robot that he had saved previously. The robot responded, and rode up the elevator. "Can you fix my arm?" asked James. Robby nodded, and he led James by the hand down the elevator.

They came into a room that James wasn't sure he had seen before, though he'd thought that he'd seen every room in the lab. Apparently, he was mistaken. Robby led James over to a small table, and James lay down on it. Robby set about patching up James' arm, and he set the bone that had been forced out of whack by the bullet.

Soon, James' arm felt as good as new, but it still hurt to move it, and every time he tried, Robby tugged on his pant legs, as if to say, "Please don't, master." And every time, it made James smile.

James rode down the elevator with Robby, looking for some kind of new weapon to use against the darkness. With a start, James remembered the space ship a couple of floors down, and rode down to that floor.

He and Robby got off of the elevator, and walked over to the ship. Robby became very excited as he looked at it, and seemed to want to turn it on. James shook his head, and Robby looked sad. James stored away in his memory the fact that Robby could operate the spaceship.

James found what he was looking for soon enough, however: a weapon cache. He took out some kind of ray gun, like the one he'd found before, and shot it at the wall. Light burst out the end, and though it didn't seem quite as powerful as the prototype light laser, James was sure that it was powerful enough.

He rode the elevator back up to the recreation room, and placed the ray gun on the couch. While he had watched Ajax' video, the unconscious bodies had somehow disappeared. He vaguely recalled hearing something behind him as he had watched Ajax's video, and wondered if Robby had something to do with it.

He turned to Robby, and didn't really want to know what he'd done with the bodies, as he could see no other possible culprit. James turned back towards the elevator.

Robby and he rode the elevator down to the room where he had found the electronic suit. There were no more suits around, but there was a room filled with weapons next to the suit room.

He tested various different weapons, some more useful than others. He picked up the ones he thought would serve him best, and brought them up to the recreation room. It was now about noon, and James decided to take one more trip down.

Making sure he was headed in the correct direction, James went back to the room where he had first met Robby. He didn't linger long, but instead headed to the room with the giant computer. Robby seemed just as in awe of it as he had been before. James logged in, though it took him a few times to guess Ajax's password, and went to the lab database. James wanted a suit, like the one he had found before.

He discovered that there was indeed another suit in the lab, though James assumed that it was most likely filled by another robot, so he rode the elevator back up, and grabbed a spear-like weapon, and rode the elevator to the room where another suit was said to lie.

Robby went behind James, keeping an eye out for danger from behind him, and James suddenly ducked as a large barrel went flying past his head. He looked ahead, and saw that he saw staring down a considerably bigger cyborg. It was about twice James' height, and there was no seemingly human face, just a robot inside a robotic suit.

James ducked as the robot lunged, and Robby rolled to the side. The robot missed both of them, and as it crashed to the floor, James stabbed it with the spear. The tip seemed to be electrocuted, and, like last time, electrocution seemed to trigger the ejection mechanism.

The smaller robot was hurtled out of the suit, and though it was smaller, it was still about James' height. James and the robot circled each other for a few seconds, and then Robby took some actions of his own. He zipped up behind the larger robot, and zapped him with electricity. The robot froze, and James stabbed it with the spear. The robot crumpled to the floor in a defeated heap.

James then set about the tricky business of getting into the suit, which lay on the floor. He sort of crawled in, and then, when that failed to accomplish much, he crawled in backwards.

It took James a few minutes to figure out how to use the suit. Once he did, he pushed himself up, and rode the elevator back up to the recreation room. He lay down in the suit, and crawled out.

James looked at the time, and saw that it was considerably later in the afternoon, and he was very hungry. He discovered that there was a mini-fridge in the room, and lay down in front of the couch to watch TV while he ate.

"And now, reporting from Washington DC, this is reporter Craig Jones," smiled the announcer at James. "Following up on our previous report about the strange goings on in Pilfershire, the small New England town, the SWAT team has come back. They are missing two of the four members that were sent out, and they are mysteriously refusing to speak to anyone about the incident. Soon after their arrival, the president scheduled a meeting with the prime minister of England. We have no idea what this is about, but we do have some theories..."

The rest of the reporter's words were lost on James as he thought about what he had just heard. "The president must be corrupted," thought James aloud with a feeling of horror growing in the pit of his stomach. "He's going to spread the corruption. Oh, this is bad!"

James thought for a few moments before deciding what his next course of action would be. He had amassed enough weapons to hold his own against the darkness again, and the obvious next step would be to retrieve the twilight crystal.

James wondered where it would be for a few moments before the answer struck him: the observatory. Where else? James realized that he had left the sheet detailing Shadius' plans in the forbidden room, and raced back in. He looked them over, and saw that he must be right: the only use Shadius had for the twilight crystal was this: he planned to use it to power a device in the observatory, opening up a wormhole leading to Alchema, where he would then spread the darkness virus.

It was still daytime, and James thought it would be wise not to strike at night. On the other hand, Shadius probably wasn't planning to get to work until night, so the possessed people were probably mostly on guard duty during the day, reasoned James. The best strategy, therefore, would be to attack in the morning, right at dawn, when most of the possessed were still working, but Shadius' powers were no longer at their peak.

Walking back into the recreation room, James told Robby to wake him up when the sun was beginning to rise, and James went to sleep.

***

"So, Ajax, you still think that you have a chance?" cackled the dark voice of Shadius. "Well, if you do, you are grievously misled. I possess the twilight crystal, James is missing, and tomorrow night, I shall open the portal to Alchema!"

"I have faith," whispered Ajax, weak from the days without food. "Photosia's spirit will protect the side of good. You will not win, Shadius."

"Oh, but I will," he laughed in reply. "What can you do to stop me? What can anybody do to stop me?"

"Well, there's always Adrian," smiled Ajax. Suddenly, Shadius' confidence seemed to waver.

"Adrian is still in the Deadwood Forest," shrugged Shadius dismissively, trying to hide the fact that he wasn't as sure of himself as he sounded. After Adrian had attacked his necrossis with lightning at Light's End, mere days ago, Shadius no longer was able to write Adrian off as a distraction.

"Well, I have faith in my grandson, and he will get you," smirked Ajax. "Shadius, know this: you will fall at the hands of Adrian Lightseeker."

***

James yawned as he slowly woke up. He wondered what time it was, and he suddenly jolted wide-awake as he realized that Robby had neglected to wake him up. James sighed, and leaped off of the couch.

He raced over to a clock, and saw that it was, indeed, about eight o' clock in the morning, and James thought that his best bet would probably be to go back to sleep, since everyone would be guarding the building. Whenever he next awoke, he would stay awake until dawn.

James awoke around seven PM, and entertained himself on a video game system for a few hours, until it was about three in the morning. He crawled into his suit, and picked up the weapons he had assembled a few days ago. He was feeling slightly tired, but he was awake enough to reclaim the twilight crystal.

Robby was nowhere to be found, so James walked out alone. He rode up the elevator in his robotic suit, and entered into the world of night.

A few minutes later, James was nearing the observatory. It wasn't quite dawn, so James lingered around for a half-hour or so. As the sun rose over the horizon, James prepared to go in. There didn't seem to be any guards, and James walked in the front door. There was really only one hallway, and that led to the dome, which comprised the vast majority of the observatory. However, there was a wall between the inner and outer sections of the dome. In the outside portion, someone was waiting for James.

"Hello, son," smiled Mrs. Cantor, looking at James with her head tilted. "I saw you lingering around outside the building, but it's good to see you. How is Adrian?"

"Cool it, Shadius," shouted James. "I know you're the one controlling the possessed."

"In a sense, yes," mused Shadius. "However, I assure you that this is still Mrs. Cantor through and through. She still retains a bit of her personality."

"Quite right," smiled Mrs. Cantor in a different voice. "I allow Shadius to control me, but I'm still myself. I believe Kronos made a similar deal."

"He most certainly did," agreed Shadius. It was interesting to James, since it looked like Mrs. Cantor was talking to herself in two different voices. However, that did not convince him to show any mercy towards the possessed woman.

James threw the electrified spear at Mrs. Cantor, but she dodged to the side, and a tendril of darkness appeared for a counterattack. James grabbed his ray gun, and blasted the tendril back.

James then lunged for Mrs. Cantor in his suit, but she caught him in mid air, and flung him to the ground, with a tendril of darkness. James felt something snap in the suit, but it still seemed to work just fine. His arm now hurt, though.

James crawled to his feet, but before he could reach his full height, another tendril of darkness shoved him back to the ground. James felt something else in the suit break, and he was unable to move the suit's legs. Adrian pushed himself into a sitting position with his arms, and then, without warning, his hand shot out, and engulfed Mrs. Cantor. She screamed, and a tendril of darkness tore apart the hand of the suit.

With the one remaining operational limb on the suit, James swung the suit around, and hit Mrs. Cantor with the full force of the suit's fist. She was knocked back, and slumped to the ground, unconscious.

With great difficulty, James extracted himself from the suit. He pushed himself upright, and picked up the weapons he had stored inside the suit. The ray gun was still intact, and since it emitted light energy, James assumed that it had the power to dispel some darkness, but not as effectively as the prototype.

James also picked up a sword and shield of some type, and the spear still seemed to work. James held on to the shield with his left hand, and put the ray gun in his pocket. He held the spear in the same hand as the shield, and clutched the sword in his right. He assumed that it was not merely a sword, but there was some kind of advantage to it that elevated it above other swords.

Weapons in hand, James kicked down the door to the inner dome. Well, truth be told, he kicked it open, as it wasn't locked. James gasped. There were easily two hundred possessed people in the inner dome. They had all been watching expectantly the giant laser, which seemed to have been built around the twilight crystal. Now, though, their attention was directed at James.

James saw Mr. Cantor operating the laser, and the man gave James a smile. As he did, the possessed surged to life, and swarmed James.

James held up the sword, and beat back the offending forces. He seemed to be dealing with the foot soldiers of the army of the possessed, for no tendrils of darkness emerged to shield them from James' relentless blows.

Suddenly, one of the possessed grabbed onto James' sword, and James started to lose his grip. His hand slid down the hilt, and found a hidden button, which he accidentally pushed. A beam of light formed around the sword, ending at the tip. It wasn't anything dangerous, just light, but that was indeed harmful to someone under the control of Shadius.

The possessed man screamed as the darkness was expelled from his body. He stumbled backwards, and fell over. James leapt over to the place where he lay, making sure that the man didn't get trampled underfoot.

With the light surrounding the blade, James' sword was a much more potent weapon. The pile of unconscious people began to double, and then triple, in size, and James had given up on trying to protect them all from the feet of the oncoming soldiers. Shadius seemed to decide that foot soldiers weren't good enough, and sent instead his more powerful men to take down James.

James' blade no longer freed his enemies from Shadius' control on contact, and he was forced to resort to brute strength to keep them at bay.

One of the enemies grabbed on to James' sword, and this time, there was no hidden switch to keep him from grabbing it. The sword was yanked out of his hands, and James grabbed the spear. Anyone that came near him was shocked into submission.

James slowly made his way towards Mr. Cantor, who seemed to be nearing the completion of whatever task he had in mind. James assumed it was the activation of the wormhole, but he couldn't be sure. James saw that he needed to buy himself more time, and he hurled the spear at Mr. Cantor. The man ducked, but the spear became firmly lodged in the machine. Mr. Cantor frantically set about repairing the damage the spear had done.

As he now had no weapon, James reached into his pocket, and pulled out the ray gun, blasting anyone who came close with light. He was now nearing Mr. Cantor.

Suddenly, someone else who James recognized jumped in his path, blocking the way with her aged arms. "Hello, sonny!" cackled the old crone that had spied on James and kidnapped Ajax days ago. "How are you?"

"Better now that I've got a chance to get even!" shouted James, firing the ray gun at the old lady point-blank. She staggered backwards, but the blast was not enough to free her.

"Well done, sonny," panted the old crone. "But I've got a few tricks up my sleeve too!" Suddenly three tendrils of darkness lunged for Adrian, originating from the old lady's body.

James blasted two back with the ray gun, but the third connected solidly with him, knocking him backwards. It stood over him, preparing to possess him, while James' mind went blank. As the tendril lunged, James brought up his left arm to defend himself, and the tendril bounced off of the shield, which he had completely forgotten about. James took the opportunity to blast both the tendril and the crone with his ray gun.

She sprawled onto the floor, dead. The excitement had proved too much for her old heart, and James now had a clear path to Mr. Cantor.

James raced forwards, but he was too late. Mr. Cantor pushed a button on the control panel, and the top of the observatory opened up, filling the room with moonlight. The laser that would soon create a wormhole opened fire, and spacetime was wrenched apart directly over James' head.

A wormhole opened up, and James made certain not to look into it, as he didn't know what he would see. Had he, he would have seen the fifth dimension, but he would not have taken it as well as Adrian.

"At last!" cried out Mr. Cantor in triumph, though James realized that it was truly Shadius that was speaking. "Now, Alchema shall feel my wrath!" Darkness flowed from Mr. Cantor into the portal, and was about to launch itself to Alchema.

Suddenly, there was a screeching noise, and Mr. Cantor looked up to see Ajax's spaceship, piloted by Robby, open fire on the laser, and it was blasted apart as the wormhole snapped shut.

The twilight crystal fell into James' hand, expelled from the machine by Robby's antics, and James' finger closed on the trigger of his ray gun as Mr. Cantor joined the rank of unconscious figures.

"Robby!" shouted James joyfully. "Thank god you arrived! Now let's get out of here!" The spaceship flew low to the ground, and James crawled in.

***

James stood in the recreation room, staring at the T.V. Moments ago, he had heard a report that spoke of how most of the world had succumbed to the strange mind control that had originated in Pilfershire. Shadius may have failed to claim Alchema, but he most assertively held earth in his command.

James walked into the forbidden room, and sat down to pull up the document that explained how to build the light laser. James looked at it, and saw that it would at least take a month or two to finish it.

"Better get started, then," smiled James as he got to work.

25

The Battle of Cloudhall

Adrian stared up at the rather formidable peak that he knew he must scale, but his eye caught a long and winding path that would lead the way for him. He instead turned his attention to the magma re-router.

It truly did take up half the mountain base. It towered over the small army, threatening to engulf them. However, Adrian didn't think it would be particularly well protected, and once he found the central power source, the entire facility would go up in smoke.

"Advance!" ordered Adrian, and the army marched forwards. Falcon walked up behind Adrian, and looked in awe at the magma re-router.

"Good god!" exclaimed Falcon. "That thing's enormous! I hope there aren't any guards. It'll take a while to find the central power source."

"So you need me to find it, and attack it with lightning?" clarified Adrian. "What would that accomplish?"

"Well, according to the limited information we could find, it should cause a chain reaction, which would lead to the facility exploding," explained Falcon. "You'll have to give me some kind of signal, though, since we'll need to get the troops out in time. I don't think that the councilmen are going to be in the re-router. It's too dangerous. Plus, according to Blaise's information, they're in Cloudhall."

"What exactly is Cloudhall?" asked Adrian. "I've never heard of it."

"Well, that's not exactly surprising," laughed Falcon. "It was believed to be a mythical ancient temple of the druids, but apparently, the corporate council actually found it, though they kept it to themselves. However, a rumor escaped that the council had turned it into a prison. We think that's where they're keeping Barge."

"Hey, speaking of the council," began Adrian, "the seats that we held, are they still ours? Technically, they gave the seats to Arrow. Are they back in the hands of the council, or did we keep them?"

"They're still ours," replied Falcon. "Arrow gave his positions to the Third Order, so we are still in control of most of Maltesque. Anyhow, returning to the subject of Cloudhall, it was supposedly a temple of the druids, though it was lost far before the first war of the druids. So, it looks like we're getting nearer to the magma machine. I think that you should take Rose with you. I can handle the attack myself."

"That's a good plan!" exclaimed Adrian. "Hey, Rose, come here!" Rose scurried over. "You and I are going to solo it. We need to find the central power source of the magma re-router. I'll attack it with lightning, and then you can cover me. I mean, I'd get lonely if I went in alone!"

"Okay," nodded Rose. "So we're going in by ourselves?"

"Well, no," replied Adrian, "but we are heading in separately. Our job is to find the central power source, like I said. Falcon and the troops are just going to do as much damage to as many things as possible."

"Sounds like a solid strategy," sighed Rose, rolling her eyes. "But if that's our plan, I'll stick to it. Say, what exactly are we walking on here?" Rose looked down, and Adrian saw her eyes narrow, as she seemed to attempt to scrutinize the surface upon which they walked.

"It's ancient ice," replied Falcon. "It's frozen all the way to the bottom of the lake basin. It hasn't received the slightest amount of heat for years." "He speaks the truth," nodded Vitalius, materializing in front of the party. "I'll stay with Falcon for the attack, right?"

"That's a good decision," replied Adrian, and Falcon nodded. "Vitalius, when is the spirit army arriving?"

"It should be here by the end of the day," shrugged Vitalius. "Say, we're getting pretty close to the magma machine!"

"Yep," smiled Adrian. "So once we destroy it, all the lights in the city are going to go out, right?"

"And everything else electrical," nodded Vitalius. "God, this machine is nearly as old as the city itself!"

"Indeed it is," nodded Adrian. "Well, let's make sure that the city lasts longer than the machine!" There was a general comment of agreement, and Adrian and Rose walked away from the army to prepare their separate assault.

"Is there another way in?" asked Rose, looking at the seemingly impenetrable wall.

"No, but the second Falcon leads the army in, I'll make one!" smiled Adrian, preparing a light attack, as he no longer needed the crude instrument of lightning to enforce his whims. Now, mere light was enough.

There was a crash, and Adrian heard Falcon give the command, "March!" Adrian blasted down the wall with his lightning attack, and he and Rose raced through the opening.

338

They emerged in a small closed room that Adrian took to be a closet. This was an incredible stroke of luck, as they hadn't been seen yet, and they didn't have to reveal themselves until Falcon had them amply distracted.

***

Falcon and Vitalius led the army in through the front door. Moments ago, a few well-placed gunshots had shattered the locks, and there was now a wide-open path inside. Falcon stepped into an entry hall. It was completely black, except for red glowing lines that formed unusual patterns on the floor.

Vitalius looked about suspiciously. It seemed to be some kind of entry hall, and there was nobody guarding it, which was a gigantic oversight, in Vitalius' opinion. Maybe there was actually no one in the entire facility.

"Falcon, maybe we overestimated these guys," suggested Vitalius. "It looks like they left the facility abandoned. Maybe they figured that we'd never go after it, since it supplies the city with power."

"I doubt it," frowned Falcon. "I think that's what they want us to believe. It seems like a trap to me. MARCH!" shouted Falcon to the soldiers, and the army moved forwards.

They stepped into a large chamber that was pretty much the opposite of the entry hall. The walls were red, with splotches of orange, and Falcon wondered who had decorated the facility.

In the center of the chamber was a large mechanism. Falcon walked over, and saw that it was a holographic display of a map of the facility. It pointed out the location of the central power source, and Falcon hoped that Rose and Adrian would find it.

"Attack anything you see, except the computer," ordered Falcon. He was hoping that it would force the enemy to spring the trap on his terms, instead of theirs, but he was disappointed. Everything in the chamber seemed to be bulletproof, and the only thing that looked like it wasn't was the computer, and since it projected the hologram, it could prove important to Rose and Adrian.

The army barely fit into the chamber, so Falcon was relieved when he saw a door off to the side. However, Vitalius saw another such door, and they were stymied about what to do.

"We could split the forces up," suggested Vitalius, but Falcon shook his head.

"That's what they want," he frowned. "It's still the best option, though, I'll at least concede that. You take half the troops through the door on the right, and I'll take my half through the one on the left. Deal?" Vitalius nodded, and they split up the army.

Adrian and Rose sat crouched in the closet. Adrian slowly opened up the door, and peered outside.

"Do you see anything?" whispered Rose.

"No," replied Adrian. "Actually, yes. I see some kind of a map on the wall, and an elevator. We're only a couple of floors above the power source, according to the map, and we're a little to the left. There aren't any soldiers around."

"Good," sighed Rose with relief, and they stepped out of the broom closet. The room was a dark shade of deep grey, with glowing red patterns everywhere, which provided the room with light. The two allies walked over to the elevator, and got in.

They rode down a few floors, and stepped out. They were in a long hallway that seemed to lead to a room with a red glow. The door was shut, though and Adrian could only see the glow from the crack beneath the door. He could only speculate as to what it would be, but he was fairly sure that it was the central power source.

***

Vitalius slid through the door, literally, and looked around. It was yet another empty room, and it seemed fairly safe. There was a lightning bolt design that ran down the length of the room, and there was a small crack in the middle of the lightning bolt. Vitalius deemed it unimportant, opened up the door for the soldiers to come in.

"Come on in!" ordered Vitalius. "There's nothing dangerous, but I still suggest that you get to the other door quickly. I don't want to give the council a chance to prove me wrong."

The soldiers poured into the room, and ran for the other door. The second the first soldier opened the far door, the floor began to open up. The floor was actually split along the lightning bolt, and the two sides were slowly retracting into the wall.

Panic engulfed the soldiers as they watched some of their friends tumble through the crevice, and down into the molten mantle of the planet.

"Retreat! Advance!" ordered Vitalius in a panic. "Whichever gets you to a door first!" The soldiers rained into the ever-widening pit, and Vitalius swiftly floated to the far side and helped soldiers through the door. The floor had split along the lightning crack that Vitalius had seen before, and Vitalius noticed this. As the bolt ran from one door to the other, the doors were quickly out of reach for many soldiers. Only twenty survived the trap room, and only ten were on the far side of the room. Vitalius turned around to face the new room, feeling sick from the loss of so many soldiers.

Vitalius stood in the doorway, stunned. In the room with Vitalius and the soldiers were hundreds of guards were aiming their guns at the ten soldiers.

***

Falcon was in the middle of a shootout. He had led his men into a trap, like he had thought he was, but the enemy forces thankfully did not outnumber his own. His men were well prepared, and had immediately opened fire on the opposing forces. The enemy had responded likewise, and the result was a shootout, which Falcon had hoped to avoid.

The enemy appeared to be shrinking in number, and Falcon smiled. He picked up his pistol, and ran forwards, firing at all enemies within his sight. His killing spree was almost a surreal experience, and it was one that Falcon had to admit that he sort of liked.

Suddenly, a bullet grazed his shoulder, and he stumbled backwards. He shot down the guard that had injured him, but he still was unable to advance further. Another bullet grazed his cheek, and the force of the near miss knocked him backwards, even though the bullet hadn't actually connected with him solidly.

The doors at the far end of the room slid open, and another hundred troops poured in. Falcon was stunned, as his side had just lost its advantage. Heading the new charge were two men with guns that did not fire bullets, but instead fired large rays of energy. One of the energy rays obliterated twenty-odd of his soldiers at once. Falcon saw that the fight had suddenly become a losing battle.

***

Adrian and Rose opened the door and stepped out of the hallway, and saw that there were easily a thousand troops between them and the main power source. Rose seemed surprised, but Adrian didn't miss a beat, and immediately summoned a blast of light, and knocked about ten of them down in one shot. Ten down, nine hundred ninety to go.

The remaining troops were each equipped with some kind of gun, and they all opened fire. Adrian created a wall of light to disintegrate the bullets before they reached him, but even so, the spray of disintegrated bullet still stung his cheeks.

Rose recovered from her temporary shock, and decided to use her powers to help get rid of the soldiers, since Adrian seemed busy defending them. Rose picked up the tube of seeds, and sprayed one out beneath the light screen. An enemy seemed to notice, and crouched down to take advantage of the opening.

Adrian made the light screen extend downwards to shield them further, and Rose was unable to shoot out any more seeds.

Rose concentrated, and the seed flared to life, growing into a giant herbal monster. It quickly grew from a single seed into a vine, which wrapped itself around the closest soldier. With a snap, it broke the soldier's back. By that time, Rose had forced it to nearly triple in size, and about twenty vines wrapped around one another to become the core of Rose's plant creation. Several other vines reached out from the core, and destroyed multiple soldiers. The gunfire suddenly vanished as the soldiers took evasive action to avoid the creature's sweeping vines, and Adrian lowered the screen, and blasted all of the nearby enemies with light. Suddenly, Adrian heard something from behind him.

The door crashed back open, and a giant magma creature oozed into the room. The guards seemed just as frightened of it as Adrian and Rose were. One of the guards shouted, "This is suicide! I'm out!" Multiple other guards seemed to agree with him, and a good portion of the enemy forces retreated. However, the rest of the guards took advantage of the situation, and opened fire once again.

Adrian raised the light shield once again, resorting to the defensive role once again, and Rose's mind was strained as she attempted to do something she'd never been taught: manipulating two plants at once. She shot another seed at the magma monster, and it sprang to life, engulfing it in a web of vines.

The magma monster ripped the vines off, and Rose fell to the ground screaming in agony. She hadn't know that she felt the same thing as her plant minions, but apparently there were still a few things that the Great Sage had neglected to tell her.

Adrian looked behind him in panic as the magma creature raced forward. He tried to maintain the light screen, but his focus became blasting apart the magma monster. As a result, the soldiers had clear shots at Adrian and Rose, and a couple of bullets just barely missed them. None of Adrian's lightning attacks seemed to do the slightest bit of damage, and, in a last bid for victory, summoned lightning, and blasted the central power source.

There was a small explosion, and then a larger one, and then Adrian shielded himself and Rose with light as the central power source became the center of a giant conflagration.

***

Vitalius concentrated, and green energy flashed out from his body, blasting back all opposing troops. Suddenly, he heard a rumbling from beneath him, and the floor began to heat up. The ten troops under his wing began to bounce up and down to try to keep their feet at a decent temperature.

Suddenly, twenty ghosts materialized in the room, and they teleported the troops out of the room. Seconds later, the entire facility exploded. Virda's army had arrived.

Similarly, the two men with the energy blasters facing Falcon were suddenly evaporated in a flash of light green light. Hundreds of spirits materialized, and teleported the troops out right before the facility exploded.

As the facility exploded, Vitalius warped in, grabbed Adrian and Rose, for he knew where they were, and warped out to a point sort of in between the exploding building and the mountain. Confusion enveloped the group as they all tried to both absorb what had happened and tell their own story at once.

"Thank you!" exclaimed Adrian tiredly, wrapping his arms around Vitalius. "We nearly died!"

"We were outnumbered about five hundred to one," laughed Rose. "Now, we could have handled that, but then a magma creature appeared, and attacked us from behind!"

"Something similar happened to us!" exclaimed Falcon. "We were ambushed as we stepped into a room, and then two men with laser guns came after us! It was ridiculous!"

"The floor opened up under my troops, and nearly all of them died," whispered Vitalius morosely. Everyone stared at him for a moment, but Falcon seemed to dismiss the comment.

"It doesn't matter. We won!" he exclaimed happily. "The magma re-router is no more!"

"Say, doesn't the machine sort of power itself, since it provides power?" asked Adrian. "I mean, since it creates power, why does it have a central power source?"

"Well, it's technically not the source," shrugged Falcon. "It's where the energy is focused, and sent to the city."

"But the router itself is also going to be destroyed, not just the power source?" asked Rose to clarify.

"Well, yes," replied Falcon. "You see, the way the re-router works is this: it sucks heat from the magma and turns the heat into power, but it also works like a water mill. The flowing lava turns a wheel, which is shielded by energy. With the power out, though, the shield will be gone, and the lava will destroy the wheel. Plus, the machine that stole the heat from the lava and turned it into energy should also be gone."

"Doesn't that mean that lava will flow back into the area?" asked Adrian. Falcon nodded. "But aren't we standing on *ice*? You know, that could *melt*?"

"Adrian, it would take years for—" Falcon was never able to finish that comment. The ice began to break apart at his feet, and he leapt back. Suddenly, a huge piece of ice broke off of the rest of the Frozen Lake, with the back end sticking up, and it then plunged back down. Falcon seemed to have been misinformed. The ice, in fact, did not run all the way to the bottom, but it was only a few meters deep. With the return of lava to the area, it did not take long for those few meters to start to melt.

"Everyone! Run onto the mountain!" shouted Adrian, for Mount Icecap protruded from the lake in an island-like fashion, and they were at the foot. Only on the mountain would they be safe from the melting ice.

Chunks of ice began to fracture off, before falling into the lake with one side sticking up. Adrian and Rose held hands as they ran over the breaking ice. Spirits grabbed onto soldiers and teleported them onto the mountain, but they weren't able to get everyone in time.

The two partners felt water lap at their feet, and realized that the piece of ice they were running across was slowly sinking into the water. They raced even faster, running for their lives. As they were at the edge of the piece of ice, it upended, and they were sent splashing into the water. Behind them, they saw the ice sink into the water. The climbed onto another ice piece, and kept running.

Adrian and Rose felt the texture under their feet change, and realized that they were safe, for they were now walking on stone. The mountain was now in island in the middle of a sea of ice melt.

Adrian and Rose found Falcon. "I thought you said the ice was solid!" shouted Adrian angrily, gesturing towards the lake. "We lost about half our troops!"

"I thought it was safe!" replied Falcon. "I've read numerous times that the ice extended all the way to the bottom! This isn't my fault!"

"It's completely your fault!" replied Adrian. "You told me the ice was solid. You made me linger on the ice. In fact, it first started to crack when you were in the middle of a sentence about how it wouldn't do that!"

Falcon didn't seem to be able to argue with that, and he sat down to brood. Adrian saw that the remnants of the Third Order's army consisted of about two hundred fifty soldiers, a fourth of what they had set out with.

The soldiers had regrouped on a flatter part of the mountain, where they could rest for a while, and not have to worry about falling back off. It was a sort of plateau, and looking up at the mountain, Adrian thought he saw a few more of them.

On the plateau, a carved out path that seemed to stretch much deeper below the surface of the water seemed to provide the only way to scale the mountain. Adrian looked up, and saw that the path twisted all the way around Mount Icecap, and it led to the top.

Adrian thanked his lucky stars that he had found the very path he had been looking for while trying to save himself. He had done a tiny bit of research on Cloudhall, and there was a wide path carved out of the very mountain itself that led to the legendary druidic temple.

Adrian suggested that they camp for the night, and was met with much assent. Everyone was cold, tired, hungry, and confused, so they pitched their tents, built a fire, and ate what food they had remaining. They went to sleep, and dawn came too soon for Adrian's liking.

***

The army aroused themselves, and Adrian was the one who wanted least of all to get up, but he had to keep pressing forwards. The spire of Mount Icecap loomed over him like the geometry test he realized that he had missed.

Adrian laughed as he thought about how he had been skipping school for the past few weeks. Then again, with all the earthquakes that had wracked his home town recently, Adrian didn't know if school had been cancelled, or what. He imagined that winter break had been over for about a month or so, but he really didn't know. He recalled his teacher mentioning a geometry test, and he hadn't really had much time to study.

Another laugh escaped Adrian's lips as he realized just how unimportant school had become to him. Regardless, he turned his attention back to scaling Mount Icecap.

Adrian woke up Rose and Falcon, and with their help, they woke the remaining few soldiers that were sleeping. In a half-hour, the army had eaten breakfast, and they were ready to move. Adrian led the group up the long path, and it got considerably colder the further up they got.

About an hour after they had broken camp, Adrian realized that it was getting foggy. He wasn't entirely sure why, until he looked down. Adrian realized that he was much higher than he had realized, and they were actually in Maltesque's cloud layer. Adrian let out a nervous chuckle as he realized why Cloudhall was called what it was.

Suddenly, the path took an abrupt right, and it seemed to lead into the mountain itself. "HALT!" commanded Adrian. The army came to a sudden stop, and Adrian turned to consult with Falcon. "Falcon, what do you make of this? The path leads to a tunnel that goes straight through the mountain."

"I believe that I'm better qualified to answer that question," smirked Blaise, stepping out from the crowd of soldiers. Adrian jumped, as he had forgotten that Blaise was with them. "It means that we've found the prison. I read in their secret online files that the jail is in the mountain itself."

"Excellent," smiled Adrian, and he turned around to address the army. "Everyone, watch out. There's a thousand or so foot plunge right here. Instead, head to the right, and keep you eyes on the ground at all times. I don't want to lose any more soldiers." There was a bit of grumbling at this, and Adrian realized that his soldiers were starting to lose faith in him.

Adrian dismissed this fact, as he didn't know how much longer he would be with the soldiers. "MARCH!" he shouted, and the army moved forwards once again. Adrian felt vaguely claustrophobic as the walls closed in on him.

Adrian looked forwards, but there wasn't enough light in the tunnel for him to see where he was going. Adrian didn't let that be a problem for very long though, and he summoned a small orb of light so he could see where he was going.

He was in a fairly large tunnel, which seemed natural to him, but he imagined that it had been created by the druids thousands of years ago. Thousands of years of exposure were bound to destroy any man-made signs. Adrian followed the tunnel for a while, and he saw something flare up behind him, and he turned around. Falcon seemed to have lit a torch, and Adrian was glad that everyone else would be able to see as well.

The tunnel opened into a huge cavern, and Adrian saw something that was definitely man-made, and fairly recent. In the middle of the cavern was a giant box-like building made of steel, with one guard patrolling. Some of it seemed to be cement, though, but Adrian was unconcerned with what it was made of. It was only about fifteen odd feet tall, for its main dimension was length.

Adrian walked towards the large building, and prepared to deal with the guard. Rose walked behind him, while Falcon led the army forwards. A guard raced out of the building, and commanded, "Halt! Turn around, and you will be faced with minimal charges in a court of law!"

"Come again?" asked Adrian uncertainly.

"Turn back!" ordered the guard, who clearly did not see the army approaching behind Adrian and Rose. Adrian laughed, and the guard drew his weapon, which was not a gun, as Adrian would have guessed, but a sword, which he waved threateningly at Adrian.

"Well, someone's clearly not up with the times," chuckled Adrian as he advanced towards the guard. "I don't think I'll go away. I think that I'll stay." "Says you and what army?" asked the guard with a hint of nervous laughter in his voice.

"Well, I'm my own army," shrugged Adrian. "But in case that's not good enough for you, I've got another one too." Adrian summoned a small sun of pure light, which lit the room, revealing the Third Order. The guard screamed, and ran back inside the building. "Well, that was entertaining," laughed Adrian to Rose. "Well, let's head in, shall we?"

Adrian and Rose raced in through the front door, and were met with a small army of guards. The first guard seemed to have assembled the best defense force he could, but it was still pathetic. There were only about twenty guards, and not a single one of them had any sort of a threatening weapon. Adrian blasted one of them down with lightning, and the rest fled in panicked disarray.

Adrian smiled as he and Rose investigated the small building. It was far less impressive than Adrian had thought it would be, but he noticed something strange: a couple of the cells had levers on the walls. Feeling under whelmed and suspicious, Adrian tried pulling a few of them, and a hidden trapdoor slid open in the back of the building, revealing that the small jail was not what it seemed. A small staircase led down from the trapdoor, as if inviting Adrian and Rose to come down. Adrian and Rose walked down the small staircase, and entered a much more believable facility, and they were suddenly surrounded by about twenty guards, all toting pistols or shotguns.

Adrian summoned three walls of light to protect him and Rose, and though it was a strain, it kept them safe. An idea possessed Adrian, and he expanded the walls outwards, and they connected with the guards with a scream and a flash. They disintegrated, but one of them seemed to be impervious to the lightning. Unbeknownst to Adrian, he had a specially designed suit, and he was unaffected by the walls of lightning.

He crept through the screen, and was about to open fire on Adrian and Rose, but Rose caught him in the corner of her eye, and right before he fired his pistol, she shot a seed at him, and he was rapidly swallowed by vines.

The fight over, Falcon led the troops down. "Well, Adrian, it looks like you've found the real prison," mused Falcon. "Why don't we use the strategy from before: we split up, and I attract the guards, while you look for Barge."

"Sounds good," nodded Adrian. "I can take Rose with me, right?" Falcon nodded. "Okay. There seems to be one large pathway, and I think that you should bring the troops that way. There are smaller hallways leading off of the bigger one, and I think that's where they keep the prisoners. Rose and I can check there." Falcon nodded again, and Rose and Adrian left the main forces.

The general design of the prison was similar to the magma machine. The walls had the same sleek look, but they were a brilliantly polished silver with green strips of light running the length of the hallway.

Adrian and Rose stepped into one of the smaller passageways that seemed to have some inmates contained. So far, all of the smaller hallways had been empty. The smaller hallways were not a particularly dramatic departure from the larger one, but there were silver bars lining the side of the hallway. There were multiple prisoners, but Adrian didn't see Barge.

"Adrian!" shouted a voice, and Adrian whirled around.

"Democritus!" gasped Adrian. "I thought you were dead!"

"No, I survived!" grinned Democritus. "My insane side ran rampant in the Poisonsap for a while, but Arrow eventually found me, and he brought me here. What happened to him?"

"He turned traitor," sighed Adrian. "It's a long story, and I don't have time to tell it. I'm just so glad you're alive!"

"And something else good came of this," grinned Democritus. "Arrow has provided me with a common enemy. My other side and I are both united against him, and I think that now I've got control over him, I can be a much more effective ally."

"Well, that's great," smiled Adrian impatiently, "but what I need is a way to get you out of here. Do you have any—"

"That's no problem," nodded Democritus. "See that keypad over there? It opens up the cells. All of them. It could be a little risky, but I think that most of the people here would be willing to help you, and the ones that aren't would be taken down by the ones that would."

"Great. Do you know the password?" asked Adrian.

"K47-IZZ-16T," replied Democritus. "Hurry, though. Someone's coming." Adrian nodded, and he walked over to the keypad. While he was opening the doors, Rose walked over to talk to Democritus.

"I'm so glad you're okay!" exclaimed Rose ecstatically. "I've felt terrible about your death ever since we left the Great Sage. I blame myself. Had I been conscious, I could have stopped it."

"Rose, it isn't your fault," comforted Democritus. "Besides that, I'm fine! Better than before, in fact. My dark side and I have made peace out of a unanimous hatred of Arrow." Rose considered his words, though she knew that Arrow was not truly to blame for his actions.

Adrian finished entering the code, and the metal bars to the cell slid open. Rose gave Democritus a hug as he came out. All of the other prisoners stepped out of their cells uncertainly, unsure of what to make of their sudden release.

A guard had been coming back to check on the prisoners, but nothing could have prepared him for the onslaught of prisoners that suddenly found themselves free. They saw the warden that had tortured them for years, and did not hold back.

"HEY!" shouted Adrian, and everyone turned to look at him. "Listen up, everyone! I've got a proposition to make! I freed you, so I'd like for you to help me. After that, you can do whatever you want. Is that fair?" There was a general muttering of assent.

"And what if we don't feel like listening to you?" snarled a tougher looking man towards the back of the hallway. "I think that I should lead the little group here! We've endured torture, and we're not about to become slaves of you!"

"Don't worry!" sighed Adrian. "I just need you to help me attack the council's stronghold."

"We're going after the council?" asked the man. "Well, in that case, I'm in. Who's with me?" There was a roar, and Adrian felt that he had struck a nerve. The council had locked them up, and the council was going to pay. These men were out for revenge.

"Hey, I've got a question for all of you!" shouted Adrian. "Have any of you seen a man named Barge?"

As the crowd was preparing to answer, Falcon burst into the corridor. "They're all down!" he exclaimed happily. "Now we can get out of here, and attack the council!"

"Yes we can, old friend," smiled a man from the crowd, stepping forwards. It was Barge.

"Barge!" exclaimed Adrian and Falcon simultaneously, darting over to him. Rose had never actually met Barge, so she was somewhat unresponsive. Democritus didn't even know that Barge was a name.

Barge had changed. His hair was longer, and he was a good deal skinnier, though he still filled up a good deal of space. He had some stubble on his chin, and he didn't look quite as intimidating to his friends.

"Barge, is there another way out?" asked Adrian.

"Yeah," nodded Barge. "If you follow the large passageway all the way down to the end, you should find a door that leads outside. It's just a short walk from there to the council stronghold."

"Excellent," smiled Adrian. "Well, what are we waiting for?!" The freed prisoners roared, and Adrian led the charge out of the prison.

***

Adrian and the prisoners walked out of the second stone tunnel into a truly majestic sight. They were in the cloud layer, so they couldn't see particularly well, but Adrian was able to discern large pieces of stone sticking out of the mountain, though the mountain seemed oddly flat. Adrian realized that they were no longer on the path, but they were instead on a flat area carved out of the mountain. There was grass planted on the sudden plateau, and Adrian saw that the pieces of stone he had seen were really the ruins of an old building. Adrian was in Cloudhall. In the center of the ruins, Adrian saw that the corporate council had made its base.

Adrian led the army through the ruins, towards the council's base. Everyone seemed to be anxious to get there, so Adrian picked up the pace. After a moment of jogging, the army was assembled around the stronghold.

Adrian gave the command "ATTACK!" The prisoner surged forwards, a hundred strong, followed by the two hundred fifty members of the Third Order. Though it was surrounded by about a thousand guards, the Third Order's army was making good headway towards the building. Adrian led the attack with Rose and Democritus, closely followed by Falcon.

Suddenly, out of the building rose a glider, with Arrow aboard. The glider swooped down, dropping air bombs on the crowd. Adrian blasted them apart in mid air with lightning bolts, creating difficult cross-breezes. Arrow was forced to fly to the side, so as not to be knocked to the ground by the sudden explosion of air from the bombs, and he circled about for another round.

"Follow me!" shouted Adrian to Rose and Democritus, who left the battle against the soldiers. The raced over to where Arrow hovered above the ground, suspended on his glider.

"Well, if it isn't little Adrian Lightseeker," scowled Arrow. "Looks like it's rematch time, buddy."

Arrow pressed the yellow button, and gas flowed out of the front of his glider. However, Democritus was familiar to this trick, and seeing it in action again unleashed his dark side. It was a very visible transformation, and not one that Adrian particularly liked.

"Kill you yes I will!" shouted Democritus, pretending to prepare to leap, but he instead rolled to the side to avoid being engulfed by the gas. Adrian ripped the gas apart with light energy, and he leapt at Arrow. Rose fired her seed gun, and Arrow pulled back to avoid the attacks.

"Not so fast, Lightseeker!" he hissed, pressing the blue button, causing electricity to spark from the tip of the glider. He dive-bombed Adrian, who countered with a lightning attack of his own. Arrow was forced to retreat.

Democritus had grown very tired of waiting, and though his sane side still had a say in things, the insanity that gripped him overwhelmed him, and he leapt off the edge of the cliff at Arrow.

Arrow screamed as Democritus knocked him off his glider. However, Democritus had caught his foot on the electrified tip that protruded from the tip of the glider, and he crashed into Arrow like so many pounds of dead weight. Adrian looked in horror as they plummeted towards the ground. Rose jumped after them, firing her seed gun at the cliff.

Rose grabbed onto Arrow's shirt, and forced the seed to bloom into a vine, which reached down towards them. Rose caught the vine, and she and Arrow jerked to a halt. Democritus plummeted to earth with a sickening crunch. This time, he stayed dead.

Adrian helped pull Rose up on the vine. Eventually, she stumbled back onto solid ground with Arrow in tow.

"Why'd you save me?" asked Arrow softly. "I almost betrayed you to Kronos, but you saved my life. Why would... Who can forgive that easily?"

"I can," smiled Rose, but she ran back over to the edge of the cliff. She began to cry as she spotted Democritus lying spread-eagled on the path below.

"Well, Adrian, you won," laughed Arrow quietly. "What are you going to do? Kill me? Exile me?"

"No," frowned Adrian. The loss of Democritus did not strike him as deeply as it struck Rose, since he hadn't really known the man's sane side. "I intend to keep you as a prisoner. After this, I think that I can go back to fight Kronos, and once I defeat him, you'll be free."

"Thank you, Adrian," whispered Arrow, lying down. "What happened to my glider?"

"It crashed over there," replied Adrian, gesturing to his left. "It's still in good shape, though. It should still work just fine." Adrian got a piece of rope, and tied up Arrow.

Adrian walked over to Rose after tying Arrow up. "Why didn't you save him?" asked Adrian gently, putting his arm around Rose. The sounds of battle still raged behind him, but he ignored them, for all he was aware of was Rose's pain. "It would have saved you this agony."

"He was already dead," cried Rose bitterly. "He caught his foot on the electrified tip of Arrow's glider, and the current killed him."

"I'm sorry," whispered Adrian, holding Rose in his arms. Slowly, he recalled that he had a battle to fight, and he left Rose lead his troops.

Adrian left Arrow tied up on the ground, and ran back to the battle, with Rose staying behind to look after him. The Third Order had overrun the defense forces, and they were now forcing their way inside the building.

Adrian joined Falcon, and they raced into the council's base. Inside a room to the left, they found one member of the council.

"Please don't hurt me!" squealed the man desperately. "Please, I never wanted to fight the council! My peers bullied me into it!"

"Then surrender your position on the council to us!" ordered Falcon.

"Yes, yes, it's yours!" cried the man desperately. "Just leave me be!" Adrian and Falcon obliged, and left him sitting in his chair.

Falcon was not convinced that they were safe yet. He was correct, as Adrian found out when he burst through the door at the back of the council's stronghold. There was a large man sitting in an armchair. He looked vaguely familiar to Adrian, but he wasn't quite sure why.

"Hello, Adrian," smiled the man with an evil gleam in his eye. He was the final member of the council, not counting Kronos, and this was the man who had initially declared the Third Order a threat.

"Hello," scowled Adrian, looking the man over. "If you're planning anything, I'd suggest against it. I'm not in a good mood right now, and you'd do best not to try my patience. Just surrender, and I'll let you off the hook."

"What, you mean give you my position on the council?" laughed the councilman. "I don't think so, Mr. Lightseeker. In fact, I think that I'll leave."

"Well, we've got the building surrounded," laughed Falcon. "I don't really think that you've got anywhere to escape to."

"Once again, you're quite wrong, Falcon," laughed the man, pressing a button on the arm of his chair. The chair dropped into a hole that opened in the floor right beneath, and the councilman disappeared from view.

"Where'd he go?!" shouted Falcon, hurrying over to the hole in the floor where the chair had been. Suddenly, the hole closed, and the man was lost from view.

"What did you see?" asked Adrian,

"The chair only dropped a few feet, and it landed on a mattress," scowled Falcon. "He was in a tunnel. It must lead to another stronghold somewhere else. I saw a few soldiers in the tunnel with him, and I think he'll attack again."

"Well, it's getting late, Falcon," sighed Adrian. "I vote we just leave him be for now, and find him in the morning. Besides, we control over half the council! We don't even need to find him! We can disband the council!"

"No," scowled Falcon. "This is personal. I know that man, and we've never been friends. Besides, he'll no doubt plot against us like we did to him, and it's best if we don't allow that to happen."

"Well, we should camp for the night," shrugged Adrian. "We can search for him in the morning. There's no rush."

"True," sighed Falcon. "Well, I guess you're unswayable in this. Let's camp."

***

It took Adrian an hour to organize the army into assigned sleeping positions, and he found Rose near Arrow.

"Rose, why don't we move Arrow?" suggested Adrian. Arrow was in a partially intact ruin. It was three run down stone walls, though the roof was missing, and it actually seemed like a good place to keep Arrow, now that Adrian thought about it. "Actually, on second thought, let's keep him here. Hey, Rose, can you sleep here too? We need someone to keep an eye on him, and I need to sleep near the troops. Say, did any of them find out what happened to Arrow?"

"No, they didn't, yes I can, and Adrian, I can't believe that Democritus is dead!" cried out Rose. "We just found him, and now he's dead again! What was the point of finding him?"

"Without him, Arrow would still be on the loose," sighed Adrian. "I feel bad about losing him too, but we have to move on. There's still someone else loose, and we need to find him tomorrow."

"Okay," sighed Rose, and she and Adrian parted. Adrian laid his sleeping bag by the troops, and drifted off to sleep.

***

The confused sounds of battle awoke Adrian, and he realized that the last councilman must have attacked. He jumped to his feet, and a blow nearly took his head off. He retaliated with lightning, but he was still half-asleep, and the attack nearly hit his own teammate.

"Adrian!" shouted Blaise, running over to him. "C'mon! We have to wake Rose! Without her, the army doesn't stand a chance, and we have to make sure she's safe!" Adrian nodded, and Blaise led him to the small ruined building where Rose and Arrow had slept.

Adrian looked around confusedly. Rose wasn't there, and neither was Arrow. "They're not here!" exclaimed Adrian confusedly. Behind him, he heard a metallic clicking sound.

"I know," smirked Blaise. Adrian whirled around, and saw that Blaise had a gun leveled at his head. "They're right here." He motioned behind him with the gun, and Adrian saw Arrow, with Rose held to him with his left arm, while he held a gun to her head with his right.

"Blaise?" asked Adrian. "What…"

"Did it ever occur to you that there might be *two* traitors to the Third Order?" asked Blaise. "I'm going to kill you, Adrian Lightseeker. If you try anything, anything at all, Arrow will kill your friend."

"Why did you save Rose if you're a traitor?" shouted Adrian angrily, aware that the sounds of battle were dying down around him. Maybe someone would come looking for him, and come to his aid. He just had to buy some time.

"Well, to clear my name!" chuckled Blaise. "Arrow was sort of a scapegoat, and since we serve two different masters, I had no qualms about exposing him. I had to stop him, or no one would trust me, and I never would have gotten this opportunity. Now goodbye, Adrian Lightseeker." A gunshot pierced the morning air, and all was silent.

26

Into the Light

James grinned. Just a few more seconds, and a month and a half of hard work would pay off. The light laser was nearly finished.

James had followed Ajax's instructions to the letter. The result wasn't particularly larger than the prototype, but it felt a good deal heavier. Then again, James supposed that it might have something to do with the fact that he hadn't exercised since he had retrieved the twilight crystal. All he had done was work on the laser and lounge around in the recreation room for the past month and a half.

However, James was still skinny as ever. His hair hung down to the back of his neck, and his glasses were still in perfect condition. Robby was as chipper and ready to help as ever. Really, in that month and a half, not much had changed for James.

The same could not be said for the rest of the world, sadly. James had been watching the news with increasing frequency, and the entire world had been corrupted by the darkness corruption. Only a select few countries had been able to keep the corruption away, and even those were beginning to succumb. James did not let that deter him; instead, it renewed his determination and strength.

The last piece of the light laser fell into place, and James let loose a whoop of triumph. He stepped back to look at the completed marvel. There was not a single ugly aspect of the device, for the exterior was made solely of smoothed metal. It looked like a very small medieval cannon, except there were no wheels, and there where none of those ridges. Had James not built it himself, he would have assumed that it was only one piece of metal, as opposed to many.

"Robby, I'm finished!" shouted James triumphantly, and his faithful robot came into the room. "Check it out! It's done!" So far, the only things James knew that could impress machines were other machines, and the light laser seemed to greatly impress Robby. James stared at it for a moment to try to figure out how to work it. He finally spotted a patch of glass that looked touch-sensitive, and he motioned for Robby to step back. James pressed the patch of glass, and light blasted out of the front of the laser. It was not quite at full power, otherwise it would have blinded James, but it left him blinking for a few moments afterwards even so.

Now James was confronted with the problem of getting the laser through the ruins to the orphanage without attracting too much attention. A small smile crossed his face as he recalled the manner in which Robby had saved Alchema a month and a half ago, and he and Robby rode the elevator down to the room where the spaceship was held.

***

In the nanosecond when Adrian heard the gun being fired, his life flashed before his eyes. He deemed it satisfactory, though he had a few nagging regrets as a matter of course, but he had kissed a girl, killed a demon, made a friend, and saved a world. And aside from that, what else really mattered?

Suddenly, Adrian realized that he was not dead. He wasn't even bleeding. He hadn't been shot! His first thought was that the bullet had missed him, but as he opened his eyes, he saw that the reality was otherwise.

Blaise lay on the ground, dead. Blood poured from a bullet hole, and his face was twisted in his final smirk. Adrian looked up, and saw tears running down Arrow's cheek as he held the gun that had dealt Blaise his final blow. In that instant, Adrian realized who else Incarcerus had been talking about when he had said that Adrian was to be Maltesque's second-biggest hero.

"Arrow!" exclaimed Adrian. "You saved my life! Does that mean that Kronos' spell is broken?" Suddenly, Adrian realized that Arrow's attention was not on him, but he was looking over his shoulder. Adrian turned around, and did a perfect double take.

"Well, it looks like I've been missed!" smiled Joshua, walking towards Arrow. He was a ghost, like Vitalius, but he looked somewhat more solid. "I'm sorry, Arrow. For everything my death put you through. But understand this: I cannot stay. Virda made a deal with the lord of death so that I could come and break the spell Kronos placed on you, but since I'm not technically a Green-keeper, I'm not eligible for Virda's spirit army, and won't be able to stay any longer than this."

"Joshua," whispered Arrow. "I'm sorry, oh god I'm sorry!"

***

"Joshua wasn't the traitor!" shouted Arrow. "I'm sorry, but I can't believe that!"

"Then you're smarter than I gave you credit for," smirked Kronos. "The other traitor is Blaise. However, I can't let you know that, so I think I'll remove these last few seconds from your memory.

A tendril of darkness suddenly shot into Arrow's body, and his mind went blank.

* * *

"Kronos forced me to believe that you were the original traitor!" wailed Arrow. "I was an idiot! Deep down, I'm sure I knew it was Blaise, but Kronos brainwashed me! I'm sorry for abandoning the order!"

"I think you just made it up," replied Joshua, glancing at the fallen figure of Blaise. "Well, brother, what you need to do is take down Kronos, so you'll be free again. You can't do it alone, and I can't help you. Instead, I suggest you turn to someone whose agenda matches yours." Joshua's ghost pointed to Adrian.

"Arrow, I will definitely help you fight Kronos," nodded Adrian. "He's the reason I'm here in the first place, and I need to rescue my sister from him."

"Very well," nodded Arrow. "But can you at least stay a little longer? I've got a couple of questions about the afterlife!"

"I'm sorry, but the lord of death is calling me back," sighed Joshua. "I must leave you now. I'll see you again someday."

"Joshua, don't go," pleaded Arrow. "Please! You can't leave me here alone! You can't!"

"Going for the spoiled infant approach, are we?" laughed Joshua. "I'm sorry, Arrow. I don't want to go either, but I've got no choice. I just got to come back to say goodbye. Goodbye, Arrow."

"Goodbye, Josh..." replied Arrow in a strangled voice, trying to hold back tears. "Oh, just give me a hug, at the very least!" Arrow hugged the spectral form of Joshua, who held him back, though Joshua's body began to disintegrate into particles of light. The light particles drifted upwards, and Arrow fell to the ground, sobbing. Rose sat down next to Arrow, and held him in her arms. Adrian supposed that was acceptable.

* * *

Adrian left Rose to comfort Arrow, and headed back to tell Falcon what had just happened. Adrian found Falcon talking to the troops, and congratulating them for their incredible victory.

"Falcon, may I have a word?" asked Adrian, pulling Falcon away.

"Sure," nodded Falcon. "By the way, a fat lot of help *you* were in the battle! Where the hell were you, anyway?"

"Falcon, you were right," began Adrian. "Blaise was a traitor. There were two."

"What happened?" asked Falcon, immediately both curious and alarmed. "How did you find out?"

"He and Arrow trapped me," replied Adrian. "He was about to shoot me, but Arrow saved my life by shooting Blaise right before he could kill me."

"Why did Arrow come around?" inquired Falcon. "I mean, I thought that he was against us!"

"Well, you know how Virda amassed a spirit army?" asked Adrian. Falcon nodded with a small laugh. "Well, she brought back Joshua."

"He's back?!" asked Falcon incredulously. "Can I talk to him? Thank god! Now everyone will rally, and victory will be ours. Oh, I'm just so glad he's back!"

"He's gone now," hurriedly explained Adrian. Falcon's face fell. "The lord of death said he couldn't stay for long, or something like that. Regardless, Arrow's back, and Blaise is gone!"

Falcon sat down to attempt to absorb the rather startling knowledge, when suddenly four members of the corporate council's army emerged from their hiding place in the ruins, escorting the last councilman.

"Aha! There you are, you—", exclaimed Falcon, including various names which would not do to be printed. "So you've decided to give yourself up, have you?"

"No, Falcon," sighed the councilman quickly. "I just wanted to talk to Adrian. Lightseeker, is it true that my brother is dead?"

It took Adrian a minute to realize who the last councilman was talking about. "You're Blaise's brother?!" exclaimed Adrian. The councilman nodded. "Well, that would explain why he stayed loyal to the council even though the Third Order was clearly winning the war. Sorry, I talk to myself sometimes. Anyhow, yeah, Blaise is dead."

"Then let me at the bastard who killed him!" shouted the councilman. "Who was it? Arrow? Let me at that slime!"

"I did not act under my own control," replied Arrow forcefully, walking towards the last councilman. "I was under the influence of the very man who you trusted with a seat on the council: Kronos."

"Then he will pay!" shouted the councilman. "I hereby denounce him and the council, since he and I are all that's left of it, and give you my seat on the council. In return, I ask for safe passage off of the mountain."

"You can have your safe passage," nodded Arrow, much to Falcon's annoyance. "Anyhow, do you have a name?"

"None that would concern you," scowled the councilman. "Don't think this is over, Falcon. I'll get even with you and the rest of the world. You'll see." The last councilman turned and walked away.

"Why did you let him go!?" shouted Falcon. "He's dangerous!"

"I let him go because he's no threat to us," replied Arrow coolly. "By the way, I would like my position back as leader of the Third Order. Adrian, will you grant me that?" Adrian nodded. "So, Falcon, how exactly do you know that man? You two seem fairly well-acquainted."

"We used to be friends," sighed Falcon. "He rejected me once he got a spot on the council, though, and we became enemies on that day. I don't think any more detail is necessary."

"Fair enough," nodded Arrow. "And what I said was partially true. Kronos did play a part in what I did, but it was mainly the appearance of Joshua."

"Say, he wanted safe passage off the mountain, right?" asked Rose suddenly. "Well, um, how is he going to get off? There's nothing below us but water, after all. How are any of us going to get off?"

Falcon prepared to give his answer, realized it was no good, thought, and then shrugged.

"I could fix the helicopter," suggested Arrow. "I could fly to the crash sight, fix it up, and fly it back. In the meantime, the spirits can teleport some of us off the mountain. How does that sound to you guys?" No one had any argument, so Arrow prepared to leave. Suddenly, he turned around, and asked, "Actually, do you two want to come with me? We can deal with Kronos now, and that way I'll be completely free. I don't think all the soldiers in the world would make a difference in the battle against that man."

Adrian and Rose nodded. "Well, then, come on!" smiled Arrow, and Adrian and Rose boarded his glider. Falcon waved to them as they flew away.

***

As Adrian and Rose neared the city, dusk began to fall. They were both starving and tired, but they felt prepared.

"Arrow, have we repaid our debt to you?" asked Adrian. "Are we free to leave the order?"

"At this point, I think you are," nodded Arrow. "You are free to leave. Why, what do you want to do?"

"If we really are free to leave," began Adrian, "then this will be our last day on Maltesque. If we defeat Kronos, the gateway to other worlds will be opened, I just know it! And we need to free any other worlds from darkness. Plus, defeating Kronos will save my sister, Serena. I need to take her back home."

"Then this battle culminates your journey on Maltesque?" clarified Arrow. Adrian gave a word of assent. "It culminates everything for me, too. The second we defeat Kronos, we've won the war. He is the last enemy for all of us."

"Then Rose and I will defeat him," smiled Adrian grimly. "I think it would be wise if you stayed in the air, Arrow. We don't know if he still controls you, and if he does, to what extent."

"I'd agree, but we're out of air bombs," sighed Arrow as they flew over the city.

"So?" asked Adrian, but he was unable to get an answer, as another sight distracted him. All around Kronos' building were thousands of people, mostly holding torches to light the way.

"They're blaming Kronos for the blackout!" exclaimed Arrow happily. "It's like a riot! Check it out!"

"Incredible," breathed Adrian. Suddenly, about ten figures flew out of the building, and drove away the crowd. "The necrossis!" gasped Adrian. "They're driving the rioters back!"

"We've got to hurry!" exclaimed Arrow. "If we don't, there's no telling what the necrossis will do!"

Adrian looked down, and gasped in horror. Tendrils of darkness were flowing out of the necrossis, and possessing the rioters. "He's possessing them!" exclaimed Adrian with horror. "He's taking over the minds of the people, like he did to you."

"So Kronos makes his last move," snarled Arrow. "He'll pay for this! He'll pay for everything a thousand times over!" The glider was now but a hundred feet from Kronos' building.

Arrow had been wearing a strange backpack the entire ride. Adrian and Rose did not know what it was for, but Arrow seemed like he was about to use it. "Hold on, everybody!" he shouted, as he pressed the red button on the glider. He jumped off, grabbing Adrian and Rose, and pulled a small cord that extended from the backpack. The backpack opened up, with a large piece of fabric dangling behind it, and Adrian realized that it was a parachute. The glider flew into the side of Kronos' skyscraper and exploded. Arrow drifted into the building through the hole he had made.

The three of them landed smoothly on the floor of Kronos' building, not quite on the top floor, but a few floors below. Adrian wracked his brains to try to remember which way led to Kronos' floor, since Adrian was sure that Kronos was on the top floor.

"Guys, I think the stairs are this way," directed Adrian, pointing the party a little to the left. "I'm pretty sure that Kronos is on the top floor, in that carpeted room that you blew apart, Arrow. And I'm of the opinion that the elevator seems kind of risky, you know?"

Suddenly, a cloud of darkness billowed up in front of Adrian, and Kronos stepped out. "There's no need for you to look for me, Adrian Lightseeker," smirked Kronos. "I'm looking forwards to this contest of abilities as much as you are. Now, speaking for my master Shadius, I would like to offer you one last chance. You can surrender, and be made a member of my master's army, or, you can fight, in which case you will be used for my master's sacrifice!"

"If I subject myself to his will, then won't I be sacrificed any way?" asked Adrian forcefully.

"Adrian, you are not the last Lightseeker in the multiverse," assured Kronos. "So your choice is...?"

"I think this should answer that question for you," grinned Adrian, blasting Kronos with light. He stumbled back, caught off guard.

"Here, Adrian, allow me to lend a hand!" shouted Rose, shooting three seeds at Kronos. They lodged in his cape, and they each grew rapidly into a different vine cluster. "You are not my father, Kronos! My father was destroyed ten years ago, when you kidnapped him. My father would never surrender to Shadius!"

"Very well, then," growled Kronos. "Well, I suppose that you're going to fight me now no matter what, now that you've successfully weakened me?" Adrian readied another light blast, and Rose held up her seed gun in preparation for another attack.

Kronos grinned, which seemed strangely unbecoming of the situation. "Very well then," he smiled. "Then your friend shall pay the price!" A tendril of darkness flowed from Kronos' hand, and knocked Arrow back out of the hole he had created with his glider.

"Arrow!" shouted Adrian, sprinting over to the shattered wall. The second his back was turned, Kronos disappeared again. Adrian lunged forwards to grab Arrow's hair, but he was too slow. His hand instead caught the parachute, which began to tear under the weight of Arrow's body. Swiftly, Adrian pulled Arrow back up.

Suddenly, a bolt of black lightning nearly hit Arrow. It missed however, but it cut the strings attaching Arrow to the parachute.

"Arrow!" screamed Rose, firing her seed gun at Arrow's dropping form. The seed attached to Arrow, and grew into a vine, which grew towards Rose much faster that she would have thought possible. Even so, Arrow was dangerously close to the ground.

Adrian's instinct warned him that something dangerous was behind him, and he whirled around to see a necrossis staring coldly at him. A tendril of darkness reached out for Rose, but Adrian blocked it with a burst of light.

Five tendrils of darkness flew at Adrian, but he deflected them all with his light attacks. The necrossis then lunged at Adrian, but Adrian threw up a wall of light. Despite the wall, the force of the lunge still knocked him back, and he bumped into Rose, and the two of the toppled out of the building. Thankfully, Adrian caught the edge of the hole with his hand, and he grabbed onto Rose with the other one. All of his arm muscles were screaming in agony, but he succeeded in holding on.

Rose was too focused on saving Arrow to truly notice that she had fallen out of the skyscraper, and she gave herself a mental pat on the back as the vine reached the hole in the building, and held. She looked down, and saw that Arrow was safe.

Adrian reached out and grabbed the vine, and used it to climb back into the building. He pulled Rose up behind him, and he sat there for a few minutes to try to regain his breath.

"Adrian, what happened?" asked Rose, who had only just realized that she had fallen out of the building moments ago. "I was too absorbed in saving Arrow. Were we hanging out of the building?"

"A necrossis knocked me out," replied Adrian, slowly getting to his feet. "I think now would be a good time to face our friend Kronos. Come, the stairs are this way."

Adrian turned around, and discovered that five necrossis blocked his path. "Not so fast," hissed one. "We need to repay you for killing our brother back in light's end."

"And for the brother you destroyed just now," whispered another necrossis. "Adrian Lightseeker, prepare to join our brothers in the grave!"

The necrossis each summoned five tendrils of darkness, and they all aimed at Adrian. Adrian was able to deflect most of them, and he attempted to throw up a light shield to defend himself.

Rose jumped back to avoid being enveloped by the tendrils. She launched a seed at one necrossis, and vines erupted around the creature of darkness. It went down quickly, and Adrian was able to hold back the tendrils, for there had just been five too many for him. Now that it was down to twenty, Adrian was able to throw up a light shield and save himself.

Adrian tried a new strategy, and walked forwards with the light shield. Slowly, he plowed through the necrossis with Rose right behind him, and within minutes, they were in the clear.

Adrian and Rose raced up the stairs, their pulses pounding with anticipation. They both knew that the battle with Kronos would inevitably decide the fate of Maltesque, and the burden fell on their shoulders to get rid of the world's biggest threat.

If they fell, Kronos would continue to possess the citizens, and he would doubtlessly overthrow the Third Order to subjugate the world. There was no telling what might happen to the environment, and once Kronos took over Maltesque, might he not move on to other worlds, and conquer those, as well?

Adrian and Rose did not feel the need to share these thoughts with each other, but they both understood the magnitude of the battle which awaited them.

At the top of the staircase stood another necrossis. "Take this!" shouted Adrian, pelting it with light blasts. Within seconds, the necrossis was down.

Adrian and Rose stepped out of the stairwell, and suddenly found themselves in a room that they had not seen for at least a month and a half. It was the room at the top of the skyscraper, the one that Arrow had attacked with an air bomb, allowing Adrian and Rose to escape into the river.

The brilliantly red carpet still sat in the middle of the room, and though it no longer drove Adrian mad with the intensity of its color, it still hurt his eyes slightly to gaze upon it.

"Welcome back, Adrian," sneered Kronos, sitting upon the very chair that he had rested upon when Adrian and Rose were summoned for their journey to Genesis. "Do you remember this room? It's where we first parted ways, back before you got mixed up with the Third Order. And now, months later, you return, eager to finally embark upon your journey to Genesis, where my master awaits you."

"Rest assured, Kronos, I will go to Genesis, but only once I am ready, and your master, not I, shall be the sacrifice," hissed Adrian. "Now, though, is not the time. Neither your master nor I shall die, but the one who falls shall be you!"

"So be it!" roared Kronos, getting to his feet. "You will pay, Adrian Lightseeker!" A black wind whipped towards Adrian, tossing his hair back. "You shall feel my wrath!"

Kronos concentrated, and an orb of black lightning formed in his hands. He threw it at Adrian, who dodged to the side. Rose shot seeds at Kronos, but he swatted them away with tendrils of darkness.

Adrian launched a blast of light at Kronos, only to have it deflected by a tendril of darkness. Rose, though her seeds had been deflected, created a writhing mass of vines. Each seed that had fallen to the ground sprouted into a plant covered in vines, and they joined together to form one giant entity, which attacked Kronos.

Kronos retaliated in kind, spewing tendrils of darkness every which way.

Adrian was forced into a defensive stance, with a glowing wall of light shielding him from the blows, while Rose fought with her vine mass.

Kronos grew irritated, and launched black bolts of lightning at Adrian's shield. Adrian, without realizing it, absorbed the black bolts with his shield. Adrian felt his power returning, even though he was using nearly all of it to maintain the shield.

Adrian readied an attack from behind the light shield. Every iota of energy he could spare went into this. The form of his attack was an orb of light, which he assumed he could hurl at Kronos from behind the shield.

Adrian suddenly lowered the shield, and launched the orb of light at Kronos. Kronos did not have time to create a defense, for all of his focus had been on penetrating the light shield. His overpowered attack sailed over Adrian's head, but Adrian hit Kronos dead-on.

There was an explosion of energy as an orb of light contacted a being of darkness. The walls and roof of the room was shattered, and Adrian and Rose suddenly found themselves standing on the new roof of the skyscraper. Adrian felt a strange feeling of satisfaction as he watched the spire crash to the ground.

Kronos stumbled back, but he was not finished. He concentrated, and darkness flowed into the sky from his body. Suddenly, it began to rain, and bolts of black lightning crashed down in front of Adrian. Rose, still fighting with her vine creation, screamed in agony as her vine mass was struck by a bolt of lightning. She fell to the ground, unconscious.

Adrian was now fighting Kronos alone. Kronos summoned up all the strength he had left, and summoned an enormous tendril of darkness. Adrian met the attack mid-way with a beam of light energy.

The two forces collided, providing another explosion of energy. The ray of light met the tendril of darkness, and light and shadow fought for supremacy. In near-perfect synchronization, Adrian and Kronos were both knocked off-balance, and fell to the ground, still maintaining their respective side of the collision of energy, and they both stumbled to their feet.

They were perfectly matched, the two of them, and neither one would give in until the other fell. There was, however, someone to play tiebreaker. Rose opened her eyes, and saw the stalemate. She hoisted up her seed gun, and fired it at Kronos' feet.

Kronos looked at his feet, and screamed. Twin vines were devouring his legs, and he refocused his attack to attempt to free his legs. In that instant, Adrian's beam of light purged all darkness from Kronos, and he slumped to the ground, defeated.

"Well, Adrian, you won," chuckled Kronos. "Kronos is no more. Shadius has been purged from my body, and I am now no one but Ulysses. However, without the protection of Shadius, I'm afraid that age will catch up with me. Rose, I'm sorry, I was a terrible father. Please, forgive... me..." Adrian and Rose watched in horror as Kronos' body succumbed to the flow of time, and he disintegrated into sand.

"He's gone," whispered Rose. "My father, he's... gone..." Rose fell to her knees, tears streaming down her cheeks. "Shadius will pay for this!" she shouted suddenly. "Shadius will pay for what he has done to my family, and to me! He will pay!" With that, Rose burst into sobs.

"Oh will I, now?" smirked a cold voice. Adrian looked around, but there was nobody there. "I'm right here, Adrian," sneered Shadius, materializing in the form of a dark cloud, from which thousands of darkness tendrils poured.

Adrian stood up, and prepared to fight the ultimate manifestation of evil. "Are you ready to die?" laughed Shadius. "Your sister provided me with ample energy to fight you with, so prepare to fall!" Two massive tendrils of darkness appeared, and prepared to crash down upon Adrian.

***

James sat in the back seat of the spaceship, waiting for Robby to turn it on. Apparently, there was some way to get the spaceship out of the lab, and James entrusted Robby with the task of achieving just that.

With a banging sound, the rocket burst to life, and flew forwards at an alarming rate. Robby pressed a button, and the ship stopped moving, and just hovered. He pressed another button, and the roof of the room opened up, and Robby flew the spaceship straight up.

James looked down at the town he had known for so long with a feeling of despair. It was beyond disrepair, beyond destroyed, beyond devastated. James was surprised to recall that there had actually been life in the town before.

The spaceship flew towards the orphanage, where the heart of all of the darkness lay. James suddenly ordered: "Stop!" to Robby, and the spaceship went into hover mode. "We'll wait 'till those go away." James pointed to a couple of tendrils of darkness that surrounded the heart of darkness.

As the day passed, James began to wonder if the tendrils would ever disappear. He resolved that if they had not vanished by the end of the day, he would attack the heart of darkness, regardless of any other factors.

As noon approached, James' attention wandered. He checked out the spaceship, and saw that there was what looked like a minifridge attached to the back of the pilot's seat. James was smart, though, and didn't trust the spaceship enough to open it. He continued looking around, and couldn't really make head nor tail of any of the strange runes he saw printed everywhere.

James glanced downwards, and saw, with a start, that the guarding tendrils were gone! "Step on it, Robby!" ordered James, and the ship flew forwards. Without warning, a tendril sprang up, and attempted to attack the ship. However, Robby was too good a pilot for the tendril, and it couldn't hit them.

Even so, James was starting to get nervous. "Robby, fly low to the ground," he ordered, and Robby dropped the spaceship so it was but feet above the ruins of what had formerly been Pilfershire. "Open the cockpit." Robby obliged, and James wince from the force of the wind that whipped past his face as the glass top was lowered. "Slow down. I'm getting out." Robby nodded, and flew fast enough to avoid the tendrils, but slow enough so that James could get out.

"Get to the heart of the darkness!" ordered James, and Robby flew slightly faster. In about a minute, they were right at the heart. James ordered Robby to slow, and he braced himself, and jumped out.

James screamed as he hit the ground, but he quickly regained control of himself. Keeping away from the shadows, he raced towards the heart of the darkness.

"Hello, James," smiled a weak voice. James looked carefully, and he saw that two tendrils of darkness were holding Ajax against the heart, and using him as a shield. "Please, James, I'm begging you. Forget about me. Just fire the light laser. It'll kill me as well, but that's a necessary sacrifice. Please, James! The tendrils are coming!"

"I can't," whispered James. "I'm sorry, Ajax, but I can't."

"Well, if you can't do it for me, do it for Adrian!" ordered Ajax, "Do it for the entire human race! FIRE THE LIGHT LASER!"

James squeezed his eyes shut as he pressed the trigger, and an incredibly bright beam of light pierced though Ajax, and flowed into the heart of darkness.

***

Shadius screamed as light used his body as a conduit and came to Maltesque. In Shadius' moment of weakness, Adrian blasted him with the full force of a light attack. Between the two blasts of light, Shadius succumbed, and he vanished. In his place, a tear in spacetime appeared, linking Earth to Maltesque. In that instant, everyone who had been under the control of the darkness regained their senses, and light returned to both earth and Maltesque.

"Rose, we did it!" screamed Adrian with joy. "Shadius is dead!"

"Not dead, just weakened," wheezed the voice of an old man. "Hello, Adrian. I am Ajax, your grandfather." Adrian recognized something in the man's voice, and realized who he was speaking to.

"Mr. L?" exclaimed Adrian incredulously. "You're Ajax? The man who wrote *Legend of Darkness*?"

"Indeed I am," laughed Ajax. "But I'm afraid my time is short. The darkness used me as a shield, and as such, I am.. paying the price... Adrian, you must... destroy... the Deathstone..." Ajax's voice faded away into nothingness, and a face appeared in the beam of light.

"Serena!" exclaimed Adrian. "Thank God you're okay!"

"Adrian," whispered Serena, "I'm not. The darkness absorbed too much of me, and I'm afraid that this face is all I have left." Adrian saw that Serena was right; she was nothing but a face. "Adrian, in the time that I have left, I would like to apologize for making your life so miserable. And I would like to thank you for putting up with me. In retrospect, I can see how much of a monster I was, and I'm proud of you for pulling through."

"Serena," began Adrian, but Serena cut him off.

"Goodbye, Adrian," smiled Serena, as her face began to vanish. Adrian raced up to her, and kissed her lips, brother to sister, friend to friend. Then Serena vanished.

"Hello, Adrian," smiled a voice from behind the curtain of light. Adrian looked up, and saw James. "It's good to see you again."

"James!" exclaimed Adrian, and he raced over to hug his adopted brother, who stepped through the rip in spacetime. "Boy, another victory like this, and we'll be finished!"

"So who's your girlfriend?" asked James, pointing to Rose. Suddenly, a look of comprehension spread across his face, and he exclaimed, "She's the girl that kidnapped Serena! What's she doing here?"

"Her name is Rose," smiled Adrian. "She was the girl that vanished in the dark district along with her father years ago."

"So who was the father?" asked James.

"Kronos," replied Adrian somberly.

"So that was true!" exclaimed James. "Ajax told me that." James' face suddenly fell. "Speaking of Ajax, I can't believe he's dead! He was my friend!"

"He was my neighbor," sighed Adrian. "I knew him as Mr. L. I didn't know him particularly well, but he was a kind person."

"I haven't seen him in a month and a half, so I guess that's not why I'm breaking down in tears now," sighed James. "It's sad, though, because I killed him. He forced me to, though. I had no choice!" James' courage seemed to be breaking down, and a tear dripped down his face followed by another one."

"Ugh, what happened?" groaned a voice from the stairwell. Arrow stumbled into the room to see Adrian, Rose, and one other boy all crying. "What happened?" he asked. "It looks like Kronos is dead, and I can't feel him in my mind any more, but why is everyone so upset?"

"Three people died," explained Adrian, though tears streamed down his cheeks. "His friend, her father, and my sister." He motioned respectively to all parties involved. "But Kronos is dead, and Shadius is beaten for now. Shadius was Kronos' master."

"So it's true?" asked Arrow. "I guess you'll all be going, then. Still, couldn't you say goodbye to everyone first? They'll be furious if you leave without wishing them well."

"That's true," smiled Adrian, wiping the tears from his eyes. "But your glider's broken! How are we exactly supposed to get to everyone?"

"Well, the, um, whole point of my coming back was to get the helicopter and fix it up," replied Arrow. "It's a long walk, but if we start now, we should be able to fix it up and get you to everyone within about two days."

"Sounds good," nodded Adrian. "James, I guess it'll be a day or two before I can head back. Would you be willing to wait?"

"He can come with us," suggested Arrow. "We need all the help we can get rebuilding the helicopter."

"I am pretty handy at building things," smiled James, holding up the light laser. "I'm not very strong, but I should still be able to help. So I guess we should get walking, then?"

"Yep," nodded Adrian, the tears finally ceasing to cascade from his eyes. "Lead the way, Arrow. You're the only one who knows where the helicopter crashed." Arrow turned, and walked away from the tear in space-time. James and Adrian followed him, but Adrian suddenly realized that they were forgetting someone. Rose still lay on the floor where she had fallen from the death of her father.

"You two go on ahead," suggested Adrian. "We'll catch up in a few minutes." Arrow nodded, and James followed him out of the room.

Adrian walked over to where Rose lay, and sat down next to her. "Rose, I—" Adrian was suddenly at a loss of words. Rose had suffered a loss so deep, Adrian knew no words could possibly heal her heart and soul. Instead, Adrian just put his arms around her, and held her.

"Adrian, thank you," sobbed Rose. Adrian was taken aback. "Thank you for freeing my dad, even if it meant his death. And thank you for being here for me." Rose stopped talking, and kissed Adrian again and again, and Adrian kissed her back.

***

Adrian and Rose met up with Arrow and James at the northeastern edge of town, near the river.

"So, Arrow, which way is the helicopter?" asked Adrian. Arrow pointed to the north, and began to walk away. Adrian and Rose followed close behind, with James in between them and Arrow.

It was nearly midnight, and Adrian and Rose were exhausted by the time they reached the helicopter. Arrow and James took it upon themselves to fix it up while Adrian and Rose slept.

***

Adrian and Rose looked eagerly out the side of the helicopter at it approached the large tree. They hadn't seen the Great Sage for weeks, and looked forward to the reunion.

The helicopter lightly touched down, and Adrian and Rose jumped out, racing over to the Sage. They threw their arms around him, and the Great Sage chuckled as he mentally embraced them back, and they all shared their thoughts for a few minutes.

***

The helicopter approached the ruins of the Rocky Outcrop, touching down on the beach. Virda waited for them at the edge of the ruins.

"Thank you, Virda," smiled Adrian, approaching her. "You were the one that set me on the right path, and now I am eternally in your debt."

"Ah, but I was not alone in shaping your future," smiled Virda. "Without Vitalius, you would have perished at the edge of his sanctuary. It seems only fitting that you should thank him as well."

"I didn't just come to thank you," continued Adrian awkwardly. "I must return to my old world now, but I have to say goodbye first. So, goodbye, Virda."

"Yes, goodbye, Virda," said Rose with a small smile. "We'll miss you."

"I shall miss you two as well," smiled Virda kindly. "Oh, but first I must ask this: should you ever return to Maltesque, please don't interfere with my workings. You know, like you did with Democritus and Chronicle."

"No problem there," smiled Adrian.

***

It had been nearly a day and a half since Arrow and the party had left Mount Icecap to rebuild the helicopter, and all of the troops were beginning to get a bit nervous.

"Stay calm!" ordered Falcon. "Arrow will be back any minute now!"

"How do we know he didn't betray us a second time?" demanded one soldier. "He might have just left us here to die!"

"He didn't," smiled Falcon, pointing at the helicopter that had just flown into his field of vision and was heading straight at the mountain from the north. It landed in the clearest area that Arrow could find.

Adrian and Rose descended from the copter, and walked over to Falcon. "We found a way back," smiled Adrian, and Falcon understood immediately.

"Then I guess this is goodbye," Falcon sighed. "How can you get back?"

"We destroyed Kronos," replied Rose quietly, choking back a small sob. "A rift opened up in space-time, and we can use it to get back to our world. We just wanted to say goodbye."

"Well, I don't see any reason why I can't come back with you to the city," suggested Falcon, smiling.

"Well, I can't come with you," sighed Vitalius, approaching Adrian and Rose. "Now that the Third Order has won, Virda is disbanding the spirit army, and I have to return to the afterlife. Goodbye, Adrian, Rose. I'll miss you both. It was a privilege fighting along side you two."

"We'll miss you too, Vitalius," smiled Adrian, offering his hand to Vitalius. The ghost shook it, and then Adrian, Rose, and Falcon got back into the helicopter.

"Stay here!" ordered Falcon to the troops. "We just need to make a short journey to the city, and then we'll come back. It shouldn't take more than two hours or so." The soldiers nodded as the helicopter flew away.

***

"Thank you, Arrow, for taking me around Maltesque, like you did," smiled Adrian, taking a step towards the portal. "I don't imagine you two will have much trouble picking up the pieces of Maltesque. Good luck."

"Good luck to you as well, Sir Adrian," laughed Arrow, giving him a mock-salute. "I'll miss the two of you." Falcon merely nodded at them, but that expressed just as much as all the words in the world could have.

As they turned to leave, Rose steeled her resolve, and ran towards Arrow. He turned around, and they kissed for half a second. "Goodbye Arrow," sighed Rose, and she gave him one final kiss on the cheek. Arrow and Falcon left, and no one in the room was destined to see them again. Rose fell to the ground.

"Well, I guess we should be going, then," stated Adrian. "Goodbye, Maltesque. I can't say I'll be missing it overmuch, but I guess I've just gotten kind of used to it."

"Adrian, we should go," suggested James. "I don't know how long this portal will stay open, and there's no telling if we could get back if it closed." Adrian nodded, and walked towards the light. He turned around, and saw that Rose was not following them.

"Rose, come on," said Adrian gently, extending his hand for her to take. Rose took it, and she stood back up. Hand in hand, Adrian and Rose walked into the light.

About Teen Author

Teen Author, an imprint of KidPub Press, is devoted to helping teens develop their writing skills by giving them a safe, fun, supportive place to express their creativity. At Teen Author we understand that teens have great ideas and plenty of stories to tell. In addition to our web site, we publish books, like this one, written by authors ages 8 to 20. You can find many more books to enjoy, written by young authors, in our online bookstore at http://bookstore.kidpub.com.

Thousands of visitors come by each day to read the stories posted by our members, and to post their own writing. We invite you to visit KidPub Press and Teen Author to browse our books, read new stories, and find out how you can publish your *own* book with KidPub Press. We're on the web at www.kidpub.com and www.teen-author.com.

Made in the USA